THE
PARADISE
CLUB

THE
PARADISE
CLUB

Hugh Miller

S T A R

A Star Book
published in 1989
by the Paperback Division of
W. H. Allen & Co. Plc
Sekforde House, 175/9 St. John Street
London EC1V 4LL

Printed in Great Britain by
Cox & Wyman Ltd, Reading, Berks

ISBN 0 352 32587 9

PROLOGUE

The cemetery was on a sloping elevation to the south of Rotherhithe, with a view of tower blocks and warehouses and railway lines. Mature trees, most of them elms, grew at intervals along the paths, softening the outlook, their dense-leafed branches muffling the sounds of traffic beyond the perimeter walls.

It was a beautiful day. The skyline's hazy shimmer merged to a rich clear blue and the sun blazed, heating the air, thickening the scent of flowers stacked high on boards by the graveside.

'And God shall wipe away all tears from their eyes,' the purple-robed priest said, reading from his book, the sun glinting gold on the frame of his glasses; 'and there shall be no more death, neither sorrow, nor crying, neither shall there be any more pain: for the former things are passed away.'

Lily stood apart, away from the others, the tight knot of family and friends and employees, the hard-eyed watchers come to make sure Jack went safely underground to leave them to their devices, to their greed and their plundering and their black-hearted malice. Some of them were watching Lily. Especially the old one, the hard-faced matriarch in her silken mourning, clutching her prayer book with bejewelled red fingers. Ma Kane was wondering about Lily. If the curiosity and speculation caused her any heartache, any pain, Lily would be grateful for that, glad she could do Jack this last service.

'And he that sat upon the throne said, Behold, I make

all things new. And he said unto me, Write: for these words are true and faithful.'

The younger son was at Ma's shoulder, glowering about him, ready to pick on anybody, anything. He was handsome in his gaunt way, but nothing like as handsome as his father, Lily thought; he had none of that beautiful warmth in the eyes, nor the mouth's readiness to smile. There was too much of the mother's vitriol in that young man's veins. It could be the death of him. Lily smiled behind her veil, thinking with a rush of feeling that at least the old cow hadn't killed Jack. No, she hadn't managed that. To bring about his death had been Lily's privilege, hers and hers alone.

'I am Alpha and Omega,' the priest intoned, 'the beginning and the end. I will give unto him that is athirst of the fountain of the water of life freely.'

The son said something in the mother's ear and they both stared at Lily, openly, the old one showing her venom, her poisonous hate. *You know, you old bitch. You know and it's eating your bowels out. Good*.

Lily looked at the shining plate on the lid of the coffin.

JACK KANE
1916–1973

All over now, Jack. That was it, my love. A few thousand days, countless pains and occasional chunks of pleasure. That was called a life. Given the chance he'd have made most of it turn out different, Lily knew that. But at the end he had been happy. In that respect he had the edge on most people.

'He that overcometh shall inherit all things; and I will be his God, and he shall be my son.'

Lily was glad they couldn't see her face. The look she had was for Jack. She was smiling, crying too. She gazed at the mound of gaudy flowers and saw him, the brightest projection of memory, and he was smiling. He was at peace with himself and everything around him. Even

6

when the stiffness of death took him and filmed his eyes he had been like that. Blissful. *God*, did he look happy . . .

PART ONE

GLASGOW: 1932–1946

ONE

Constable David Bryce came down Buchanan Street on the last leg of his shift on Central Division's north quadrant. It was a cold Friday night in March, starless and damp. Gusting wind swirled rubbish along the pavements and kept late stragglers close to the walls, huddled in on themselves as they made their way home.

Bryce turned left into Argyle Street, stiff-backed, looking to left and right, maintaining the regulation pace. On the corner of Glassford Street and the Trongate he stopped by a street lamp and inspected his pocket watch. Later his inspector would say that if Bryce hadn't checked the time at that precise moment, he wouldn't have been pensioned out of the force at the age of twenty-four.

The time was 11:53. Bryce finished at twelve. If he walked steadily back to the station, maybe a fraction slower than the rules required, he would be able to step through the swing doors on the stroke of midnight and sign off.

He put his watch back in his pocket and looked round sharply. Somewhere in the shadows across the street there had been a sound, like metal scraping on stone. He stayed where he was, listening. After a couple of seconds he heard it again. He fancied he heard a grunt, too, somebody exerting himself. The sounds were faint, he wouldn't have heard a thing if the wind hadn't been blowing from that direction.

'Damn it . . .'

He wasn't an officer to go looking for work, but he couldn't ignore something like this.

He stepped to the edge of the pavement, straining his ears. The building opposite was a coal and oil merchant's, a lockup shop with a walled yard at one side. The shop front was invisible in the shadows of the second-storey overhang, but Bryce could see it clearly in his mind. Two hours ago he had shone his torch through the windows, checked the doors and the yard gate. Everything had been in order.

Bryce waited. The wind blew spots of rain in his face. He turned his head aside and was sure he heard a voice.

He crossed the cobbled road soundlessly, cat-treading on thick rubber soles. On the far side he stepped into the shadows in front of the building. Reaching behind him under his cape, he slid his thumb through the thong of his truncheon and drew it halfway out of the special pocket in his trousers. He adjusted his fingers on the grip, getting the thong taut round the heel of his hand so the truncheon couldn't be snatched away. He heard the grating sound again and pulled the truncheon clear of his pocket.

Somebody was in the yard. Bryce stepped close to the wall, inched his way along to the gate. It swung inwards at his touch. On the other side a man was panting, moving something heavy over the soft ground, hitting an occasional stone. Bryce unclipped his torch, got his thumb on the button and drew back the truncheon.

He held his breath and put his head into the foot-wide opening. At a guess his target was seven or eight feet away. *Step up close, get the light in his eyes and baton his shoulders – one, two, hard, close to the neck . . .*

Bryce opened the gate wider, staring into the inky dark as he stepped forward on his toes. He heard a grunt and a muttered curse, a young voice, maybe even familiar . . .

There was an explosion, or so it seemed. It was deafening. Bryce saw blinding white and felt himself go down. His elbow hit the ground and pain tore along his arm. He howled but couldn't hear himself for the noise in his head. Something hit his face, then his chest. He tasted salt warm blood, tried to cry out again but he had no wind. Maybe he was lying on his face, he didn't know, there was grit mixed with the blood in his mouth. A blow harder than anything he had ever felt landed on the back of his head. The noise in his ears stopped. There was silence.

Bryce knew he was there, on the ground, hurt. But he knew it without hearing or seeing, without feeling anything.

A street sweeper found him seven hours later, curled on his side with his head in a congealed puddle of his own blood. A wheelbarrow stood six feet away. Beside it a small safe lay on its back, green and gilt-banded with a shiny brass door handle. The roadman believed the constable was dead. His face looked caved-in above the nose and his skin beneath the purple smears of blood was the colour of butter. One eye was half open. There was no sign of breathing.

The enormity of his discovery caught up with the man. He ran out into the street, shouting. A policeman across the road stopped and the man began jumping up and down, yelling, pointing at the yard gate. Within minutes there were eight policemen there and not long after an ambulance came. Constable Bryce, who was still alive, was put on a stretcher and whisked away to the Royal Infirmary in Cathedral Street.

Shortly after noon the following day, in the gloomy charge room of a men's surgical ward, a harassed young doctor delivered the verdict to Chief Inspector Laurie and Detective Inspector MacKay of Central Division.

'He's in a bit of a mess. Fractures of the frontal and occipital bones of the skull. They're not massive, only hairlines really, but they're fractures all the same. Two nasal bones are smashed and the orbital bone of one eye's cracked. He has two fractured ribs. We think he was attacked with some kind of club, possibly made of metal.'

'There was an iron bar lying beside him in the yard,' MacKay said. 'A Christ-awful sight it was, too. Blood and hair all over the end of it. They've got it at the lab.'

'Thank the Lord for the lab,' Laurie said. 'I've no doubt

they'll exhaust the resources of forensic science to prove the bar was *probably* used to batter Bryce. Clever people, our lab boys.'

Laurie was a man of imperious height with sad, deep-set eyes and a habit of pushing one end of his curly moustache into his mouth and chewing it. He looked at the doctor, chomping softly on the dark bristles.

'Is he conscious?'

'He came round about tea time last night. He's slept on and off ever since.'

'What are his chances?'

'He's strong,' the doctor said, 'otherwise he wouldn't have survived lying out in the cold so long. We'll need to wait and see how things settle down. The left eye's damaged, we can't assess the extent of it yet, but if the sight's gone . . .' He shrugged. 'The other one could go. It happens often enough. Sympathetic reaction, not fully understood.'

'What else?'

'We get a weak reflex response in his left leg, so there's some kind of nerve damage, and the neurologist thinks he might be partially deaf on the left side.'

'Can we talk to him?' MacKay said.

The doctor nodded.

'Try not to tire him. And don't expect too much. His head's giving him a lot of pain and his ribs are strapped. He'll find it hard to speak.'

They were led to a screened bed. Chief Inspector Laurie went in first with MacKay a step behind. The constable who had been sitting by the bed got up and left. Laurie's eyes turned a shade sadder as he gazed at David Bryce. He was propped on a sloping metal backrest with his chest, neck and head cocooned in bandages. The exposed oval of face was puffy and discoloured, the left eye covered with a pink celluloid shield sprouting cotton wool at the edges. There was a grooved, horizontal bruise across the eyebrows. Red rubber tubes descended from his nostrils and disappeared over the side of the bed.

'Name of Christ,' MacKay breathed.

'Can you hear me, son?' Laurie said.

The good eye flickered, opened wide. It stared at the police tunic, then at Laurie's face. The lips moved dryly, stopped, tried again.

'Yes, sir,' Bryce croaked.

'Are you in a lot of pain?'

Bryce made a fractional nod.

'We won't stop. We just wanted to see how you were.'

'And ask you one question, Davey.' MacKay moved forward and leaned over the bed. 'Have you any idea who did this? From the footprints we think there were three of them. Any names?'

The tip of Bryce's tongue poked through his lips and slid from side to side.

'I thought I knew a voice.' He stopped, wincing as if his words had scraped something raw. 'I was trying to think, a while back. My head's that sore, though . . .'

'Think *now*,' MacKay said, leaning closer, his beer belly pressing on the sheets. 'Picture it happening again. See it in your mind. Try to hear the voice and put a name to it. Try hard, Davey. It's important – '

'Steady,' Laurie grunted.

MacKay stayed where he was, leaning over Bryce, waiting.

Bryce's eye closed. He was motionless for nearly a minute, then he moved his head back an inch, inhaled sharply and tried to cough. There was a frothy rumble in his chest. The eye opened again.

'I can't be sure about this,' he said.

'You don't need to be. Just give us a name, eh?'

'Well . . . It was dark, mind. Pitch. And he wasn't talking out loud, he was nearly whispering. Swearing.'

'Who?' MacKay demanded.

'Could've been young Kane. Him from Monteith Row. Hard wee bugger, never out of trouble.'

'Jack Kane?'

'Aye. But I can't swear to it.'

MacKay nodded once, a sharp chop of the head. He

stepped back from the bed and looked at the Chief Inspector.

'I'll get on to it,' he said. 'We'll have him in the station that fast he'll think he's got wheels.'

Laurie hadn't taken his eyes off Bryce.

'If he happens to fall on his kisser a couple of times on the road round,' he said, chewing gently, 'and if he hurts his knackers that bad he's got to get carried, we'll not complain about the delay.'

Barrowland, known commonly as the Barras, was a market occupying roughly three acres near Glasgow's city centre. It was a sprawl of carts, barrows, stalls and open-backed vans laden with everything from clothes, food, crockery, toys, and bed linen, to rare stamps, cameras, herbal cures, and furniture. It started in a roofed enclosure on the Gallowgate and spilled out southward along back turnings and side streets as far as the London Road. On Saturdays the streets were choked with shoppers and sightseers, churning their way among the stalls, looking and listening as traders yelled at them about revolutionary novelties, suicidal price cuts and once-in-a-lifetime offers. It was a great place to do the weekly shopping, as long as you were careful, and if you were at a loose end there was no cheaper diversion than a walk round the Barras.

But you did have to be careful. Nobody knew that better than Detective Constable Loudon, a heavily pock-marked man in his forties whose chances of promotion had been submerged by his love of drink. Loudon was an authority on the market's criminal undertow. He was there most Saturdays, keeping an eye out, observing old patterns of criminal activity, noting the evolution of new ones. He made prowling circuits of the market, doling out eye-threats to thieves, whores, touts and molesters, verbally warning bookies' runners and making occasional arrests. The point of the drill was containment, never cure. A man's expectations had to be reasonable – some scourges were rooted too deep to be eliminated.

'Even if they gave us guns,' Loudon would tell younger

detectives, 'we'd never wipe out the three Ps – pickpockets, prostitutes, and poofs.'

Today Loudon was looking for a particular pickpocket, a boy who had learned his trade here when he was ten years old. He was sixteen now and so good you didn't dare blink or you'd miss him making his move.

'Jack Kane's talent puts him in the expert league,' Loudon said, addressing DC Fraser, a recent transfer from uniform branch who had come along to assist with the arrest. 'He learned the hard way. Practice, endless practice. Right from the start he knew there were no quick roads, no shortcuts or easy methods.'

'What does the inspector want him for?'

'No idea. He's playing at grim-and-silent today. He just said to pick up Jack Kane.'

They pushed their way through a crowd who watched, rapt and silent, as a grizzled little man demonstrated the shine they could put on faded chrome if they bought his secret-formula polish, sixpence a tin.

'How does a kid learn to pick pockets?' DC Fraser said.

'Some of them are self-taught. They don't tend to last. Jack Kane was privileged. He was a pupil of the mighty Barry MacLaren.'

'Never heard of him.'

'Oh, he was something special. King of the lifters. A dazzler. He worked round Glasgow for thirty years and was hardly ever arrested. He died a couple of years back, but he lives on through Kane's nimble fingers.'

'So what's the secret?'

'Nothing mysterious,' Loudon said. 'He uses the classic method, but he's refined it to something like an art.'

'I don't know anything about these things,' Fraser said. 'It can be a sheltered life, wearing a uniform.'

Loudon stopped, peering over the heads of the diminutive punters around him. He pointed to the right and they started walking in that direction.

'MacLaren taught his pupils never to *take* victims' wallets or purses off them,' he explained to Fraser. 'The trick, you see, is to attach yourself to whatever you want

17

to pinch, then at the right moment stand still and let the mug walk away from his valuables. Get it?'

'I think so.'

'That's the telltale sign if you're out to catch Jack at his trade. He'll get in among a moving crowd and walk beside a man, or just a wee bit behind, matching the fella's pace, not looking at him, and at some point he'll stop in his tracks and gaze about the place, all vague-faced and innocent. When you see that happening – *if* you see it – you can bet he's got a wallet or a wad clipped between his fingers.'

'Does he come here every week?'

'He's about the place most Saturdays, but he's not always working. I think he's temperamental. A real artist, y'know? If the inspiration's not on him, he doesn't try.'

'In my book,' Fraser said, 'a crook's just a crook. It's too easy to romanticise them.'

'Dead easy to underestimate them, too,' Loudon said.

They walked on past a radio-parts stall and a chip van with its heavy smell of over-used fat. At the corner a bearded man in filthy rags sat on the ground with his knees drawn up to his chin. He appeared to be asleep. By his feet was a cap with three coppers in it and a hand-lettered card that said SUBJECT TO EPILEPTIC FITS.

'I wouldn't have thought your master thief would do too well round here,' Fraser said. 'This isn't the place it used to be.'

Since 1930 Glasgow's fortunes had followed the general downward spiral. The shipyards were struggling, textile manufacture was at a fraction of pre-war output and the steel works had empty order books. For people in work the wages were low: bricklayers could pick up £3 10/-, engineers and mineworkers got £3 on average for a seventy-two-hour week.

For the unemployed things were a lot worse. The dole paid a single man seventeen shillings a week and a married man with three children got less than thirty shillings. To survive they had to learn to beg, steal, or improvise. Enterprising men with families to feed often did all three.

In most working-class homes soup was the main meal of the day; bones were boiled five or six times to extract every atom of nourishment. Bread was a staple too, and when it couldn't be bought it was made from anything that would rise in an oven. Men made forays into the countryside to steal wheat which they ground up – husks and all – to make a kind of flour that was mixed with water, then shaped into loaves, or flat scones that were baked on the kitchen range. Heat, above all, was central to survival. In the cold weather an open fire could be kept going with street rubbish, old shoes, broken boxes, twigs, potato peelings. If hard cash was needed the pawnbrokers would offer money on anything that was saleable.

The stalls at Barrowland reflected the times. There were plenty of quality goods for the out-of-town specialist punters, but the majority, the mainstay domestic customers, were offered what they were looking for and could just about afford – second-hand clothes, day-old bread and buns, meat pies with mysterious grey-brown fillings, bruised and spotted fruit, and cheap alcohol-based medicines to alleviate the symptoms of everything from tuberculosis to manic depression.

'Kane never thieves off his own kind,' Loudon said. 'He goes for visitors – antique collectors on the lookout for a bargain, jewellers hunting for spare bits, publicans taking a breather. I'd say he does all right for a kid.'

Loudon stopped. He tapped Fraser's arm.

'There he is. At the corner. He's the one not leaning on the wall.'

Fraser looked and saw a muscular young man in a grey fisherknit jumper with a black woolly scarf showing above the neck.

'I thought you said he's only sixteen.'

'He is. The life he leads would put years on anybody.'

Kane was talking earnestly to two other boys, his head making gestures. His stance – feet spread, hands clasping his elbows – suggested compact, restrained energy. He had a squarish, even-featured face, the nose flattening towards the tip. As the detectives drew nearer Fraser

19

noticed Kane's eyes. They were usually what people noticed first. They were an angelic blue and disquietingly steady.

'Aye then, Jackie,' Loudon said, nodding to him. 'How's it going?'

The two leaning on the wall looked at their feet. Kane turned and stared.

'Ma name's no' Jackie,' he said. 'It's Jack. Jackie's what folk call their budgies.' He passed his fingers through his cropped dark hair. 'It's Mister Kane to strangers, anyway.'

'Right, right. No offence.' Loudon smiled tightly. 'I'm not exactly a stranger though, am I?'

DC Fraser glanced at Loudon. What was going on here? He was talking to this ned like he was something special. They were here to arrest him, not crawl into his favour.

'I'm on an errand from Mr MacKay,' Loudon explained. 'He'd like a wee word. Over at the station.'

'What about?' Kane demanded.

'He didn't say. I suppose he'll explain when you get there.'

'Tell him I'm busy.'

'Aw, come on now, Jack. No need to make an issue out of this, eh? Just come across to the station and have a word with the man. He's not going to take no for an answer, you know that.'

Kane's jaw tightened. He hooked his thumbs in his trouser pockets.

'I've not done anythin',' he said.

'Well you've nothing to worry about, have you?'

'Once the swing doors shut behind *anybody* they've *everythin'* to worry about.'

'Och, you're exaggerating. I'm sure the inspector just wants a chat. He didn't seem to be in a very bad mood.'

'Ah'm no' worried about his mood. He can feel any way he wants. Ah just don't like bein' picked up every time the notion comes up his back.'

'Look – why not come along with us and get it over and done with?'

'It's a nice day. I'm enjoyin' the fresh air.'

DC Fraser's patience ran out.

'Come on,' he said, grasping Kane's elbow.

'Paws off!' Kane jerked his arm away. He looked at Loudon. 'Who's yer pal?'

A few people had stopped to watch. Loudon waggled his hands placatingly.

'Now, now, we don't want a sideshow.'

'This yin started it,' Kane snapped. He glared at Fraser. 'If you want to play at bein' a hard man pick on a wee lassie. That'd be more yer mark.'

The boys by the wall grinned. Fraser, incensed at losing face, tried to grab Kane again. The lad stepped back sharply and Fraser grabbed thin air.

'Tell him,' Kane said to Loudon. 'He keeps his hands off me or else.'

'Or else what?' Fraser demanded.

'Ye'll wake up with a crowd round you.'

'Cheeky wee bastard!'

Fraser lunged with both hands. Loudon caught him by the wrists.

'Pack it in, for Christ's sake!'

'You're letting him treat us like shite!' Fraser yelped. 'Maybe you don't mind, but I do!'

'Put a lid on it,' Loudon hissed, pushing Fraser back. He turned to Kane. 'Are you coming?'

Kane slid his hands into his pockets. He glanced at his two friends, then at Loudon. He shrugged.

'I was gettin' bored hangin' about here, anyway.'

They went off, Kane sauntering beside Loudon. Fraser gave the pair by the wall his hard look, the slow burn, nemesis in a gabardine raincoat and a soft hat. As he turned away he was sure one of them muttered something, but he didn't have enough composure to turn back and challenge them.

* * *

21

The Cockit Hat was a small gloomy pub halfway along the Bridgegate between the Saltmarket and Clyde Street. As Glasgow pubs went it was quiet – which meant that in 1932 the place was nearly always deserted. Men didn't often have the money for drink, and when they did they weren't likely to spend it with Dougie Meickle, the pub's wheezing gaffer. He was a bad-tempered man, forever preoccupied with his ill health and convinced, moreover, that people would always try to cheat him if he didn't keep his mistrust burning full flame.

The place was old and badly maintained. The floorboards were buckled and split – strangers invariably tripped over them. Dougie never bothered to change the sawdust and it had clotted in rat-grey dollops round protruding rusty nailheads and in the corners under the seats. Airchie Cairns used the Cockit Hat because Dougie needed the trade and so he wasn't fussy about the age of his customers. Airchie sat at one of the less ancient tables, an oblong unpainted plank on iron legs. He nursed a pint while he waited for Jack Kane. Because the table was relatively new there wasn't much to read. *Jimmy Nicholl 1919* was carved boldly in the centre, and beside it *Murdo MacIver, Perth. God Bless Partick* was inscribed in passable gothic nearer the edge, and below that was *Fuck the Pope* in coarse penknife.

'Quiet, the night,' Airchie said amiably as Dougie came to the end of the bar and wiped it with his rag.

'Quiet every night,' Dougie rumbled, glowering through the fronds of his eyebrows. 'Ye'd think the bliddy plague had landed out on that street.'

Airchie, a seventeen-year-old with the kind of flat-nosed, bulge-eyed, thin-lipped ugliness that people somehow found likeable, sat back on the rexine-covered bench and looked at his beer. It was cloudy. Flat, too, because he'd hung on to it for twenty-five minutes. He could only afford one pint and if he drank it down fast, which he'd love to do, Dougie would come and stare at him until he ordered another one.

Jack was late. He'd said seven o'clock and now it was

after half-past. He was usually on time. This was supposed to be a special Saturday night, too. Jack had forecast he was going to be flush, with enough cash on him for the two of them to have a good night out. He hadn't said how he'd manage that, and when he didn't volunteer information you never asked for it.

'A nose stickin' in my business,' he'd once told a Govan lad, 'is like a hand crawlin' up ma shirt tail. Ah don't like it, so don't do it.' For a youth not quite seventeen he could be uncommonly brittle and fixed in his views. And candid. 'Talkin' to you,' he said to a doorman at a Maryhill dance hall, 'is like washin' a hankie.'

Airchie had put on his good jacket tonight – and a tie – because Jack had said he fancied going to the dancing. What he really fancied was picking up a couple of girls, but you couldn't do that if you didn't go to the dancing because most Glasgow pubs didn't let women in. The few that did seemed to attract all the ferret-faced skelly-eyed old disease-carriers between the Broomielaw and Cowcaddens. So Airchie was spruced up and brilliantined for the bright lights. Where the hell was Jack?

'Yer friend's not with you the night, then?' Dougie said.

'He'll be here in a wee while.'

'I was in the army wi' a lad the image of him.' Dougie paused to cough and spit the product on the floor behind the bar. 'First time I saw yer pal it gave me a turn. I thought he was the one I used to know. Daft, that. He'd be my age now, if the Jerries hadnae blew his head off at Passchendaele.' Dougie drew his rag absently across the pump handles. 'There's a strong similarity, all right. Same kinda walk, same manner. Same look. He's got a face for the gallows, that pal of yours.'

Jack turned up at a quarter to seven. He had on his brown suit with the bum-freezer jacket, a cream shirt and a dark green tie with black racehorses on it. His stubbly hair was smarmed flat and shiny. At the bar he asked Dougie for two pints of heavy and brought them to the table.

'Where've you been?' Airchie demanded. 'Ah've got pins and needles in ma arse.'

Jack sat down opposite. He put his glass carefully to his lips and took four gulps, half emptying it. He put down the glass and wiped his mouth with the back of his hand.

'I was at Central Division until half-six.'

'Eh?' Airchie's face clouded. He leaned forward. 'What happened?'

'A polis got battered last night. Bryce. Know him?'

'Oh aye,' Airchie nodded. 'He's no' a bad yin, considerin'.'

'He copped his whack in the dark, couldn't see a thing, but he thought he heard ma voice.'

'*Was* it you?'

Jack shook his head solemnly.

'I was there, but I never touched him.'

'Who, then?'

'That numskull Liddell.'

'Bert Liddell?'

'Him. The one an' only. All he had to do was keep an eye on the gate an' handle any trouble. Simple lookout job. Me an' Wullie Mather was shiftin' a safe out of Culligans. The polis showed up before we could get it into the barra. So Liddell lays into him with an iron bar.' Jack shook his head. 'Can ye credit it? He's got to be fourteen stone, six feet if he's an inch, but he goes an' uses an iron bar.'

'So what did they say to you at the station?'

'The usual. I might as well confess, they've got proof, all that keech. So I said they better just use their proof if they want to bring charges because I'd got nothin' to tell them. MacKay tried gettin' heavy. I waited until the other polisman went along the passage to get their tea, then I told MacKay if anythin' happened to me, he'd get a tap on the shoulder one night an' end up with a spare mouth halfway down his neck.'

'Did he believe that?'

'I made him believe it. I think *he* thinks I've got gang connections.' Jack grinned. 'He's just a big pudden. He put on some more of the hard chat an' the bluster, but his eyes were kinda wobbly by then. At five o'clock he went away an' they sent in another guy to question me. I gave him the same story – I'm innocent, I don't know what this is all about, an' the more I say it the more he spills – how Bryce is in the Royal with his skull cracked, his eye damaged, ribs broken, an' all they've got to work on is him sayin' that *maybe* he heard my voice. They had to let me go. They've nothin' on me.'

'D'ye think Bryce did hear you?'

'Maybe. We were havin' a lot of trouble with that safe. It was a wee one but it was heavy. We near ruptured ourselves gettin' it across the yard – I might have been cursin' a bit.' Jack emptied his glass and stood up. 'Ready for another one?'

Airchie nodded, handed over his glass.

'Was it worth all the strife?'

'I should have stayed in the house,' Jack said. 'We had to leave the safe an' run for it. Even if we'd got it out we'd've been no better off. The second guy that questioned me, he says there was nothin' in it but ledgers.'

Jack went to the bar and ordered two more drinks. He was still there when a tall man in a belted raincoat came in and spoke to him. Airchie watched, fascinated by the way the man chewed the end of his moustache while he talked. Jack was half smiling and his eyes were hard, defiant. He said something, the man glared at him, muttered something back, then turned and walked out. Jack came back with the fresh pints.

'Who was that?'

'Chief Inspector Laurie. A big turd if ever there was one.' Jack sat down. 'He wanted to let me know he's got his eye on me. I told him I was dead glad I'd put on brown trousers. His partin' message was that I'll soon learn not to be cheeky to my betters.' He sat back and sighed. 'It's not been the kind of week I thought it'd be, Airchie. But we're fixed for tonight, an' that's all that matters.' He took three folded pound notes from his breast pocket and handed them to his friend. 'Don't spend it all in the one shop.'

Airchie looked about him and pocketed the money.

'How come ye're flush? You were skint on Wednesday. An' the thing wi' the safe went wrong. What gives?'

Jack looked at him, his blue eyes wide and steady.

'Is it any of your business?'

Airchie took the reprimand with a little nod and a swift spread of the hands. With Jack you didn't ask questions. He'd forgotten.

'I dipped Torrance,' Jack said. 'I was goin' to tell you, anyway.'

'What?' Airchie looked incredulous, then delighted. 'The rent man?'

'He asks for it, carryin' that baton everywhere with him. That's a challenge, intit? So I took the challenge. Pure accident how it happened, though. When I came out the polis station I thought, Christ, I could go a pint. So I went in the Dalrymple. Who should be standin' there at the bar but Torrance. Havin' a sherry, readin' the paper with the baton stickin' out his coat pocket. Our Lady's lookin' after me, I thought. The place was busy so I got myself tucked in nice an' tight beside him. I gave the barman my last shillin', got ma pint an' waited. After about five minutes Torrance went for a piss an' I got out of it.' He patted his breast pocket. 'Eight quid.'

'Jesus!'

'Up till then, I thought I'd be round here tellin' you we couldn't go anywhere tonight.'

'That's great,' Airchie said. 'Terrific. I hate that Torrance. Everybody hates him. Who'd have thought we'd get a night out on the bastard?'

They decided they would have a few pints in the Cockit Hat then go up to a dance hall on St Vincent Street where Jack had been lucky a couple of times. The first girl he'd picked up there with was a slumming university student who believed him when he told her he was twenty-two and a shipping clerk from Greenock. The second one was a married woman. She didn't care what he did or how old

26

he was so long as he kept buying her drinks. She had been a lot more uninhibited than the first one, but the encounter had resulted in Jack paying six visits to the Black Street Clinic. He'd lied about his age there, too.

Over the third and fourth pints they discussed the parlous position their solo status put them in. It was a subject they talked about often. Neither of them was mob-minded, but they had to admit that only the gangs gave a man the kind of protection he needed in these days of increased police presence, trade depression, and shrunken options.

'It's not easy bein' a hired hand or goin' it alone any more,' Jack said. 'You're the lonely man in the middle an' both sides lay into you when they feel like it. The polis can lift you without anybody puttin' the warnin' on them or givin' you an alibi. The gangs'll pick on you if they think you're trespassin' on their territory. An' there's the wars – the bastards *make* you take sides, an' if you happen to support the wrong one you get a kickin', with nobody to back you. Maybe we should think about joinin' up, Airchie.'

There was security in the gang life. Members rarely went without. It was a demanding existence and at times highly distasteful, but it was better than being a ready-made target for whichever outfit decided you were due for chastising. The writing was on the wall, anyway; all over the city private criminal enterprise was amalgamating with the combines. Jack had had offers, so had Airchie. They were both known to be hard lads, and reliable. They could see in straight lines and each had an impressive capacity for reactive loyalty. Jack had more practical experience than Airchie, but when Airchie did get involved in anything he showed initiative and guts. The Kingston Clan's one-armed scout, Mad Harry McColl, had approached them in a south-side pub and told them they would be welcome to join his prestigious outfit any time they wanted.

'We'd have no trouble gettin' in,' Jack said. 'What do you think?'

'I think what you think. I'd sooner stay my own man, but it's no' too practical any more. An' I'm fed up bein' skint all the time.'

'Right.' Jack slapped the table. 'We'll leave it at that, for now. Tonight we'll go out an' have a wee bit of fun. Monday we'll get ourselves sorted out.'

They left the pub at ten past nine. At the corner of the Saltmarket, hunched against the cold, they stopped when three tall men stepped out of a closeway and blocked the pavement in front of them. The trio were only silhouettes, but Jack recognised the shape of Chief Inspector Laurie.

'So what's the score?' Jack said. 'Are ye goin' to let us past, or what?'

The man nearest the kerb pushed Airchie into the road.

'Stay there,' he said.

Airchie made to resist. The man brought up a truncheon and tapped him on the chest with it.

'Stay,' he said.

The other two already had Jack. One was behind him, holding him in a choke grip. The other man stood in front.

'Spread his feet,' he grunted.

Airchie saw the man's arm swing out, his truncheon glinting dully. The arm flashed back. There was a sound like wood hitting a pillow. Jack gurgled against the pressure on his neck. The man in front moved in close and brought up his knee. Jack groaned. The knee was sunk in his groin three more times, short stiff jabs, then he was released. He fell and the big man with the truncheon kicked him in the chest. Without another sound the three men regrouped and walked away along the Saltmarket.

Airchie helped Jack to his feet. He couldn't make out his features in the gloom.

'Are ye all right? Anythin' broken?'

Jack said nothing. He panted for a while, bent over, clutching his chest with one arm, the other hand rubbing his crotch.

'Feels like ma balls caught fire,' he panted eventually.

'No serious damage?' Airchie said.

'Only my plans for tonight,' Jack panted. 'Give us a hand.'

Airchie helped him into the mouth of a close. Jack stood with his hand on the wall for a minute, then he vomited. Groaning, he leaned back on the wall, fumbled in his pocket and handed Airchie a shilling.

'Go back to the pub an' get us twenty Kensitas. A fag'll settle ma stomach.'

Another twenty minutes passed before he felt he could move. He dropped the burning end of his second cigarette and pushed himself away from the wall. He put his arm round Airchie's shoulder and they stepped out of the close.

'This way,' Jack said, pointing back along the Bridgegate.

'Where are we goin'?'

'Down to the lavvies on Clyde Street. Ah want to get cleaned up.'

'What – are we still goin' to the dancin'?'

'Bugger the dancin',' Jack grunted. 'We're goin' over the river to look for Mad Harry.'

TWO

Changes were happening in the world that made Jack wonder, now and again, if his grandpa had been right when he said there would be another war before the thirties were over.

Jack didn't fancy the idea of fighting in a world war. He couldn't imagine being any good at it. There could be nothing personal, no angry thrust in the guts, because a war was somebody else's fight. And there were no benefits. Survival was the one and only bonus.

Some bonus.

Glasgow had a fair few examples of men who put on khaki, faced the hun and survived. There were the ones who'd been gassed and could hardly breathe, lots of them, standing outside pubs and on street corners gulping air as if they were trying to eat it. One-legged men were everywhere and the legless variety weren't exactly scarce. 'Counting the limps' was a game Jack and Airchie had played when they were younger – they stood on a busy street and one of them made a tally of how many cripples went past while the other one counted to a hundred. Men had come back in their thousands with bits missing and faculties impaired. There was a blind clarinet player who begged in St Enoch's Square; he was thirty-two, but the war had made him a gaunt old man with dark holes in the front of his skull that you could see if you sneaked a look through the side of his black specs. And there were all the widows and the kids with no fathers, hardly a street without them. War was very bad for people. But it looked like the world hadn't learned that lesson.

Jack didn't look at the papers much but other folk did, and they talked about the news all the time. The older people could read warnings of a conflagration from the stories of little fires smouldering all over the world. In Britain there were hunger marches, and late in 1932 somebody called Oswald Mosley formed the British Union of Fascists – that story worried some of the older heads very badly. At the beginning of 1933 there was big trouble with the anarchists in Spain. In Germany a deranged-looking character called Hitler had been appointed Chancellor; old men sitting on the benches in Glasgow Green were unanimous in the view that everybody should watch that bugger Hitler. He'd be the real trouble, just wait and see. Every week the papers carried stories about the swelling power of the Nazis – in Glasgow they called them nazzies, black-uniformed men with thrusting jaws and holy zeal in their eyes. To Jack they looked like advanced, super-powered police.

In spite of the troubles at home and abroad, in 1934 trade began to pick up. In Glasgow more ships were being built and the steel works were busy. Foreign customers were lining up again for textiles and engineering goods. The dole queues shortened. Jack's father, Alistair, after being out of work for four years, got a job reading gas meters in the new council houses out at Uddingston. There was money about, shops and pubs did a healthy trade and people began to look more cheerful.

World news remained ominous. There was a general strike in Spain and the papers talked about the likelihood of civil war. In Britain Winston Churchill warned Parliament about the menace of Germany's air power. On the other side of the world Japan was denouncing old treaties made with America, while the Russians were rounding up political leaders and putting them in prison for treason. Everywhere, it seemed, there was snarling unrest. In the words of Dougie Meikle, gaffer of the Cockit Hat, the world was in a bad mood.

If Jack had known the word 'microcosm' he might have used it to describe how the politics of his own world mirrored the global state of affairs. By the middle of 1935 he had been a member of the Kingston Clan for three years. In that time he had seen the neutral territories shrink, the viciousness steepen, the all-or-nothing policies proliferate.

It was an exhilarating life, profitable and dangerous. A Kingston Clan boy died when he accidentally trespassed on another gang's sacred ground: a man had stepped up to him in a Cathcart pub and shoved a knife into his stomach. The Kingstons' reprisal – a daylight raid on a wedding reception – produced seventeen casualties, nine of them serious, with one man paralysed and two disabled for life. In terms of overall violence that hadn't been exceptional. Glasgow had mob fights every week and there was at least one gang death a month. Maiming and disfigurement became common as more of the lads started carrying knuckledusters, razors, bayonets. Jack himself got a three-inch battle scar on his cheek six weeks after he joined the Clan, though in three years he inflicted much more damage than he sustained. In common with Airchie he acquired the disciplines and instincts of the street warrior. He learned that anger could be switched on, that hate could be conjured from his chemistry to boost the skill in his fists. By swift degrees the conviction had grown in him that fighting – war – was an impulse inside every man who wasn't a coward, and no amount of sweet reason would ever drive it out. Men, he could sometimes believe, were born to fight.

On a muggy day in October when his father brought home the weighty news that Italy had invaded Abyssinia, Jack was standing at the living room window, gazing down into the well made by the walls of other tenements. Children were playing in groups on the flagged court two storeys below. He had played down there himself when he was a toddler. The scene was heavy with nostalgia if Jack had cared to notice, but he wasn't looking at the children. Over in the far right corner a girl in a pinnie was pegging out washing on a line. She was Jessie Young, a lissom sweet-faced eighteen-year-old and Jack's current

32

passion. She was a current problem, too. He would be seeing her tonight, they would talk about it, he would reassure her and try to come up with an answer, if she hadn't found one by herself. There were things to be done before then, though; as he watched Jessie, seeing the muscles tense on her bare calves as she reached up to the clothesline, he thought of her as his reward for a good night's work. If things didn't turn out so well, she could just as easily be his consolation.

'Aye, it'll come to war yet,' Alistair Kane said, hanging his jacket on the back of the door and easing himself into his chair by the fire. 'The Germans an' the Tallies between them'll see to that.'

The remark died on the air. Jack said nothing; his mother, at the table with her mixing bowl, rolling pin and mounds of dough, didn't seem to hear.

Alistair crossed his legs and sighed importantly.

'Give it a year or two, there'll be no holdin' them.'

He was passing on somebody else's opinion. There was no talent in him for formulating views of his own. Life had scraped its way past Alistair, taking away more than it imparted. He was passive, friendless, a man of no discernible character. At forty-four he looked ten years older. He was tall and stooped, empty-faced with perennially watering eyes. He could sit and stare at the fire for hours. When he read at all it was always the same book, his wife's copy of Pierce's *Lives of Ten Saints*. In spite of that he never opened his mouth about the saints.

His wife did, however. Marie Kane, a drab, skeletally thin woman, was an authority on saints. On the Holy Family, too, and all the apostles and popes. She knew what was worth knowing about the Roman ritual and the hierarchical order in the Vatican. Litanies were no mystery to her, neither were catechisms. She was versed in the procedures governing the sacraments of Baptism, penance, Eucharist, marriage, holy orders, confirmation and the anointing of the sick. Marie was, in short, a rabid Catholic, one whose religious knowledge was less a source of spiritual enrichment than a club for battering Protestant heresy. She despised Protestants. That didn't make her unique in Glasgow, where many Catholics and Protestants regarded each other as subhuman. But Marie's knowledge of her faith was unusual, since most religious bigotry in Scotland was based on tribal traditions that took no account of Christianity, apart from the labels. Marie had inherited her distaste for Protestants from her father; the learning had come later, prompted by her uncommon need to know what she was shouting about.

'Pope Pius wouldnae let the Italian people go to war,' she said now, shaping a bun. 'He's a man of peace.'

Hearing that, Jack smiled at the window. She managed to bring religion into everything. It coloured practically every utterance she made. Her head must be like a wee cathedral. When he had once told her he was going out with a girl – the first time he admitted such a thing, a year ago when he was eighteen – his mother's immediate response was, 'I hope she's not a Protestant.'

He turned from the window and looked at himself in the mirror above the mantelpiece. The hair was just the way he wanted it, at long last. For two years now he had worn it longer, though short at the back and sides, with a centre parting. Keeping it in place had been a struggle until one of the lads had put him on to gum arabic. His hair felt as stiff as a board these days but it stayed in place in all weathers.

'Any signs of a job?' his father said.

'I'm still lookin'.'

'There's work to be got, if you really want it. Things are a lot easier now.'

'I know.' Jack took his jacket from the back of a chair and slipped it on. 'But I'm managin' to keep body an' soul together. Don't worry about me.'

'That's all very well – ' his father began, but Jack put out a stiff warning finger.

'Skip the lecture, Da.'

'I think I've a right to state my views in ma own house,' Alistair piped, glancing at his wife.

'Sure,' Jack said, 'go ahead. But leave me out of whatever you've got to say.'

'A father can have an opinion about the son he's raised . . .'

'Do me a favour, eh?' Jack stood over his father, compact, resolutely separate. 'Spare me that kind of patter. I've looked after myself since I left school. I've paid my own way. I never had a button off you, but I've put money in your pocket an' seen ma mother all right for the housekeepin' all the time you were out of work. I put that shirt on your back.'

'Oh, well, if that's the way it's to be . . .' Alistair folded his arms and waggled his head at the fireplace. 'Throwin' it in my teeth . . .'

'Ah'm no' throwin' anythin' in your teeth,' Jack said. 'You were welcome to every penny I could give you. All I'm sayin' is, you're in no position to spout at me about the company I keep an' the way I earn my money. If you'd ever refused to take it, then you'd have a right to shoot yer face off.'

Alistair tightened his arms around his chest and glared at the ash pan.

'Are you not stoppin' for your tea?' Marie said.

'Ah've a lot to do.' Jack buttoned his jacket, checked his hair in the mirror again. 'I'll see you the night.'

As he went down the tenement steps he thought about the impulse he'd had just before he came out. He had wanted to put his hands on his mother's shoulders and peck her cheek. It was something he had never done, though the desire to commit the act was often there. He could imagine the fluster if he ever gave in and did it, if he plonked one right on her face. She would be a week getting over the affront. In Glasgow a lot of men grew up without ever hearing their parents address each other by their first names. Open displays of affection were never encouraged. To kiss somebody or cuddle them where other people could see was somehow indecent. If that was how the majority in Glasgow really felt then Jack had to be an oddity, for he would often have loved to give his daft old lady a hug.

He walked south and crossed the river by the Victoria Bridge. A brisk ten-minute walk took him to the corner of Norfolk Street and Gorbals Street. He went through one of the sooted doorways and up a flight of stone stairs. At the top he knocked twice on a chipped brown door and waited. A man opened it a crack, the visible parts of his face clenched with suspicion. He recognised Jack and pulled the door wide.

'Right on time,' he said. 'Ye're a brammer. Ah'll no' be late for my tea, just for a change.'

Jack stepped into the narrow hallway. The man closed the door, took his jacket off a wall peg and put it on. Jack took his jacket off and rolled up his sleeves.

'Many in?' he said.

'Sixteen. There'll be more later. It's Friday. Some fellas can't wait to get separated from their pocket money.'

The man left and Jack dropped the catch on the door. He went into the big converted living room beyond the hall. The windows were blacked out. Lights hung over three trestle tables set up in the middle of the room, each one covered with green baize, tacked at the edges with drawing pins. Three games were on offer – dice, roulette, pontoon, presided over by three members of the Kingston Clan. They nodded to Jack as he came in. The punters, their faces shadowy beyond the perimeter of the low-slung lampshades, kept their eyes on their money.

Jack took up his position near the door. His function for the next three hours was to keep an eye on the road – which he could do by peering through the edge of the blackout – and to answer the door. He was also expected to handle any trouble, which usually only happened when men lost more than they could afford. Occasionally one would realise he was being cheated, and say so, but that didn't happen often. The table operators were experts, lads who had worked the markets up and down the country doing the three-shell game, Find the Lady and Prick the Garter. They could, as Mad Harry put it, steal your eye-teeth while you were talking to them.

This stint always dragged, but whenever Jack got bored

he reminded himself he was on a good thing. He would make a fiver for the shift and there was a bonus if he had to manhandle any of the customers.

'Car,' he said, peering down at the street.

Everybody froze. The punters knew the drill: if it was the police they could leave by a door at the back of the room that took them into the building next door.

It didn't look like a police car. It was a nearly-new Crossley, bottle green with a cream running board. Jack fancied one of those. He had made inquiries about prices and hadn't been too discouraged. The model down there cost £560 new, but there were other models, not quite so luxurious, from £375. Maybe next year . . .

'He's away again.'

The car moved on and the games resumed. In the two months since the Kingstons commandeered this house there had been no sign of the police. That didn't mean they could be complacent. Disgruntled punters sometimes turned informer, in spite of knowing what could happen to them if they ever tried it on. The risks involved in running the operation were always high, but the same went for the dividends. The ban on gaming, like any ban, produced a powerful demand for what was forbidden. The scarcity of venues kept the prices steep. The door-fee here was two pounds a head, there were minimum wagers and IOUs were anathema. No one was allowed to spectate, everybody had to play. On a good Saturday night the take could top £800.

Jack looked at the road again. It was quiet, growing dark. In the litter-strewn streets between the scruffy buildings the denizens of the Gorbals came and went in their mufflers and anonymous bunnets, hands in pockets, gazing at the ground with no need to see where they were going. It looked like a scene of grubby life fixed in its ways. That was only because the real currents down there were invisible. The Glasgow seen by outsiders was a black-and-white picture of backdrop buildings, cranes, statues, tall chimneys and more buildings, a colourless smoky context for a drab citizenry. Yet it was nothing like that. There was eternal fire in this city. Unseen colours fizzed and sparked. Operatic passions flared. Dreams, many of them wild and extreme, were born and often materialised. But always away from sight, behind the dour front dictated by a need, eternally unexplained, to keep the real life of this city a secret.

'You win, sir. Well done.'

At the dice table a man in overalls – dress here was optional – was beaming as he drew a pile of pound notes towards him. It beat Jack how anybody could fall for that game. But they did, in fact it was very popular. Results were quick, which could have something to do with the attraction – you could get rich or skint in a hurry. And an idiot could follow the rules of play. The numbers from two to twelve, omitting seven and eight, were crayoned in squares on a board in the middle of the table. Punters laid their money on the numbers of their choice and took turns at throwing a pair of dice from a cup. The house paid out even money on the numbers three, four, five, six, nine and ten; odds of two-to-one were given on numbers two, eleven, and twelve; if seven or eight was thrown, the house took the pot. On the face of it the rules were generous – gamblers had six chances to double their money, three chances to treble it, and they could lose out to the house on only two numbers. But if anyone took the trouble to work out the odds, as Jack had done long ago, they would realise they were more likely to throw a seven or an eight than any other number – it was four times as likely as throwing a two, eleven, or twelve. The even-money numbers would turn up twice as often as the two-to-one shots. But the kind of gamblers they got in here never analysed the odds. Instead they believed in intuition, in omens. They would even trust a lucky feeling, and they all knew there was such a thing as a run of luck; men would forfeit a lot of money waiting for one to start.

There was a knock at the door. Jack went out and opened the door a fraction. It was Mad Harry. He slid into the hall and waited for Jack to lock the door again. Harry was a short muscular man with tufted red hair and puffy, friendly-looking features. When he smiled he showed stubby white teeth with a gap at the lower left where he frequently lodged a cigarette.

'Got a job for ye,' he said. 'It came up kinda sudden.'

'I'm supposed to meet Eric in the Dalrymple at ten past nine,' Jack said. 'He wants to talk about settin' up another shebeen.'

'Eric sent me. He's had to go up to Buccleuch Street. His sister's man's been knockin' her about again. Eric's not a fella to interfere between a couple, but the lassie's got a black eye an' a burst lip, so in the circumstances . . .'

Eric Ross was their leader. He was a man who never remained in one spot for long and passed on most of his messages through a lieutenant.

'He hates anybody pickin' on women,' Jack said. 'God help his sister's man. It'll be a long time before he can piss without screamin'.'

'Right enough.'

'So what's the job?'

'It'll be what you make it. Eric says you're not to feel you have to follow through nor nothin' like that . . .'

Jack got the feeling he was about to be asked to do something riskier than usual.

'It came up sudden, like I said. About half-past four this afternoon one of the boys spotted Hector Kemp goin' in the side door of the Kelvin on Maxwell Street.'

'Christ. He's got a cheek.'

Maxwell Street was on the extended Kingston territory north of the river. Hector Kemp was head man of an Orange gang from the west of the city.

'There's a private party upstairs at the Kelvin tonight,' Harry said. 'It's a family do of some sort an' Kemp's a relative. From what Eric could gather, he slipped into the district early so there'd be less chance of any of our lads seein' him.'

'How did Eric find that out?'

'He knows the head barman. Went round to see him. Seems Kemp's a guest of honour at this shindig. The family's an Orange bunch an' it's a feather in their hats to have him at a party right on our territory. He's stayin' in a room at the Kelvin until the ball gets rollin', but he'll be leavin' when the party breaks up.'

Harry got out his tobacco tin and a packet of papers. Which meant there would be a short interval. Making a cigarette was a silent ritual with him. He had a tendency to do it at awkward moments, as now. Jack was anxious to know what Eric wanted him to do, but he'd have to wait until the one-handed ceremony of rolling the fag was completed. It was unthinkable that anyone should try to rush Mad Harry. He was an institution and his foibles were accommodated. He was the oldest man in the Kingston Clan, a founder member, one of the original twenty who colonised a wedge of the Gorbals from Kingston Street to the River Clyde, back in 1930. Originally from Maryhill, he came south of the river in 1924 when he was eighteen. He gained the Mad Harry title a year after that, following a running battle with the police at Laurieston Road, during which he felled eight constables. Reinforcements turned the tide and Harry made his escape through a brewery yard. As he made for the far perimeter wall he was set upon by a ferocious alsatian dog which mauled his left arm so badly it had to be amputated. The day after he left hospital Harry went back to the yard and killed the dog with a bread knife.

'There,' he said, sticking the misshapen roll-up into the gap in his teeth. He took a match from his box and tucked the box into his armpit. With a dexterous flip of the wrist he lit the match and applied it to the cigarette. He puffed hard, making sparks of burning shag fly up around him. 'That's better,' he muttered through the smoke. 'Where was I?'

'Kemp's leavin' the pub when the party breaks up.'

'Oh, aye, right. Well, Eric thinks it would be a good idea if you took him aside an' warned him not to bring his arse on to our turf again.'

'Kemp's not goin' to take kindly to that.'

'Definitely not.'

'There could be trouble. Tonight, and later on.'

Harry nodded, winked.

Jack understood. Eric felt there should be a confrontation with Kemp's bunch. It was understandable. Few members of rival gangs would have the nerve to walk right on to Kingston turf. For one of their leaders to do so was an act of extreme provocation – whether he did it discreetly or not. Eric was forever conscious of maintaining standards. A slight must never be overlooked. No man should be in a position to brag that he had put one over on the Kingstons – not even a hard bastard like Hector Kemp.

'Any worries?' Harry said.

'None I can think of.'

'Remember what Eric said, though. You don't have to follow through . . .'

It was a nice touch for Eric to say that. He knew Jack never held back, but the message was a way of saying things had come a long way, that Jack was not only a special emissary these days, he had the authority to make up his own mind how he handled sensitive business.

Harry went to the door again and unlatched it.

'Let us know how you get on,' he said, stepping on to the landing.

'You'll hear,' Jack promised. 'One way or another.'

When he finished his stint in the Gorbals he had a couple of drinks in the Cockit Hat with Airchie. Over the second pint he explained about his mission at the Kelvin.

'You'll have to watch it with him,' Airchie said.

'I know. I watch it with everybody.'

'Talkin' of watchin' . . .' Airchie nodded his head a fraction towards the corner behind Jack. 'There's a very tidy lookin' fella sittin' over there. He hasn't took his eyes off you since he sat down.'

'Detective Sergeant Fraser,' Jack said, without looking.

'Done business with him, have ye?'

'Nothin' much. The first time I came across him was at the Barras, two or three years back. He was a DC then.

41

Doesn't like me. We've had words now and again. He likes warnin' people.'

'They all like doin' that,' Airchie said. 'They'd work without wages as long as they could carry on warnin' every poor bugger that looks at them the wrong way.'

Jack glanced at the clock.

'I'll give it ten minutes,' he said, 'then I better go round to the Kelvin an' hang about.'

'Have another pint, then.'

'No, no more for me. I'll need a clear head.'

For a couple of minutes they listened to Dougie Meikle telling three of his regulars what it was like to 'catch gas'. Dougie had been gassed twice during the war. He explained that gas masks were highly unreliable. So was gas, which was subject to the wind's currents and often drifted back into the faces of those who used it.

'That's what happened tae me, the second time,' Dougie said. 'Our gas drifted back. I got one whiff and thought, Christ, gas, an' I sticks on ma mask – but if you even sniff the stuff it makes you sick, an' ye've got to take off the mask to spew, an' by the time ye've spewed ye've sniffed up a lot more an' you've had it. It burns yer lungs, yer eyes . . .'

'He's such a cheery soul, isn't he?' Airchie said. 'A laugh a minute. If it's no' gas he's on about it's gangrene, or trench lice, or syphilis . . .'

'It's a ploy,' Jack said. 'He drives the punters to drink.' He looked at the clock again. 'I think I'll make tracks. Kemp might decide to leave early.'

He emptied his glass and stepped away from the bar.

'I'll see you on Saturday, as usual,' Airchie said.

'As usual,' Jack nodded.

He slapped Airchie's arm and walked away, but instead of going straight to the door he went to the corner table where Detective Sergeant Fraser was sitting alone.

'Excuse me, sir,' he said, putting his hands on the table. 'Am I wearin' somethin' of yours?'

Fraser was halfway through swallowing some beer. He gulped it down, glared at Jack.

42

'I was just askin',' Jack explained, 'because you don't seem to be able to take your eyes off me.'

'Don't be smart, Kane.'

'What's the game, then? D'you think it'll make me all nervous an' jittery if you sit there an' glare at me? If that's what you think, I can tell you you're wastin' your time. All you're doin' is makin' everybody else think you fancy me.'

Fraser touched his tie and glanced around to see if anybody was listening.

'Don't think being in a gang gives you any kind of immunity,' he said, his lips hardly moving. 'You're on my list of people to be watched. So I'm watching you. And when you put a foot wrong, I'll land on you.'

'You better have company when you try it. A company of the Highland Light Infantry at least.'

Fraser tried for a derisive smirk.

'You've got a big head on you, Kane.'

'Maybe I have. But if I stuck it in your mouth it'd rattle.'

Fraser made to rise from the chair.

'Go ahead,' Jack said quietly, stepping back. 'Take me outside for a talkin'-to. It's a nice night.'

Fraser sank back. He had gone pale.

'I'll get you, you mouthy little bastard. Bear it in mind. I'm making it a priority.'

'Snap,' Jack said, he smiled and winked. 'Be seein' you.'

He waved to Airchie as he went out. He stopped on the pavement for a minute and breathed the air. It was warm, with a trace of a breeze coming off the river. He felt just right now, braced tight, ready. He was glad Fraser had been there to sharpen himself on, to get him in the mood.

He was in position across the road from the Kelvin five minutes before last orders. Behind him was the unlit waste ground between two tenements, terrain he knew well, even in the dark. He stood back in the shadows, whistling softly, wondering what kind of mood Jessie would be in tonight.

43

The bar's electric bell started ringing. It would go on ringing until the place was cleared. Landlords were transformed at closing time. The nice man who was joking with you a minute ago turned into a roaring, menacing bugaboo, demanding empty glasses, threatening to take away unfinished drinks and to bar the offenders from coming there ever again. The gaffer in the Kelvin was a short-fused character with a bitch of a wife and ulcers. Jack reckoned the place would be empty inside ten minutes. He stepped further into the dark, whistling, watching.

People came out in twos and threes. Jack strained his eyes, watching for known faces. After a couple of minutes he saw three, all known to him, all enemies. They were the Murphy brothers, Protestants in spite of their name, all members of an Orange Lodge and sworn to visit misery on the lives of as many Fenians as they could in one lifetime. Bigotry was another area where Jack found he was an outsider. He had a lot of enemies who were Protestants, but he couldn't think of anybody he hated or mistrusted *because* he was a Protestant. To the Murphy boys and their kind, all Catholics were automatically targets. Jack's mother thought along the same lines where Protestants were concerned. He could never view any human issue in such uncomplicated terms.

As he watched, another handful of Protestant worthies came out of the pub, shouting farewells, laughing, shaking hands and slapping each other on the back. The party was breaking up. Jack glued his eyes on the corner door. When Hector Kemp came out there was no mistaking him. He was taller than the others, fair-haired and good-looking, oozing his broken-nosed charm. The way people started slapping his shoulders and clapping his back it could have been mistaken for an assault. Jack noticed a car had appeared and was waiting five or six yards from where he was standing. It was Kemp's royal blue two-seater, a Swift Chummy. He showed up in it regularly at dance halls and football matches.

Jack eased closer, trying to get a look at the driver. A

44

match flared obligingly behind the steering wheel. He saw wee Angus Shaw light a cigarette. He was nothing.

Kemp finally broke away from the wellwishers and came across the road. Jack watched to make sure nobody was behind him. Nobody was. They were all walking away, talking to each other again. As far as they were concerned the guest of honour had departed.

As Kemp reached the pavement Jack stepped forward. There was three yards between them.

'And who's this?' Jack said, nice and loud. He took two steps closer. 'Well blow me down. It's Hector Kemp.'

Kemp had stopped. He stared, tilted his head, finally recognised Jack. He straightened up and squared his shoulders.

'Was there somethin' you wanted?'

'I've got a memo for you.'

'Who from?'

'Me. On behalf of Eric Ross an' the rest of the lads.'

'I don't talk to message boys,' Kemp said, turning to the car.

'Ye'll talk to this one.'

Kemp stopped, faced Jack again.

'You're Kane, right?' he said.

Jack nodded. In the greenish lamplight Kemp's face looked demonic. He was scowling in a way that suggested he knew exactly the effect he created. A mirror man, Jack thought. Fond of himself. The line between self-respect and self-worship was easily crossed.

'Well listen, Mr Kane – '

'No, *you* listen.' Jack took a step closer, narrowing the gap to a couple of yards. 'You've been trespassin', an' you know it. It's not to happen again.'

Kemp took a deep breath and let it out.

'Are you tired of livin'?' he said.

'Shove yer wisecracks. Ah've said ma piece an' that's that. Now get in your wee motor an' fuck off.'

Kemp's stance and the tension in his face showed he wanted to grab this man and hammer him. But Jack's

45

stillness deterred action. The way he confronted you was too quiet, too understated to be only what it seemed.

'You better learn to control your tongue, Kane.'

'Is that what you reckon?'

'If yer cock was as big as yer mouth you'd be a legend.'

Jack stepped closer still and that seemed to surprise Kemp.

'Get into the car, Hector. While you still can.'

That was too much. Jack stood motionless, inhabiting the gap between spark and explosion. He saw it coming. *Always watch the eyes*. Kemp's arm moved as his body swung. The hand went into the jacket, was out again in a flash. The razor sliced the air an inch from Jack's cheek. It cut the shoulder of his jacket the instant his fist cracked Kemp's chin. Kemp staggered back, swung the razor again, missed. Jack leapt, left the ground and brought down his head on Kemp's nose. Blood spurted, black in the street light, smearing Kemp's face. He dropped to his knees. Jack kicked the razor out of his hand, brought back his foot and kicked him in the crotch. Kemp gurgled from a throatful of blood and curled forward on the dirty road.

The narrow-shouldered figure of Angus Shaw was half-way out of the car. Jack stabbed a finger at him and he got back in.

'Right, Hector, let's look at you.'

Jack took him by the tie, pulled him up on his knees again. His face was clenched with pain. There was blood all over his shirt and the front of his jacket.

'Is that us finished?' Jack said. 'Come on, tell me.'

'Fenian fucker!'

Jack swung his hand and cracked it across Kemp's cheek. On the way back it smacked the other cheek.

'I can keep this up, Hector. You let me know. Is it finished, or what?'

Kemp's lips moved. He was preparing to spit. Jack hung on to the tie and bunched the other hand. As Kemp's lips pursed he punched them. A tooth cracked with a sound like something trodden underfoot.

'Hey! You! What the fuck is this?'

Across the road three men were shuffling to the kerb. The Murphy brothers. Jack straightened and let Kemp go. He landed on all fours, then rolled on to his side.

'Mind what you were told,' Jack said. 'Keep off, Hector.'

'Hey, pal! C'mere a minute!'

The tallest Murphy was crossing the road.

Jack turned, faced the darkness between the tenements and slipped into it, walking until he was sure the Murphy boys couldn't see him any more. Then he started to run, grinning, knowing every bump and hillock, feeling the breeze skid across his stiffened hair.

THREE

'Nothing's worked,' Jessie Young said, her voice glum. 'I was sick all day on Thursday. It was that bad I thought I was going to die. Yesterday morning I felt better but it was still there.' She touched her stomach through the rough tweed coat. 'Somebody's bound to notice soon.'

They were on a bench in Glasgow Green, a favourite sheltered spot where the wind-rustled leaves of bushes and trees muted the sounds of the Saltmarket and the streets beyond. Saturday morning sun warmed their shoulders. Jessie had brought a bag of crumbs and chopped-up crusts to feed the pigeons. So far the starlings had stolen most of them.

'You look all right,' Jack said.

'Wrapped up like this I do. I can't go about with my coat or a baggy pinnie on *all* the time.'

It was hard for Jack not to think of her as a victim, even though she insisted he didn't. Last night, coming to her jubilant and exhilarated, all he could do was hold her and stroke her hair. Little had changed, visibly, but everything about her seemed so fragile now, even her voice. She spoke uncommonly fine English for a Glasgow girl. Her mother came from Argyll, where they spoke in a sing-song lilting way and sounded every consonant, crisply, without ever committing a glottal stop. The voice blended with her looks and the way she carried herself. Jessie was as delicately formed as bone china, fair-skinned and blue-eyed with dark honey hair. Her body, which Jack had viewed dimly in a curtained room on six occasions during the past four months, was curved and creviced so near to perfection that he was sure he'd never again find anybody like her.

'Something drastic's got to be done,' he said, wishing his voice didn't sound so rough.

'I've been doing drastic things.'

'I know. But if the high jinks an' potions aren't goin' to work, we'll have to face the other two alternatives.'

Jessie had tried everything she and Jack had ever heard about how to shake loose an unwanted pregnancy. She had run up flights of stairs until she was exhausted, jumped off tables and landed on her heels to jar her insides, skipped with a rope in the flour store at the bakery where she worked until she was exhausted. The exercise had only made her feel fitter. So she'd tried drinking double measures of gin, which made her violently sick. She lay in scalding hot baths, ate slices of soap, chewed slippery elm bark, swallowed aloes, pennyroyal, cough mixture, tobacco – which also made her ill – and finally tried a mixture of olive oil and lead oxide, bought from a quack at the Barras who told her it never failed. With Jessie however it did fail, though she believed it nearly succeeded in killing her.

'We can get married,' Jack said. 'Or we can arrange a visit to Mrs Begbie.'

'But you don't want to get married.'

'Och, I'm no' so sure about that, now. It wouldnae be the end of the world. I want to get married some time in my life, an' I don't think I'd find anybody better than you.'

'We're too young,' Jessie said firmly. 'We've years of things we should do before we settle down. I don't want to get married yet – and neither do you, whether you admit it or not. We've talked about all this before.'

They looked out across the green-brown expanse towards the People's Palace, inspecting their private misgivings.

'Well . . .' Jack looked at her. 'You don't want to have a baby and *not* be married . . .'

'My da would kill me.' Her small fingers twined

together in her lap. 'Anyway,' she said, 'I don't want a baby.'

'What – never?'

'Never. I don't want to be anybody's mother.'

Here was the strong side of her, the independence under the fragile shell. She was determined to be a free person, making her own choices. Traditional considerations of a woman's place and function never occupied her. She had told Jack she liked sex, even admitted she looked forward to it – but she didn't confuse what they did with a desire for offspring. The pregnancy was a serious nuisance, but she would never let it drive her into the anchored life her mother lived. One day Jessie hoped to leave Scotland and travel, perhaps never come back.

'It's Mrs Begbie, then,' Jack said.

'If she's the only answer.'

They had both heard terrible stories about backstreet abortionists. A girl who had lived near them in the Calton died the Christmas before of septicaemia. Another one bled to death. Jessie knew of a woman who was paralysed after visiting an illegal practitioner in Hamilton, and girls where she worked kept hearing about others and were always talking about them. Success stories were rarely circulated, but it was known that Mrs Begbie, who had never been prosecuted, was a qualified nurse and although she was expensive she was reckoned to be the best.

'Are you sure about this, Jessie?'

'Yes. Will you arrange it?'

'Sure. Leave everythin' to me.' Jack touched her hand and squeezed it. 'I'm sorry, darlin'.'

'Don't be daft. It's not your fault. We both did this.'

He wanted to cuddle her.

That afternoon he approached Mrs Begbie in her local tavern, a rough but strictly managed bar on Carrick Street near the Broomielaw. Dockers and sailors used the place; when Mrs Begbie was present the language was moderated without anyone having to be asked. The woman's looks commanded deference. She was in her sixties, tall and broad-shouldered with sharp, severe features and hooded eyes that moved from side to side when she spoke. Her hair was dyed raven black, scraped into a bun at her crown. She wore the kind of long dark clothes that had been fashionable at the turn of the century and never took off her gloves in public. Her tipple was port and brandy; Jack took one with him to her table. He cleared his throat and waited until she looked up from the little book she was reading.

'Mrs Begbie?'

She nodded.

'Could I speak to you?'

She looked at the drink he was holding and nodded again. Jack sat opposite her and pushed the glass across the table. Mrs Begbie swallowed the drink she had been nursing and picked up the fresh one.

'What is it you want to talk me about?'

She wasn't Scottish, Jack noticed. Her accent was foreign, maybe Polish.

'A friend,' Jack said. 'A young lady. She's, um, got a problem. I was told you could help.'

'And who told you that?'

'Well, I just kinda heard.'

Mrs Begbie took a sip and put down her glass. She laid her forearm along the edge of the table and leaned forward.

'Before you say any more, I have to tell you that if you're up to any mischief you are wasting your time.'

'Oh, no, nothin' like that,' Jack assured her.

'I'm telling you, all the same.' She pointed at the landlord. 'That man and a couple of others will say you were never in here, if they have to. Should money change hands, nobody will see it. And if I agree to help your friend with her problem I will take no responsibility for anything unfortunate that may happen afterwards. I don't know her now, I will not know her then. Do you understand what I have said?'

'Sure,' Jack nodded.

'Very well. Now tell me about your friend's difficulty.'

Jack explained. He pointed out that Jessie's tenacious

51

pregnancy was reaching a point where it was beginning to show. A termination was urgent.

'Is she in good health?'

'Oh aye, she's fit.'

'Does she understand that if I help her it will be painful? Very painful?'

'I think she understands that.'

'Make sure she does,' Mrs Begbie said. 'I use nothing to ease the pain. The operation is dangerous enough without anaesthetics, which make matters more complicated. Be absolutely sure she knows that. It will be painful and very dangerous. I don't want her to come to me expecting to have an easy time. She must be properly prepared.'

'I'll see she knows the score,' Jack promised.

Mrs Begbie asked how soon Jessie could come to her.

'Any time. As soon as possible.'

'Tomorrow morning? Ten o'clock?'

Sunday, Jack thought. An abortion on a Sunday. He had none of his mother's strictures, but the rudimentary Catholic in him had qualms.

'I'm sure that'll be fine,' he said.

Mrs Begbie told him her address, a tenement flat two streets away.

'I require you to give me three pounds now,' she said. 'That will be forfeited if the young lady does not come at the time we have agreed. If she does come, I will want a further seven pounds before I help her.'

Ten quid. He had expected it to cost a fiver at the most. A man he knew, a bus driver whose wife couldn't face having another kid, had shelled out three guineas for the services of a woman in Anderston. When he told Jack and a couple of the other lads they said he had been robbed.

Ten quid. But this old character's the best, Jack reminded himself as he slipped her the deposit. Nothing but the best for Jessie.

That evening, when he had seen Jessie and explained about the time she was to show up at Mrs Begbie's, and

52

how she was to expect an ordeal and nothing less, and after he had agreed – without showing his terrible reluctance – to go with her and stay until it was all over, he met Airchie in the Dalrymple.

The place was jumping. Now that the working men of Glasgow had jobs again the old rituals were being revived. Saturday night was a time for herd revelry, for drinking with both hands and spending as much in three hours as the old lady was given to keep the house for a week. By half-past seven rapturous men were spilling into the street, yodelling drunk. Others lolled in corners of the pub with moist and faraway eyes while their pals at the bar tried to catch up.

'I feel like gettin' guttered myself,' Jack said, squeezing in beside Airchie at the angle of the bar and the wall. 'It's been a rough day.'

'Ye'll get drunk all right,' Airchie said. 'Even if ye hadnae wanted to, tonight you're a certainty to get plastered.'

'How come?'

'Ye're Eric's hero. Ye're *everybody's* hero – everybody that matters a toss, anyway. I met Eric on the Gallowgate this mornin' an' he was beamin' all over his face. He filled me in on yer performance last night. He was lookin' for ye, wanted to pin a medal on yer chest.'

'I was goin' to go over the river an' see him later, fill him in on what happened.'

'No need, Jack. He's been told. Did ye know Hector Kemp landed up in hospital?'

'Honest?'

'The job ye did on his bugle – it gave him breathin' complications. That's what they say, any road. An' he's had to have a root dug out his jaw, an' have his lips stitched – the word is he's got a face like six poundsa mince. Eric told me, then Mad Harry, then Tam Fisher. They'll all be here to fill ye wi' drink, kid. Kemp's out of the game. It's a great excuse for a celebration.'

'It'll no' stop there, though,' Jack said. 'Kemp's crowd'll be lookin' for a return match.'

'Oh sure. An' everybody's ready for it. Ye've lit the fuse, Jack. The bomb'll go off, nothin's surer. I fancy it's what Eric wanted, anyway. He needs to register a victory. Got to keep the flag flyin'.'

Jack couldn't feel the zest of this situation. He kept thinking about Jessie, about her soft-warm little body, what it was going to be put through tomorrow. He thought about the baby, too. He wished he didn't have to see it. Until he had made arrangements with Mrs Begbie, Jessie's lump had been a nuisance. Now that it was condemned it was something else. It was his first child, alive and growing in Jessie's womb, but tomorrow it would be in the dustbin.

By the time Eric Ross, Mad Harry McColl and Tam Fisher appeared, Jack had sunk three pints and was feeling less intensely about Jessie. The three-man leadership of the Kingston Clan buffeted him between them, hugging him, pumping his hand, telling him what a great lad he was. Three double whiskies were set on the bar in front of him.

'Ye're a bloody natural, Jack,' Eric told him.

'Nothin' special,' Jack said. 'Just doin' ma job,' he added, making the disclaimer appropriate to a seasoned hard man.

There was unrestrained admiration in his leader's eyes. It was something to see. Eric had stiff belligerent features that seemed to offer permanent rejection. He wasn't prone to dish out praise, not even the half-hearted kind. It was generally agreed that he revered nobody, not even his mother, and could find shortcomings in the finest acts of decency, self-sacrifice or valour. His leadership hinged on the need people felt, against the odds, to please him.

'Ye knew what was needed, an ye did it,' he told Jack. 'That's special, all right. Plenty other fellas would just have attended to the bare bones of the job. They wouldnae have put in the right kind of effort, the finishin' touches. Ye always give us that wee bit more than we expect, Jack.'

Eric loved finishing touches and he was a believer in

practising what he preached. At twenty-four he already had one murder to his credit; a not-proven verdict had saved him from prison, possibly from the rope. For a number of his other distinctions – among them the single-handed mutilation of three Govan men who had robbed a south-side café protected by the Kingstons – he had been denounced from the pulpit of St Andrew's Cathedral. A tight-lipped priest had told Eric that if it had been in his power he would have had him excommunicated.

'I'll tell ye Jack,' Mad Harry chimed in, 'ye're madder than me. Ah'll have to watch my title.'

Tam Fisher, who never said much, simply put his battered face close to Jack's and winked. There was a great sense of security in having such a man on your side. The only thing better would be if he ignored you. Known to admirers and enemies alike as Tam the Crippler, he was a trained boxer who had been sorely mismanaged in the early days of his career. He had drifted into gang life in the late twenties; in 1931 he gained forefront status by executing a child molester with a single punch below the heart. The police, grateful to be rid of a felon they had never been able to convict, took no pains to find out who had despatched him. The murder was officially unsolved and would remain so.

'We're havin' a wee party for ye,' Eric told Jack. 'No' the night. I think we need to be on the alert. But next Saturday, for sure.'

'That's good of you,' Jack said, vastly relieved that no immediate celebration was planned.

'But ye get yer bonus right now.' Eric moved close and took a bulky, folded brown paper bag from his pocket. 'Ye've earned it, kid.'

'Och, Eric . . .'

Jack stood shaking his head, staring at the bag. It was mandatory to refuse a reward, or at least make a show of reluctance.

'On ye go, take it,' Eric commanded him. 'I'll be offended if ye don't.'

'Ye're an awfy man,' Jack said, taking the bag and stuffing it in his inside pocket.

'Now drink yer medicine. We're goin' on a crawl round the city centre. The five of us. We need tae draw a bit of attention.'

Jack raised the first glass of whisky, toasted his companions and swallowed it in one go. He kept his lips clamped against the fire for a second, then exhaled slowly.

'Are we covered?' he asked.

'Absolutely,' Mad Harry said. 'There's a shadow army out there. Sober as Edinburgh ministers, every one of them.'

'They're none too pleased about bein' sober,' Eric added. 'But it'll put that bit extra spite in them, if it's needed.'

When Jack had swallowed the rest of the whisky and was beginning to feel pleasantly numb, they left the *Dalrymple* and walked to Glasgow Cross. Among the pedestrians on either side of the street Jack could see the familiar shapes of other Kingston men, randomly walking, stopping to look about them, neatly spaced and ostensibly separate, ready for open attack or ambush. If Kemp's men stuck to form they wouldn't be far away. Jack, Airchie and Eric walked three abreast with Mad Harry and Tam Fisher behind them, a grinning, chattering phalanx, exuding carefree bonhomie, expecting war to break out any second.

They visited four pubs, having one drink in each, without a sign of trouble. They walked slowly back towards the Gallowgate, their attendant shadows spread out to the sides and behind them. In the spacious Lorne Bar they presented themselves as a wholly visible target, occupying the curved end of the horseshoe bar, laughing and talking, drinking liberally, their faces unmistakable. Still no one came; no hint of a reprisal showed itself. At closing time, politely refusing the gaffer's obsequious invitation to take a late one in the back room, Eric led his men out on to the street. Gathered under the light of a lamp post, they listened as their leader stated his conclusion, raising his voice to make himself heard over the noise of the trams.

'They're frightened tae show,' he said. 'We gave them too much credit the night. Big Kemp's been actin' the bulletproof hero for years without havin' tae prove it. So now he's out the game they're buggered, they're in shock. Nae morale.' Eric slapped Jack's arm. 'Ye did us an even bigger favour than I realised, kid. Ye fucked the whole bunch of them.'

As they dispersed for the night Eric declared he would walk Jack home. It was an honour, rarely bestowed. As they walked along the dark turnings of the Calton, Jack felt a swelling of pride. Here they were, two men strolling easily through the Glasgow night, one of them a dire legend, the other his well-favoured lieutenant. They were a force. Jack knew petty toerags and policemen alike would see them and nudge each other.

After five minutes of idle chat, Eric suddenly asked Jack if anything was wrong.

'There was somethin' missin' the night. You looked a bit low.'

Jack was aware that his leader was watching his face, alert to any deception.

'Ah've been a bit worried,' Jack admitted.

'Is it a big secret, or what?'

Jack told him about Jessie, her attempts to terminate the pregnancy, and explained they had finally decided to go to an abortionist.

'Who did you pick?'

'Mrs Begbie. Ah heard she's the best.'

Eric was silent for a minute.

'They call her the Lithuanian Butcher,' he said finally. 'She was a nurse at the Southern General, years back. My old man told me all about her. Got her jotters for hittin' one patient an' strappin' another man's mouth shut with tape because he kept talkin' in his sleep. A real hard bitch, by all accounts.'

'Is she as good as they say?'

'None of them's good, Jack. They do a job an' some of them's better at it than others, that's all. Begbie knows a bit about medicine, so Ah suppose she's got the edge. She costs a bit – ye'll know that by now.'

'Ah suppose that's because she's good,' Jack said.

'That's what a lot of folk think. But it's not the reason. She pays off the polis, Jack. She's got protection. They leave her alone, an' if any of her cases goes wrong there's no come-back on her.'

The news brought back the uneasiness in Jack's stomach.

'If there was any other way,' he said, 'I'd take it. But Jessie doesn't want a kid. Doesn't want to get married, neither.'

'She's got her head screwed on.'

They stopped outside the tenement where Jack lived.

'There's one thing ye should get yerself ready for,' Eric said. 'Maybe it'll not happen, but there's a good chance it will. This Jessie of yours, she might go off you. Don't ask me what for, but she might. It's happened tae me.'

'What – ye mean after the lassie's been to have herself seen to?'

'Uhuh. All lovey-dovey before, then didn't want to know me after. Not at any price. Other fellas have told me the same thing.' Eric patted Jack's shoulder. 'Just prepare yourself, in case.'

When Jack got in his father was sitting at the fireside, staring at the coals.

'There's tea in the pot, if you want a cup,' he said.

Jack said he was tired.

'I'll just go to bed.'

He looked at his father. Guilt twitched. Alistair was a lonely man. His wife hardly spoke to him any more and he couldn't even rely on having a bedtime natter with his son. But that was something neither he nor Jack could do anything about. Some distances were too wide to be bridged.

'Good night, Da.'

In his room he took the folded paper bag from his

58

pocket and tipped out the contents. A wad of notes fell on the bed. He counted them slowly. Fifty pounds. His feelings tumbled and mixed. He was a hero, highly valued. He was on the threshold of helping his girl friend to kill their baby.

Through the wall he heard his mother's voice. She was praying again. When insomnia plagued her she talked to God. Jack took off his jacket and hung it up. He opened the top drawer of the chest by the door and looked at the rosary lying on his folded jumpers. Hypocritical, he thought, to want to pray now. He never did it when he was feeling good, when everything was on the up and up. Closing his eyes he pictured Jessie, imagined her lying awake, frightened. When he saw her earlier she had tried to put on a brave face, but he could feel the apprehension, the tremor in her hands when he squeezed them.

He took the rosary from the drawer and went to the side of the bed. He knelt, bowed his head and clasped his hands, the rosary wound around his fingers.

'Sweet Jesus, lover of obedience,' he whispered, 'be our succour and support, that leaning on thee we may safely pass through all dangers . . .'

The room where Mrs Begbie worked was bare except for an old hospital trolley in the middle of the floor, minus its wheels, and a rickety card table with two buckets under it and an enamel bowl on top, covered with a dish towel.

'This is not what we agreed,' she complained as she showed them in. 'It is not usual for the man to stay.'

'I want him to,' Jessie said.

'Then you mustn't get in the way,' Mrs Begbie told Jack sternly. 'If you get sick or feel faint you must go outside.' She turned to Jessie, pale and cold-looking in her heavy coat. 'Take off your clothes and lie on the table.'

The room was cold. Jessie glanced at Jack. He tried to look encouraging, supportive. She took off her coat and looked at Mrs Begbie, who was tying on a rubber apron.

'Put the clothes on the floor,' she snapped.

Jessie undressed quickly, not looking up. Jack stared at the tall curtainless window. When Jessie was naked he helped her on to the cold rubber sheet on the table. As she lay down Mrs Begbie came forward and grasped her feet. She pulled them apart sharply and pushed them through leather loops attached to the ends of rods sticking up at the bottom of the table. When Jessie's feet were firmly tethered Mrs Begbie reached under the end of the table and pushed up the rods, hoisting Jessie's legs two feet off the table, wide apart.

'Stand there,' Mrs Begbie ordered Jack, pointing to the head of the table.

Jack did as he was told. He reached forward and patted Jessie's arm. She was trembling. He watched Mrs Begbie prod the pale narrow body, frowning as her fingers dug into the edges of the little swell on Jessie's belly.

'You should have come to me much sooner.'

Mrs Begbie turned and whisked the cloth off the enamel basin. It held a clutch of ugly-looking metal instruments and a jar of Vaseline. She unscrewed the jar, put three fingers inside and scooped out a lump. Without warning she swung round and plunged the fingers inside Jessie, who cried out with the shock and pain.

'You must make no noise,' Mrs Begbie snapped, her fingers working vigorously in and out. She reached with her free hand and picked up the tea towel. She flipped it on to Jessie's chest. 'Fold that and bite it when you have to.'

Jack touched Jessie's shoulder again. He felt helpless. Her eyes were wide and scared. He squeezed the fragile shoulder bone, smoothed it and tried to smile down at her.

Mrs Begbie withdrew her fingers and snatched up one of the instruments. It clanked coldly against the side of the bowl. She paused, making no effort to hide the ugly implement, looking sternly at Jessie's face.

'I will begin now,' she said.

Before Jack had time to register what she said she plunged the head of the instrument inside Jessie. The girl's body stiffened and twisted sharply to the left. She shoved the towel into her mouth and screamed against the muffling folds. Mrs Begbie worked with frowning intensity, her elbow jerking back and forth. She pulled out the instrument again and dropped it on the table. As she did, bloody fluid began to pour from Jessie and splash on to the linoleum. Mrs Begbie slid one of the buckets under the flow.

'The waters,' she murmured.

Jack looked at Jessie. Her face had turned grey. She was still biting fiercely on the tea cloth, her knuckles standing up white through her skin as she clutched its edges. Her body was sheened with sweat.

Mrs Begbie picked up another instrument. Jack stared, feeling he wasn't quite there. The flow of blood and mucus from Jessie was unbelievable. It splashed into the bucket in a clotted stream. Mrs Begbie pressed on the abdomen and the flow increased. It gushed and spattered the bucket. Jessie roared against the towel. Her head thrashed on the rubber sheet.

Jack closed his eyes tightly, feeling a wave of nausea. *God let it be over soon, let it finish . . .*

His eyes opened as Jessie screamed again, the towel falling from her slackened grip. Mrs Begbie had the instrument right inside her and was working it in a harsh circle. She glared along the length of Jessie's tortured body, her severe ugly face tight with disapproval.

'Quiet!' she barked. 'You must make no noise!'

Jack put the towel in Jessie's hand again and guided it to her mouth. He noticed that his own hand was shaking. He gulped, frightened, fearful that Jessie was going to die. She looked terrible. There was a harsh sucking sound and he looked at Mrs Begbie, saw her pull out the instrument and insert her entire hand, up past the wrist. She set her teeth, wrestling with something unseen. Jessie moaned and her blood-smeared abdomen convulsed. Mrs Begbie went motionless for a second, then drew her hand out sharply. Jessie bellowed against the cloth and Jack's stomach lurched as he saw the bloody, mangled foetus dangling from Mrs Begbie's fingers. She glanced at it, turned it over once, then dropped it in the bucket. Jack swallowed hard, fighting down the bile in his throat.

He stroked Jessie's sopping brow.

'It's all over, darlin',' he said shakily.

Mrs Begbie stared at him.

'Put your hands on her shoulders,' she snapped, picking up an instrument that looked half scoop, half spoon.

The next three minutes were a nightmare. Using the wicked-looking scoop, Mrs Begbie pulled slimy chunks of scarlet tissue from Jessie, flicking them into the bucket, working with clockwork steadiness until Jack was sure she would scoop the girl's life clean out of her. Jessie was only half conscious, whining softly, looking like the victim of some brutal, sadistic assault. Her lower body and thighs were smeared with mucus and blood. The smell in the room was terrible. Jack couldn't believe he would keep from being sick.

But then, suddenly, it was over. Mrs Begbie took the second bucket out of the room and brought it back full of steaming water with a strong antiseptic smell. She bathed Jessie's body with a cloth and dried her with a rough hand towel. When she lowered the stirrups, Jessie lay splayed and motionless. Her eyes were open and she made no sound. If it hadn't been for the slight rise and fall of her breasts, Jack would have sworn she was dead.

Mrs Begbie took away the bowl of instruments and the buckets. When she came back she had removed her apron. She looked as tidy as a woman who had just come from church.

'You must take her away soon,' she told Jack.

'But she's in no fit state,' he said. 'I mean, look at her . . .'

'She will be better when she is out in the air.'

'Have you not got some place she can rest? She can't go home like this. You never warned me she'd be this bad.'

'You didn't tell me she had been pregnant for so long.' Mrs Begbie folded her arms. 'There is a room upstairs where she can lie down for a few hours. But it will cost more. Three pounds.'

'Three quid? Christ, I could book into a good hotel for a week for that much . . .'

'Go to a hotel, then, if you prefer.'

Jack looked at Jessie. Her own mother would be hard pushed to let her in looking like that. He fished three pound notes from his pocket and thrust them at Mrs Begbie.

'Here. Now you can give me a hand to get her dressed. And I think the fee should cover a pot of tea, don't you?'

They dressed Jessie and got her sitting on the edge of the table. Jack asked her if she thought she could walk. She said nothing, slid down off the table and tried to stand. She fell back and he had to catch her. He lifted her in his arms, cradling her like a child.

'Lead the way,' he told Mrs Begbie.

In the stuffy upper room he laid Jessie on the bed. She had rallied and a trace of colour had come back to her cheeks. Jack kissed her gently.

'A nice hot drink'll make you feel a lot better,' he said.

She looked at him and the thing he had feared was right there in her haunted eyes, as clear as day. It was an unfocussed mingling of pain and resentment and anger. Eric's warning. There it was, already. She tried to smile but she couldn't mask it, the ordeal had put her outside the framework of whatever had held them together. Jessie, whether she quite knew it yet or not, was preparing to be a stranger.

'I'll go and see what's keeping the tea,' Jack said, and kissed her again.

He went to the door, remorse and sadness blocking his chest, choking him. For the first time in his life he felt utterly heartbroken.

FOUR

In November the police picked up Airchie Cairns on charges of serious assault and theft. A scrap-metal dealer in Parkhead had been thumped on his way from his yard to the bank and his wallet containing £250 had been taken. The battered trader gave a description of his attacker that left the police in no doubt about his identity. Airchie's hair was the giveaway – the vivid colour and the new style he had adopted, a fashion that prompted Eric Ross to observe that nowadays Airchie looked like he was wearing a shiny brass helmet.

The attack was in retaliation for the scrap dealer's mean-spirited treatment of an employee, Paddy Reardon, a mongoloid boy who worked hard but was easily confused. He had accidentally mixed ferrous and non-ferrous scrap in the sale yard; when the dealer found out he grabbed Paddy and made an example of him in full view of the other workers. He kicked his backside, twisted his ears, made him sort out the mistake and then fired him. The story had a strong element of pathos, quite apart from the fact that Paddy was a mongol. He was the sole support of his old mother and the loss of his job put the pair of them in a financial fix. Eric heard the story when he was in a Robin Hood frame of mind and instructed Airchie to do what was necessary. Paddy's mother had the scrap dealer's money well tucked away before the police began their follow-up on Airchie's arrest. The job had been a success within the terms of Eric's brief, but Airchie was put away for three months. He had been out of circulation only two days when Jack Kane began to understand how much he was going to miss him.

Airchie had always been around. They grew up together, he and Jack, they had learned everything as a team and actually made their first appearance in juvenile court on the same day. Since childhood neither of them had ever been at a loose end, because when there was nothing else to do one could always catch up with the other. They were closer than most brothers. They shared every difficulty and hardship, except when either of them felt a particular worry was too much of a burden to put on his pal.

'I try not to believe in luck an' all that,' Jack told Mad Harry. It was the Sunday morning following Airchie's incarceration. 'Just lately, though, I keep feelin' I'm on a black streak.'

'Depends how ye look at things,' Harry said. 'Ma old lady always used to say, "Count up the good things that happen an' don't count the bad things at all." Mind ye, my old lady was an idiot.'

They were minding the Clan's shebeen on Monteith Row, which occupied two adjoining rooms of an empty house two hundred yards from where Jack lived. The shebeen was open for business whenever the pubs were shut. For a price, anyone in need of a drink could come here and have one. Although the prices were high and there wasn't the range a punter would find even in the smaller pubs around the district, the place did a good trade – particularly so, Jack believed, because there was a brothel two doors away. A lot of men didn't like going through those satin-curtained doors without a drink in them. One of the shebeen's regular punters was an old school teacher who put the point succinctly: 'Dutch courage,' he said, 'is often necessary to engage the gears of wayward libidos.'

'Inside three weeks,' Jack said, 'I've lost the girl friend, ma mother's been put in the hospital an' now Airchie's in the jug. It definitely looks like a run of back luck, doesn't it?'

Mad Harry agreed that things could have gone better.

'It's definitely over with the lassie, then?'

'Finished,' Jack assured him. 'She's cleared off down the coast somewhere.'

On pained reflection he'd decided the relationship was dead by the time they left Mrs Begbie's premises. Jessie hardly spoke a word to him. Next day her mother said she was feeling poorly and wouldn't be able to come out. Five days later Jack saw Jessie on the street and watched her make a detour to avoid him. When he called at her house the following night her mother told him she had decided to go and find work at a seaside hotel. No, there was no forwarding address.

'Women are a fuckin' mystery,' Harry said with some feeling. 'Ah've never been able to weigh them up. Ye treat them like muck an' they can't do enough for you. Show them a bit of consideration an' before ye know it they've got yer tadger in the wringer.'

They were interrupted by a man who wanted a half bottle of rum. He was a fussy little punter who kept his money in a purse. When Harry passed him the hip bottle and took his cash, the man held up the bottle to the window. He tutted softly.

'Anythin' the matter?' Harry demanded.

'It doesnae look like the full measure tae me,' the man muttered. 'It's as if somebody's had a drop out of it, know what Ah mean?'

'Right.' Harry reached across the makeshift counter with his one and only arm. 'Sees it back.'

The man blinked at him.

'Ah was only makin' an observation,' he said.

Harry snatched the bottle off him, put it on the floor and slapped the man's money back on the counter.

'Now bugger off.'

'But I told you, I was only makin' an observation – '

'An' Ah'll make one, too,' Harry said. 'If ye're not out that door in five seconds, ye'll be on yer hands an' knees huntin' for yer teeth.'

The man left, the latest customer to learn that service-with-civility was not a trading principle with the Kingstons.

'So what's up with yer mother?' Harry asked Jack.

'It's her ticker. She's been havin' wee turns for months, on an' off. Last week I went round an' talked to the doctor about it. He came an' had a look at her an' decided she should have a rest an' a bit of treatment at the Royal.'

'Does he think it's serious?'

'He says it's not too bad – she's got somethin' called congestive heart failure.'

'Christ, that sounds desperate.'

'Och, she'll be all right, as long as she looks after herself. They'll put her on a special diet an' give her drugs an' stuff. To tell ye the truth, it's the old man that worries me. Since she went into hospital he's like a lost kid.' Jack shook his head. 'She was the same when he had his appendix out. Went about the house dabbin' her eyes with a hankie all the time. Amazin', intit? They never talk to one another unless they have to, but as soon as one goes out the game the other one's snookered.'

'Aye, love's a bloody odd thing, too,' Harry said.

At two o'clock Jack visited his mother. It was a disheartening half hour. All she did was complain. The nurses didn't pay any attention to her; the food was terrible; the women in the beds on either side were Protestants; none of the doctors realised how ill she really was – they were too young to be doctors, anyway. Jack was grateful when the bell sounded. He patted his mother's hand and left, promising to bring her the *Universe* and her book on Saint Theresa.

Life was *weird* without Airchie. Having the other lads around wasn't the same as having access to the one-and-only lifelong pal. At odd moments during the afternoon Jack caught himself halfway to the door, off to meet Airchie.

That evening he made the tea for himself and his father. They ate in silence. The heart had gone out of Alistair. If food hadn't been put in front of him, it was quite believable that he would sit in his chair and starve to death without a word.

Jack washed up, got changed, then stood at the window wondering where to go. Other Sunday nights it had been no problem. The pubs were shut of course, but he and Airchie knew a dozen places to go and have a drink and a crack. And if he hadn't been seeing Airchie he would have been going out with Jessie. He sighed at the window pane. He would go for a drink, anything would be better than staying in with his mourning father. But it wouldn't be the same on his own . . .

Going along Monteith Row, he glanced across to the darkness of Glasgow Green, picturing the bench where he used to sit with Jessie. That period had turned golden in his memory. It was in the category of cherished times. It took no effort to conjure up their closeness, its sensations; he could still smell the sweet aroma of Jessie's hair and the astringent scent of her skin. To date, Jessie had been the finest girl he had known. He could never be sure if he had loved her, but he wasn't sure if love was necessary, or if it even existed. To go on liking her as much as he did – that would have been enough. The heartbreak had passed, its tearful sharpness had gone, but there was a recurring ache of emptiness. He missed Jessie badly and would give anything to see her again. It was just as true, of course, that he'd give plenty to spend half an hour with Airchie.

On Greendyke Street somebody waved from across the road. He was a tall man, standing a yard from a lamp post with the light behind him. Jack stood for a moment, trying to make out the face.

'All right then, Jack? How's it goin'?'

Jack crossed the road. The man walked up to him and too late Jack saw the sheath knife, sharp and glinting, pointing straight at his belly.

'Been lookin' for you, Jack.'

The man was smiling. Jack didn't recognise his face. He was young and just wild enough round the eyes to be the kind to use the knife without stopping to think. Jack could have run, there was plenty of room. But when it was one-to-one he never ran. Nobody could ever say that about him.

'I'm frozen, know that?' There was whisky on the man's breath. 'Been hangin' about here ages, so I have. I was sure you'd be along, mind you. You're what they call a man of habit.'

It occurred to Jack that it was probably true. Most Sunday nights he came along here with Airchie, or on his way to meet him.

'What do you want?'

'Oh it's no' me. I don't want to see you at all. It's a friend of mine.'

Jack heard the sound behind him, a soft shuffling of feet, then four hands seized him, forced his arms up his back. He felt something cold clamp his wrists and heard the *crick* of one ratchet, then the other.

'This way,' the man with the knife said.

Handcuffed and feeling like an idiot for walking into this, Jack followed with the invisible men behind him. There was an old Rover parked on the corner of Turnbull Street. He was guided towards it and pushed into the back seat. The one with the knife got behind the wheel, the other two sat on either side of Jack. He could see their faces now, hardbitten, expressionless, as young as the driver and probably, like him, enjoying playing at deadly menaces.

As they moved off Jack sat back in the seat, watching the route, trying to guess the cause of the incursion on his liberty. They drove slowly up the Saltmarket to the cross, turned left along the Trongate and Argyle Street, then right at Union Street. After that it was hard to tell where they were; the driver kept to the back streets, taking long unlit stretches that opened on to wider thoroughfares for ten or twenty seconds at a time before they were back into the dark, following the cone of the headlights past the backs of shops and warehouses. After ten minutes

Jack's best guess was that they were somewhere north west.

'And here we are,' the driver said, braking outside high double wooden gates. 'Help Mr Kane out, lads.'

He was pushed out on to the cobbles and held by the arms while the driver unlocked the gates and swung them inwards on to blackness. Jack was prodded between the shoulders. He walked, listening to echoes, noticing the traffic sounds were very faint. They walked on in darkness, then a light came on ahead. They were in a covered courtyard, maybe a loading bay. A door at the back of a platform opened. A man in a tight brown double-breasted suit stepped forward. He was in his forties, Jack guessed, a beefy man with neat side-wings of silvery hair and pink, babyish skin. He was smiling but it was a show smile, a device to step up the menace.

'You'll be Mr Kane, of course,' he said. His accent was Irish. 'I'm Dermot Kennedy. Glad you were able to come.'

The man turned and they followed him through the doorway into a corridor. At the end was a lift. They got in, Kennedy pushed a button and the cabin rose shakily. Jack stared straight ahead, mouth tight, eyes relaxed. It was hard to do, but he knew it was his best expression for circumstances like these.

When the lift stopped and the gate was opened they stepped into another corridor. Kennedy led the way to a door and ushered Jack inside. It was an office with a big rosewood desk and a couple of deep armchairs. Kennedy marched briskly to the desk and sat down. Jack was marched to the front of the desk and left there. The three men who had brought him withdrew to the french windows and stood looking out at nothing.

'So.' Kennedy folded his hands on the desk. He was still smiling, but not so broadly as before. In the bright light from the ceiling Jack noticed he had fine blue scars on his cheeks. He had probably been a coal miner at one time, or a steel worker. 'You'll gather I'm not a Glasgow man, Mr Kane.'

'Aye, I noticed.'

'I'm the manager of this company, as it happens. We make metal boxes.'

'Fascinatin'.'

'I came here eleven years ago from the Belfast branch. I have to tell you I didn't want to come. But a fella's got to follow the road of promotion, hasn't he? So I put my head down and dug in, and I'm quite used to Glasgow now.'

'Very interestin',' Jack said. 'What am I here for?'

Kennedy's smile faded.

'Have you not guessed?'

Jack shook his head.

'I want to have a word with you about a man called Hector Kemp. You remember the name, do you?'

'It rings a bell.'

'Oh, I'm sure it does,' Kennedy said. 'Now, I'm not related to Mr Kemp, but in a sense I feel I am. I'm his boss, for one thing, and we're affiliated in other ways.'

'You mean you're an Orangeman, same as Kemp,' Jack said.

Kennedy nodded.

'Yes, I'm a follower of King Billy. I'm not in a Lodge or anything like that – I don't like joining things, not since the Army. But I'm as loyal in my way as any man that wears the sash. I'm loyal and I'm very quick to put right a wrong. In the case of Hector Kemp a very great wrong's been done.'

Jack was wishing he didn't have the handcuffs on. Something deadly serious was developing here.

'I had a lot of trouble finding out your identity, Mr Kane. You probably don't know it, but when you attacked Hector just over a month ago, you inflicted damage that's caused him terrible pain and distress. Bones in his face were fractured, you see. They were operated on to put them right but the operation caused nerve damage, and that in its turn produced a kind of palsy. The upshot is that Hector's disfigured and he's in constant pain.' Kennedy sat back and folded his arms. 'You can imagine how

71

I felt, knowing that a man I think of so highly was knocked into such a state by a snot-faced little Glasgow Fenian, of all things.'

Kennedy stood up, dug his hands deep in his pockets. He was glaring at Jack now.

'He wouldn't let his friends pay you back for what you did to him. He wouldn't say who you were. He wanted to attend to you himself. He still does, I suppose. But he's not well, you see, he's not likely to be for a long time. I decided to have a good hard talk with him. I got your name out of him, and I managed to make him see my point of view.'

'An' what's that?'

'You should be punished. More than that, what happens to you should be a terrible warning to the bunch of scruff you belong to. I convinced Hector he needn't put his freedom at risk. I promised him that if he left it to me, the job would be done well and there would be no recoil on anyone. Certainly not on him, nor on me.' Kennedy put his hands flat on the desk. 'You asked me why you're here, Mr Kane. I think you'll have a rough idea by now.'

Kennedy nodded to the three men by the french window. The silent pair who had handcuffed Jack came and stood on either side of him. The other man unlocked the window. Jack stiffened as his arms were gripped.

'Don't try any heroics,' Kennedy said, coming round the desk. 'You'll only make things worse for yourself.'

Jack was marched out on to the landing beyond the windows. He was convinced now about the turn his luck had taken. He was on a black streak that was getting blacker. Kennedy stepped past him and walked to the end of the narrow balcony. He climbed a short flight of steps to the parapet. Jack was pushed along behind him. On the roof Kennedy turned to him, his grey hair flapping in the wind.

'We're taking a little walk now. Across the roofs. Can't have anybody thinking you were ever in my office. Heaven forbid.'

As they walked, following the parapet around the

corner of the building, Jack decided his position was hopeless. He was hemmed in, there was no room to manoeuvre. Even without the cuffs restraining him he wouldn't stand a chance.

After two or three minutes shuffling along the stone walkways they came to a flat stretch of roof. Kennedy stopped, stark-faced in the moonlight. He pointed at the edge and the three men grabbed Jack. He stiffened. They slid him forward, his heels scraping the stone. At the edge he looked down. The lighted yard was a greenish oblong, five or six storeys below.

'When you tore into Hector Kemp,' Kennedy said from behind him, 'I bet you never thought you were setting this up for yourself. Funny how things work out, isn't it?'

Jack forced his head round, glared for one instant at Kennedy.

'Fuck you!' he snarled.

The three men closed in tight around him. He looked at their faces, dwelling a fierce second on each.

'I'm rememberin' you bastards!'

All three pushed at once. Jack felt his feet slide and slip. The support vanished from under him. He fell, spun, the air tearing upwards against his face. For a moment he saw the yard flying at him. There was a thump and roaring darkness. Then nothing.

Airchie Cairns was released from Barlinnie prison on the morning of 23rd December, a freezing dark Monday with grey slush underfoot and sleet on the driving wind. By half-past nine he was home at Lanark Street in the poky single-end he shared with his father, Tommy, a retired worker with the Parks Department. Early as it was, Tommy was out in the shed at the back, scrubbing mud-caked terracotta plant pots in a tub of soapy water. Since the time his wife died six years before, he hadn't been able to sit still. He glanced up as Airchie put his head through the door.

'So ye're back,' he grunted, and returned his attention to the pots. 'I hope the sojourn did ye some good.'

Airchie realised it was as much of a welcome as he could expect.

'Merry Christmas to you too, Paw,' he said, going back to the house.

In the narrow scullery he fried himself two eggs, a couple of rashers of bacon and a slice of bread. He brewed a pot of tea, filled a mug with it and spooned in plenty of sugar. Five minutes later he had demolished the lot and finally felt he was back home. In prison he'd missed the breakfasts as much as his freedom.

By 10:15 he had shaved and changed into warm corduroy trousers and a heavy sweater. In Barlinnie they had cropped his hair and there wasn't much he could do with it, so he contented himself with a generous application of Brylcreem and brushed it flat. He was back out on the street and running to catch a tram less than an hour after he arrived home.

At the Royal Infirmary he met resistance.

'There are rules about visiting,' the sister at the orthopaedic ward told him. 'The hours are two to three and seven to eight on visiting days. Monday isn't a visiting day.'

Airchie countered with a heartfelt story about having to be back at the Clyde Street Mission by twelve to help feed the old people.

'The mornin's are the only time I get off,' he said. 'I promised Mr Kane's old grannie I'd visit him for her, so I could tell her how he is.' He shook his head sadly. 'She's not got long, by the look of her. She's pinin' for a bit of news.'

Sister showed a glimmer of sympathy.

'I could be in serious trouble if I let you into the ward,' she said. 'Couldn't you just tell the old woman you'd seen him, and that he's coming along fine?'

'She'd never believe me,' Airchie said. 'Anyway, I don't think I could tell her a lie. She's such a nice old person.' He shrugged helplessly. 'I'd hate doin' anythin' like that.'

Sister consulted the fob watch pinned to the bib of her apron.

'You can speak to him for five minutes,' she said, sighing heavily. 'He's in the third bed along on the left. Five minutes, mind. Not a minute longer.'

Airchie went into the ward, noticing how the green and yellow walls gave the light the same hopeless, jaundiced tint that hung over the cell he had vacated that morning. He stopped inside the doorway, looking along the rows of beds. The patients in here were like sculptures of people captured in unbelievable poses. They were strapped, wired, plastered and half-suspended at all angles, some with their arms sticking up in the air, others their legs, some both. He moved along to the third bed and wondered if Sister had got it wrong. This didn't look like Jack.

But it was him. The eyes opened and the intense blue was unmistakable, although the rest of him still looked like a stranger. Airchie went to the side of the bed.

'Jack? How're ye doin'?'

'No' bad,' Jack said, his jaw barely moving.

'I'd like to say ye're lookin' great, but Ah'm not that much of a liar. Ye look like a tenement fell on you.'

Jack's head and neck were bandaged. There were broad strips of adhesive tape on both cheeks. His eyelids and lips were bluish black and his fingers, the only other parts of him uncovered, were taped to thin wooden splints. His back, hips and legs were bedded in plaster. The left leg and arm were hoisted in traction.

'It's good to see you, Airchie. I've thought about you a lot.'

'Aye, an' Ah've missed you, Jack.' The confession was a small embarrassment. A joke was needed. 'Listen, how come you're talkin' like an Englishman?'

'My jaw's broken, both sides. They've wired it.'

'Ah'll have to try that myself.' Airchie glanced over his shoulder at the doorway. 'This is a flyin' visit. I had to use ma charm to get in as it was. Just tell me, is there anythin' I can get you?'

'No, I'm fine. There's bugger all I can do, anyway. Have ye seen any of the lads?'

'I just got out this mornin'. You're my first social call. Eric's the only one I've seen in ages – he came to see me pretty regularly. He visited just after this happened. He was mad enough to walk through walls that day. They'd told him they didn't think you'd pull through. He's kept me posted ever since, but it seems they weren't sayin' much up here.'

'He came in yesterday,' Jack said. 'It was the first day I was allowed visitors.'

'Ye've been pretty bad, then. How long's it been?'

'Nearly six weeks. I don't remember the first three.'

'An' what's the forecast?'

'Nobody'll tell me.'

A couple of minutes later Sister came to the door and tapped her watch. Airchie left, promising to visit soon. When he had gone Jack closed his eyes again. He was exhausted. The least exertion, even talking, wore him out. He knew now how old people felt, how they had to cope on skimpy rations of energy. It was no wonder so many of them were bad-tempered. The frustration was hellish. His brain throbbed with energy, but the least bodily effort took the heart out of him. At night, when he lay there without an ounce of strength and yet couldn't sleep, he worked on schemes for his future, skirting the suspicion that he might not have one.

In his early days of awareness, when he learned he'd been nearly dead for weeks, all he could think of was his stupidity. It burned him. A doctor explained that he'd had a long operation to relieve the pressure of a clot on his brain; he'd had two more to realign the bones in his legs. His spine was damaged and one hip was still dislocated. There had been some internal bleeding and the gashes on his face had needed skilful stitching to restore the muscle function. The legs would still need a lot of work. He was a loosely assembled jigsaw puzzle, weaker than a kitten, vulnerable as a newborn baby. And all because he had been stupid.

He still didn't know how he had let it happen. To other people, if he had to, he could make excuses: he was distracted by the loss of Jessie, by the imprisonment of his best mate, so his alertness was at a low ebb. To himself he could offer no such extenuation. Nothing short of being struck by lightning excused the kind of distraction he'd dangled in that night. The lack of caution was ridiculous. An amateur would have done miles better than he had. He'd been unarmed, strolling along like a blameless kid, instead of carrying a set of brass knuckles and treading the streets with the kind of alertness appropriate to a man who had made bad enemies. And when that joker had waved him across the road – *he'd gone*! He walked right up to him! The molester that Tam Fisher killed got his hands on most of his young victims that way – he just waved them across. Lambs to the slaughter.

And how about standing there with the knife pointing at his belly, refusing to let himself run from a one-to-one confrontation, without even checking to see if it *was* one-to-one? He'd been ambushed on a wide-open road. It was a disgrace. When they grabbed his arms he could have used their support and kicked the guy with the knife right in the balls with both feet, then used the back of his head to put at least one of the other two out of action. *Then* it would have been one-to-one, a situation he could have tackled easily. But he'd done none of that. He had stood there and let them shackle him up. If he'd heard of anybody else doing what he did in that situation, he would have choked on his contempt.

As the days had passed and the shame of his performance hurt less, he remembered something Mad Harry had said in one of his half-drunk philosophical moments: *Hardly anybody scratches the surface of what he could learn from his own experience.* Since Jack had nothing else to do but lie there, and since the time would be passing anyway, he began carefully to scratch the surface.

What had he learned lately? Things were getting more dangerous, that was for sure. A few years ago a gang member might have been treated to a hammering or a kicking by way of revenge; nothing worse than that. But look at the picture now – a Kingston lad knifed to death in a Cathcart pub, Jack himself handcuffed and thrown off a roof. What did that teach him?

Rule One: Always know the worst that might happen; be ready for it.

He recalled the motto blazoned on the badge of every Glasgow Police helmet – *Semper Vigilo*. Latin's high-sounding mystery intrigued him, he had found out what the words meant: *I am always watching*. Too good for the police, that. He would make it his own. *Semper Vigilo*; he could mutter it like a charm, just to remind himself of Rule One.

So what else did recent experience teach him? That he was a lot more fragile and vulnerable than he had imagined. He would be dead now if he hadn't fallen on dustbins that scattered and softened his impact with the ground. The lesson?

Rule Two: Be harder, as hard as it's possible to be, and never believe you can afford the deadly luxury of trusting people.

Lessons had begun to crowd his head then, beckoning for attention.

Sex wasn't a game or a bit of fun: he only had to think of Jessie's agony, picture the torn-up foetus; one dear life stained and the other destroyed before it had begun.

Rule Three: Take great care of what you love, it's too easy to hurt, and lose.

Then there was reliance: just who could he lean on, depend on, turn to when the black streaks brought him to his knees? Nobody. There was no harbour, not in the long run. Already his father wanted nothing to do with him – and what good would *he* have been, anyway, what succour or support could that poor soul offer? His mother, having decided now to be a permanent invalid, was preoccupied with her religion and the spiritual preparation for her call to glory, which she believed was imminent. No chance of an enveloping solace there. What about the gang? Hardly something to rely on, since it could bring on more trouble than it prevented. He wouldn't be lying there if he hadn't been one of the Kingston Clan.

Rule Four: Be sure you can rely on yourself, you're all you've got.

Four good rules were enough to be going on with, he decided, enough to live by in whatever future he might have. They would take every ounce of resource and determination. Jack memorised them and in his crippled immobility swore he would honour them to the letter. Given the chance, of course.

On Friday night Eric Ross came to visit. He noticed at once that Jack's bed had been raised at the foot and that both his legs were now in traction. Catheters emerged from various parts of his dressings, leading to a clutch of bottles under the bed.

'Another operation on the legs, one on the jaw, too,' Jack told him. 'I feel worse now than I did two weeks ago.'

Eric took it in grim-faced, slowly scanning the length of his fallen lieutenant, as if he had to remember every detail.

'You thought maybe you would remember a name,' he said. 'Any luck?'

Jack nodded. He had known the name all along, of course. But he'd wanted time to think, to consider. He had decided he would make do with the three who heaved him over the edge; Eric was entitled to something to feed his anger.

'Dermot Kennedy. He said he's Hector Kemp's boss. He was very free with the information. I suppose he expected it to die with me down in that yard.'

'He'll be shittin' himself now,' Eric said, his eyes distant.

'Listen, Eric . . .' Jack winced as he moved his head to a better angle on the pillows. 'I might as well face this now – I'm not goin' to be much use to you any more.'

'Don't talk soft.'

'I'm just bein' practical. I mean, look at me. I've two or three more operations to go yet, and even then they don't think I'll be up to much. I'll have a lot of problems, so there's no sense me askin' you to suffer them as well. I'll bow out gracefully, glass jaw an' all.'

'What'll ye do?'

'For a livin'? Oh, I thought maybe a nice wee business. Nothin' that needs much effort. Money-lendin', somethin' on those lines. I could just about cope with that, if I'd Airchie to help me.'

Eric sat thinking for a minute, then he nodded sharply.

'Fair enough. I'll give ye a hand tae get goin'. A bit of capital for starters.'

'Aw, Eric, there's no need – '

'It's the least Ah can do.'

Eric changed the subject then, brought Jack up to date on what had been happening and outlined a few schemes he had brewing.

'Our biggest problem right now is the polis,' he said. 'They keep interferin'. Things would run smoother all round if they'd stick to traffic duty.'

'They've been here,' Jack told him. 'Two of them. DS Fraser an' Superintendent Laurie. Two of my biggest admirers. Fraser's been tryin' to catch me for a long time. Laurie once gave me a thumpin' outside the Cockit Hat.'

'What were they after?'

'Well they made out they wanted to know who did this to me. But they knew I wouldn't say. What they were really here for, I think, was to gloat. Laurie told me I'd been workin' for somethin' like this for a long time. Fraser said it did his heart good to see me really sufferin'.'

'Their time'll come,' Eric said, grave with certainty.

When the bell rang he stood up, pushed back the chair, then leaned down over Jack, putting his face close.

'You concentrate on gettin' better. Leave me to do the debt-settlin'. When ye get out we'll talk about gettin' you set up in yer independent business.'

When Eric had gone Jack realised he felt better. He was still as weak as water and everything hurt, but his head was buzzing. Things were moving. He would be out of the gang with Eric's blessing. He'd be a free man, free to move and manoeuvre. He had no inspiring expectations of sudden stamina when he got out of here, but he was sure his determination to be a loner again could build strength where medicine never would.

And now, on top of the rules he was preparing to live by, there was a goal he had set himself, something to nurture and get well for. By some means yet to be decided, Jack Kane would become a terrible force in Glasgow. He would do it before he was twenty-one. It was a treat he owed himself.

FIVE

At three minutes past ten on the morning of Monday 30 March, 1936, Airchie Cairns accompanied Jack Kane through the side gates of Glasgow Royal Infirmary and helped him into a waiting taxi. It was a slow, awkward operation and by the time Jack was seated he was sweating with pain. Airchie held on to the crutches, keeping a wary eye on Jack and putting an arm round his shoulders as the cab jerked away.

'Ye shouldn't have come out yet. Ye're still in a bad way.'

Jack nodded at the Infirmary's receding facade.

'They've done all they can for me in there. Anyway, if I'd stayed any longer I'd have gone off ma crust.'

'Ye still need the care, Jack. The nursin'. There's nobody at home to give you that kind of help. An' you'll no' get the treatment now, either.'

'The cure's in my own hands, Airchie. The hospital's had five months hackin' an' choppin' at me, an' I'm still a bloody wreck. I'll try it my own way from here on.'

He had signed himself out against the surgeons' wishes. They argued with him and issued grim warnings. His body, they said, was structurally and chemically out of balance. The fractures to his legs, the dislocations, the deep bruising of internal organs, the sheer number of injuries that aggravated and complicated each other had weakened his physiology as well as buckling his spine, legs, and arms. His muscles had wasted from disuse. He needed more operations to correct the alignment of his hips and knees. There was concern, too, about his erratic arterial blood flow. In the teeth of all that Jack had still insisted on leaving. He signed a form absolving the medical staff of any blame for what might happen to him now.

When they got to Monteith Row he sat on the steps outside the tenement while Airchie went up to the house with the crutches and made sure Alistair had the bed ready.

'An' I know it's none of ma business, Mr Kane,' Airchie muttered on his way out again, 'but try an' give him a bit of support, eh? He's in a bad way. He'll need as much help as he can get.'

'He's turned down the expert help that was on offer,' Alistair said, dourly addressing the door jamb rather than look at Airchie. 'He'll have to learn to manage for himself. I've enough to do,' he added as Airchie went back to the stairs, 'what with runnin' an' fetchin' for his mother.'

'It'll be tough goin', Jack,' Airchie announced as he hoisted his pal on his shoulder and carried him to the stairs. 'Your old man doesn't want to know.'

'They've written me off as a bad job, the pair of them,' Jack grunted.

When he was in his room and sitting on the side of the bed, Airchie said he would have to go, he was the runner that day for the Kingstons' off-track bookie operation.

'But Ah'll come round every day,' he promised. 'I can try an' see you don't starve, at least.'

'Be here at ten tomorrow then, eh?' Jack said. 'I want us to have a wee council of war.'

'Should you maybe just get better first? There'll be time enough for business later on.'

'I want to do both at the same time,' Jack said. 'Ten o'clock, Airchie. Try to be on time.'

Airchie nodded and went to the door, then stopped.

'I nearly forgot. Eric said to give you this.' He took a folded newspaper from his inside pocket and threw it on to the bed. 'Kind of a homecomin' present. Ye'll find it on page two.'

Airchie went out and Jack spread the paper on the bed beside him. The banner headline announced that ninety-nine per cent of the German electorate had voted for official Nazi candidates in the weekend elections. The British defence budget had gone up by thirty-six million; the money would be spent to strengthen the Fleet Air Arm, add 250 aircraft for home defence and create four new infantry battalions in the Army. Jack turned the page, scanning the headings. There was something about the Hoare-Lavall pact, whatever that was. A civil defence anti-gas school was to be opened. In Japan the armed forces had taken control and somebody called Koki Hirota was the new prime minister. Elsewhere on the crammed page there were advertisements for Ovaltine, Player's cigarettes and Bovril. What was Eric talking about? Jack wondered. Nothing here concerned him in any way he could think of. Then a heading at the bottom of column three caught his eye.

GLASGOW DEATH FALL HORROR

A man fell to his death yesterday from the roof of the Muirpath Glass Bevelling Plant at Timpson Street in north Glasgow. The dead man, later identified as Dermot Kennedy, a works manager from Dover Street, fell into a skip filled with shards of broken glass. Mr Kennedy sustained injuries so severe that it was some hours before he could be identified.

Last night a police spokesman said they still had no idea why Mr Kennedy had been on the roof in the first place. He was described as a man of regular and sober habits who was well respected by his neighbours and those who worked with him. His widow Kathleen, 39, told our reporter, 'I still can't believe this has happened. I'm stunned, just stunned.'

Police are appealing for witnesses. They stress that they do not suspect foul play at this time.

Jack folded up the paper again as Alistair came into the bedroom. He looked at Jack sideways, not quite facing him.

'I think we should clear up somethin' right at the start,' he said gruffly.

'Are you not goin' to say hello, just for openers?' Jack said. 'It's been months, Da. Did you realise that? I've been lyin' in that flamin' hospital five months. In all that time I haven't seen hide nor hair of you or ma mother.'

'I wrote you a letter,' Alistair said, apparently addressing the carpet now, standing with his hands bulging the pockets of his baggy brown cardigan. 'I think that said all that needed sayin'.'

'Oh aye, it was just the tonic I needed. Dear son, we're finished with you, sincerely, Mum and Dad. That was the gist of it, right? I don't think I've ever met a man as empty as you, Da. Ye must have been standin' behind the door when they dished out the hearts.'

'We've always been respectable,' Alistair said. 'How do you think I felt at ma work with that story in the paper, an' all the details about your record an' how you're connected with that Kingston gang? Your mother didn't have an easy time, either. I thought it'd finish her.'

'All right,' Jack said, 'I'm sorry if I caused you a red neck or two. What is it you want to clear up?'

'Well it's not a thing Ah like sayin' . . .' Alistair was trying to look assertive. He extracted his hands from his cardigan pockets and folded his arms. 'Your mother's behind me on this as well, mind you . . .'

'Spit it out, then.'

'We don't want you stayin' here.'

'I gathered that much from your letter,' Jack said. 'But I'm sure Airchie passed on my message – I'm only stoppin' here until I'm fit enough to go some place else.'

'Aye, but how long's that goin' tae be?'

'As long as it takes.'

'Damn it!' Agitated suddenly, Alistair shifted his weight from one foot to the other. 'Your mother doesnae want ye here at all. We had a row about you comin' here this mornin'.'

Jack started nodding.

'Say no more. I get it, loud an' clear. As soon as she

heard I was comin' out of hospital she turned on you an'
told you I wasn't settin' a foot in this house. But you
didn't have the heart, or the guts more likely, to tell
Airchie he wasn't to bring me up here. Right?'

'It's upsettin' her,' Alistair whined. 'She's not to get in
a state, the doctor warned me about that.'

'What's really gettin' you down,' Jack said, 'is the way
she's pickin' on you. Ye can't take it.'

Jack turned his face to the window and caught sight of
himself in the dresser mirror. He hadn't realised he
looked so ill. The journey in the taxi, short as it was, had
exhausted him. The skin round his mouth looked blue
and his eyes seemed to have sunk halfway into his skull.

'Let me put your mind at rest,' he said wearily. 'I'll get
out of here by the end of the week. That's a promise.' He
tilted his head, trying to make his father look at him.
'Feel better now, do you?'

'Well, if it's only goin' to be for a few days . . .'

'Rely on it.'

'Where'll ye go? How will ye manage?'

'What the hell does that matter to you?' Jack braced
his arms on the quilt and swung his legs up on to the bed.
'Look, Da, get me a cup of tea, will you? I'll not bother
you after that. Ye'll hardly know I'm here.'

Alistair left and Jack lay back on the bed. He had
learned by now that illness could drain the heat and
colour out of everything, even anger. What happened, he
believed, was that constant pain and weakness wore the
ends off a person's responses – no extremes were left, just
the flat middle ground. If it had gladdened his heart to
learn that Eric had despatched Dermot Kennedy, he
hadn't noticed anything. The fact was agreeable, that was
all. As for his mother hating the thought of him being in
the house – well, that was just a fact too, it didn't induce
much feeling. Illness had plenty to do with his reaction,
but so had her letter. It was handed to him two days
before the note from his father – which she had probably
made him write. By now Jack knew most of her letter by

heart. There was no hurt left in the message, he had read it over and over until the pain was gone.

Father Pierce made me understand that you are bad in your spirit, she wrote. *I know only too well that evil contaminates even the righteous, and I have felt your taint in our house, threatening us. You have never been a son of mine, you have never behaved like one. Now I learn that somebody wanted to kill you, and I know I shouldn't be shocked or surprised. You have always put a stain on people's lives.*

Cleared of emotion, empty of resentment, he could see the only fact that was significant: his mother was crazy. That certain knowledge had helped his fondness for her to dry up and blow away. She was beyond love or condemnation. With the connivance of Father Pierce her religious mania had run wild – and sanity had been standing in the way when the stampede happened. Exit clear-headed reason, along with any human warmth she'd had left. Jack was as vile in her eyes as any blaspheming Protestant.

'It's a good job I don't get depressed easy,' he murmured.

Naturally, everybody believed the equation of his existence was bleak. On one side there was life, bristling with challenges, demands, dangers; on the other there was Jack, imminently homeless, devoid of his old defences, so badly broken in body that he was barely capable of an independent existence. His situation and outlook, in the words of his long-dead grandfather, were as black as the Earl of Hell's waistcoat.

But that was the visible equation. People didn't know about the Four Rules. Nobody could read his ambition to be one of the legends. They couldn't suspect the humming determination that would countenance no setback. All that other people knew about Jack Kane was what they saw, and what they saw told them a lie.

He drifted into sleep and woke up again sharply when his father put the cup and saucer on the table by the bed.

'Maybe ye should get under the covers,' Alistair mumbled. 'Ah'll help ye, if ye like.'

'No, no need.' Jack pushed himself up. 'I'm goin' to drink the tea, then I'm goin' out.'

Alistair stared at him.

'Don't worry,' Jack said, 'I'll not need your help to do that, either.'

'But ye're no' fit enough.'

'I'll only get fit if I start makin' my body do its stuff.' Jack picked up the cup and took a sip. 'A fella's got to fight back. Only mugs an' old women don't fight back.' He cocked his head at Alistair. 'That's right, isn't it?'

Murdo McKechearn was a Barras trader who specialised in new and secondhand bicycle parts, with a healthy sideline in primus stoves, waterproof jackets, groundsheets and general camping equipment. His business thrived because he believed in spending a bare minimum on stock and never carried any lines he couldn't be sure of selling. His grasp of supply and demand was the envy of other traders. They could never analyse his technique or imitate it. Among themselves they concluded that Murdo simply had a knack of knowing what people wanted, and was always in a position to find supplies of the right items.

The fact was that Murdo's success hinged on his cordial relationship with a half dozen skilled young men who could get him anything he needed in double-quick time, for prices that satisfied them and kept the cheerful grin on Murdo's chubby face. Until Jack Kane was seventeen he regularly obliged Murdo whenever he needed a particular type of dynamo or gearshift, a length of brake cable, sets of cotter pins or a specific brand of tyre. Jack could produce the goods, new or used, within an hour of being approached. Murdo always paid on delivery and at Christmas he never failed to come up with a bonus for the members of his supply network.

When Jack stopped working around Barrowland and moved on to other things, he took the trouble to leave a replacement, a whippet-fast lad who could strip a bike of every accessory in much the same time it took the owner to park it in a back court or shed. Murdo was grateful to Jack for appointing such a competent successor. He told him as much.

'Any time I can do ye a good turn, son, just give me a shout.'

The shout came on Wednesday April 1, two days after Jack left hospital. Murdo came to the door of his lockup and stared in open shock at his visitor.

'Christ almighty. I heard you'd got done up, but I never imagined it was anythin' like this.'

Jack hung thin and gaunt between his crutches, panting softly from the effort of getting here. He had dragged himself the length of Monteith Row, along the Gallowgate and up Spoutmouth to this modest row of traders' warehouses. The journey had taken more than an hour. He was sweating and deathly pale.

'Can I come in an' sit down, Murdo? Ah'm buggered.'

Ten minutes' rest in one of Murdo's latest line in camping chairs made a difference. So did a mug of tea spiked with whisky. Pale but visible sparkle came back. On the second cup Jack explained why he had come.

'I was wonderin' if you could do me a favour, Murdo.'

'Name it.'

'Ye've got a house on Steel Street, haven't you?'

'To ma cost,' Murdo sighed, leaning his bulk on the door frame.

'It's done out in flats, is that right?'

'Four of them,' Murdo nodded, 'each with its own bathroom, full electric wirin', stairhead lamps, the lot. It was to be my goldmine, Jack. I was goin' to retire on the yield.'

'What went wrong?'

'People,' Murdo said. 'As usual. Trouble is always people. I insisted on references, mind you, only the most respectable tenants for me. Families, reliable units.' He sighed. 'I should have had my head looked at. They've wrecked the places. People have no respect for what isn't their own. An' gettin' the rent out of them's like shovellin' steam with a billiard cue.'

'I'd have thought you were on to a good thing.'

'Aye, me too. But listen. Take my advice, if you ever consider goin' straight an' havin' a nice tidy wee business to support you, don't even *consider* bein' a landlord. Of the four flats I've got, I collect rent regularly from one. Just one. I have to issue threats to get it out of another two, an' the fourth one's a dead loss. They've got a dog with the temper of a fuckin' werewolf an' when I threatened to get the bailiffs on them the fella said he'd come round here an' burn down my lockup. He looks just like the kind that'd do it, too.'

Jack looked interested.

'Anyway,' Murdo said, 'what's the favour ye're after?'

'We'll turn it the other way round, Murdo.'

'How d'ye mean?'

'*Ah'll* do *you* a favour. This character with the dog – I suppose you'd like to get him out?'

'Aye, you're right I would. I'd also like to throw my leg across that Bette Davis, but I've about as much chance of one as the other.'

'If I get him out for you, can I have the flat?'

'What – to live in?'

'Sure. An' you'd have no trouble gettin' your rent off me.'

'Well . . .' Murdo scratched his beefy neck thoughtfully. 'I'd be happy tae let you have the flat, Jack. Delighted, in fact. But I mean, don't take me wrong, it's just that the way you look, you'd exhaust yourself if you blew your nose too hard, never mind throwin' out that bloody gorilla over on Steel Street.'

Jack smiled, drawing his crutches towards him, positioning the rests in his armpits. He lurched forward sharply and was upright, spreading his feet to balance himself.

'Just tell me we've got a deal, Murdo.'

'Sure.' Murdo shrugged. 'It's a deal.'

'Fine.' Jack pointed himself at the doorway and swung

forward into the sunlight. 'A friend of mine'll come round later. Give him the name an' the flat number. Then forget about the whole business.' He made to move off, then paused. 'One thing – will it be all right for me to have the keys as soon as this other guy's out?'

'Certainly,' Murdo said. 'Ah'll throw in a few bob for the house-warmin', too.'

At five o'clock that evening Airchie Cairns knocked on the door of a groundfloor flat in Murdo's house in Steel Street. A dog started to bark. Feet came thumping along the passage and Airchie heard the animal snarling behind the door panelling. The deadlock was turned and the door opened. A big unshaven man in a vest and moleskin trousers was standing there. His fingers were curled round his Alsatian's collar, restraining the animal.

'Mr Peter Drummond?' Airchie said.

'Who wants tae know?'

'Me.' Airchie looked down at the dog. It was snarling again, eyes slitted, its lips drawn back from its big yellow teeth. 'That's a hungry-lookin' dog ye've got there.'

'What's this about?' Drummond demanded.

'I'm here on behalf of the landlord,' Airchie said. 'He wants you to leave.' He slid his hands into his jacket pockets. 'Soon as possible, actually.'

Drummond did something with his mouth that made it sneer on one side and scowl at the other. He bent forward a fraction, letting the dog get nearer Airchie.

'Ah think you better fuck off, pal, before this hungry dog of mine helps itself to a bit of supper.'

'Nice doggie,' Airchie said, taking his right hand from his pocket and thrusting a big chunk of beef at the dog. The animal snatched it and chewed it furiously.

'Hey!' Drummond looked at the dog, then at Airchie. 'What's the game?'

'I gave your dog a treat. It's good beef, that. He'll enjoy it. He'll get a nice sleep after it, too. In fact he'll sleep for about twelve hours, Mr Drummond. Consider yerself lucky I didn't poison him. It would have been just as easy.'

91

Drummond looked at the dog again. It was still chewing, but its back legs were trembling, buckling.

'Acts like lightnin', that stuff,' Airchie said.

Drummond let go the collar. The dog lurched sideways and slid down the wall. It lay on its side, whining softly, eyes glazed as it swallowed the remainder of the meat. Drummond grabbed Airchie's lapel.

'Ya fuckin' – '

Airchie's brass-knuckled left hand came up and jabbed the angry mouth. Blood spilled out over Drummond's chin. He staggered back too late to dodge another jab that tore open his cheek. Airchie followed him into the hall, stepping over the comatose dog. A woman in curlers came to the living room door and screamed as Airchie dropped her husband with a well-aimed punch in the solar plexus. Airchie pushed past Drummond, strode into the living room and pulled open one of the windows. Without breaking his rhythm he picked up a vase and a couple of ornaments and threw them down into the street. As they smashed on the road a chair followed them, then a picture and a heavy oval mirror. The woman ran round the room screeching and clutching herself. Drummond had crawled along the hall and was pulling himself upright against the door. Airchie glanced at him, crossed the room and dragged him by the hair to the window. He pushed him halfway out, doubled over the ledge.

'Now listen,' Airchie said, his mouth an inch from Drummond's ear. 'If you're not out of here when I get back, this is the way you'll leave. For sure. You, your missus there, an' the dog. At least he'll feel nothin'.' He shook the big ugly head, banging it on the side of the window frame. 'Did ye get all that?'

Drummond's broken mouth burbled something.

'Right. Ye've got three hours. Make sure you leave the keys under the mat.'

Airchie turned and marched out.

That evening five members of the Kingston Clan turned up at the abandoned flat with ladders, dust sheets, wallpaper and tins of paint. They all worked for the council and were well used to this kind of job. They cleared the premises of abandoned refuse, furniture, and clothing, then washed down the walls and covered the rugs and linoleum with dust sheets. They then set to work redecorating, supervised for the first hour by Eric Ross himself. By two-thirty the next morning they were finished. Before they left they opened windows to help air the place and speed the drying of the fresh paint and paper.

At his house in the Gorbals Eric sat into the night with Jack Kane, reminiscing over tots of whisky, expressing faint hopes and solid good wishes.

'Ah have to admire you, Jack. Goin' it alone like this. A lot of men with half yer problems would have packed in their hand.'

'I've had help,' Jack pointed out. 'It was good of you, Eric.'

'Treat it as a retirement present. This, too.' He took down a fat envelope from the sideboard by his chair and threw it into Jack's lap. 'Four hundred in there. Will it be enough?'

'Ah told ye before – '

'Take it an' use it. Get yer business on the go.'

'Fair enough.' Jack patted the envelope. 'I'm payin' it back, though.'

'No need,' Eric said sternly.

'Just tae keep ma standards up. Within the year you'll have it back.'

'If it'll make ye happy, then.'

Eric refilled their glasses.

'We'll have this last one, nice an' slow, then I'll drive ye home.'

'No, I'll walk,' Jack said. 'I'm gettin' better at it. No sense lettin' up when I'm startin' to win.'

Eric sat back, staring at Jack, shaking his head.

'What the hell is it that's drivin' you? Airchie tells me you'll not rest an' give yerself a chance to get better. He says you get up an' down the stairs at Monteith Row on yer arse. Ye do exercises that make ye howl with the pain. An' now ye're determined to move into your own place an' fend for yourself. I'm all for fightin' setbacks myself, but there's limits.'

Jack swirled his whisky, looking at it against the light.

'Rest's for the dead, Eric. If a man's able to move then he should move as much as he can. I've got to make the best of what's happened to me. I'll never be what I was, but I can make sure the loss is as small as I can make it. I'll not let myself get any worse. Does that sound daft?'

'It certainly does,' Eric said. 'Ye could kill yerself at this rate.'

Fifty minutes later, hearing birds begin to sing on the roofs and in the back courts, seeing light in the sky over by Coatbridge, Jack clomped his way on his crutches across the Albert Bridge. He was exhausted and not at all sober, but the drink had taken a lot of the pain out of his back and legs. As he went he smiled from time to time, reflecting on the way Eric had revised the old days, laying sentimentality over memories of events that had been savage, bloody, dangerous. He had talked wistfully about the destruction of Dermot Kennedy, painting a picture of sweet and honourable vengeance, a heartfelt act of recompense committed out of one man's respect for another.

And I was no better, Jack thought, nodding to a dour-looking night-shift constable measuring his way across the bridge in the opposite direction.

Eric had been presented with a picture of a brave warrior determined to make the most of a bad job. Jack had expressed the most modest hopes for his future: it would be a quiet stretch of time, pain-wracked no doubt, but profitable, even though it would lack any hint of challenge or adventure.

Lies, lies . . .

If he couldn't come out of this twice or three times the man he'd been, then he was badly misjudging himself. He didn't think he could do that. He looked about him at the sleeping streets, sniffed the breath of his city and felt its assent. He *knew* he would make it.

Handing Eric all the guff about hobbling on bravely, about never again being what he had been, et cetera –

94

that was a necessary part of the total scheme. The last thing Jack wanted was old allies suspecting he was free-lancing on their territory. Much better to encourage pitying respect, their sentimental approval of his poor stumbling efforts to carve a way for himself in this cruel jungle they all inhabited.

The constable stopped at the end of the bridge and looked back at the lad on the crutches, wondering what the hell somebody in his condition could find to laugh about. And so loudly, at that.

On Saturday morning, again with the help of Airchie Cairns, Jack moved into the freshly decorated flat on Steel Street. Murdo McKechearn was there, waiting with a cheery welcome and a couple of his friends to help get Jack's stuff into position. The furniture – a three piece suite, four dining chairs and a gate-legged table – was from the man who had the lockup next to Murdo's. He had taken pity on Jack and let him have the lot for five pounds. The three-quarter size bed was Jack's own from Monteith Row, the same bed he had slept in since he was four.

By noon everything was in position. Murdo and his friends left to get back to their stalls at Barrowland. Jack and Airchie sat opposite each other at the tiled fireplace, relishing the brightness of the place, its new-decorated smells.

'This is where it starts,' Jack said. 'Clean and fresh. A beginning, Airchie. By Christmas this place'll be furnished like a palace. An' remember, any time you want to move in there's a bedroom for you.'

'Ah fancy Ah'll stay with the old fella a while yet,' Airchie said. 'He hasn't much time for me, but I don't think he'd like me movin' out. I'm somethin' for him tae moan at. Old folk need that.' He stretched out his legs and sank back in the armchair. 'The word from Eric is that I'm to do all I can for you. I'm still one of the boys, but I've no duties for the time being. So what's on the programme?'

'I've talked to Dougie Meikle. We can operate the money-lendin' out of the Cockit Hat. I'll give him three quid a week for accommodatin' us. It'll be a good business an' there'll be no competition – Eric's promised me that.'

They had worked out most of the scheme already. Jack had made his ambitions plain at the first council of war in his bedroom at Monteith Row: 'The money-lendin's only goin' tae be a smokescreen, Airchie. I want everybody tae believe it's the only thing I do.'

Airchie had been doubtful at first; he couldn't see Jack keeping control of all the ventures he planned to set up – dice games, stacked-pack pontoon, pitch-and-toss schools, a racing book. But Jack's confidence was swiftly contagious. He had spent weeks working everything out in the hospital. As he explained it all to Airchie, he radiated an intense, nervous certainty of where the pair of them were headed. Venues, rotas, timetables had all been planned. Security was mapped, down to the finest detail. So was control, which would be maintained by the only reliable means, the mailed fist, the solemn threat that one attempted swindle meant immediate catastrophe for the individual concerned. Minions, who would be kept to a handful and wouldn't really know who employed them, would be encouraged to stay content with what they were given. If they got any other ideas they would have no future in Glasgow.

But even those ventures were to be part of the smoke-screen, a second shield in case anybody noticed that Jack was getting richer than any man could from simple money-lending.

The real business, the serious stuff, would be conducted by himself and Airchie. Nobody else would know. They were uniquely placed to make a mint.

'For the time bein',' Jack said now, 'we'll stick to the games and the money lendin'. The other stuff's all planned up here . . .' He tapped the side of his head. 'But I've got to get myself fit before we do anythin' about it.'

He saw Airchie run an inventory with his eyes.

'Ye don't think Ah'll make it, do you?'

'It's a tall order ye've set for yourself,' Airchie said.

'I know. It's taller than you realise, too.' Jack drew himself to his feet, using one crutch as a support. He stood there clinging to it. 'I went through hell up in the Royal, Airchie. They did everythin' to me, every bloody thing that hurt. Half the time I'm sure they couldn't work out how I went on livin'. I wondered myself at first. But after a while I stopped wonderin'. Busted an' broken as I was – as I *am* – there's somethin' at the centre of me that'll not go out. I know it surer than I know my own name. A clear blue flame, Airchie. Hot an' strong. That's what saved me, kept me goin' while they were shakin' their heads an' despairin'. The way for me to get right again, to get strong, is never to deny that flame. I've got to keep rememberin' it's there. It'll see me through as long as I'm prepared to help myself.' He stopped and stared at Airchie. 'What're you grinnin' at?'

'Ye sound like one of the evangelists that get up on their soap boxes in the park.'

'Maybe I do. They're burstin' with faith, those guys. I can understand what faith's all about. The say it moves mountains. Well, I've got faith in *myself*, Airchie. Keep your eyes peeled. Watch the fuckin' mountains start movin'.'

They eyes met and for a second the intensity was shared, a spoke of energy passing from one man to the other. Then they burst out laughing. Jack gripped his crutch and lowered himself into his chair, wincing with the pain of his mirth. It took them a whole minute to recover.

'Christ, Jack, If anybody can do it, you're the man.' Airchie stood up, still grinning. 'Ah'll put the kettle on. Do ye fancy anythin' tae eat?'

'A cup of tea'll do me for now,' Jack said. 'I'm goin' out for a while.'

'More exercise?'

'Aye. A bit of practice, too. I can't let myself get rusty.'

Later, dragging himself along the Saltmarket, he stopped outside an ironmonger's and studied the goods strung out along the shop front. He stayed there five minutes, fingering pots and buckets and spades and watering cans, hobbling from one end of the window to the other. Eventually the shopkeeper came out.

'Can I help you with anything, son?'

Jack shook his head, smiling.

'Just lookin', thanks.'

The man went back in. As he turned his back Jack made his move. His hand flashed out and shot back again. He straightened, braced himself on the crutches and shuffled away, leaning forward so his coat flaps covered the nice new hatchet tucked in his belt.

SIX

Without making ripples on the surface of everyday life, the volume of illegal leisure activity in central Glasgow grew significantly during the late spring and summer of 1936. In the Calton district covert dice and card games became available to those with gambling fever; an alfresco pitch-and-toss school appeared, too, tightly managed and open only to those who didn't gamble from motives of financial desperation; the temporarily hard-up, meanwhile, could borrow money with minimal security three mornings a week, simply by approaching an amiable, puffy-featured young man in the public bar of the Cockit Hat and providing some proof of identity; men who wanted to back the horses suddenly found it easier, with four new bookies' runners around the Calton ready to take bets and deliver winnings promptly. Subtlety was a keynote of all these activities. Anyone not involved was unlikely to notice the change.

Towards the end of August one very obvious change became a talking point. Until then Jack Kane hadn't been seen, apart from a time or two in April following his release from hospital. He had been a pathetic sight at that time, and when he finally disappeared from the streets people assumed the worst. Rumours circulated during late spring and early summer, mostly to the effect that Jack was now a crippled recluse, out of the game and living off handouts. Even the police decided he was a part of history, a flame that had blazed briefly and swiftly faded. Out of sight for more than four months, Jack was soon out of the enforcers' minds.

Until he reappeared. Then a lot of them could think about nothing else.

'What do you make of it?' Superintendent Laurie asked Detective Sergeant Fraser. 'I wouldn't have given a carrot for his chances back in April.'

They were sunning themselves on the steps of the High Court on a slow afternoon when the jury, it seemed, had fallen asleep over their deliberations on a robbery case.

'He looks like something out of those stories you read in the papers,' Fraser said. 'You know, the ones about people nipping over to Switzerland to get rebuilt.'

'He looks like a cod-liver oil advert. But he doesn't seem as cocky as he used to be.'

Fraser clasped his hands behind his back, carefully examining his reaction to the new Jack Kane.

'I spoke to him. Just in passing. He even sounds different, you know.'

'How?'

'It's something about his accent. I didn't talk to him long enough to work it out. It's still a Glasgow voice, but it's smoother. Not Kelvinside or anything like that, not pan loaf. But proper. Tidier.'

'So what's brought about all the changes?' Laurie said, chewing the end of his moustache.

'Search me, sir. It usually takes religion or money to transform a man to that extent.'

'He's a pape,' Laurie said. 'Religion's just a habit with them. It *could* be money, though. He's driving a car now, I notice.'

'Where would he get the money?'

'Insurance.'

'His folks, you mean?'

Laurie nodded. In June Marie Kane had suffered a heart attack and died. Eleven days later Alistair was found dead on the floor of the gas-filled scullery; it wasn't possible to prove he had committed suicide, but it was generally assumed he had.

'If you think about it,' Fraser said, 'that's not a far-fetched conclusion. Say Jack Kane's mother and father were well insured – a lot of these quiet old-fashioned types go through life skimping and saving and then when they die the Prudential shells out a packet to the next of kin. So there might be money in the picture. And then there's the shock of them both dying. Look at it that way and you've a combination of factors that could change a man overnight.'

'Kane's looking well on it, anyway, whatever the reason. I suppose we better start keeping an eye on the bastard now he's back in circulation.'

'As if we hadn't enough to keep us busy,' Fraser sighed.

They observed a moment's silence over the current workload.

'The Chief Constable's put round another sour memo about the burglary rate,' Laurie said. 'Too many break-ins, too few arrests. Prostitution's on the climb, too, according to the lads on the dirty squad. And the murder rate's nothing to get complacent about.'

'At least our percentage of arrests has gone up in that area,' Fraser said, ever the promotor of CID ratings. 'We've made a good showing on violent crime, too.'

'Mm,' Laurie grunted. 'Any developments yet on the Garscube Road shemozzle?'

'Not a whisper.'

The case was perplexing, since no motive could be uncovered, and the mode of execution didn't help to pinpoint suspects. Three young men, all employed at the same metal-box manufacturer's, had been attacked as they left a pub the previous Saturday night. According to witnesses and the victims themselves, the shadowy, solitary attacker had moved with alarming speed. He left two of his victims lying on the pavement and one in the road, all with their legs smashed. One man had already had an amputation and it looked like another one might lose both his legs. All three would be disabled for the remainder of their lives. The weapon used was thought to be an axe.

'Getting back to Kane,' Fraser said; 'I don't think he'll be half the bother he used to be.'

'You've a touching faith there, Fraser. What makes you so hopeful?'

'He's not connected any more, sir. It's been noticed. He's been spotted at six or seven locations in the past week and each time he's been on his own. Even in the pubs. My guess is he's out of the gang life and he's staying out. Easy enough to understand, when you think what his membership got him.'

'I'd like to believe you're right,' Laurie said, snipping off a couple of bristles between his lateral incisors. 'But we'll keep an eye out, just in case.'

A few miles from where the two officers stood, to the south-west of the city in a secluded hollow of a park called Rouken Glen, Jack Kane was sitting on a slope facing the sun, his jacket carefully folded over a low branch of a tree behind him. He had been coming to this spot three times a week for four months. He had decided that today would be his last visit for a while. It seemed approrpiate that this was the first time the sun had shone on him in this place. He grinned as Airchie came out from a clump of trees at the bottom of the slope, shaking his head. He was carrying a hatchet.

'What do you think?'

Airchie came up the slope and dropped down beside Jack.

'Ah think,' Airchie said, 'that if the parkie ever saw what ye've done to those trees, he'd tell your teacher on you.'

'The trees can take it,' Jack said. 'They'll survive.'

'It's more than I'd say for any poor bugger that ever got in the way while ye were practisin'.'

'For some reason, Airchie, nobody else ever comes to this corner. Maybe it's because you've got to struggle to get to it. People take the easy roads most of the time. In everything they do.'

The thoughtful content of Jack's patter still surprised Airchie. They could be talking about anything – horses, women, anything at all – and suddenly Jack would go all reflective and come out with a remark that must have taken some thought to put together. Airchie found it surprising because Jack had always been a come-off-it merchant, a debunker of lofty thoughts and wise remarks. On the whole most of the changes in him surprised Airchie, even though he had been present at every stage of Jack's transition from the crippled ex-strongarm to the ascendant organiser he was today.

'Show us it again,' Airchie said, passing Jack the hatchet.

'One more time, then.' Jack stood up, gripping the hatchet a third the way along its short handle. He hefted it. 'Same tree?'

Airchie nodded.

'What's the bet?'

'Christ, I owe you four pints already. How about a free shot?'

'I need a reason,' Jack said. 'Incentive.'

'A whisky, then. A double.'

'You're on.'

Jack drew back his arm slowly, staring fixedly at a gap in the trees twenty yards away. The blade of the hatchet came up past his ear, stopped a second and rose above his head, maintaining its angle as he straightened his arm. He drew in his breath, held it, then jerked his arm forward, letting go the hatchet at the instant of maximum thrust. It shot down into the trees, spinning twice and curving past the nearest tree to slice into the one behind. The crack echoed round the hollow like a pistol shot.

'Ah still don't believe it,' Airchie said. 'How did you learn to do it like that?'

'I learned because I wanted to.'

Airchie went down into the trees and retrieved the hatchet.

'I needed two hands to get it out this time,' he said, coming back up the slope. 'It's some bloody weapon.'

'In the right hands,' Jack said, 'it's the best.'

He took the hatchet from Airchie and pushed it into the canvas pouch on his belt. They sat down again, turning their faces up to the hot sun.

'Ah used to think ye were just gettin' away for a while on your own,' Airchie said. 'It never occurred to me ye were trainin' tae be a hatchet man.'

'Well, now you know.'

Until today Airchie hadn't even known Jack owned a hatchet. As often happened, Jack said nothing until he had mastered the task in hand. It had been the same when he revealed he could walk without the help of his crutches: one day he had hoisted himself out of his chair, clinging to the crutches for dear life, then he said, 'Look, Airchie!' He threw the crutches across the room then did a little jig in the middle of the rug. For weeks before that, Airchie learned, Jack had been walking round his flat, hour after hour, falling and sometimes hurting himself, refusing to lean on anything, fighting to bring back the strength to his legs and restore his sense of balance.

'Ye're full of big surprises these days,' Airchie said, lying back on the grass. 'They're comin' out at a rate of about one a month.'

'I'll try to improve on that.'

Some surprises were discussed, some were not. It was easy for Airchie to know which ones to avoid mentioning; they were the ones Jack never mentioned himself. Like his complete lack of visible response to the death of his parents. And the change in his speech.

'What made you want tae get expert with the chopper anyway? Was it all the Tom Mix pictures we used to watch, the ones with the Red Indians in them?'

Jack laughed softly, staring at the green ridge above the hollow.

'It came to me while I was in the Royal,' he said. 'One bad day, worse than most, I was thinking to myself how wide open I'd always been, without knowing it. So lying there, hurting like hell and not able to move a muscle, I started to think about ways I could make myself less defenceless – and more of a threat at the same time. I didn't fancy guns, I've never liked them. Bang-bang merchants always come to a bad end. But the idea of

104

doing damage from a distance was a bit seductiive, all the same.'

'I know the feelin',' Airchie said.

'A knife wasn't a very good answer, either. Throw a knife wrong and it just bounces off. But a *hatchet*. If one of them bounces off somebody he's still a wounded man. Just imagining the feel of the tool, the weight and the balance – I don't know, I got excited. I promised myself I'd learn to use one.'

'An' that's what you've been doin' out here all these months?'

'Not just that,' Jack said. 'There's been the exercise. Regular visits here sorted out the troubles with my spine. I've swung and dangled on most of the trees round here.'

'Your own outdoor gym, eh?'

'Definitely. The first five or six weeks were torture, mind. It was hard enough getting on and off the bus. Then I had to come all the way across the glen and struggle down this slope.'

'It knackers me just thinkin' about it.'

'And don't forget, every time I threw the hatchet I had to go down and get it and bring it back here before I could have another throw. I'll tell you something – at the end of the first month I felt like giving up. One day I lay here roaring with the pain. Everything cramped. My whole body begged me to pack it in. But I didn't, and I'm glad I didn't. I got myself fit and I picked up a bit of skill while I was at it.'

Airchie sat up. He looked at the hatchet in Jack's belt.

'I notice ye can throw it with both hands. Does that mean what I think it does?'

'Indeed it does, squire,' Jack said. 'I'm having two hatchets tailor made at a foundry in Cambuslang.'

'Ah might have known. Ye never did believe in half measures.'

'Just wait till you see them. Tool steel heads, hickory shafts. Balanced just right. A saddler on Argyle Street's making a special belt for them, too.'

'The fastest hatchet in town,' Airchie said. 'There's worse titles.'

Jack patted the hatchet and looked at Airchie.

'This is more than just another weapon. It's a discovery. I can't explain, it's complicated the way I feel about what I can do now. But I'll tell you this – I just *knew*, the very first time I aimed it and sunk it in a tree, I knew I was a natural.' Jack winked. 'No two ways about it, Airchie. I was born to use a hatchet.'

The trip to Rouken Glen had been a surprise for Airchie, but the rest of the day was planned in advance and he knew the whole timetable. It was a special day, the first ever when he and Jack would get down to their real enterprise, the lucrative heart of their partnership. Before that, though, there were a couple of business calls to make and for once Jack was getting personally involved.

The first call was at six o'clock in a Maryhill pub. By any standards the place was a dump. The floor was covered with dark green carpet, shiny bald in places and ripped here and there. Stains made the remaining green bits look like diseased moss. The bottom of the bar was splintered from decades of toe-contact and higher up its varnish was pitted and flaked. Hundreds of cigarette burns and sticky rings from the bottoms of glasses marked the bar surface. The lights, covered with dusty fly-specked globes, gave off a spiritless glow the colour of nicotine. The gaffer was bleary-eyed and grossly fat, a man as scruffy as his premises. The customers, too, might have been recruited to match the surroundings.

Airchie ordered two half pints of heavy and brought them to the corner by the side door, where Jack was inspecting an ancient framed print of a gormless-looking kilted highlander.

'I'll hang on to this for show,' he said, taking the drink from Airchie. 'I don't fancy drinking it. I might catch something off the glass.' He looked about him. 'Any sign of our man?'

'Not so far. But Ah'm told he's here about this time every night.'

They watched a drunk old man weave his way through an invisible crowd to get to the bar.

'How does a fella get that drunk so early?' Airchie said.

'Stairhead dynamite. You can tell by their eyes. They've got white lines round the pupils.'

Stairhead dynamite was not for men who had plans to be survivors. The usual method of making the stuff was to steal a pint of milk off a doorstep, then take it to the nearest tenement landing with a gas light that could be reached by a man of average Glasgow height. The bottle was then opened, the gas mantle was broken off and the bottle held up to the jet, so that the gas could bubble through the milk. The strength of the drink depended on how long a man could hold the bottle up before his strength gave out, or somebody chased him. Stairhead dynamite tasted vile but the drinker got intoxicated on three or four gulps. The effects of a whole pint lasted for hours, and the effect could be renewed by drinking half a pint of water.

'Christ, there he goes,' Airchie breathed.

A yard from the bar the old man swayed sideways, put out his hand for support and found none. He hit the floor with a bump, groaned and coughed for a minute, then scrambled to his feet again. He happened to be facing the door and that was the way he went, straight back out on to the street.

'Every picture tells a story,' Jack muttered.

Airchie nudged him.

'There's the bloke. Just came in the other door.'

Jack looked across the bar and saw a heavily-built man with cropped grey hair and a bullet-shaped head, narrower at the forehead than at the jaw. He had small mean eyes and a nose that looked as if it had been reshaped a time or two. He strode to the bar with his hands in the pockets of his docker's jacket, swivelling his shoulders in a swagger that was probably habitual. He nodded to several people as he waited to be served.

'This is his local, all right,' Jack said. 'You did business with a tourist, Airchie. Bet you he thinks he's a right fly man.'

Jack crossed the bar with Airchie behind him. They hovered near the best looking piece of furniture in the place, a polished wooden cigarette machine, until the man got his drink and took it to a table. As soon as he was seated and unfolding his paper at the racing results, Jack went and sat down opposite him. Airchie took the chair on Jack's right.

'It's Mr Allander isn't it?' Jack said, smiling tautly.

The man stared at him.

'What if it is?'

'My name's Kane. Jack Kane. We came to a business arrangement two weeks ago, you and me. You seem to have forgotten the terms of the agreement so I'm here to jog your memory.'

'What're you talkin' about? Ah've never seen you in ma life before.'

'No, but you've met my associate here. This is Mr Cairns. Remember him?'

Allander looked at Airchie and shook his head.

'There's some mistake, pal,' he said.

'No mistake,' Jack said. 'You borrowed money. My money. Five pounds, to be repaid at ten shillings a week over the maximum repayment period of twelve weeks, which covers our interest at twenty per cent.'

Allander's expression went through a swift medley of reactions.

'Ah've told ye, son, ye've got the wrong man.'

Jack shifted in his chair, getting himself closer to the table, setting his hands on top.

'Can we scrap the bullshit? You went out of your district and borrowed money off Mr Cairns, then you came back here where you live, thinking you were well out of our reach. That's really insulting, Mr Allander. Do you think we're stupid or something? Did you take one look at Mr Cairns and decide his head buttons up the back?'

Allander decided it was time for belligerence. His little eyes narrowed. He jutted his chin.

'I think ye'd better clear off, the pair of ye. Ah've got friends in this pub. If ye don't scram double-quick *you'll* be makin' their acquaintance too. Get it?'

Jack stood up sharply. Airchie did the same. Without pausing he walked to the open door and went outside. Jack followed him, but as he passed Allander he grabbed the back of his collar and dragged him backwards out of his chair. For three desperate rearward gallops the man managed to stay on his feet, then he fell heavily and Jack dragged him the rest of the way out of the pub. On the pavement he let go the collar and switched his grip to the lapels. He hoisted Allander against the wall, pinning him there. The belligerence was gone from the big face now. There was shock in its place, and fright.

'For Jesus' sake, steady on . . .'

Jack's moved in close. The vivid blue eyes were wide, transmitting a warning.

'Just listen, Allander. Absorb.'

Airchie went to the pub door and wagged a no-no finger at two half-hearted rescuers. They backed off, trying to look reluctant about it.

'You'll start the repayments right now,' Jack said, his face inches away from Allander's. 'One pound, right in my hand. Then you'll pay back the rest at weekly intervals as arranged, starting this Saturday. But now it's a pound a week, seven Saturdays on the trot.'

'Hey, hang on – '

'If you miss any payments the interest goes up. You missed two, so now you owe us at a rate of fifty per cent. You were told the rules. And don't bother asking to see the prospectus – all the options are fucking agony, I promise you.'

Jack stood back and held out his hand. Allander looked as if he might take a swing. Jack stared at him, ready. The moment passed. Allander fumbled in his pockets and found a ten-shilling note and four half-crowns. Jack took the money and pocketed it.

'A word in parting,' he said. 'Don't give us any more trouble. If you do it'll go on your bill.'

'But Ah cannae afford a pound a week.'

'Can you afford busted ribs?'

'Aw, come on . . .'

'Don't be late on Saturday, Mr Allander. And don't think you can hide from us. You can't. Have you got all that, now?'

Allander moved away from the wall, mouth churning, eyes troubled.

'The wife'll bloody murder me.'

'That's your problem.'

Jack turned and walked away with Airchie beside him. At the corner they looked back. Allander had gone.

'Ah knew he was goin' to try it on the minute he walked up to me in the Cockit Hat,' Airchie said.

'You've always had a nose for that kind,' Jack said, grinning.

The drill with suspicious cases was either to refuse the loan, or to grant it and have the man followed when he left the pub. In this case Airchie had taken the second course, because Allander fulfilled the requirements of a potential warning to others. He was big and he looked hard, but there were a dozen signs that told the informed observer a different story. So they had waited two weeks, confident enough that Allander wouldn't show up again without persuasion. Now he had been attended to, and other men who might have been tempted to try his game would think twice. Word travelled fast.

'It's getting a bit late,' Jack said as they got into his shiny little Morgan. 'The other call's Tommy Sykes, right?'

'That's it,' Airchie nodded. 'Three quid still owin'. He's missed a payment.'

'Wait till tomorrow, then you go and see him yourself.' Jack turned the ignition and revved the engine. 'Tell him to forget it.'

'Eh?'

'He's a desperate case, Airchie. I've watched him

110

struggling since the days at the Barras. There's a difference between him and Allander. Sykes wouldn't try to fiddle us. He's just a poor old bugger. Never had any luck. Tell him the debt's clear and he needn't ask us for a loan again. Not even if he's starving.' Jack looked at his watch. He turned to Airchie. 'Ready then?'

'Ah'm ready.'

'Fair enough.' Jack put the engine in gear and drove away from the kerb. 'Craigiehall Street, here we come.'

The sky was clouding and threatening rain as they drove down through the city and across the river, into the narrow streets of the Gorbals. They were both nervous, though not from misgivings, or any fear that they would run into trouble. This was a threshold time. Nerves were appropriate.

Jack parked the car just off Paisley Road West. He locked the doors and they walked through the back turnings to Craigiehall Street. At the corner they stopped, looking up and down the street as they pretended to talk casually.

'Deserted,' Jack said.

They started walking again. Two thirds of the way along the street they turned into the mouth of a close and walked clear through to the back court. Keeping to the wall they moved to the near corner and went down a flight of steps. There was a heavy door at the bottom, secured with thick steel hasps and two heavy padlocks. Jack passed a bunch of keys to Airchie. They had tossed a coin to see who should perform the inaugural break-in.

'Somebody should warn old Lewis to be more careful where he buys this kind of stuff,' Jack whispered.

Airchie muffled a laugh. He put a key in the upper lock and turned it. For a second there was resistance, then something clicked, the key moved and the lock fell open. He did the same with the second padlock, removed them both and swung back the hasps.

'Now the heavy stuff,' he murmured.

He pulled up his trouser leg and unwound a length of insulating tape that held a ten-inch crowbar against his calf. He put the flattened end of the crowbar into the gap between the door lock and the jamb. Three sharp taps on the other end of the crowbar sprung the lock. The door opened. The holy moment had come. Airchie stood aside and let Jack go in first.

He found a switch and put on the light before Airchie closed the door again. They were in the back room of a shop. Bulging boxes were piled to the ceiling around three walls.

'The stuff we want's through in the front.' Jack opened the adjoining door and stuck his head into the shop. 'No need for a light,' he announced. They went through.

The shop was small and crammed with goods, most of them far from new. Practically everything – prams, rugs, wireless sets, suits, dresses and even false teeth – belonged to local residents. The items were deposited here in exchange for cash and were redeemable on a repayment, with modest interest.

'You look up that end of the counter, I'll work down here,' Jack said. 'It'll be a box of some kind, quite a big one.'

They searched for nearly twenty minutes until Airchie discovered that a pile of twenty or thirty old newspapers in a dusty corner were actually glued together and hollowed-out to make a cover. Beneath it he found a big metal cash box, its black and gold paint chipped and scored.

'This could be the item we're after,' he said, holding it up.

Jack stood at the front of the counter and steadied the box while Airchie prised open the lid.

'Jesus,' Airchie breathed. 'I never realised there was that many married women livin' round here.'

The box was full of rings, dozens of them. There were gold and silver wedding bands, diamond and ruby and emerald engagement rings, eternity rings, old-fashioned clusters and solitaires in every imaginable combination of stone and setting. They were unredeemed pledges that

112

had been left beyond the date when they could be claimed back.

'They're nearly all antiques,' Jack said. 'Inheritances from better times. It's guys like Lewis that end up inheriting the lot. All they've got to do is wait for a depression.'

Old Lewis had been incautious enough to brag about this cache, his insurance for his retirement. Mad Harry had mentioned it to Jack two years ago, after he heard Lewis and a friend talking in a Trongate pub.

'I knew his mouth would get him in the shit one day,' Jack said, taking a handful of rings and dropping them in his pocket. 'Cheers, Mr Lewis. All the best.'

They filled their pockets and put the empty box back under the cover.

'Anythin' else?' Airchie said.

'Well . . .' Jack looked around him. 'According to local legend he keeps money here. Banks it once a week.' He pointed to the alcove where Lewis kept his tea-making bits and pieces. 'I think I'll have a look at the floorboards back there.'

He went into the alcove and got down on his knees. He ran his fingers across the smooth boards, pressing the joints, tapping with his knuckles. After a minute he looked up at Airchie.

'I think we've found his hip pocket.'

With the edge of the crowbar they raised a short board and Jack put his hand into the gap beneath. He brought out a dark blue drawstring bag.

'Definitely a bonus, Airchie.'

He stood up and opened the bag. The wad inside was so thick he had to tug to get it out. He dropped it on the counter.

'What's your guess?'

'No idea.' Airchie shrugged. 'I'm not used to seein' bundles that size.'

'I'd say three hundred,' Jack said.

He flattened the wad and counted the notes carefully from one pile into another.

113

'Three hundred and forty-five,' he announced, tucking the bundle into his inside pocket. 'That'll do us, Airchie. We'll go back to my place and put all this away safely. Then we can drink ourselves silly.'

Airchie checked that the back court was clear, then they slipped out and relocked the door. When they were finished there was no sign that anyone had been there. Even the spot on the door where Airchie had used the crowbar was camouflaged by natural weathering on the surrounding wood.

'Marvellous workmanship, those padlocks,' Jack said solemnly, making Airchie laugh again. 'Never buy less than the best, that's what I always say.'

The padlocks were of the highest quality. They were two from a batch of ten Jack had bought a couple of months earlier. They cost him two pounds each. He put them on sale again through a box-number service in the city centre; they were advertised as bankrupt stock and were offered at an irresistibly low price. They were sold in a week. Jack knew where they had all gone, and he had duplicate keys for every one of them.

When they got back to the flat on Steel Street they put away their haul. The rings were packed into a pair of socks and stuffed up the insides of two holy statuettes Jack had taken from his parents' house at Monteith Row. The money was packed into a bogus waste pipe soldered among a cluser of other plumbing under the sink.

'Right,' Jack said, brushing off the knees of his trousers. 'Let's have our break. We've earned it.'

He produced a bottle of whisky and six screwtops of beer. They retired with them to the living room, where they sat together until midnight, celebrating quietly, getting gently inebriated as they discussed business and speculated on the prospects for the future.

Tonight had been the first and last time they would conduct their business on the Kingston Clan's territory. Lewis's pawn shop had been the primary target for reasons of certainty – they had keys, they knew the location and layout, and Lewis was the busiest pawnbroker on the south side, so the haul was bound to be worthwhile. His shop had also been picked for reasons amounting to vendetta. In their boyhood Jack and Airchie had been forced by circumstances to use the shop. They'd had to accept skinflint offers for their watches, bicycles or items of clothing. They had both been stung countless times by Lewis's tight-mouthed reminders that he was what stood between them and empty pockets, so if they didn't want to take what he offered they could go without.

'We've had our wee bit of revenge,' Jack said, 'so that's that. From now on we stay off Kingston turf. There's plenty of other places to trespass.'

Plans were already laid. They would raid warehouses, pawnbrokers' shops and whisky bonds right at the heart of other gangs' territories. Being a two-man team they were a criminal rarity in Glasgow, they could travel light and succeed where the heavy machinery of big gangs often failed. They had no fears of treachery, since they trusted each other completely and told no one else about their business. They were experienced and wise enough to avoid the risk of over-reaching. Best of all, the proceeds would be split only two ways. They would prosper swiftly.

'The only tricky bit,' Jack pointed out, 'will be remembering to keep up appearances. As long as we put on a placid front and don't get seen in each other's company too often, we'll be all right.'

'The polis are bound to have noticed you're out an' about again,' Airchie said.

'They're watching me now,' Jack told him. 'It's what I want them to do for a while. They've got to believe I'm strictly a loner, not looking for trouble, just leading a quiet life. And while they're coming to that conclusion the gangs'll get blamed for the robberies. All loners will be left alone, because the boys in blue know that nobody would be daft enough to trespass for profit on gang territory.'

'An' God help us if any of the gangs ever catches on,' Airchie said.

'Do you think they ever will?'

'Well . . .' Airchie sniffed. 'Ye want ma honest opinion?'

Jack nodded.

'Not a chance of it, Jack. We're bomb-proof.'

That night Jack had trouble getting to sleep. His thoughts were a jumble, an over-tired reaction to the day's events. At the centre of his mind, though, there was an area of calm, a small cool certainty. He had made it, he had started out on his chosen road and the omens were good. He wasn't yet twenty-one and he had done what he promised himself. Jack Kane was a power, the dictator of his own future. All he had to do now was maintain his withdrawn front as he reaped the lush harvest.

Eventually he fell asleep. He dreamed about his mother. He saw her from a high place where he stood alone – it was important to stand apart now, to be separate and distinct from the toerag herd; he even spoke differently nowadays because that gave him separateness, too. In the dream his mother was dead, a gaunt figure head-bowed in a stiff shroud, refusing to look at him when he called to her. She turned her back and went frowning off through the shadows to wherever the dead went. As he watched he saw his father shuffling after her, whimpering. Jack felt a great wave of sadness. Whether it was for them or for himself, he couldn't tell.

Maybe if he'd tried harder, he thought, if he had shown them more consideration, he could have enjoyed something like the closeness of a family. If he had made an effort . . .

'Sure,' a cold voice said, familiar because it was his own, 'and if your auntie had balls she'd be your uncle.'

SEVEN

During the autumn of 1937 Airchie Cairns briefly courted a girl who had a fine talent for embroidery. She worked in a Catholic Church furnisher's where she decorated altar cloths and priests' vestments. She monogrammed Airchie's shirts and handkerchiefs for him and even stitched his initials inside his overcoat. In November Airchie persuaded her to do a special tapestry; he got it nicely framed in mahogany and presented it to Jack Kane for his birthday. Thereafter it hung in pride of place above Jack's fireplace. Gold letters on a dark purple background proclaimed GLASGOW BELONGS TO ME. Jack was tickled with it.

In that first year their fortunes grew at nearly twice the speed they had anticipated. By exploiting the diversions caused by increasing numbers of gang wars, and taking advantage of overtaxed police manpower, Jack and Airchie were able to make two raids a week for forty consecutive weeks. They worked to no pattern and left none of the city's commercial districts untouched. By the spring of '37 two lockup garages in Kent Street were full to the doors with contraband. The goods in one garage – furs, carpets, canteens of silver-plated cutlery, gramophones, china and glassware – were regularly sold to traders and replaced. The other garage was stocked with crates of whisky, rum, and gin, boxes of tea and thousands of cigarettes in anticipation of the war everybody said would come.

One afternoon in early December Jack was approached by an Italian immigrant, a man called Elliot Rossini. He was younger than Jack and taller, a hard-eyed individual given to glancing around him warily as he spoke. Rossini was obviously a poor man, but he carried himself proudly nevertheless.

'I been here two years,' he told Jack. 'My English not so good, but it will be better. And I want to get better – *do* better.'

'So what can I do for you?'

'A man in Maryhill talked to me . . .' Rossini screwed up his face, trying to remember. 'Tarranter?'

'Tranter,' Jack said. 'Mick Tranter. He's an old acquaintance of mine.'

'He said you have a big piece of Maryhill, where I am living.'

'He said that, did he?'

In commercial terms Jack now had big pieces of lots of places. Nobody quite knew how it had all come about, but by the diligent use of money and muscle he now had guardianship of areas that would have fallen, otherwise, to the scruffier undisciplined mobs that roamed Glasgow looking for easy territory.

'Mr Tranter said maybe you help, if I mention his name to you.'

'How? Are you interested in doing business in Maryhill, or what?'

'In Maryhill for now, yes. Later the Gorbals, if I can.'

'You're ambitious, anyway. What business are you in?'

'Ice cream.'

'I'm not connected in that line,' Jack said.

'No, but I need space to . . . ah . . . operate. Mr Tranter said that if I speak to you, you could make space for me in Maryhill.'

Jack understood. The street ice cream barrows in Maryhill were all owned by one Irish outfit, the Gallaghers. Jack didn't get on with them, they were bullies rather than hard men, though so far he'd had no sound reason to work against their operation.

'Have you had trouble getting started?' he said.

'For three weeks I did good. People like my stuff. Then

one day a man come and push over my barra when I am in my shed. The ice cream runs out on the road, it is *rovinato* . . .' Rossini waved his hands. 'How you say . . . Spoiled. It was spoiled. I say to him, why you do this, and he says to me, *vaffanculo* – in my own language he says it. He learn the word somewhere.'

'I don't speak Italian,' Jack said.

'In English is fuck off. He say I fuck off out of Maryhill, I can't sell my stuff there.'

'What did he look like, this man?'

Rossini described a bear-like individual with a scar dividing his left eyebrow.

'His name's Bob Gallagher,' Jack said. 'He sells ice cream in Maryhill.'

'But Mr Kane, my stuff is best, in Palermo where I was born the ice cream of Rossini is *gelato supremo*.'

'And you still want to make a living selling it in Maryhill, yes?'

'*Si*. I have family to support, my mother, my brothers and little sister, I need to sell as much as I can make. I have one barra. Only one. I want to have more. Many more.' Rossini put his hand in the pocket of his loose coat and brought out an envelope. 'I do not have much for your help, but there is this . . .'

Jack took the envelope, peered inside and estimated the wad at twenty notes. He pressed it back into Rossini's hands.

'No need for money,' he said.

'But Mr Tranter say – '

'I'll speak to these people. I'll explain to them. Tell me where you live, so I can let you know when to start selling your ice cream again.'

Rossini looked perplexed.

'Why you don't want money?'

'Give me help instead,' Jack said.

'Help? *Certamente*. When? In what way?'

'When I need it. *If* I need it.'

Rossini went away, trailing effusive thanks. The next day Jack spoke to a couple of the Gallaghers. They didn't like his suggestion that they let Rossini share the turf. The territory was theirs, certainly as far as selling ice cream was concerned. That weekend, out of instincts too complicated for him to analyse, Jack got Airchie to help him destroy the Gallaghers' ice cream plant and cripple their barrows. To drive the message home Jack called on the head of the family, Liam Gallagher, and told him that if he didn't learn to co-exist with Mr Rossini, he would have to leave Maryhill. When Liam flew off the handle, as Jack knew he would, he was taken outside and thumped. As he lay bleeding and cursing, Jack – who knew how the man worshipped Tara, his prize-winning greyhound – leaned down over him and made a promise.

'If you don't do what I say, Liam, I'll get hold of whatever you love most in this world, and I'll kill it.'

Later, when Airchie asked why Jack had gone out of his way like that for some big Tally he knew nothing about, Jack shrugged.

'I'm not sure. Maybe he's got the look of a lucky charm about him.'

No more was said about the matter.

Business continued to thrive. By Christmas Jack had salted away three thousand pounds of personal capital. Weekly spending money averaging twenty times an ordinary working man's wage was drawn from the proceeds of gambling and money lending. Eric Ross was paid back the £400 he had given Jack to get started; he slapped Jack's back, hugged him emotionally and complimented him and Airchie on the efficient and discreet way they ran the business.

'If only he knew the half of it,' Airchie said later. 'Or a tenth, for that matter.'

'He'll never know,' Jack assured him.

And he never would. In February, 1938, the body of Eric Ross was fished out of the Clyde at Prince's Dock. He had been savagely beaten before he was thrown into the water. His hands had been bound behind his back with baling wire, the trademark of a powerful gang called the Covenanters. The long-smouldering dispute between the Kingston Clan and the Covenanters flared into war.

For a month there were sporadic street battles and house burnings on the south side. Extra police were drafted in. Local curfews were declared and regularly violated. *More* police were drafted in. While all that was going on, Jack and Airchie robbed three warehouses, two jewellers' shops and a Buchanan Street department store. They had to find more and bigger storage space. In April a deal was struck for the supply of 400 gallons of bonded whisky to a public-house chain in the north of England. Without ever meeting the customer, and without letting him know who his suppliers were, Jack and Airchie depleted the stocks of four bonded warehouses and doubled their cash resources in a space of eight weeks.

That summer, for the first time in their lives, Jack and Airchie went on holiday. They left their various smoke-screen ventures in the hands of trained and trusted minions, men so bewildered by the go-between system that they had no idea who their bosses actually were, let alone that they were going to be absent from the city.

In Blackpool Jack discovered the pleasures of sea and sand, clean streets and naturally friendly people. He learned to respect Boddington Ale and made sexual contact with more women in two weeks than he'd had in the previous two years.

For Airchie the holiday was a much more profound and life-enhancing event: he met Jessica, a raven-haired choc-olate-box beauty from Darlington. The courtship was swift and intense. Airchie treated Jessica like a lady, taking her to good restaurants and the best seats in the variety theatres; every day he sent round flowers to her boarding house. He learned that she was eighteen, a Catholic by birth but not at all by inclination; she was a trainee book-keeper in a wholesale confectionery manu-facturer's but would have preferred to be a school teacher if her family could have afforded to have her trained. Airchie, she said, was only the third young man she had ever gone out with. He was just as candid with her: he told her he was twenty-two, an independent wholesaler dealing in general goods, a Catholic of the same lukewarm kind as she was, and until now he had been kept so busy making a dazzling success of himself that he'd had no time for girls. In less than a week he was sure he was in love. Jessica coyly admitted she felt the same way.

By the time the holiday was over the pair were engaged. Airchie returned to Glasgow sunburned and lovesick. Jack, arriving in considerable pain, visited his doctor and was referred to Stobhill Hospital, where he began a course of outpatient treatment for a chronic sinus condition, a relic of his ordeal three years before. It had been aggravated, he was told, by the bracing salt air of England's north-west coast.

Business was resumed. Jack and Airchie operated as before, like phantoms, spotting opportunities in daylight, taking advantage after dark. They had no need to work so hard any more. They restricted themselves to two, sometimes three well-planned raids a month. Even so, Jack soon realised that Airchie's sharpness had diminished. On one job he came near to getting caught. Jack, making a swift diagnosis, took him aside for a consultation.

'Stop mooning about,' he said. 'Stop daydreaming. Stop *wishing*. Marry your wee Jessica and get yourself back to normal.'

'Ah've already asked her, Jack. But she won't go against her folks. They say she should wait until she's older. Her mother thinks she might change her mind by the time she's twenty.'

Jack didn't understand how people could come so severely under the sway of their parents, although he acknowledged that it happened.

'Give her an ultimatum,' he said.

'How d'ye mean?'

'Tell her she can either marry you, or she can obey her folks and forget she ever met you.'

'Aw, Christ, Jack – Ah couldn't do that. Ah don't want tae risk losin' her.'

122

'Do you want to keep her while her folks have got her on a leash? Let them win on this one, Airchie, and they'll overrule you right, left, and centre.'

'Aye, well . . .'

'You've got to be firm. If she feels as strongly about you as you do about her, there'll be no contest.'

After a lot of hesitation Airchie sat down with pen and paper and put the plain take-me-now-or-leave-me-forever proposition to Jessica. For a week there was silence, then on a Saturday morning in late September he had a telegram asking him to meet her that evening off the Darlington train at Glasgow Central Station. When she arrived she explained, tearfully, that she had split with her parents and left home. She wanted to be married to Airchie as soon as she could.

Remembering their boyhood struggles and the modest boundaries of their long-ago ambitions, it pleased Jack deeply to see Airchie go into action as he created the setting for his wedded life. He bought and furnished a house out at Springburn, a real one with a living room, kitchen, bathroom and two bedrooms; it even had a small garden. The place cost him £650. He paid cash.

At the wedding reception, in a Co-operative Hall round the corner from the church where Airchie and Jessica were married, Jack made the best-man's speech that he had rehearsed for a week. He told the guests – no more than a dozen and most of them Jessica's relatives, including her parents who had undergone a swift change of heart – that the bride could have found no better companion with whom to share her life. 'He's an upright man with a good grasp of business and the skills to take him to the very top before he's much older.'

Jessica's people were from the upper end of the working class. The speech left them in no doubt about how lucky they should think themselves to have a man of Archibald Cairns's stature marry one of their number.

'Ye made me sound like some kinda tycoon,' Airchie complained when he and Jack met in the toilets later. 'It's a hell of a lot to live up to.'

'Listen, Airchie, this game of ours is all make-believe. It's acting, isn't it? We can never let other folk know what we're really about. So if we're going to act, we might as well act as if we're the whole cheese, not just the smell. Anyway, the older you get and the better you eat, the more you look the part. You're like a bank manager in that suit.'

'I look like an insurance man,' Airchie said, appraising himself in the pitted mirror above the sinks. 'I keep worryin' Jessica's goin' to want to know a bit about the business. She's no' daft, Jack. She's bound to get curious.'

'You're worrying about nothing.'

'That's easy to say.'

'You've got money, right? Jessica knows it, it makes her happy. She knows all she needs to know about you. Face the facts – money's part of the reason she married you.'

'Ye think so?'

'Definitely. You're a man with more cash than she's ever smelt before. It's bound to have influenced her. Remember, nothing's more likely to keep a woman content than having a husband that's well heeled. Just make sure you've got plenty of complicated-looking paperwork lying about the place. She won't want to know any of the details.'

In the following months it became clear that Jack was right. Jessica displayed no curiosity about Airchie's business. She wallowed in her status. She enjoyed being a housewife with watertight security and a husband who doted on her. When she discovered she was pregnant Airchie believed he'd never known a happier or more contented female in his life.

'The baby's due next September,' he told Jack. 'If it's a boy we're callin' it after you.'

Jack declared himself flattered. Airchie pointed out it was the least he could do.

'If it wasn't for you,' he said, 'I'd still be puttin' my neck on the block for the Kingstons five nights a week. I've got a good life now Jack, an' it's all down to you.'

The child, a girl, was born on September 7, 1939. Four days earlier Britain and France had declared war on Germany. While the rest of Britain prepared for the Nazi onslaught, Jack and Airchie got ready for their forthcoming black-market operation. In the first quiet months of the war they worked long hours building up their stocks and enlisting people they could blackmail or otherwise coerce in the event of unrest. As men went into the forces in their hundreds, police manpower dropped; security at warehouses and shops took second place to fire precautions. Jack and Airchie used both circumstances to advantage: van-loads of goods were nightly liberated from the premises of their rightful owners to enhance the stocks held in Jack's newly-acquired south-side warehouse. By January 1940 they believed they were ready, stocked to the teeth with essential supplies and luxury goods ready to go on the streets when shortages put the prices up.

'This war's going to be the making of us,' Jack said. 'If Hitler wins we'll be able to bribe the bastard to leave us alone.'

Jessica's euphoria ended with the news that bombing raids were expected on Clydeside. She began to fear terribly for her daughter, Angela. She begged Airchie to let her and the child go and stay in the Midlands; her father now worked as a foreman in a munitions plant there, with a tied house in a quiet town a few miles away. Airchie didn't want them to go, but in March he gave in to the pressure, which was becoming hysterical. Jessica and baby Angela took the train to Birmingham, leaving a chapfallen Airchie waving from the platform at Glasgow Central.

Jessica wrote a lot of letters during 1940. In November she admitted that the whole year had whittled down her capacity to feel safe anywhere. She read the papers compulsively, terrified of what she would learn next. In April, when Germany invaded Norway and Denmark, she had felt the enemy were surrounding Britain and she began to imagine what it would be like to live under the Nazis.

125

Winston Churchill's National Government had seemed to her like a good idea, and his Blood and Toil speech in May cheered her up, but only for a time. The Dutch surrendered soon after that, then Amiens and Arras were captured. Belgium fell and the next day the British forces were evacuated from Dunkirk. Jessica admitted she wept when she heard about Dunkirk; her father had told her not to be such a defeatist, she was British and she should remember it. The British were different, they always came out winning.

When Italy declared war on France and Britain she said nothing about it and didn't let her panic show. She tried to ignore the war news altogether, but the year was full of disheartening events and wherever she turned there was new distress. John Buchan died that year; she had been trying to get through one of his books at the time she read the news, so she saw his death as a black omen.

'Ah should hang on to these letters,' Airchie told Jack. 'They're a wee history of the whole bloody war, so far.'

On the first night the Germans bombed Coventry, Jessica came close to caving-in. She told Airchie how she had clung to little Angela in the Anderson shelter, feeling the ground shake as explosions tore down buildings and extinguished lives a few miles from the market town where they were living. The only bright thing she could recall from the whole year was going to the local pictures to see Charlie Chaplin in *The Great Dictator*.

'I just wish she'd find somethin' pleasant to write about,' Airchie complained. 'It's bad enough not havin' her an' the baby here with me. The letters are all I've got to look forward to, but when I get one an' read it I wish she'd never bothered.'

On the whole Jack was having a better time of it, even though the police had renewed their interest in him. The curiosity rose from nothing more than their ignorance. Policemen didn't like being kept in the dark. They wondered how Jack managed to live so well without doing useful work. They weren't satisfied when he told them that as an officially disabled person he didn't *have* to do anything. They pointed out, rather huffily, that he didn't look disabled, whatever the medical records said, and what they really wanted to know, anyway, was where he got his money. Jack wasn't a conspicuous spender – nobody was, now there were universal shortages – but he gave off an air of affluence all the same. He told the police about money his mother and father had saved over a period of years and hidden away in the house. He even produced a bank book to back up the story.

The police didn't believe him, but there was nothing they could do, since his life these days seemed to run on blameless lines. To deflect their interest he got a job at a Red Cross packing station, which left him plenty of free time to carry on his business. There was also time to pursue a new-found obsession, a pneumatic little blonde nurse called Annie Kempson.

It hadn't begun well. Annie was a staffer at the Stobhill clinic Jack still attended. When he had first shown an interest in her she snubbed him. But he persisted. Eventually she agreed to let him take her out for a meal and was obviously surprised by the quality of the surroundings and the respect with which the staff treated Jack. His gentlemanly behaviour caught her on the wrong foot, too; Annie's looks and figure were of the kind that prompted more lust than respect, and she had learned to accept that a lot of her dates would culminate in carnal struggles – especially when the man spent a lot of money on her. But Jack had driven her straight back to the hospital after dinner and watched until she was safely at the door of the nurses' home.

By Christmas they were going steady, though intimacy had gone no further than lingering farewell kisses by the gate before Jessica returned to the nurses' home. Annie knew very little about Jack's background, but she liked his company and preferred him to the housemen and senior registrars who had occasionally taken her out. He was funnier, he was better looking, and he didn't wince when he was presented with the bill at the end of an evening.

He wasn't her ideal man, though; she preferred them

taller, more aristocratic – the kind who never showed any interest in her. Even so, Annie would have been content to let her relationship with Jack glide along at the easy, close-friends level it had attained by December. Except that the highly practical side of her saw hope of consolidation here. Jack Kane had money, plenty of it as far as she could tell, and she had always planned to land a man with a fortune to spend on her. Airy dreams of godlike creatures had to be seen for what they were: fantasy. The fact was, Jack Kane might be her only chance.

Two days before Christmas Jack saw his doctor for his quarterly check-up and was told that his arterial system was still a cause for concern. He had made a completely unexpected recovery from his injuries, but the heart and its nearby vessels hadn't come on so well as his bones and muscles.

'Take it easy,' was the doctor's advice. 'You're young, I know, but try to remember this – because of what happened to you when you were chucked off that roof, your heart and arteries are a bit older than the rest of you.'

Jack tried not to let the news depress him. It did no good to dwell on negative things, he reminded himself. A man had to think positively, winning where he could and ignoring the losses. That night he was taking Annie to dinner, so he had to put himself in the right frame of mind. He had decided it was to be a very special evening. The gentle courtship was over. He knew he could always put up a good show of self control, but the truth was he couldn't look at Annie any more without wanting to jump on her. Fears about how a girl like that would react to his carnal side must be suppressed. It was all or nothing. The relationship had to move forward because he couldn't hold out any longer.

Jack might have been disconcerted to know that Annie had decided the same thing.

They were meeting at the Baddiscombe Arms, a special place out in the country near Loch Lomond. Annie was working late so Jack had arranged for a taxi to take her there ahead of him, so she could have the benefit of his grand entrance and see how well he was received. Lately, some of his heftier black market negotiations had put him in touch with The Big People, society's wheels. They needed him, so he was in a position to enter their world occasionally without being frozen out. He had dined at the Baddiscombe a few times on his own, picking up pointers, learning to read a good menu and to decipher a decent wine list. Tonight he would put the training into action. Annie had to be impressed, at all costs.

After a long soak in the tub he dressed carefully in a light grey suit, grey cotton shirt with a thin blue stripe, a dark bue waistcoat and a wisteria silk tie. He oiled his hair and brushed it, dabbed on cologne and stepped into a new pair of patent-leather pumps.

In the hall he took one more look at himself in the new mirror by the front door. In his Crombie overcoat he looked very substantial.

'Good for another sixty years,' he said, and winked at himself.

Driving out of Glasgow he thought of the future, probing the mist for certainties. If he retired some time in the next five years he would take a lot of pressure off his arteries; he could afford to do it, so why run risks with his health when he could be enjoying himself? He wouldn't vegetate in retirement. He'd still be a young man. He would travel, and he would spend much more time with Annie Kempson, if she'd have it. He thought of her and got a sharp tingle of excitement. An insight came to him: *She's right for me, she's all the medicine I need.*

Annie was waiting in the foyer at the Baddiscombe Arms when he got there.

'I'm not late, am I?' he said, bending to kiss her cheek, a thoroughly un-Scottish gesture.

'No,' she said, 'I was early.'

She wore a silky gold-and-green evening dress. Her blonde hair was combed down straight on either side, shifting softly on her bare shoulders when she moved her head. She had used make-up in a way that suggested she

129

used none at all. The sight of her made Jack's throat swell. She always took some trouble over her appearance, but this was something else. She stood and he took her arm.

'I think we'll go in right away,' he said. 'We can have drinks at the table while we look at the menu.'

The Baddiscombe Arms was a hotel with a restaurant favoured by business people and semi-rural gentry. It was so heavily patronised by wealth and influence that shortages were unheard of. The only thing hard to get here was a table, and for Jack, who nowadays supplied a lot of the hotel's meat, that was no problem. The *maître d'hotel* smiled discreetly as he led them into the spacious dining room. They were seated at a table in a corner, near an ornamental fountain ringed round with greenhouse flowers.

'Merry Christmas,' Annie said demurely. She put a small box in front of Jack. It was wrapped in pale blue paper and tied with gilt string. 'I hope you like it.'

'Annie . . .' He shook his head at her. 'You don't have to buy me presents.'

'I wanted to.'

He unwrapped the box carefully, took off the shiny lid. On a velvet-covered card inside was a tie pin, an undecorated bar of gold no wider than a matchstick.

'It's a beauty,' he said.

'I'm glad you like it.'

Jack took the pin from the box and attached it to his tie.

'There,' he said. 'How does it look?'

'Just the way I imagined it,' she said.

He took her hand and kissed it, astonishing himself.

'Thanks again. I'll really treasure this.'

The waiter brought menus. As Annie opened hers Jack told her not to be surprised.

'I'm told they haven't changed a thing since 1936.'

They sipped dry sherry as they decided. Annie thought she would like the *vichyssoise*, followed by grilled Dover sole, then roast loin of pork with gravy and a pear-and-potato purée. Jack settled on tomato soup with basil, then poached trout; as a concession to the doctor's warning about fatty food, he decided to follow with roast chicken, a watercress sauce, roast baby potatoes and glazed onions. He ordered a bottle each of claret and Rousillon vin vert, which he had taken a long time learning to pronounce.

'It staggers me the way they've managed to keep such a good cellar in times like these,' he murmured, hoping that he wasn't overdoing things.

All the time his attention was divided between the menu and a covert, charmed appraisal of Annie. She was a dazzler. And here she was, his dream girl. She was right here with him. *She was going to be his*. His determination hardened as the sherry went down.

'How are your parents, Annie?'

'They're fine.' She smiled, a trace of sadness. 'I wish they could get about more, though. I'm always imagining them sitting there with their old wireless set, not able to leave the house.'

She had told him, before, that her father was crippled with arthritis and her mother had a hernia from an old operation scar. Neither one was particularly mobile. It was a lie Annie told with ease, one of a number of devices that cast her in a sympathetic light. Her parents were in fact habitual drunks from Auchenshuggle who were always being pulled in by the police for fighting. Annie never visited them.

'All they have to look forward to is me visiting them.' Her voice was soft, unmistakably Glasgow but with an endearing lilt. 'I'm their window on the world, and I can do things about the house they can't manage.'

'It's a big responsibility,' Jack said. 'Having to manage two old folks' lives. Constantly having to do the best for them.'

The parents, he could imagine, were a bloody nuisance, giving in to their ailments and making Annie feel guilty that she couldn't do more for them. He had his share of people like that. More than half his older runners and

131

fetchers were humanity's submitters, content to lie down in the path of events. They did nothing to help themselves or shape their own lives. People like that were born without savvy and never gained any. They just gave in, never noticing what Jack knew for sure: people who submitted to life got mangled by time as it rolled over them.

'How did they feel about you coming out with me tonight?'

Annie had told him she'd planned to spend the evening with the folks, but decided she would come out with him, anyway.

'I could see they were a wee bit disappointed when I told them.'

Jack thought of the stored black market luxuries in cupboards at the flat. *Would she come back there*?

'We'll stop by my place on the way home,' he said. 'I'll give you a treat to take back for them. Something to make amends.'

Annie gave him a look that would have put a pang across hearts tougher than his. It was an expression she managed with perfect spontaneity: grateful, gracious, almost adoring, a blend of subtleties amounting to the finest regard. Jack felt like he was floating. *Flying*.

Some time past midnight a lorry backfired down near Glasgow Green, startling the birds and making them chirrup and screech louder than any dawn ever would.

In the darkened bedroom at Steel Street Jack rolled on to his back, hearing the rasp of his breathing and the thudding pulse in his eardrums. Beside him Annie moved sinuously, curling to fit herself to his side. She felt warm and moist. Her breath fanned his cheek as she put an arm across his chest and kissed him.

What a woman! When she moved about the Stobhill clinic she was the picture of starched propriety. Even on their dates she'd been delicate and withdrawn in her manner, a picture of decorum and modesty. She was often shy. That was his habitual mental image of her, a shy, shapely, demure wee blonde. It had made him keep the brakes on far longer than he had with any other girl.

But now the change in her was staggering. Jack put his hand on his chest and felt the heart muscle hammering. Between the sheets she was totally transformed. Jack could believe there was nothing she wouldn't venture, no impulse she would hesitate to follow. He had been with young women and older women, he had known them inhibited and repressed, and he'd been with one or two who revelled in sex like dockside whores. But none of them, *none* of them carried so much as a hint of Annie Kempson. Her ingenuity and her energy were breathtaking. Literally.

When they came back to the flat they had gone straight to bed, even though Jack had planned to open a bottle of champagne and play records on his new American electric gramophone. Annie changed his plans without a word. It was in her eyes, in the heaviness of her contact as they walked up the steps together. She wanted sex and she didn't want to wait.

So for an hour they had thrashed and twined on the bed. In silence, her shuddering breath the only audible clue to her mood, Annie brought Jack to the point of release a dozen times; then, time and again, she led him off down another road, using her mouth and hands, making him a delirious nervous wreck. The game went on to a point where Jack actually pleaded with her, beseeched her and begged until she relented and granted a stopping place, a climactic terminus. By some instinct – it had to be an instinct, some dark sense in her – she fathomed his deepest relish and needed no instruction. Lying motionless with arms and legs spread wide, she became lifeless, submitting totally until he lay spent and moaning on top of her. Then and only then she closed her arms and legs round him, stroked his neck and waited until he regained enough of his senses to roll over on his back.

'Excuse me a minute,' he whispered in her ear. 'Got to pay a visit.'

He slipped out of bed. When he had been to the bathroom he went into the kitchen and pulled a bottle of champagne out of a bucket of cold water in the sink – he had put it there before he went out, just in case. He took two glasses off the shelf and went back along the passage. At the open bedroom door he stopped. The light was on. Annie, eyes demurely averted, was standing naked by the bed, feet spread, fastening a wispy black girdle around her hips.

'What's this?' Jack went in, clutching the bottle and glasses. 'Are you going?'

She looked at him and shook her head. Her face was beautiful, serious, almost grave.

'You're not tired already, are you?' he said.

She slid on to the bed and lay back with her shoulders on the pillows, legs extended.

'We'll have a drink first though.' She smiled through strands of hair. 'Since you've brought a bottle to the party.'

Jack put down the glasses. He managed to get the bottle open and fill the glasses. He brought them to the bed, sat down and handed Annie hers.

'Cheers,' he said.

They touched glasses and drank.

'It's shaping up to be the best Christmas I've ever had, Annie.'

'Same here,' she said.

In the following weeks Annie found that consolidation wasn't going to be as straightforward as she hoped. It had never dawned on her that Jack might be a crook. But he was, by the end of January she was sure of it. On the two nights a week she stayed at his flat, she tried to find out what he did for a living. His explanation that he was a general wholesale merchant, a buying-and-selling man, didn't convince her. She made discreet searches of the drawers and cupboards in his flat whenever he was asleep. She went through his pockets. She found cryptic codes and figures in notebooks tucked away behind dressers and under the edges of rugs. She noticed the eye language that often passed between him and his thuggish-looking friend Airchie, who visited from time to time for no apparent reason. Oh, Jack was a crook all right. But that wasn't the problem. The problem was that he was a Catholic.

Annie didn't like Catholics. She had been brought up to detest them. She would certainly never marry one, not even one who said, as Jack did, that it made no difference to him if he was married in a church or a registry office. He wasn't an active Catholic, he added, because his belief in Christianity was flimsy; it followed that he had no intention of taking up an alternative faith. So there was no chance of him 'turning', as they put it in Glasgow. But he wanted Annie to marry him.

So she had a dilemma. Knowing Jack would never change his Catholic label, however loosely it was attached, Annie simply wouldn't marry him – not even in a registry office, which would result in a marriage all right, but she would have a Catholic about the house and that would never do. She simply couldn't live with an arrangement like that.

On the other hand she had nothing against his money. She explained matters to Jack in a way that wouldn't offend him, nor cut off her chances of doing well out of him.

'I want to wait a while,' she said. 'I promised my mother I would finish my training. It's important to her, and to me. I want to be qualified, Jack. Can you understand that?'

'How long would it take?'

'A few more years. I want my Sister's badge.'

Jack was obviously disappointed.

'Maybe if I had a place of my own, in the meantime,' Annie went on, 'we could see each other as often as we wanted, not just on my nights off. That would be something, wouldn't it? It would tide us over until I'm qualified.'

Jack thought it was a great idea.

'I'm not suggesting we live together,' Annie added. 'I don't think I could do that, and it would break my mother's heart if she ever thought I'd set up house with somebody without being married.'

'No, of course not.' Jack was now putty in her hands. Warm putty.

'I'd need to save for a while, to afford the rent of a flat.'

Jack's cup overflowed.

'Listen,' he said, 'I'll buy you a place. And I'll support you, too. I know the kind of wages nurses get. It's time you had a bit of luxury in your life, Annie. Let me do it for you, eh?'

Annie looked hesitant.

'I don't know,' she said. 'I mean, it'd make me a . . . a kept woman, wouldn't it?'

He told her not to be daft.

'You're my lady, Annie. As much of a lady as any married woman. And me buying a place for you – that ties you to nothing. When I give it to you, it's yours, no strings.'

And so it was settled. In March Annie left the hospital and moved into a plush little flat in the West End. Jack let her furnish it to her own taste and he paid the bills without a murmur. He set up a bank account for her. He couldn't do enough. He had never been happier in his life and for once he felt he was spending money to a completely worthy purpose.

But although Jack believed his arrangement with Annie was perfect, Airchie couldn't see it that way. He said nothing to Jack about how he felt. It was none of his business.

Jack was his pal, though, and Airchie felt that as a friend he deserved protection. Annie Kempson was a baddie. That wasn't a hunch of Airchie's, it was a fact, established by carefully-observed fragments of her behaviour that added up to a crystal-clear picture. Far from adoring Jack, as she claimed she did, Airchie believed she actually despised him. She was using him, milking him.

136

The subject of money was never off her lips, in all kinds of roundabout ways; she encouraged lavish spending on herself and the flat, always making it sound as if it was for Jack's direct benefit. Airchie had noticed that when Jack wasn't facing her she had a coldness in her eyes that cunningly vanished the instant he looked her way.

Jack, of course, would never buy that. It would take a tree to fall on him before he would ever catch on.

'She's a gem, Airchie. I just wish you could see the dinners she makes me. And she waits on me hand and foot. I always thought I'd never come across another lassie like wee Jessie Young, but see this one . . .'

Annie was his blind spot. The fact caused Airchie some pain. Jack knew the score where business was concerned, he was a kingpin when it came to applying the commercial screw or the mailed fist. He was hard, shrewd, alert, nobody's fool – except Annie Kempson's.

'Jack looks like he's walkin' on air since he took up with that lassie,' Mad Harry remarked to Airchie over a pint in the Cockit Hat.

'Aye,' Airchie nodded. 'He's caught love bad.'

'He's cunt struck, ye mean?'

Very likely, Airchie thought, without saying so.

He decided to keep a sharp eye on that little woman in case she tried anything that would really hurt Jack. If she ever did, then Airchie would act. He had no clear idea how, but he would. He would have to. Nobody was going to hurt Jack Kane and get away with it. Not while Airchie Cairns was around.

EIGHT

For those who could provide the unobtainable there was always a late drink available at the Cockit Hat. For men like Jack Kane and Airchie Cairns there would have been a red carpet, too, if Dougie Meikle could have laid hands on one. At a time when women were scouring Glasgow for fresh fish and men were queuing for an hour or more to get hold of ten cigarettes, Dougie wanted for nothing. Jack and Aircihe regularly dropped in – though never together – and left little parcels. A couple of times a month Airchie would call at the back door in a plain van and leave boxes of spirits and the occasional barrel of beer. Dougie's response was always a nod and a thumbs-up, the shorthand reminder that it was always open house here for those who looked after his interests.

On a Friday at the beginning of April, 1942, Airchie received a letter that gave him strong reason to celebrate. He turned up in the Cockit Hat at ten minutes before the official closing time, grinning hugely.

'Ah'll have a triple whisky, Dougie,' he said, planting his elbows on the counter.

'Keep it down, son,' Dougie urged, his lips scarcely moving. 'The ration's one single per person, per night.'

'Sorry, Dougie.'

'It's all right. I'll slip it tae ye when the place is a bit quieter. Have a beer for now.'

There were ten or eleven people in the place, drinking moodily, muttering their despair in little knots at tables and against the bar. The recent news had been depressing: the Japs had sunk three British warships in the Bay of

138

Bengal and that morning it had been officially announced that there would be no more white bread available in Britain in the foreseeable future. Public morale was in the gutter. Airchie had already drawn a few dark looks, as if his cheerful expression was an act of blasphemy.

'What's the celebration, anyway?' Dougie asked, putting a lifeless half pint in front of Airchie.

'My wife an' daughter are comin' home,' Airchie said. 'Tomorrow mornin'. It's finally dawned on Jessica that she's in as much danger down in the Midlands as she would be up here. So she's decided she'd as soon risk her life with her old man around as do it without him.'

'That's nice,' Dougie said through a rumbling cough. 'Got the place all ready tae welcome them, have ye?'

'I've dusted an' polished everywhere at least twice,' Airchie said. 'Got some new toys for Angela, as well. And a new cot, a bigger one.'

Airchie had been drinking already, going the rounds of the pubs, trying to find Jack to pass on the news. But Jack was nowhere to be found. He would be away somewhere with his Annie, as likely as not; he never seemed to have the time any more to sit and chew the fat over a drink with Airchie. Nowadays they were hardly more than business associates. Since the business was largely black market now, and since it practically ran itself, they made very little contact in the course of a week. Any spare time Jack had he spent either with Annie, or chasing round for this or that item she wanted for the flat. Airchie had been up there a week before; the place was like a palace. Jack went on living in his modest flat at Steel Street while his woman dwelt in Babylonian luxury up the West End. It still burned Airchie to think of what that little tart was doing to his pal. In the circumstances it was just as well that Jessica and the baby were coming back. They would take Airchie's mind off Annie Kempson's systematic shafting of Jack.

'Here,' Dougie said, sliding what looked like a quadruple whisky across the bar. 'If anybody asks how ye

139

managed tae wangle this much, kid on ye've got lotsa water in it.'

Airchie drank the whisky swiftly, in three sharp gulps. He chased it with a huge swallow of beer.

'There's no' a fire or anythin',' Dougie told him. 'Ye can take yer time.' He turned, coughed once loudly, and addressed the clientele at large. 'Let's be havin' yer glasses, now. It's time ye were in yer beds.'

The punters trickled out in twos and threes. Soon there was only Airchie at one end of the bar and three vaguely-familiar men at the other. From the unhurried way they sipped their drinks he gathered that they, like himself, were among the privileged.

When Dougie had locked and bolted the doors one of the men at the far end of the bar helped him put up the shutters without disturbing the blackout curtains.

'Right,' Dougie said, coming back to the bar, rubbing his hands. 'What's yer pleasure, gents?'

'Let me get these,' Airchie said, waving a pound note. 'Whisky for everybody, Dougie.'

The three men studied him with interest.

'Whatever ye say.' Dougie got behind the bar again. 'Mr Milroy here drinks rum . . .' He raised his eyebrows at the broad man leaning on the curve of the bar. He nodded at Dougie. 'So that'll be three whiskies and a rum.'

'Four whiskies,' Airchie said. 'Have one yerself, Dougie. An' make them all doubles.'

The drinks were served and the three men raised their glasses solemnly to Airchie. He raised his own, nodded, and swallowed it in one go.

'Christ almighty,' Dougie grunted. 'Ye're certainly puttin' it away the night, Airchie.'

'No more than the average sponge, Dougie.' Airchie put his glass on the bar. 'Same again, I think.'

In the next half hour he had four more large whiskies. The men at the other end of the bar made no attempt to buy him a drink. That didn't bother Airchie. He was celebrating. Petty violations of courtesy didn't concern him tonight. He leaned on the bar, swaying gently, listening as the man called Milroy discussed septic tanks with Dougie.

'If ye're not connected to a sewer ye've got to have one.'

'It's always sounded like a filthy idea tae me,' Dougie said, shaking his head.

'Ach, it's only a place for the sewage to collect until the council can pump it out,' Milroy told him. 'Ah've been told all about it.'

'But that's what Ah mean. All that shit an' stuff, packed intae a wee tank. Christ, it must smell hellish.'

Milroy shook his head solemnly.

'Not at all. The sewage gets broken down by the germs. It kills itself off. Ye can stick yer head in under the cover an' it smells as sweet as a garden.'

'Ah'll take yer word for it,' Dougie said.

'You a plumber, then?' Airchie enquired brightly.

Milroy and his two companions stared at him.

'Who's askin'?'

'The fella that just bought ye all a drink,' Airchie said, still smiling.

'No, Ah'm not a plumber,' Milroy said, pointedly turning away to talk to his companions.

'Very friendly, Ah must say,' Airchie muttered as Dougie took his empty glass.

'Ssh.' Dougie leaned close. 'They're Baltic Street lads. A rough bunch, Airchie. Very rough. Ah'm not helluva fond of them myself, but I let them drink here as an alternative to havin' the place burned down.'

Airchie knew of the Baltic Gang. They were one of the smaller and more vicious outfits that had sprung up since the beginning of the war. As military service took away more and more young men the bigger gangs had splintered and disintegrated. Outfits like the Baltic mob were able to flourish openly without serious opposition. They were a nasty development; they didn't simply make war on other gangs, they picked on the public, too, and usually at random. Their crimes were petty, ill-planned and usually messy. In circumstances where a man like Jack

Kane would need no more than a screwdriver, they would use a bulldozer. They were also very badly informed. They didn't know who to respect, they stepped on the wrong toes all over the place. In their ignorance, Airchie reflected, they probably didn't believe they needed to show respect to anybody. God help them the day they learned different.

Dougie put another drink in front of Airchie. He paid for it, held it to his lips and paused to yawn before he gulped half of it down. He was tired. He was also drunk. The wisest move now would be to get into the van and clear off home. Six or seven hours' sleep would put him in the right condition to meet Jessica and Angela at the station in the morning. He was swirling the remainder of the drink, preparing to despatch it, when a remark from the other end of the bar made him stiffen.

'I still say Hector Kemp's the man that'll rule the roost on the north side when all the dust dies down.'

It wasn't said for any provocative reason, Airchie realised. The man next to Milroy had said it, and not at all loudly. But it *was* provocative, all the same. Hector Kemp, who was still the worse for what Jack Kane had done to him years ago, was one of the five people Airchie held in deepest contempt. Kemp had nearly caused Jack's death, after all – and he hadn't even been there when those men threw Jack off the roof. Nowadays he ran a lowdown bunch of Catholic-bashers whose methods were so reminiscent of the jungle that they had been openly disowned by all the official Orange bodies in Glasgow. In Airchie's estimation Hector Kemp was twenty stone of shit in a twelve stone bag.

'Hector Kemp,' he heard himself say, 'is a balloon.' He was aware, too, that he was glaring at the man who had spoken. 'He's a bigger bum than two arses.'

The three men were staring at him. At that moment Airchie was two people. One, small and feeling quite ineffectual, was trying to tell the other one to exercise a bit of self control.

'Who asked your opinion?' Milroy demanded, speaking softly.

'Hector Kemp has the guts of a butterfly.'

Was that me? Airchie wondered. He was swaying. He gripped the edge of the bar.

'Ye want to watch yer tongue, son,' Milroy said.

'Now, now, boys, steady on . . .' Dougie shot a pleading look at Airchie. 'We don't want any trouble, do we?'

'Tell yer wee pal that, then.' Milroy took a swig from his glass, keeping his eyes on Airchie. 'With a bucket like that for a mouth, he shouldnae be out on his own. He could get his head kicked in.'

'Away an' fuck yerself.'

Airchie was *positive* he'd said that. As he stood swaying Milroy came along the bar. Dougie was tight up against the back shelf. Milroy stopped a yard from Airchie and spread his feet.

'Ye must have a lot of power behind ye tae talk like that,' he said. 'Some kinda bit shot, are ye?'

'Beside you anybody's a big shot,' Airchie said. 'But since ye ask, Ah think Ah've got some clout. Enough, anyway.' *Don't*! he warned himself. *Button it*! 'Enough to see off the likes of Hector Kemp and the bubble-brains that think he's special.'

'Oh aye.' Milroy stepped nearer. 'So ye're callin' me a bubble-brain, is that it?'

This was all wrong, Airchie thought. Only dummies started this kind of thing. But his mouth was running away with him. He couldn't do anything about it.

'In ma experience,' he said, 'people that follow the Hector Kemps of this world have one thing in common – they're all as thick as shit in the neck of a bottle.'

Milroy put down his glass. Dougie shot forward and took his arm.

'Leave him, Roddie,' he hissed. 'He's drunk, ye can see that. His wife an' kid are comin' back the morra, he hasnae seen them in a long time. He's excited an' he's had a few too many. Leave him, eh?'

Milroy stood frozen for a second, then he picked up his

glass and walked back to the other end of the bar. He rejoined his companions. They all stared at Airchie, waiting for him to open his mouth again.

He decided not to. At last he felt he was in control of himself again. He finished his drink, nodded to Dougie and made his way carefully to the back door.

'Ah'll let myself out,' he said.

He had his hand on the door handle when he heard Milroy's voice from the bar.

'It'll do ye no good lettin' silly bastards like that in the place, Dougie.'

Airchie was back at the bar before he knew it.

'Silly bastards like me,' he said, 'are the saviours of this place. It *needs* silly bastards like me. Me an' that other silly bastard, Jack Kane, are a fuckin' lifeline hereabouts.'

Wrong! his brain screamed at him. *You don't mention names*! *You don't provoke*!

'Oho!' Milroy came away from the end of the bar again. 'So ye're a follower of the man Kane, are ye?'

'If ye were anybody, pal, ye'd know exactly who Ah am. But ye're just another toerag, right? A Baltic Street upstart.'

Airchie wasn't sure what happened after that. He was aware of being bundled out through the back door. Dougie shouted something and he sounded scared. Then it was dark. Airchie felt the cold air on his face, then he felt wet ground. He was rolling about, moving without trying to. He was being kicked, that was it. Above him he saw three shadows, he heard them grunting and cursing as they laid their boots into him. He couldn't feel anything. They couldn't hurt him. On an ordinary day he could have handled them, sent them crashing like skittles. But right now he didn't know how to stand up, so it was just as well he couldn't feel pain.

'Right then, fuck-face.'

Airchie felt himself hoisted and slammed against the wall. They were in close to him, one on each side and one, Milroy, in front. His arms were being held. Milroy stepped back, looked like he was aiming a punch. His hand swung, swept past without making contact. A second later there was searing pain. There *had* been contact, but what? Airchie heard himself howl. The hand swung close again and this time something terrible happened, he didn't know what, but something was taken away, he felt the loss. His howl was like a dog's now, long and thready and full of hurt. Now his head was tugged back, he heard hair roots tearing. Something was pushed in his mouth, rammed back into his throat.

They let him go and he fell. As he tried to spit the thing from his mouth the world swam away from his closing eyes.

Jack Kane woke up to the hammering on his front door. He looked at his watch. Ten past eleven. He shook his head, felt a throb near the back of his neck.

He remembered. Brandy, lots of it. They had celebrated Annie's birthday across in Edinburgh, first in a restaurant and then at a club. He'd slept most of the way back. The driver had helped him up the stairs and Jack had given him a ridiculously large tip.

The door banged again. Somebody was punching it, by the sound. He stood up, saw he still had on his socks. He took his dressing gown off the back of the bedroom door and slipped it on. He padded out to the hall and opened the door.

'Jessica. What are you doing here?' At first sight he thought she was angry about something. But it wasn't that. She was scared. 'Come in.'

She brushed past him, hugging the baby close. She went straight to the kitchen, turned and waited for Jack to catch up.

'What's the matter?'

'My Airchie's in hospital.' Her voice was taut, shocked. She swallowed once, very hard. 'Somebody cut off his ear.'

Jack was alert suddenly.

'Who did?'

'I don't know.'

145

'Where is he?'

'The Royal Infirmary.' Jessica blinked rapidly and tears slid along her cheeks. 'The police were waiting when I got to the house. I thought he'd slept in, I waited nearly an hour at the station. But they were there, the police, sitting in a car outside when I got to Springburn.'

'Have you seen Airchie?'

'Yes. Only for a minute. They were taking him to the theatre.'

'Sit down, Jessica. I'll make some tea. Try to relax and tell me what you know.'

She said nothing as he boiled the kettle and spooned tea into the pot. He kept watching her, recognising shock, seeing her trying to fit back into the normal current, the real, ordinary world. He poured two cups and got a chocolate biscuit for the baby. Angela slid down off her mother's knees and sat on the floor to eat it.

'Drink your tea,' Jack told Jessica.

She tasted it, then gulped some down.

'Why would anybody do that?' she said. 'His ear, imagine . . . It was cut right off. With a razor, the doctor said. Then it was shoved in his mouth. He nearly choked on his own ear.'

She began to shake, spilling tea. Jack took the cup from her, put it down and held her hands between his.

'Do you think people at the hospital know who did it?'

'No. They asked me if maybe I knew. I told them I'd no idea, I just got back to Scotland this morning.' She let out a shuddering breath. 'What a welcome, Jack. What a thing to come home to . . .'

'When can Airchie have visitors?'

'They said I could go back this afternoon.'

'I'll go with you. I'll drive you. I need to talk to him, Jessica.'

'Do *you* know who did it to him?'

'I've no idea. But I'll find out. I'll attend to them, whoever they are.'

'Them? You think it's more than one person? Why do you think that?'

'Because one man on his own would never be able to do that to Airchie.'

'He'd been very drunk,' Jessica said. 'That's why they had to wait so long before they took him to theatre to be stitched. They couldn't give him an anaesthetic because of all the alcohol in his bloodstream. He looks terrible, Jack. Terrible. I hardly recognised him.' She put her hands up over her face for a moment. 'I didn't know he had enemies. I thought everybody liked him.'

'There's no such thing as a man everybody likes.'

Jack drank his tea quickly and put the cup in the sink. He told Jessica to go back home and wait there for him. When she had gone he ran a hot bath and sat in it for ten minutes. When he had towelled himself dry and put on fresh clothes his hangover was nearly gone. He made another pot of tea and took a cup into the living room. At the table he sat and did something he had never told anyone about. He slid back to his centre. It was an exercise he had learned during the long months of recovery, when he had set out to make himself a force. Sipping tea slowly, he sat with eyes closed, letting himself be what he was at core, without the trimmings, without facades. There were times, like now, when it was necessary.

The first he had ever known about the existence of midbrain politics was what he read in a book called *Miraculous Mankind*, from the trolley of dogeared volumes that came round the wards at the infirmary. Until that time Jack had read nothing about the brain. He was ignorant of its evolution. But that old book he'd borrowed – and subsequently stolen – told him things that made him want to know more. So he went to the Mitchell Library and learned more. In the end he was equipped with a good understanding of the primitive warrior brain, the shark brain. The knowledge related to traits he knew existed in himself. Without meaning to, he had memorised a Victorian description of the shark's existence:

'Surviving in a world that is wholly hostile, a world that challenges its right to live, the shark makes an

147

advantage of its seeming deficiences and in the process becomes an awesomely effective predator, dedicating eighty per cent of its life to tracing, catching and devouring its prey alive.'

And behind that relentless life was the shark's special brain, devoid of such distractions as compassion, mercy and sympathy. The fundamental warrior brain, Jack learned, is lethally focused, knowing that it can rely on no other creature in its constant dedication to staying alive.

Rule Four: Be sure you can rely on yourself, you're all you've got.

He had learned that the midbrain in human beings is almost identical to the shark's brain. It is a throwback brain, surrounded in man by all the refinements imposed by evolution and civilisation. Knowing this, Jack had believed it would be possible to switch over to that brain, that primitive, predatory, ruthless organ at the centre of man's lofty intellect. To be able to shut off compassion, caution, reactive fear, to focus without distraction on the establishment of territory and the elimination of obstacles – it was a talent worth pursuing, whatever the cost in time or effort. And he believed he had achieved the goal.

He waited, eyes shut, body limp, waited for the icy calm to soak through to his centre, cutting the civilised circuits, clearing the lines of thought that clogged the midbrain's function. He was sure if he ever told anybody about this they would think he was mad. So he told nobody. They didn't deserve to be told, anyway. This kind of knowledge had to be won.

At two o'clock he got into his car and drove out to Springburn. Jessica was waiting. A neighbour had agreed to look after Angela for a couple of hours. Jessica kissed the baby goodbye and got into the car beside Jack. He drove her to the Royal Infirmary without a word passing between them.

He had to wait a long time. Jessica seemed to be in the ward for an age. When she came out she was weeping.

Jack told her he wouldn't be long. He went in, saw Airchie at once and went across.

'You look a mess,' he said. 'Who did it?'

Airchie's head was swathed in bandages. His chest was strapped, too. He groaned softly and waved a hand vaguely in front of him.

'Ye'll have to know, Jack – I asked for this.'

'That doesn't concern me. Just tell me who it was.'

'I was in the Cockit Hat, I was drunk, got mouthy – I even used your name.' Airchie closed his eyes for a moment, chewed his lip. 'Christ, Jack, I'm sorry, I was that bloody *stupid*. I should never have done anythin' like that . . .'

Jack leaned down over the bed.

'*Tell* me!'

'There was three of them,' Airchie said. 'But the one that did it, his name's Milroy. I think the first name's Roddie. Baltic Street Gang.'

Jack nodded.

'When do they say you can get out of here?'

'A couple of days.'

'Rest, then. Try not to feel sorry for yourself. There's worse things you could have got cut off.'

Jack took Jessica home and promised her he would be in touch. He drove back to Steel Street, parked the car and walked across to the Bridgegate. The Cockit Hat was shut. He went to the back door and banged on it until Dougie came downstairs and opened up.

'Christ, Jack, I thought ye were the polis.'

'Can I come in?'

'Sure.'

They went through to the bar. Dougie poured them both a whisky.

'Right then.' Jack leaned an elbow on the bar. 'Tell me about the man that cut up Airchie. Who is he, exactly?'

'Roddie Milroy. A man about thirty-five, thereabouts. He's single, lives with his mother in a tenement on Hillroad Street. Works at the tram terminus on the

Gallowgate. He's somethin' halfway high-up in the Baltic Gang – razor man, if last night's performance is anythin' tae go by. That's all Ah know about him. Except he's started usin' this place, along with a couple of other fellas from the gang.'

Jack was nodding, logging the facts.

'Who's the head man with the Baltic crowd?'

'Vince McStay.'

'The one that's got a billiard hall above that tailor's on the corner of Gordon Street?'

'That's him.'

Jack finished his drink and put down the glass.

'Thanks a lot, Dougie.'

He went to the back. Dougie came after him.

'Listen, Jack, I hope there's no hard feelin's, what with this thing happenin' in here, or startin' here, any road. I did try to warn Airchie to be quiet – but he'd had a few, ye know how it can get.'

'It wasn't any fault of yours, Dougie. Airchie brought it on himself. It was a lapse. He didn't deserve what he got, mind you.'

'I know that.'

'It occurred to me, when I heard about what happened – that infirmary's been quite a feature of my life, one way and another.'

'Aye, never mind churches. Hospitals are our real salvation centres.'

'They're revenge centres, too. I wonder how many reprisals have got planned in hospital wards, eh? It's something to think about when you're writing your memoirs about hard times among the wild men of Glasgow.' Jack pulled open the door. 'I'll see you soon, Dougie. And while I remember, I'll apologise for losing you a customer for a while.'

Dougie frowned.

'What customer?'

'What one do you think?'

* * *

Nobody expected disaster in the bright light of morning. When lives changed dramatically for the worse in the tougher districts of Glasgow, or anywhere else, the change usually came under the cover of night. Morning was the birth time of good expectations. Roddie Milroy left home that Sunday morning with a spring in his step, whistling softly, ready to take on the new day with optimism in his flinty heart. A Sunday shift at the terminus meant time-and-a-half for doing practically nothing. There had been worse Sundays, he believed.

As he passed the big half-open gate of a wood yard on the Gallowgate somebody whistled. He stopped and looked inside. A man beckoned, waving urgently. He was standing beside a pyramid of timber, his head slightly bowed. Roddie couldn't make out his face in the shadow of his cap.

'You wavin' tae me, pal?'

The man nodded, waved again. Roddie went into the yard. He had never been here before. The still air within the high fence was rich with the smell of resin and sawed wood. The place would make some bonfire if anybody ever took it into his head.

'What is it, then?'

The man in the cap raised his head as Roddie got close.

'Nice morning, Mr Milroy.'

Roddie skidded to a stop. He tightened, squared his shoulders.

'What do ye want?'

Jack Kane took off the cap and laid it on a pile of planks.

'I wanted you to see this,' he said, pointing to a solid block of wood mounted on legs a few yards away. 'A beauty, isn't it? They make them here.'

Milroy glanced at the thing. He inflated his chest and stared at Jack.

'Ah'm on ma way to work. Say what ye've got to say.'

'I've nothing to say, really. I want you to look at that.'

Milroy tilted his head.

'What's the game, eh?'

151

'It's a drama, Mr Milroy. The idea is, you look at that block and get it fixed in your mind, so that any time you think about it in the future, you'll want to start bawling.'

'Have you been on the bevvy or somethin'?'

With no visible preamble Jack's right arm shot forward. His fingers closed round Milroy's throat. The other hand swung in a horizontal punch that landed on Milroy's ear. He tried to jerk free, lashing out with his hands and feet. Jack tightened his grip, stepped close and jabbed his head forward, smashing his forehead on the other man's nose. As he sagged Jack took him under the arms and dragged him to the side of the block. Milroy struggled as he was forced to his knees. Jack rammed his head on the side of the block. He stopped struggling.

Jack made his preparations. When he was ready he stood back and waited for Milroy to rally. Eventually he looked up and saw his arm was tethered to the block. He tried to jerk free.

'Don't waste your energy,' Jack said.

'You'll pay fuckin' dear for this, Kane!'

Milroy jerked violently, trying to get his arm out from under the tight coils of rope.

Jack stepped to the side of the block and pushed back his jacket. He drew a shiny-bladed hatchet from a pouch in the broad leather belt he wore.

'Aw for fuck's sake . . .'

The anger had fled. Milroy looked terrified. He gulped, nearly choked on the intake of air. Jack adjusted his grip on the shaft of the hatchet. He raised it two feet above Milroy's wrist and held it there.

'This *is* your razor hand, isn't it?'

'Don't! Please don't! *Please!*'

The hatchet went a foot higher then swept down, chopping halfway through Milroy's wrist. Blood and bone fragments spattered his face. He screamed. He was still screaming when the blade came down a second and third time, finally severing the hand. It lay splayed on the block, sprouting splintered bone and tendon. Bright arterial blood surged from the stump of his wrist. The fourth swing of the hatchet cut through the rope. Milroy fell back, mouth gaping, his throat hissing. He clutched the stump to his chest and knelt there, rocking back and forth, his face turning blue as blood spread in a crimson patch across the front of his shirt.

Jack wiped the blade of the hatchet with a piece of sacking. When every trace of blood and skin was gone he returned the weapon to his belt. Milroy's severed hand was wrapped in another piece of sack. Jack put it carefully in his inside pocket. He buttoned his jacket, smoothed his hair and walked out of the yard without looking back.

Shortly after two that afternoon Vince McStay went to his billiard hall on the corner of Gordon Street. He went there every Sunday to do his books and keep an eye on the cleaners, who came in at three o'clock. As he pushed open the heavy door he noticed a brown cardboard box on the landing. His name was written on the lid in capital letters.

Nobody had ever sent Vince a booby trap, but he reckoned there could always be a first time. He picked up the box carefully, took it inside at arm's length and put it on his office desk. Standing well back, he flipped off the lid with the end of a billiard cue. Nothing happened. Vince stepped forward and looked into the box. At first he didn't understand what he saw. Then it dawned on him. It was a human hand, chopped and bloody, with a tattoo on the back that he recognised.

That evening Jack visited Airchie in the infirmary. Without being specific he told his old pal that although his ear couldn't be put back, the right price for it had been exacted.

Airchie had news. He delivered it haltingly. Jessica had been back to see him, and they had talked things over. Or *she* had. She wanted them to leave Glasgow as soon as Airchie was discharged by the doctors. She wasn't open to arguments, there was simply no chance of her remaining in a place where something like that could happen to her husband. They had plenty of money, she'd pointed out; they could go somewhere quiet to live and run a small business, any business, just so long as it didn't involve Airchie in dealings with the kind of monsters who cut pieces off people they didn't like.

Jack offered no resistance to the plan. He could see Airchie had been turned around, as much by what Milroy had done to him as by Jessica's determination. Airchie had never been a midbrain type, anyway. Maybe it was best he got out of Glasgow. He was a hard enough man, but Jack believed the razor job had defined the limits of what he could take without buckling.

When Jack left the infirmary he sat in his car for a while. He felt low. Airchie and he went back a long way. All the way, really. He would miss his pal.

A chiming clock reminded him he should look in on Annie. She would have recovered by now from the post-celebration hangover that had kept her in bed for the whole of Saturday. He started the car and drove slowly over to the West End.

At the flat he let himself in quietly, hoping to surprise her. He was halfway into the living room when he realised something was badly wrong. The place was a shambles. Furniture had been overturned and slashed. The stuffing from chairs and the couch was scattered everywhere.

'Annie?'

He rushed to the bedroom. There was no sign of her. She wasn't in the smashed up kitchen, either. He went back to the living room. Fury was pounding his chest.

'Annie! Are you here?'

He heard something, a muffled whine, like a sound a cat would make. He listened, heard it again and ran into the bedroom. He jerked open the big fitted wardrobe. Annie was on the floor, tied up with her dressing gown cord and gagged. She was in her nightdress. It was stained with blood. She began howling behind the gag when she saw him.

'Hang on, hang on . . .'

Jack dragged her out, lifted her and laid her on the

bed. He tore the gag off her mouth. She lay panting and whimpering while he untied the cord.

Rule Three: *Take great care of what you love . . .*

'Are you all right? Annie?' He touched her shoulder. 'What did they do to you?' He looked at the blood again, long streaks of it around the front and sides of the nightdress. 'What did the bastards do?'

She was staring at him with wild eyes, her mouth open and bruised from the gag. She tried to swallow and coughed. Her hands jerked forward and Jack saw the bloody fingertips.

'Oh Jesus Christ, Annie . . .'

Her fingernails had been torn off. Jack raced to the bathroom and soaked a towel. He brought it back and wrapped it around her hands.

'Come on, I'll get you to a doctor . . .'

She raised her head off the bed and spat in his face.

'Scum!' she shouted. 'Filthy Fenian scum bastard!' She swung her legs over the side of the bed and flung herself to her feet. 'This is the price, isn't it?' Saliva dripped in a silvery string from the corner of her mouth. 'I should have known! You're a crook and I've paid for having anything to do with you! You're a filthy criminal!'

'Annie, for God's sake . . .'

'Fenian scum!'

He moved towards her and she jumped back, holding the wet towel up to her throat. She looked like she might start screaming.

'They did this to me to get at *you*, didn't they? Those rotten bastards are your kind, Mister Big-Shot. You're all animals! Bloody fucking animals!'

'Annie, you're in shock. Sit down, love. Take it easy. I'll get you a drink.'

'Get out of here!'

'Aw, now, wait . . .'

'Get out! Scum!'

'Please, honey, listen – '

'Filth! Don't come near me! Not ever!'

'Come on, you're in a terrible state, I understand that. Calm down, we'll sort all this out.'

'Get out, Jack! I'll get the police if you don't!'

Jack stared at her. She was radiating purest hate.

'Just go, will you? I don't want to see you ever again.'

When he left the flat he drove to Steel Street, switched off the engine and just sat in the car again, staring at the rain patterning the winscreen. There wasn't enough coldness in him. The predator brain had to give way under the layers of purely human pain. He sat motionless for an hour, hurting like he never had before.

Finally the damp air got through to him. He shivered and opened the door, all the feelings in him sharpening on contact with the chill breeze. He hurried across the road and into the close, desperate suddenly for a drink, something to warm him and fan the murder in his broken heart.

NINE

Hostilities between the gangs in 1942 were as numerous as the gangs themselves. The government's enlistment of young brain and muscle for the war effort meant, inevitably, a dismal drop in the quality of civilian manpower; the falling-off was nowhere more obvious than in the Glasgow gangs. Intelligence and maturity were as scarce as experience and dedication. The well-structured and disciplined factions were mostly gone, replaced by small-ish, rudderless teams who mistook viciousness for toughness and believed mayhem was the same thing as menace.

From the safety and comfort of a new flat, a mile from his old place in Steel Street, Jack spent a couple of weeks studying the picture of the gangs' individual strengths and their mutual animosities. One thing was sure: he couldn't bring down biblical wrath on the Baltic mob single-handed. He could see, however, that they had made enough enemies to get themselves wiped out, if only those enemies could join forces long enough to get the job done. They never would, of course. On the other hand it could be made to look as if they were doing just that.

Jack's plan was in three parts. Part One was put into effect on a Friday night at the end of May. Vince McStay was walking in Glasgow Green with two of his lieutenants, an arrogant show of strutting imperialism that took place once a week, just to let the lesser squads of the district see who really mattered around these parts. Bulging jackets attested to battle-readiness. The trio laughed a great deal among themselves as they made their casual progress along the carriageway that ran the length of the park.

As they passed a clump of trees towards the Saltmarket end of the road, a man in a black boiler suit and goggles appeared. He carried a galvanised bucket. He looked odd but his movements were casual and unhurried, so it was a total surprise when he stepped to the edge of the grass verge and threw the contents of the bucket over the three men.

Before they could react he followed through. He dropped the bucket, whipped a twisted newspaper from his pocket and lit it from a windproof lighter. It flared up at once and as the men turned on him he threw the paper into their midst. The petrol on their clothing caught fire. Vince's hands and hair caught fire, too. Panicking, they tried to beat out each other's flames until the pain and panic became too much for co-ordinated action. One of the lieutenants broke into a run and in seconds he looked like a mobile torch. Vince rolled on the grass, roaring. The third man, who hadn't received so much petrol as the other two, sat at the road's edge, whining with pain as he slapped at his smouldering jacket and trousers.

The man in the boiler suit and goggles had meanwhile vanished. But he had left his bucket behind. Later, when the men's burns had been treated and the police had been assured that the assailant was unknown to the Baltic boys, a messenger passed on the word to Vince that the bucket had come from the Toll Garage – the name was painted on the bottom. That was significant. The head of a rival outfit owned and operated the Toll Garage.

The next day a petrol pump at the Toll Garage blew up. The explosion destroyed the office and three second-hand cars on the forecourt. The attendant on duty reported seeing a Baltic member hanging about near the pumps earlier that morning. A green Alvis was seen taking off shortly before the blast. Vince McStay owned a green Alvis.

This meant war.

The Baltic Gang closed ranks and drew up battle plans.

Meanwhile Jack Kane stole Vince's Alvis and parked it prominently outside a shebeen operated by another of the Baltics' rivals. Wearing goggles and a black wool cap, he entered the shebeen and began smashing up the place with a claw hammer. The two men in charge could hardly believe their eyes. When they finally tried to intervene, Jack broke the nose of one and winded the other by jabbing him in the stomach with the hammer. A couple of minutes later the Alvis was seen driving away. Before the night was out the Baltic Gang had more trouble on their hands, and before daylight the following morning nine of their number had been taken away in ambulances.

Part Three of Jack's plan involved no deceptions. Dougie at the Cockit Hat had been encouraged to do some snooping, which he normally did by keeping his ears open and appearing to be preoccupied with the technicalities of his beer pumps and spirit optics. Calling on Jack to report progress over a half gill of single malt, he revealed that the person who had pulled off Annie Kempson's fingernails was one of Vince McStay's part-time cruelty merchants, a man called Peter Bulloch.

'Ah'm no' surprised it was him,' Dougie told Jack. 'He's a wicked bugger. They took his kids away from him because of the way he treated them. He put his wife in the hospital a couple of times, too.'

'Does he come in your pub?' Jack asked.

'Saturdays, like clockwork. He's been usin' the place since one or two other Baltic lads have made it their boozer. Bulloch comes through the door at eight on the dot an' doesnae leave until he's blind drunk.'

Jack's need to avenge the harm done to Annie had swelled to the proportions of a holy mission. He knew he would never undo the damage, revenge never did repair an injury. She would still be mutilated, he would still be despised. But when he dwelt on the details of her torture – and he could find no way to stop himself doing that – he could understand the motives of men who sacrificed everything, from livelihood to liberty to life itself, in order to hit back for some crime that blistered their hearts. Jack now saw himself as the direct cause of terrible agonies suffered by two young women, yet neither of them had deserved less than his affection and respect. Revenge was maybe not the name for what he wanted. Peace of mind would be closer.

'You're not thinkin' of showin' up in the Cockit Hat, are ye?' Dougie said. 'Ah'm not too keen on havin' a miniature World War Two in there, Jack. The Baltic boys are still helluva sore about what happened tae Roddy Milroy.' Dougie sniffed the malt and sighed. 'Did you know they call ye Hatchet Jack round these parts nowadays?'

'No, I hadn't heard. And no, I'm not planning to come barging into your pub, Dougie. But I'd like to have the use of your back yard.'

'As long as I don't know when ye're usin' it, Jack. It'd make me jumpy an' somebody'd be sure to catch on that somethin' was up.'

'It'll all be over before you even know I've been,' Jack promised.

That Saturday night Peter Bulloch was more expansive than Dougie had ever seen him. Ordinarily unkempt, he lounged about the bar drinking non-stop, grunting his few communications and ignoring most of the people who spoke to him. Tonight, though, he had shaved and put on a clean shirt, and he displayed the kind of lighthearted social behaviour that suggested he was a normal human being. Most people in the Cockit Hat knew he was far from normal, but they were glad enough to suffer his impersonation. At twenty past eight, well oiled and grinning to right and left, he bought drinks for himself and three impromptu companions. He collared Dougie as he pulled the drinks at the end of the bar.

'Ah've had a great day,' Bulloch revealed. 'Made a packet on the cuddies.'

'Ah backed three horses myself the day,' Dougie said balefully. 'Every one a stroller.'

'The secret's in knowin' yer horse an' knowin' the kind of course that suits it, Dougie.'

'Is that right?'

'Definitely. Take Hamilton Park, now. It's shaped like a tennis racket, did ye know that?'

'No, I hadn't heard.'

'Well it is. A tennis racket.' Bulloch wiped his fleshy mouth with the back of his hand and propped his elbows on the bar. 'An' it's very up an' down. So. The six-furlong stretch is dead straight, right? An' it's hillocky. Well, ye pick the kind of horse that's good on the straight but can handle the bumps as well. Get it?'

'I learn somethin' new every day,' Dougie said.

'An' ye bear in mind it's a right-handed course. That's important too. Right-handed. So yer horse has got to favour the right turn. There's a wee horse called Warm Cargo that just fits the bill.' Bulloch winked. 'Any time it runs at Hamilton, put yer shirt on it.'

'Ah'm obliged tae ye,' Dougie said. 'That'll be eight an' a tanner, please.'

He watched Bulloch on and off during the next ten minutes. The man was getting drunk faster than usual and his high spirits were verging on the boisterous. But there was still no sign of nastiness creeping in. To see him, anyone would think he was the epitome of the Saturday-night Glaswegian, the cheery man with a quip on his lips and a pocketful of change to spend on drinks for any stranger he came across. The truth was that Bulloch was habitually mean, belligerent and acutely paranoid. If he heard laughter anywhere in the pub, he tended to think it was derision, and that it was aimed at him. Tonight, though, some magic or other had worked on his chemistry. Dougie hoped he stayed that way until he left. He also hoped that Jack Kane wouldn't choose tonight to haunt the back yard. The way things were shaping, the evening could end on a harmonious note. Just for a change.

But Jack was already in the yard. By 8:40 he had been there for half an hour, standing in a shadowy roofed section close to the wall, a couple of yards from the door to the gents' lavatory. As punters came and went he peered at them from the gloom, watching for the bald head and protruding ears that were Bulloch's distinguishing features.

As the minutes passed he began to think that Bulloch hadn't come out tonight, or if he had, he wasn't drinking much. Or he had a powerful bladder.

Jack was rubbing the cold from his fingers when the back door swung open and he saw the dim light from the pub shine on a clean scalp. Peering, craning his neck forward, he checked the ears. They looked like the handles on the Scottish Cup. He took a folded tea towel from his pocket and tucked into his sleeve, where it would be ready when he needed it. There was already a length of rope in the other sleeve, looped and slip-knotted. He waited until Bulloch had used the lavatory and was on his way out.

'Hey, Peter.'

Bulloch stopped, swung round.

'Who's that?'

'It's me.'

Bulloch took a couple of steps towards the shadowy corner. When he was within reach Jack grabbed him by the lapels. He swung him round, putting his back to the wall. The big man resisted, but it was the sluggish, off-balance resistance of a disorientated drunk. As he feinted with elbows and fists, Jack poked him sharply on the chin with his fist. Bulloch opened his mouth to yell and Jack pushed the folded tea towel into the snag-toothed gap.

'Don't swallow it,' he said, turning Bulloch to face the wall. 'I want it back.'

Working quickly, he put his knee in the small of Bulloch's back and kept him pinned against the wall. He was a big man and strong, but any street fighter knew that a man lost half his power when he was forced to defend himself with his arms and hands flapping behind his back. Jack got the loop of rope round the left wrist, forced the right hand through the gap and pulled the end hard. The knot slipped snugly round Bulloch's wrists. Jack gave it

162

another tug, making the rope bite. He spun Bulloch to face him again.

'I've done you up like this so you'll listen to me without fidgeting or interrupting,' he whispered. 'Now I'm going to take you down the other end of the yard, where nobody'll disturb us. Don't struggle, Peter. I'll kick your nuts if you do.'

Gripping Bulloch's arm, Jack pulled him to the farthest corner of the yard and pushed him into the angle of the two walls.

'This isn't going to take long.'

Jack put himself squarely in front of Bulloch. In the late evening light he knew his face would be discernible. That didn't matter. In a way it was important. This was an occasion for open declaration, so it was fitting that he should be visible and identifiable.

'A while back, Peter, you took it on yourself to attack and seriously disfigure a helpless young woman. Now I know you'll be wondering which one I'm on about, because you've worked on a few in your time. That's the kind of shit you are. You're one of those freaks that gets a big thrill out of hurting people weaker than yourself. Women are more fun than men, I suppose, because they squeal a lot, their pain sounds better.'

Bulloch pushed himself away from the wall suddenly, putting his head down, rushing forward bent double. Jack stuck out his foot and the big man went down, cracking his forehead on the cobbles. There was a muted roar behind the towel in his mouth. Jack got him to his feet and slammed him back into the corner.

'That was stupid. You could have hurt yourself.'

Bulloch was furious now. He came out of the corner again, struggling to free his hands, trying to spit out the towel. Jack put one foot behind him and jerked his leg up sharply. Bulloch landed heavily on his backside.

'Right. Sit there and don't move. I'm going to have my say, whether you want me to or not.' Jack got on his hunkers beside Bulloch. 'As I was saying, you like torturing women. I've done a bit of checking this past couple of days. I've picked up a yarn or two about you. You're a right demon, aren't you? Broke your wife's leg once, and while she was still in plaster you broke her arm. And there was a bus conductress you had a go at – pulled out clumps of her hair with pliers. You're something special.'

Jack reached out and took one large ear between his finger and thumb. He twisted it. Hard. Bulloch roared again. 'See what it's like? Being helpless, feeling pain – and worst of all, not knowing what's going to happen next. Terrible, isn't it? That's how those women must have felt. Only worse. Because they were being tortured by a gorilla twice their weight and nastier than a bear with toothache.'

Jack stood up, took something from his hip pocket and squatted again.

'I weigh a lot less than you, Peter, but the way things are right now, I'm a fucking sight bigger and stronger than you. So I've got you right in the position of that wee girl I mentioned. Trussed up, powerless. Her name's Annie, by the way. A wee nurse, very good looking. You took out all her fingernails, Peter. The pliers again, wasn't it?' He held up his folded hand. 'Guess what I've got here?'

He heard Bulloch's breathing change. He was panting. He was scared.

'No, it's not pliers. I'm not going to pull out your nails. Or lop your ears or anything like that.' He leaned close to the big fretful head. 'I'm going to make sure that every morning you wake up, for the rest of your rotten life, you'll remember that wee girl. You'll remember her and the terrible things you did to her, and when you remember, you'll wish to Christ you'd never gone near her.'

Jack moved back. He flipped open the razor in his right hand. Steadying Bulloch's left leg, he drew the edge of blade across the back of his knee. Bulloch jerked with the pain. He was trembling. Jack steadied the other leg. Bulloch howled as the blade sliced through his muscle and tendon.

Jack stood up.

'Every day, for the rest of your days,' he said, 'when you hobble out of your bed to get your walking sticks, you'll remember Annie Kempson.'

He pulled Bulloch out of the corner, hearing the whimpering behind the towel. He was a heavy man and dragging him to the back door of the pub wasn't easy. When he was finally there, doubled over, jammed in the doorway, Jack snatched the towel from his mouth.

'Ya bastard!' Bulloch hissed.

'Don't get cheeky,' Jack told him. 'I don't want to hit a cripple.'

Somebody opened the door as Jack was halfway over the wall at the foot of the yard. He heard the sounds of shock and confusion as he dropped down on to the pavement and walked to the corner where he had parked the car.

He got home just after nine. He was in the kitchen pouring himself a whisky when the door bell rang. He waited and it rang again. Putting down the whisky bottle he went to the hall, propping a hatchet on the wall to one side of the door before he opened it. A tall, sombre-faced man in a navy blue raincoat was standing there.

'Jack Kane?'

Another man appeared, looking over his companion's shoulder, his face just as grim.

'Sure, I'm Jack Kane. What can I do for you?'

'You're under arrest, Mr Kane.' The man held up a warrant card. 'I'd like you to come to the station with us, please. And don't make it difficult. There's two of us here and four more at the foot of the stairs.'

Jack reached behind the door for his jacket, finding it hard to believe that Bulloch would set the law on him. Or that he could have done it so quickly.

At the police station they put him in a spotlessly clean cell that managed, nevertheless, to stink of urine and vomit. Old scratchings covered the pitted walls – names, initials, dates, heartfelt promises of retribution, obscenities. Jack sat on the slatted bench that was intended to double as a bed. He had the feeling he was being watched, so he sat perfectly still, hands clasped, trying to work out what slip, or lie, or act of treachery had brought him here. He could think of nothing. He had been there nearly an hour when the door was flung open and a uniformed officer beckoned him into the passage.

He was taken to a bare interview room with a tin-shaded lamp over the table. He sat down and waited again. Ten minutes passed, then Detective Sergeant MacKay came in. He was smiling, trying to look very confident.

'At long last,' he said.

He came to the table and rested his foot on the chair opposite Jack's. He leaned forward, putting his arm across his knee. Jack had seen the pose in a lot of gangster films.

'When I think about it, Kane, it's been worth waiting for you. I've always been sure we'd nail you, although I'd never have guessed what for. So I suppose each day I've had that little certainty to carry me through the shift. And now the time's come.'

'What's the charge?'

'You mean you don't know?'

'Are you going to tell me, MacKay, or are you just going to fuck about?'

'Watch the lip,' MacKay warned. 'You can get injured in here, you know.'

'And *you* can get injured out on the street. Even while I'm in here. It could be arranged faster than you can fart.'

'Is that so? How come it hasn't happened before, then?'

'Because I was never interested in you for more than ten seconds at a time,' Jack said. 'You're easy to forget, you know.' He sat back and folded his arms. 'I'm asking you again – what's the charge?'

MacKay took out his notebook and opened it.

'Enough to put half a dozen men away,' he muttered, staring at the page. 'Theft, at least twenty counts – that's for starters. Then there's illegal gaming, bookmaking, violation of War Office civil trading regulations – black-marketing, in other words – fraud . . .' MacKay looked

166

up. 'The list's not complete yet. We've been to your garages and got ourselves a vanload of evidence there, so we'll hold you on the theft charges for now. A squad'll be going through your south-side warehouse in the morning when there's a bit of light. I daresay we'll add another couple of columns to the charges when that lot's been sorted out.'

'This is bloody nonsense,' Jack said.

'No it's not. You know it's not. We've got proof. Lots of it. Names, places, dates, the goods.'

Jack thought of Airchie, tried to imagine him turning traitor. It was impossible. It couldn't be him.

'It's easy to say you've got proof, isn't it?'

'It's easy to *prove* we've got proof, Jack.'

The door opened and Superintendent Laurie came in. He sauntered across the room and stood by the table, looking down at Jack. He didn't smile the way MacKay had, but he looked pleased with himself.

'They're getting a cell ready for you at Barlinnie even as I speak,' he said. You're one bastard I'll be delighted to see sliding down the pan.'

Laurie turned to MacKay.

'Has he been charged?'

'Not yet, sir. The papers will be along in a minute.'

'Fine.' Laurie looked at Jack again. 'Have you any idea how we managed to get a case against you?'

'I've told your monkey here,' Jack said, 'I don't even know there is a case. All I've heard so far is cop talk.'

'You'll know there's a case, soon enough.' Laurie chewed thoughtfully on his moustache. 'We've been needing to make an example of somebody for a while now. It's chaos out there. The lawless city, that's what the papers have been calling Glasgow. People have got to be pulled into line. I fancy when word about your conviction and sentence gets out, a lot of them'll think hard before they break the law again.'

'That's still cop talk,' Jack said.

'Well I'll put some substance in it for you,' Laurie snapped. 'A certain young woman, whose name I'm sure

I don't need to mention, sent for us earlier today. She wanted to place evidence in our hands – notebooks, names she'd copied down, addresses, dates and so on. She's been very diligent, you know. Must have been collecting her paperwork over a long period. She even gave us impressions she'd made from a lot of different keys. All very damaging stuff, Kane. It'll knock the stilts out from under you. Rely on that.'

'You're lying,' Jack said.

'I've no need to. We've enough on you to keep the High Court busy for a month.' Now Laurie did smile. 'I bet you're wondering why she shopped you.'

Jack stared at him. It was hard to fight off the belief, bewildering or not. *Annie . . .*

'It was spite,' Laurie said. 'She's been through a bad time. The day before yesterday she spent six hours having plastic surgery on her hands. That left her in a lot of pain. Then last night the whole job went septic. Her hands are worse than ever. At ten o'clock this morning she decided to get her own back. I know you're not the one that savaged her, but she blames you all the same. Tough, eh?'

At midnight, after the charges had been read out to him and he still refused to admit anything or name any associates, Jack finally asked to have a lawyer. He pointed out he could afford the best and the best was sent for. He was called Samuel Moncrieff, a tall, stately man with curly grey side whiskers and a long Victorian face. He arrived at ten-past one and conferred with the police for over an hour. Then he came to see Jack in his cell.

'I have to tell you, Mr Kane, that the case against you is getting more watertight by the minute. I'll need time to think over our line of defence, of course, but in the meantime I think you should seriously consider an unconditional confession of guilt.'

'You call that a defence, do you?'

'In a way it is,' Moncrieff said. 'If you deny any of the charges it's my belief they'll be able to prove them, nonetheless. Denials in the face of hard evidence tend to make judges peevish. They irritate juries, too. A contrite confession of all your sins would be likely to make your eventual sentence shorter – a lot shorter, I'd say, than it might be if you insist on hotly maintaining your innocence.'

'Is there nothing I can do?' Jack said. 'No way to fight back?'

'No,' Moncrieff said flatly. 'Your only chance of avoiding prison has passed. If you'd known this was coming, you could have sidestepped it by disappearing for the duration of the war. I've a feeling that when this conflict is over, the law will find itself in the same mess as last time. The backlog of delayed and suspended cases will be a nightmare of disorganisation. Witnesses will be dead or untraceable, evidence and records lost or destroyed, identities changed.'

Now was a fine time to be told that, Jack thought. The best he could do with the information was file it away, to be retrieved and considered if there was ever another war.

He got to bed at dawn. He was exhausted. As he drifted off he dreamed of Annie. She was dressed to the throat in a gown of purest white. In her hands she had a bouquet of yellow flowers. She stood in a sunlit grotto framed by willows and banks of long, sighing, emerald grass. She was looking straight at him. Her lips were moving. He couldn't hear so he moved closer, feeling as if he were treading knee deep through water. As he got closer he heard her voice, loud and clear on the crystal air: 'I got you, you bastard! I *got* you!'

When the came came to court the file of police evidence ran to 240 closely typed pages. Chinks in one layer of prosecution material were neatly covered by thickets of proof in another; where genuine doubts occurred they were submerged by the weight of certainties that followed. For nine days the police case was put relentlessly by three barristers working in relay.

The essence of their submission was that Jack Kane was

a ruthless, cunning, thoroughly dishonest individual who had isolated himself at the heart of massive criminal dealings over a period of years. His personal isolation had been so effective that although his criminal network was extensive, there was no way of knowing how many people he had employed, or who any of them were.

When the time came for the defence to present its case, Mr Moncrieff had only one witness: Jack Kane. He had decided, against vehement persuasion, to deny everything. He argued that all the evidence was circumstantial, since he had never been caught committing any of the crimes of which he stood accused. The prosecution wearily pointed out that according to the logic of the defendant's wordy and contradictory testimony, all evidence, of any kind at all, was circumstantial.

'Being caught red-handed *is* a circumstance,' the senior prosecutor said. 'So even if Mr Kane had indeed been caught *in flagrante delicto*, I've no doubt he would call that evidence circumstantial, too.'

Jack continued to argue that he had nothing to do with the offences. The prosecution finally insisted that reality and common sense be allowed to hold some sway in the court. Was His Honour going to permit any further waste of public funds, not to mention the justiciary's time, while the defendant made it clear, at great length, that he hadn't a leg to stand on?

The newspapers carried stories about Hatchet Jack and his one-man empire of crime. He got letters asking for his autograph. One correspondent, a woman, begged him for a lock of his hair. Another wrote to say that he should be tied to a chair in the middle of Hampden Park where everyone could see, and have boiling oil poured over him.

On the thirteenth day of the trial the jury finally withdrew to consider their verdict. They came back after only eight minutes. They found Jack Kane guilty on all counts. The judge declared himself relieved that the whole wearisome business was over and done with. Almost as an afterthought, he sentenced Jack to seven years in prison. That same day he began serving his sentence in Barlinnie.

As matters turned out he served a total of four years. In all that time he had only two visitors. Airchie Cairns came only once, to thank Jack for not implicating him in the case and to say goodbye. He and Jessica had decided to go and live in Darlington so that they could be near her parents, who had moved back there on the father's retirement. Airchie talked vaguely about opening a newsagent's shop. His ear, Jack reflected, might have had some of the qualities of Samson's hair, because without it Airchie just wasn't the man he had been.

The other visitor, who came nine times between 1942 and 1946, was Dougie Meikle. He proved to be a good friend, loyal and sentimental, who never forgot any of Jack's birthdays and always reassured him he was better off inside, given the state of the country.

Jack never felt confined in prison. The need to survive diminished; he had no cause to fend for himself, so he was never hemmed-in by imperatives. Life was supported by the state, all he had to do was live it. Which turned out to be a far from dull business. Barlinnie in the war years was a quieter place than it had been. The inmates Jack mingled with were mostly middle-aged men, some of them one-time legends, like Jack Craig and John Ramensky. But the majority he met were in prison for distinctly non-violent crimes. Jack adjusted quickly to the unaggressive pace and the absence of competition. He became friendly with an old college lecturer, a historian who had been jailed for embezzling academic funds. By easy stages this man introduced Jack to the world of thought and refined curiosity. Life took on a new complexion. Without menace and opposition, Jack's days became almost idyllic. It was hard to believe that this existence was defined as punishment.

By late 1944 there were three shelves in Jack's cell packed with books. He developed an especial interest in the Crusades and read La Monte's *Feudal Monarchy in the Latin Kingdom of Jerusalem* from cover to cover, twice. He copied out whole stretches of Munro's *The Kingdom of the Crusaders* and committed most of his notes to memory. As the war in the world outside the walls drew to its bloody, apocalyptic close, Jack was discovering inner peace.

One day, a month before he was released, he listened to the lecturer, known to everyone as Uncle Brian, talk nostalgically about travel to Leslie, an accountant who was doing three years for insurance fraud. Their exchange produced in Jack a sensation which, at one time, he would have denied even existed. It was called enchantment.

'Do you know where I'd like to be today,' Brian said, 'if there was no war on and I wasn't enjoying myself here, of course?'

Leslie tried to guess.

'Paris?' he said.

'No, I think I'm too old for Paris now. Have another guess.'

'Athens?'

'That might be my second choice. But where I'd love to be, ideally, is Toledo. I haven't visited it for twenty years, but there's hardly a week goes by when I don't think about being there.'

'Your special place, is it?'

'The city of my heart, Leslie. A hill city – a granite hill at that, practically surrounded by the muddy old Tagus. Cervantes called it the sacred city, the glory of Spain.'

To a man who had been no further than Blackpool this was intoxicating. But more than that, it was a demonstration of an instinct Jack had, or perhaps no more than a hunch until now, that to know the wider world was one way of avoiding crass narrowness in the mind. Beside these men's wistful dreams, Jack believed his whole previous life stood revealed as something meaningless.

'In the fifteenth century there was no place like Toledo,' Uncle Brian said. 'It was the epicentre of Moorish art, science, and philosophy. The great cultures were blended and fused in Toledo – Arab, Jewish, Christian. It's a terribly seductive place, even if all you do is look at it.

172

But it's a spiritual city too, there's greatness hanging in the air. Some places *shimmer* with their history, Leslie. Do you know what I mean?'

'I know exactly,' Leslie said. 'One night I bored my wife to sleep talking about Florence.'

'The city of *your* heart.'

'Definitely,' Leslie said. 'Maybe I'll grow out of it, but the way I feel about Florence is roughly the way Byron felt about Greece.'

'Pure adoration.'

'Yes. And a profound sense of home. He wrote something somewhere about believing his bones wouldn't be able to rest in an English grave . . .'

Brian nodded. The space between his eyebrows narrowed as he concentrated.

'My bones would not rest in an English grave,' he quoted, 'or my clay mix with the earth of that country.' He grinned. 'He even went so far as to say he wouldn't feed England's worms if he could help it.'

Oh, this was heady stuff. Jack began to mourn his wasted life. What did it amount to, after all? He had been one rat in a community of rats, surviving by his wits and by violence, so that he could use the same wits and similar violence another day. Where was the significance, the meaning?

One piece of wisdom he had picked up from old Brian would stay with him, he was sure, for the rest of his days. During a friendly argument with another inmate Brian had said, 'It's all very well to have certainties, and to live by them. But you have to scrutinise them regularly and revise them in the light of your experience. And other people's experience. Today's truth could be tomorrow's exploded theory. You have to be alert to the possibility that your sacred beliefs can die on you. And when they do die, you have to admit as much.'

That made Jack think of all the bigots he knew – villains, policemen, the pious men of faith, too; they had their certainties and they hung on to them, regardless of whether they were still valid or not, alive or dead.

He wouldn't be like that, he swore. Not any more. When he got out of Barlinnie he would be a different man. A broader man. He'd be someone who could embrace and appreciate the wider joys of life.

Three days before he was due to leave prison, Dougie came to see him. He was agitated.

'Jack, you're goin' to have to be careful when you get out. Word about the date's got round. There's some men want to settle scores with you.'

'The Baltic Gang?'

Dougie nodded.

'They're strong again,' he said. 'An' nastier than they've ever been. They've targeted ye because of what happened to Milroy, an' Bulloch, an' because of one or two other things. They've put the word round their members. They're gettin' ready, Jack.'

'What's the score?'

'When ye get out of here, they're goin' to kill you.'

Jack considered that. It seemed to him that Dougie was talking about somebody else, not him.

'Thanks for warning me, Dougie.'

'Ah would have preferred to bring good news,' the old man sighed.

When Jack got back to his cell he sat staring at his shelves of books, trying to remember the hard, narrow man he had been before he came in here. The midbrain man. That character would have to be summoned back from his slumbers. He would need to be resurrected and set at the ready.

Rule One: Know the worst that might happen; be ready for it.

If Hatchet Jack didn't re-appear, it would be curtains. It could be curtains, anyway.

He lay back on his bed and closed his eyes. A sad certainty dawned, and it had to be faced: the new, broader man and the wider joys would have to hang about in the wings for a while.

TEN

He was released early in the morning, a June day that promised to be warm. There was a pale damp mist, a gossamer scrim clinging to trees and rolling silently over grass. No one was waiting. No one he could see. He walked down the road from the prison gates, stopping to look round every couple of minutes, caught halfway between the novelty of being out and the possible imminence of attack.

He saw a taxi and hailed it.

'Glasgow Green,' he told the driver, settling in the back with his kit bag on his lap.

'Just get out, did ye?' the driver said as they pulled away.

'That's right.'

'I can always tell. Ye get that funny kinda pale-yellow look in there. But don't worry, son. It'll wear off.'

Jack gazed as the city's outskirts sped past. Rusted railings, bent and twisted, made eerie sculptures in front of ruined gardens. Blind-eyed rows of condemned council houses sat like serried fossils, waiting to be catalogued. As they turned on to a long main road he realised something: the old grey-red stone of the buildings, the green-painted doors, the battered red pillar boxes – all of it, the mundane drabness, was the signature of this part of the city. It added up to something as individual and unchanging as a fingerprint. He had missed it, without knowing he had.

Glasgow in peace time didn't look much different from the way it did before he went inside. Except there weren't any barrage balloons hanging in the air. Getting nearer the city centre he noticed new shops, and the office windows weren't taped and blacked-out any more. The taxi stopped outside the city mortuary on the Saltmarket, opposite the gates of Glasgow Green.

'Have this one on me,' the driver said as Jack went to pay him. 'An' the best of luck, pal.'

Jack stood on the edge of the pavement for a while, just looking. Four years' absence had distorted his memory. The road was narrower than he recalled. The High Court building, standing next to the mortuary, wasn't nearly as big or imposing as he'd expected. He strolled towards it, stood on the front steps for a minute and gazed at the pillars. The last time he was in the city this had been the place they'd taken him from, by the back entrance, in a van that only let him see segments of sky and buildings through slits in its armoured sides. It felt odd to stand there now, knowing he didn't have to hide anything from the people who sat in this place, altering lives. He had paid for everything. His secrets were written off.

An important secret had brought him here. He crossed the road, looked around him casually, making sure he wasn't being followed. Going through the gates he jumped back sharply when a man reared up in front of him, arms outstretched. It was only an old meths drinker bumming a cigarette. Jack gave him a couple of Player's and accepted his copious blessings with a smile.

In case he *was* being watched, he decided to walk right round the park, playing the liberated man, breathing deeply and relishing the space. After half an hour of that it looked legitimate enough when he crossed the grass towards the carriageway and flopped down, panting. Sitting with his elbows on his knees, he eye-counted the oblong black stones along the grass verge. Taking the stone by the waste bin as number one, he located number eight and stared at it. It looked as ordinary as ever. It hadn't been disturbed. Why should anybody move it, after all? Many a night in prison he had imagined coming back here to find all the edging stones gone and a concrete strip in their place.

He only had to reach out and loosen the stone. It was socketed into earth and it would be hard to move, but it was no big job, it would be done in a minute. But Jack wondered . . .

He looked about him. It was early yet, there was hardly a soul about. But he still wondered. There was no saying who could see him. He had hidden among these trees when he was a kid; it was easy to make yourself invisible. Then he thought, to hell with it, he wasn't going to hang about any longer than he could help. He took off his coat and spread it out on the grass, as if he was making himself a groundsheet. One corner of it covered stone number eight. Pretending to smooth out the wrinkles, fussing with the folds, he got both hands on the stone through the fabric and gripped fiercely. He tugged, stopped, looked around and tugged again. It moved, but not much. He decided to wait a minute, lighting a cigarette, puffing thoughtfully, then he got a grip and tugged again. This time he got it halfway out of the damp socket. He looked over his shoulder and saw a man coming towards him across the grass. He was young and lean. The eyes were determined. Jack stiffened, got himself ready to spring.

'Have ye got a light, Jimmy?'

This had the makings of farce. Jack gave him a light and lay back on the coat for a while, waiting until there was no one at all in sight.

Right, he told himself, *get the job done and let's be out of it*.

On his knees again he gripped the stone and heaved mightily. It came clean out of the ground with a sucking noise. He dropped it on the grass under his coat and slid his hand down into the hole. He felt cold metal and fished out the box. He couldn't stop himself smiling. It had been down there since 1941. He had deposited it after dark one night, on a half-drunk whim, because he'd always liked the notion of having valuables stashed away for emergency purposes all over the city. As it happened this was the only stash he'd ever got around to establishing. But he thanked God for it, all the same. Whistling softly, looking about him again, he slid the box into the coat pocket, stood up and put the coat on.

He left the park the way he had come in. The mist had lifted now and the sun was getting warm. It felt good. He could have sat on a bench and baked himself for an hour, if he hadn't felt that would be suicidal.

On the corner of the Bridgegate he stopped, took the box from his pocket and prised open the lid. It was an airtight tobacco box and he could actually smell the dryness of the paper as the lid came off. He flipped out the wad, squeezed it from affection and gratitude for its existence. A hundred pounds. A man could go a fair distance on that.

Putting the money in his inside pocket and dropping the tin in a waste bin, he sauntered along to the Cockit Hat. Another swift reconnoitre – right, left, behind – then he slipped down the passage between the pub and the cobbler's shop. He let himself into the pub yard. He knocked sharply on the back door and waited.

After a minute Dougie opened the door a crack. When he saw Jack he pulled it wide and waved him in.

'Did anybody see ye?' he said, shutting the door again.

'Who knows?'

They went through to the bar. The jolt of recognition astonished Jack with its force. Not a thing had changed, it was like he'd slipped back in time. Even the smell was the same, the mature blend of beer, old tobacco smoke and a trace of mouldering timber.

'Christ, Dougie . . .' He looked, seeing the old tables, the sturdy no-nonsense chairs. 'It's good to be back.'

'Aye, I suppose it must be.' Dougie went behind the bar and jammed a glass under the whisky optic. 'But ye'd better not stay.'

'I know. Did you manage to get the things I wanted?'

Dougie nodded, putting the whisky in front of Jack.

'It's all in a sack behind the back door there.' Dougie

looked at the little bag Jack was holding. 'Is that all ye've got?'

'All I have in the world. That and a few quid to see me right until I get fixed up.'

'Did ye not get tae keep anythin'? Did they take the lot?'

'Everything. Four confiscation orders did it. Special wartime powers. They even took my clothes.'

Dougie tut-tutted.

'The polis are shite, aren't they?'

He turned to the optic with another glass for himself.

'So ye're startin' from scratch. That must be murder. Considerin' where ye were, what ye had.'

'At least I know the ropes in advance, Dougie. I know the mistakes I won't make next time.'

'Where'll ye go?'

'I thought about it a bit. It's either Birmingham or London. I don't think it'd be healthy for me to stay in Scotland.'

'Well . . .' Dougie turned with his glass and raised it. 'Here's tae ye, Jack. All the best.'

Jack stayed for one more drink, then he left, giving Dougie a big hug and remembering to take the sack from behind the door as he went.

The streets were busier now. It was easy to blend with the crowd, but it was easy to be watched and followed, too, without knowing it was happening.

He walked as far as Glasgow Cross and did a slow scanning reconnaissance. His heart sank. There were two of them by the horse trough across the road, sitting there watching him. McPhail and Logan, Baltic men. He turned left on to the Trongate and saw a third man, Proudfoot, walking eight or nine yards ahead. Jack didn't need to look behind him. He knew he'd be surrounded by now.

On Argyle Street he crossed the road with a crowd of other people and saw Proudfoot glance round and nip into the traffic, maintaining his position and distance. Jack turned up Queen Street, striding smartly, then stopped to look in the window of Tam Shepherd's joke and magic shop. One sharp glance to the left and he got the message. There were three of them at the end of the street. He looked right. Another three. He tried to estimate how long it would take him to run from here to the Central Station. Too long, he decided.

If he tried to get back on to Argyle Street they would jump him. If he went further along Queen Street he'd be in quiet territory and the upshot would be the same. So he walked on for half a block, then dodged into a dark close. He ran to the far end, getting himself into the shadows under the stairs. He put down his bags, flipped open the sack and pulled out a hatchet. It had been a long time since he'd held one, and this was no specialist job. Still, it had an old familiar feel. It put hope in him. He took out another hatchet and crouched with one in each hand, waiting.

Three of them came to the mouth of the close at once, crowding the opening. They were trying to look casual, drawing no attention from the passers-by. Then, in unison, they came into the close.

Jack saw them as clear silhouettes. He drew back his right hand, tensed the arm, letting them get a yard closer. His arm jerked forward. The hatchet flew straight at its target. On its second spin the blade struck the middle man between the eyes. He screamed and went down.

Jack grabbed his bags and dashed out from under the stairs. The other two were still confused, staring at their mate on the ground. They turned to face Jack too late. He swung the hatchet right and left and right, fracturing a skull, a jaw, and slicing halfway into a nose. He ran out on to the street, saw three other men waiting ten yards away. He ran the opposite way, up Queen Street, getting a warning signal as he went. There was a bread van with a big dent in its side. He'd seen it cruising near him on Argyle Street. Now here it was, going up the road ahead of him.

At the corner the van slowed. Jack could hear the other three coming behind him, their feet pounding the pavement. He stopped, looked at the van, decided to take the only opening. It was a narrow passageway between a building and a new brick wall.

He was halfway along the passage when he realised there was no way out. No gate, no stairs. Just a high wall, too high to climb. Jack ran all the way to the end, dropped the bags and got his back to the bricks. There were two hatchets in the sack, one in his hand. With a bit of luck that would be enough. He braced himself, a hatchet in each hand as before, panting, ready.

When they came for him he felt the odds slip. One had a bayonet. The other two were pulling hatchets out of their belts.

The bastards can still learn from their betters . . .

They were coming at him too fast. Jack realised he had blundered. He hadn't allowed himself time to get set, to aim and throw. They came rushing along the narrow passage and the one with the bayonet had it at the ready angle, the precise angle to shove it right through his chest.

Then an incredible thing happened. Six feet from where Jack stood the wall caved in. He shielded his face as bricks and cement flew round him. As the dust cleared he saw the back of the bread van sticking into the gap.

'Get in!' A voice roared from the cab. 'Get in the back of the van! Hurry!'

For one frozen second Jack did nothing. Then he sprang forward, dragging his bags, hearing the three men shouting and banging on the other side of the van. He threw himself up over the tailgate and landed on the back on the floor. The van was off and careering along St Vincent Street before he scrambled to his knees. He braced himself on the side panel and moved up to the back of the cab. He stuck his head through the gap. The driver turned briefly to wink at him.

'Jesus Christ,' Jack said. 'Mr Rossini, if I'm not mistaken.'

'At your service.'

Rossini drove on for another five minutes, taking back turnings at breakneck speed, throwing Jack all over the back of the van. Finally he stopped and shouted for Jack to get out.

They were in a back court with double gates.

'My brother will get rid of the van,' Rossini said. He pointed to a car parked in the corner. 'That is mine. I will take you to where you need to go.'

Jack looked at him, taking in the stylish clothes, the fatter frame. He had heard Rossini was doing well. He was still in the ice-cream game, but mostly as a cover for more profitable operations.

'You saved my life, you know.'

'I know. I owed you a favour. I heard what was to happen today. So I hung around, watched and waited. This van came in handy.' Rossini shrugged. 'If it hadn't been there, I would have thought of something else.' He slapped Jack's arm. 'Come on. You should get away from Glasgow. The climate is very unhealthy.'

They got in the car and Rossini tooled it out through the back gate, driving with flamboyant sweeps of his arms as he careered along the back streets. They were out on the road to Uddingston before he spoke again.

'How do you think my English is coming along, Mr Kane?'

'It's very good. You look like a millionaire, too. Everything's working out, eh?'

'A fair treat, as they say in Maryhill.' Rossini turned and flashed a smile at Jack. 'I'm glad you have to leave Glasgow. The way things are, we would be enemies before long.'

'You think so?'

'I'm sure of it. But you *are* leaving, so the matter does not arise. No problem. You go your way, I go mine.'

Jack saw the Glasgow boundary sign go past.

'Where are you taking me?'

'Motherwell. From there you can take a train to London. No danger of getting cut to bits on the platform while you wait.'

'I hadn't definitely settled on London,' Jack said. 'It was to be a toss-up between there or Birmingham.'

'Go to London,' Rossini said. 'It's further. And it's easier to hide there, if you ever need to.'

'Cheers,' Jack said, smiling. 'I'll give it a go.'

PART TWO

LONDON: 1951–1973

ELEVEN

'The big trouble with women,' Frog Mitchison said huskily, 'is they're greedy. Give them one toffee and they want the whole bloody bag.'

Mondays weren't easy for him. Each one was a replay. Trouble seemed to wait behind the door and jump him when he came into the office on a Monday morning. Headaches accumulated over the weekend and this was always clearing-up day. Frog Mitchison hated Mondays as much as he loathed fat women.

This Monday a particular fat woman was one of the problems. Hettie Wiseman was as broad as she was tall, and she was very vocal with it. For three months she had been warning that if conditions in the Purple Parrot didn't improve she would withdraw the girls' labour. This morning she had told Billy Sims, Frog's right hand man, that she wasn't opening the place again until the heating was fixed, the broken toilets were mended, a decent cleaner was found and a regular bouncer was put on the front door.

'She's puttin' her foot down,' Billy said. 'I couldn't get past the doorstep. She stuck her head out and told me to pass on the word – you either get the place sorted out, or it stays shut.'

'Did you get the weekend take?'

'She wouldn't give it me.'

'Bloody stroll on . . .'

Frog stood by the mirror nailed to the wall beside his desk. He patted his oiled black hair and centred the knot in his yellow-and-green silk tie. Somebody once told him he looked like George Raft and he checked regularly to see if the similarity was intact.

'How much do you reckon it would cost to get that gaff sorted out, then?'

Billy shrugged. He didn't know about the cost of things. He didn't know much at all, apart from how to win regularly on a certain make of pinball machine that had a design defect. Billy could scarcely read or write and until Frog took him on he hadn't held a job for longer than six weeks at a time. He worked for Frog because he was his brother-in-law. Frog's wife Sharon, another whining bitch running to fat, had insisted that her kid brother be given a chance to develop his talents.

'I don't suppose a plumber's time would come to much,' he said. 'Nor an electrician's. But the cost of the stuff could be a crippler. I mean they've got a toilet bowl wants replacin', two of the cisterns don't work and them radiators are knackered. The wires are all buggered up, too. You could be talkin' a fair packet, Frog.'

'Would Hettie settle for a cleaner an' a bouncer, for now?'

'I could ask her.'

It was Billy's turn at the mirror. He was only twenty-three but most of his hair had gone. He affected a ruffled style to cover the bare scalp, which it did in dark places like the Purple Parrot. In the bright morning light of the office, pink skin glowed distinctly through the thin covering. He teased the strands for a minute, then gave up.

'Where'll you get a bouncer?'

'I'll ask around. There's bound to be some handy lad that could use a few bob on the side.'

'None of them ever last with Hettie,' Billy said. 'She nags them.'

'She nags everybody, the cow.' Frog sat down behind the desk. 'Go round and see her this afternoon and tell her we're on a plumber's waitin' list. An electrician's, too. Tell her I'll get a bouncer and a cleaner this week some time.' He folded his hands on the desk's bare plywood top. 'What's next?'

'Gareth only collected thirty-five quid on Saturday.'

'How much should it have been?'

'Fifty.'

'So what's the problem?'

'People are backslidin' on the repayments,' Billy said. 'He reckons one or two of them have skipped the district.'

'But Gareth knows how to handle that kind of thing. If a punter doesn't keep up the payments, he gets a sharp reminder.'

'Yeah – but what about that one that went to the police? Shook Gareth up, that did. He thought he was goin' to get nicked.'

'I don't know what this outfit's comin' to,' Frog sighed. 'Like a bunch of old women, we are.' He slapped the desk sharply, a decisive gesture he made when he wasn't sure about something. 'I'll talk to Gareth myself. Anythin' else?'

'That bloke was round again on Saturday mornin'.'

'What bloke?'

Frog's eyes didn't show curiosity. They showed mild hope, hope that Billy wasn't talking about who Frog thought he was talking about.

'The jock. Kane. I told him you were out of town and you wouldn't be back for a while. I don't think he believed me.'

'What does he want with me, for Christ's sake? I can't be bothered with haggis bashers comin' in here wastin' my time.'

Frog had heard about Jack Kane two years before, when the wages department of a laundry on the Camberwell New Road was knocked over. Three thousand pounds was snatched. The police never made an arrest, but the grapevine was certain Hatchet Jack Kane had done the job – him and his sidekick Martin Weir, another Scottish tearaway. What held Frog's troubled interest about the laundry job was the violence of the operation. A lot of people got hurt. Guns had been in evidence. There hadn't been anything like that in this part of London since before the war. It made Frog uneasy to think there was an outfit like Kane's so close to the perimeter of his own operation. Kane's name had come up regularly since the laundry job: there had been more robberies, warehouse burglaries, a bank job and a flurry of reports about street bookies being trounced and fleeced. Frog didn't want anything to do with Jack Kane. But he had been to the office three times asking to see Frog. It could only be a matter of time before they met. Frog tried hard to avoid facing the likelihood.

'I've got a busy day ahead of me,' he said now, suddenly impatient to be out of the office. 'Can you handle things while I'm out?'

'I suppose so.'

'Right.' Frog got up and took his black overcoat with the padded shoulders off the back of the door. 'If I'm wanted and it's a real emergency, I'll be at The Dominoes. We're workin' out the details of our Sharon's surprise birthday bash on Saturday. You got her a present yet?'

'Not yet,' Billy said. 'I'll get somethin' by Saturday, though.'

'You better. She's your sister, remember. It's her thirty-fifth, a bit of a milestone. Be sure and get her a card, too.'

'Yeah, don't worry. What're you givin' her?'

Frog shrugged. His wife had most things a woman needed and most of the luxuries besides.

'Jewellery, I suppose. Somethin' tasty. She's always goin' on about a charm bracelet. Maybe I'll get her one of those.' Frog opened the door. 'Remember to go and see Hettie. I want that gaff open for business by seven tonight.'

As he left the building and stepped out on to Elmington Place he was watched from a car parked ten yards away.

Martin Weir, sitting behind the wheel, nudged Jack Kane, who was reading a paper.

'There he goes.'

Jack lowered the paper and watched Frog cross the road.

'I'll let him get clear, then I'll go up.' He yawned and

190

stretched. 'Deary me. I could use a decent sleep, Martin. I don't know when I last had eight uninterrupted hours.'

'Well, if you *will* have kids . . .'

Martin wasn't married. He was a tall, gauntly handsome man, well-spoken and always immaculately dressed. He had a noticeably fastidious manner when he was around women, but the truth was he didn't like them as people. Not that he liked men much, either. He had let it slip that he could survive happily without other people, in fact he would prefer that, although he valued his friendship with Jack Kane.

'Young Frank's as good as gold,' Jack said. 'He sleeps all night, now. It's Danny. He wakes up at three every morning. Never drops off again before half-past.' He opened the car door and stepped out. 'I'll be less than five minutes,' he promised.

As he climbed the stairs to Frog Mitchison's office he rehearsed the stiff unsmiling approach, remembering that it made people nervous when he stared at them. As time passed, he tended to forget the components of menace. He had to remind himself and make an effort to do what used to come naturally. Reaching the door he squared his shoulders and knocked once. This was the fourth visit, timed like the others to occur when Frog was off the premises. By now, Jack believed, the croaky little villain would be getting very jumpy.

The door opened. Billy took an instinctive step back.

'Mr Mitchison isn't here'

'Again? Is he ever here?'

'Not often,' Billy said, and swallowed. 'Maybe if I could give him a message . . .'

'You can tell him I want to see him. It's important. And I want to see him soon. It's not something that can wait indefinitely. Will you tell him that?'

'Oh sure, Mr Kane. Definitely.' Billy licked his lips. 'Is there any place he can find you?'

Jack shook his head.

'Is there any place I can find *him*?'

Billy thought about what Frog had said – *if it's a real*

emergency . . . Maybe this fell into the emergency category. Besides, Billy didn't like giving this man negative answers all the time. It didn't please him, and those eyes of his could turn very hard . . .

'I think he's goin' to be at The Dominoes today. He's havin' a surprise birthday do for his wife there on Saturday – they're goin' over the details and stuff like that.'

Billy hoped he hadn't dropped Frog in it. At least Kane looked less displeased with that answer than he did before.

'Fine,' Jack said. 'I might just look in on him.'

He went back to the car and got in.

'I think we'll talk to Mitchison on Saturday,' he said.

At the beginning it hadn't been easy. London was an alien city, vast and unknown, desperately unfriendly. Jack had never been in a place where he was made to feel so much like a foreigner. He spoke his words properly and with care, but people still said 'You're Scottish, aren't you?' and in pubs the barmen always called him Jock. They seemed committed to reminding him of his outside status, and a lot of people were hostile solely on the grounds of his nationality. In the first week he had a fight with a man who called him a Scotch git, and not long after that he had to lay out another one who made a crack about jocks getting their jollies wearing tartan skirts and pretending they were different from women's clothes.

For a month Jack was determined to go straight. He wanted to do an honest job where he could earn enough money to be comfortable, with enough free time to develop the fuller life he had promised himself. He wanted to improve his mind. He was sure it was a mind worth improving. Surely it was a crime to leave it undeveloped. Life, after all, had to be about more than conflict.

By the second month he had learned that a vital part of the fuller, wider life was communication. He needed somebody to talk to, somebody who would listen to him and tell him things, a companion in the process of embracing art, culture, and constructive thought. But there was no Uncle Brian in London.

Work was a problem, too. He had to take a menial job, and while he didn't mind hard work he found the boredom difficult to handle, and the wages were poor. A crisis occurred when he lost his wallet with the remainder of his £100 capital.

He was poor now, one of the faceless strugglers, a grey person indistinguishable from the ones around him. And entirely without contact. The weekend he lost his wallet the landlord announced that the rent was going up, and in future the gas meter would only accept two-shilling pieces. Jack went to bed when it got cold, rather than squander his precious pennies on gas. One night, lying there thinking things over, he began to remember the fine nights in Glasgow when he could go into any restaurant or hotel bar and order whatever he wanted, without considering the cost. It had been the same with clothes: he bought what he liked, the price wasn't a factor in his selection. He could think of a dozen things he had done regularly, all of them fulfilling, all of them dependent on a decent supply of cash.

He asked himself a question: what do you want? A tough time? Living on toast and beans and improving your mind to no apparently good end? Or do you want what you had before, the mindless pursuit of the comfortable life, without money worries, without having to do what you're told?

The answer was ready and waiting before he'd finished asking himself the question. He got out of bed, put on a warm sweater and a donkey jacket, then went for a trip on the Underground.

The job took two hours. On the embankment at Charing Cross he sat on a bench and counted his takings. He had £67. For two hours' work. If it could be called work. All he did was spot the well-off looking characters on the tube and got close to them. He dipped four in all. It was easy, miles easier than it had been in Glasgow. People might be cold and aloof down here, but they were more trusting, they kept their money where it was easy to reach.

He gave up his job and moved back into villainy full time. On the matter of mind-improvement he settled for a compromise: he would pick up what he could whenever he could, but he would never let it get in the way of situation-improvement. He'd had a taste of being hard-up in London and he didn't want to repeat the experience.

For six weeks he worked every day, from the morning rush-hour to early evening, travelling round London on buses and the Underground, being careful not to stay too long in any one area. He didn't restrict his activities to pocket-picking: tucked away on dark streets there were plenty of prosperous little shops that yielded up cash and negotiable goods. By late November he had amassed nearly a thousand pounds. It never stopped amazing him how much cash people carried on them or left lying about. London was crammed with unintentional benefactors.

By nine o'clock on Saturday night the main room at The Dominoes was packed with people, most of them dressed up in party attire, gathered to convey their good wishes and get plastered at Frog Mitchison's expense. Long trestle tables had been set up along one wall and covered with plates and platters of buffet food. The bar took up the length of the opposite wall. In the dance area a six-piece band played current hits under the revolving glitter ball.

Frog was at the door, welcoming guests. His wife, Sharon, who had known about the surprise party all along – because, as she'd told her sister, her thicko of a husband could keep nothing secret – stood with her twelve-year-old daughter at the opposite end of the room from the band. She smiled graciously, showing her large teeth as she accepted gifts and congratulations from people she hardly knew.

Given her own way, she would have spent the night with her mum and dad in Walthamstow. She hated the people who revolved around Frog, she hated his business and his whole rubbishy way of life. The older she got, the more she wondered how she'd been daft enough to get hitched to an ineffectual counterfeit of a man called Frog. She never called him that but it seemed everybody else did. He was saddled with the name because of a cut-throat wound he got in a teenage gang fight; his larynx had been injured and now he talked funny, like a frog. Once, long ago, Sharon had thought his throaty tones were sexy. Once, long ago, she had thought a lot of things she didn't think now.

'My feet are killin' me in these shoes,' she muttered to her daughter. 'First chance I get I'm slippin' them off.' She craned her neck, trying to see past the throng of guests. 'What's your dad poncin' about at? I feel like a bloody lemon stood here. Some birthday this is.'

'Can I go and get somethin' to eat, Mum?' the child said.

'Go ahead. Let me stand here on my todd. Serves me right for comin' in the first place.'

Frog came into sight, grinning and winking, waving and shaking hands as he made a weaving progress through the bodies to where Sharon stood. He was in his element, she thought. He lapped this up. The birthday party was only an excuse for him to invite all these people to come and feed his delusions about himself. The sad part, the really pathetic part, was that he couldn't see how they despised him. He was a joke and he'd be the last one to know.

He finally reached her.

'All right, love?' He kissed Sharon's cheek. 'Havin' a good time?'

'I've had better times queuin' at the butcher's.'

'Aw, come on, now. You're the party girl tonight. This is all for you, remember. Have another drink and get in the spirit of things.'

'I don't think one more drink'll do it,' Sharon murmured. 'Get me a bottle and I'll see what I can do.'

She glanced towards the door and saw a good-looking man in a smart lounge suit standing there. He didn't match the rest of the crowd, he wasn't flash, he wasn't shifty or seedy. He was staring at her. Or at Frog. There was another good-looker standing just behind him, taller, just as well dressed. He was staring, too.

'Who are those two?' she asked Frog.

'Who?'

He looked. His eyes narrowed and he muttered something under his breath.

'Let me guess,' Sharon said. 'The only two decent lookin' blokes who show up turn out to be gate-crashers, right?'

'Jack Kane and Martin Weir,' Frog said.

Sharon looked impressed. She stared back at the two men, absently touching her hair.

'You know them, do you? They're pretty dangerous people, by all accounts.'

'They're rubbish,' Frog snapped.

'Maybe you should throw them out, then.'

'Don't get smart, Sharon. I can do without you takin' the piss, just this once.'

Kane and Weir were making their way through the guests, keeping their eyes on Frog.

'Christ,' he breathed.

As Jack came forward he smiled at Sharon. She smiled back and touched her hair again.

'I didn't realise there was a party on tonight,' he said. 'The man on the door explained.' He held out his hand. 'I'm Jack Kane. Many happy returns, Mrs Mitchison.' He took her hand and squeezed it gently, then turned to Frog. 'We haven't met before, Mr Mitchison. But I've been trying to get in touch with you. You're a hard man to catch.' He gestured towards Martin. 'This is my associate, Mr Weir.' Martin nodded, staying a couple of paces behind Jack. 'I wonder if we could have a quick word, Mr Mitchison.'

Frog was doing his best to look put out.

'This *is* a party,' he said, fingering his bow tie. 'I don't think it's quite the time – '

'Only a quick word, as I said,' Jack interrupted.

'Go ahead,' Sharon told Frog, enjoying his discomfort. 'I don't mind.'

'I can give you five minutes,' Frog mumbled.

'Fine.' Jack smiled at Sharon again. 'Excuse us, won't you?'

They went to a quiet corner at the back of the room. Martin stood to one side, hands behind his back, staring at Frog as Jack addressed him.

'We'd like to talk to you about your territory.'

Even under the coloured lights Frog looked pale.

'My territory? What territory?'

'Your patch,' Jack said. 'Your turf.'

'I'm not sure I know what you're talkin' about. You're not confusin' me with somebody else, are you?'

'No,' Jack said, 'we wouldn't be likely to do that. We're too careful about our homework to make mistakes.'

Frog Mitchison first came under their scrutiny in the autumn of 1950. After a preliminary survey Martin had announced that the man was a clown. 'He inherited a wedge of Dartford from his old man four or five years ago. And it's his dad's reputation that's kept it under control ever since. Old Mitchison was a hard man, by all accounts. He was the unforgiving kind. Nowadays people on the patch submit out of habit. But Frog hasn't got what his father had, and he's losing ground. He hasn't the guts or the style to run a territory. The right people could walk in and take that stretch off him.' They were agreed that the territory was well placed. It could be just what they needed.

'I don't talk to strangers about my business,' Frog said.

Jack smiled.

'Make an exception with us. You don't have to do any talking, anyway. Just listen.' He moved a fraction closer, keeping his eyes locked on Frog's. 'We're in management, Mr Weir and me. I think I can say we're experts.'

'Oh you can, can you?' Frog said, trying for a sneer but only managing to look sick.

'Management's a very broad term, of course,' Jack said. 'It means different things in different situations. Where

197

your territory's concerned, it would mean us taking over the running of it on your behalf. Making it more efficient and profitable, expanding its borders, that kind of thing. We're prepared to do that on a percentage basis.' Jack spread his hands. 'That's it. That's the proposition. What do you think?'

'I think *you* must think I'm crackers,' Frog said.

Jack feigned puzzlement.

'I don't follow you,' he said.

'Do me a favour, mate – just piss off, the pair of you.'

'Oh, come on now, there's no need to be unfriendly about this . . .'

'Unfriendly?' Frog was shaking. 'If you want to see unfriendly, take a look at them two big lads on the door. They work for me. They're what I call unfriendly.'

'What are you trying to tell us?' Martin said.

'I don't want no trespassers, that's what. I'm quite happy with my territory, as you call it. It's runnin' fine, it don't need no help.'

'Well, that's a matter of opinion,' Jack said. 'Incidentally, one thing I should have mentioned straight away is that we provide insurance as part of the service.'

Frog's eyes widened. He looked from Jack to Martin and back to Jack again.

'Don't you fuckin' threaten me!'

'Shh.' Jack put a finger to his lips. He reached out and patted Frog's shoulder gently. 'People can hear. You don't want to spoil your wife's party, do you?'

'You're the ones bloody spoilin' it, comin' in here with your threats.'

'You're going off the deep end for no reason at all,' Jack said. 'We're not here to theaten you. We came with a business proposition. We've put it to you, and we'll go now. I can see you need time to think things over before you give us an answer.'

'You've got my answer,' Frog said. 'Keep off.'

'I'll drop by and see you some time in the week,' Jack said.

'Don't bother!'

Jack turned and walked away. Martin followed him. They nodded to Sharon as they passed.

'You've turned all pasty,' she said as Frog came back. 'Has somebody been frightenin' my little tough guy?'

'Just shut it,' he said, watching Jack and Martin thread their way out.

When they left The Dominoes they crossed the road to a friendly-looking pub and had a swift pint each. The beer was so good they decided to have another one. They sat down with their drinks at a table near the door.

'What's his best earner?' Jack asked Martin.

'I'm not sure. He's got nothing really big. It's all bitty, know what I mean? A wee money-lending racket, a wee bit of lifting and shifting, the wee club we've just been in, a wee brothel on Turner's Road. It all adds up, I suppose. But it's half-arsed.'

Jack sat back, drumming his fingers on the table.

'He's got a warehouse, I suppose?'

Martin nodded.

'Do it over, then. Take two of the lads with you early tomorrow morning. Don't make any noise. Let it come as a surprise to him. Then I'll go and see him on Tuesday.' Jack sipped his beer. 'He's got a brothel, did you say?'

'Aye, it was his father's first business, apparently. The madam, if you can call her that, was one of the girls that worked there before the war. Tough old biddy, she is. Keeps the punters well in line.'

'I was thinking . . .'

'Don't tell me you fancy having one of Frog's women? Christ, Jack, you should see them. Pigs with knickers on.'

'No, nothing like that. I was thinking the brothel might be something to keep my missus quiet.'

They looked at each other.

'Are you serious?'

'Sure I am,' Jack said. 'Our Queenie would make a good madam. The job would stop her interfering, that's the point. She shoves her nose into everything I do just lately. You must have noticed.'

'It's not my place to say.'

'Feel free to pass any comment you like, Martin. Would you not say she's itching to get in on the business?'

'Well . . .'

'Of course she is. The kids don't keep her busy enough. She's bored. So if I hand her the knocking shop and tell her I want to see it tightened up and run on profitable lines, she'll have her hands full, and I'll get a bit of peace.' He thought about the scenario again, then nodded sharply. 'Yes, I like the idea. It'd suit me just fine. I don't mind having a place like that, but I don't want anything to do with the running of it.'

'Queenie'll have a job getting old Hettie Wiseman to hand over the reins. She runs the place like it's her own. None of Frog's men like going there, she's forever shouting and threatening.'

'That'll be no problem for Queenie,' Jack said. 'She's a handy battler when she has to be – and she's at her best when she's up against another woman. Red in tooth and claw, Martin, with a voice like a rag man's trumpet.'

They finished their drinks and left. The party across at The Dominoes was hotting up as they passed. The music was louder than before; women were yelling and screaming and somebody was bursting balloons. Jack pictured Frog at the centre of it all, pale and distracted.

'I actually felt a bit sorry for him,' he said as he got in the car.

Martin laughed.

'Getting a conscience in your old age, are you?'

Jack peered through the window at the lighted front of the club.

'It's funny you should say that,' he murmured.

TWELVE

Jack had met Queenie in November of 1946. He was to realise, later, that she had been the first person in London to show him a spontaneously friendly face.

He met her in a dance hall, the Hammersmith Palais. He was taken straight away by her brassy, open charm, her energy and complete absence of coyness. There were dozens of girls there, but she was the only one he could see. After watching her for a while he screwed up the courage to ask her if she would have a dance with him. She said yes. They danced with each other for the rest of the night. Jack learned that Queenie was thirty, the same age as he was; she had grown up in Rotherhithe and now lived in Camberwell; she was a twin – her sister lived in Australia – she worked in a dress shop, and she was single because she didn't like the idea of being tied down. Judging by the way she moved against him when they danced, she liked Jack a lot.

The following weeks reminded him of Airchie's whirlwind courting of Jessica. He took Queenie everywhere and spent money on her with a spirited abandon that topped anything she had ever known. She was spellbound by his muscular charm, his quick humour, his cash. It wasn't long before she told Jack she loved him. He said he loved her too, although he wasn't sure if it really went that deep. She was good in bed and great fun to be with. Maybe that was love. He didn't know, but whatever it was, it was enough.

They spent Christmas at a hotel in Torquay. While they were there Jack told her about his past – not all of it, but he did tell her about prison, and about the days before then when he had his own sizable share of Glasgow's black market. Queenie was delighted. She confessed an unashamed admiration for successful criminals.

'I'll be straight with you, Jack,' she said. 'I've been out with one or two of them in my time. Real gentlemen they were, without a word of a lie. Half the villains in this town aren't as black as they're painted, and that's a fact.'

She went on to tell him that she'd found out her real father – not the man she had grown up calling Dad – had been a full-time villain from the East End. The truth, the rock-bottom truth, was that she had grown up knowing more criminals than any other kind of people.

Jack wondered if fate had a hand in their meeting. On reflection he decided he didn't believe in fate. Not very much, anyway. Meeting her had been a stroke of luck, that was all.

Late in February 1947 Queenie announced she was pregnant. So that was that. They were married – she didn't mind marriage now, since she didn't feel Jack would tie her down – and they moved into a roomy old terrace house in Camberwell. Their son Frank was born in August.

Meanwhile Jack had embarked locally on a modest criminal career – shop and warehouse burglary, bookmaking – until he met up with another Scottish escapee, a former safe-blower and gang enforcer from Edinburgh called Martin Weir. Martin had fled Edinburgh seven months earlier, when he learned he was on the target lists of three different gangs.

Martin had heard of Jack. 'Stories used to drift across from Glasgow about you,' he said. 'You were a bit of a folk-hero to the younger neds.' Martin was drifting at the time Jack met him; he said he worked best when he was directed. They got on well together and collaborated on a couple of jobs. Finally they joined forces, Martin falling comfortably into the role of lieutenant. They put together a modest team. Their goal, whenever the chance came along, was to control their own territory. History could be made to repeat itself, Jack said; this time he would avoid the bad moves.

Jack's second son, Danny, was born in April 1949. By that time the Kanes were living in an even bigger house, with Martin occupying the second floor. In 1951 they were still there, but Jack had warned Queenie to expect another move, quite soon.

'Rotherhithe,' he said, knowing the decision would please her. 'Back where your roots are.'

She was pleased, all right. But why was he doing it?

'I want to carve out a decent chunk of London,' Jack explained. 'But I don't want it stretching out away from us, like it's doing right now. I want to go and stay where our final boundary will be, and then take in all the ground that leads from here to there.'

'What do you want to do it like that for?' Queenie asked him.

'Just a funny notion I've got. Something tells me it'll be easier to do it that way.'

Another funny notion. Sometimes Queenie wondered about Jack. He had changed in the five years they had been married. He admitted it.

'In the old days,' he told her, 'what I was outside was exactly what I was inside. But now it's not. Inside, I'm a different man.'

'What way are you different?'

He shrugged.

'Just different,' he said.

The plans for annexing Frog Mitchison's territory went ahead at speed. Jack wanted that piece of Dartford firmly under his control before he turned his attention to an upcoming money-spinner, the Festival of Britain.

Frog was badly shaken when his warehouse got wrecked. But he still resisted Jack's overtures. He even issued a couple of threats of his own. Thinking it over afterwards, Jack decided that Frog's one open attempt at resistance could be put down to acute desperation while the balance of his mind was disturbed. The attempt came on a sunny afternoon while Jack and Martin were sitting with drinks at a table outside The Bell, a pub they had acquired for no other reason than that they fancied owning their own boozer.

Two mean-looking young men got out of a car opposite The Bell. One had an almost completely flat nose; the other was shaven-headed, with a face that looked like it had been whittled from suet. They strolled across the road. On the pavement they stopped and opened their jackets, revealing pick handles tucked into their belts. They pulled out the weapons and walked purposefully towards the table where Jack and Martin sat.

'I don't believe this,' Jack murmured.

Martin sighed.

'I was just getting relaxed,' he said. He sat forward in his chair, pretending to look alarmed. 'Know what the hardest part of this is going to be?' he muttered without moving his lips. 'Trying not to laugh.'

They both stood up as the heavies reached the table.

'What's this all about?' Jack demanded.

'Just a little warnin', guv,' the shaven-headed one said.

Jack's fist shot out and hit him on the nose. It was a complete surprise. He went down and as his mate jerked aside Martin kicked him in the crotch. He doubled over and landed on the ground beside the other one. Jack and Martin took hold of the pick handles and began battering the men, working systematically along the right and left sides of their bodies. When they were finished they bundled the pair into the back seat of their car and drove them to Elmington Place. They were dumped on the pavement outside Frog Mitchison's office.

'You should have seen them,' Billy Sims told his sister later that day. 'When we got the shirts off them they looked like they were made of corned beef.'

Sharon was amused.

'I think it's time you retired,' she told her sweating husband.

Matters were settled within the week. Frog, so frightened by now that he couldn't co-ordinate his speech or movements for more than a couple of minutes at a time, agreed to step down and pass the management of his various ventures to the Kane mob. He would become Boss Emeritus, Jack told him. He would have a salary, a good one, in return for which he need do nothing, except make sure none of his people got any silly ideas about resistance or rebellion.

'If they do, Frog, your dick'll go in the mangle as well as theirs, and you'll forfeit your income.'

Queenie was enthusiastic about being put in charge of the vice operation. Jack outlined the scale and scope of the business; he told her he wanted it knocked into shape and expanded. She promised she would make him very proud of her.

Hettie Wiseman was in the sleazy little bar at the Purple Parrot sipping a beer and reading *Woman's Own* when Queenie showed up.

'Is your name Wiseman?'

Hettie looked up and saw a shapely, strong-featured woman with peroxide blonde hair and glittery, determined eyes.

'Who let you in here?' Hettie demanded. She heaved her wobbling bulk off the stool and confronted Queenie with hands on hips. 'This is a private club, darlin'. Members only.'

'Belt up and listen,' Queenie told her. 'I want you off the premises no later than three this afternoon, right? You're fired, as of now. Just gather up everythin' that belongs to you and make sure you've got it all, because once you're out that door you don't come back.' She smiled tightly. 'I'm Queenie Kane, by the way.'

'You can be the Queen of Sheba for all I care.'

'I've heard that one until I'm sick of it.' Queenie prodded Hettie's padded breastbone with a stiff finger. 'I'm takin' over this place. Get the girls in here and I'll explain things to them.'

'Don't you poke me, you bloody cow!'

Hettie's agility was impressive. She must have weighed fifteen stone, but she moved with the speed of a dancer. She leapt to the bar, snatched up a big glass ashtray and threw it at Queenie's head. Queenie ducked and the ashtray smashed against the wall.

'Nobody comes in here and tells *me* what to do!'

Hettie followed the ashtray with a plastic ice bucket. Queenie ducked again and came hurtling forward. She grabbed Hettie round the middle and swung her sideways. Hettie's slippered foot caught on the torn carpet. She fell across a table. As she struggled to get up Queenie brought a bar stool down on her head.

Minutes later, as Hettie regained some sense of where she was and what had happened, Queenie explained the score. To Hettie it was all news. Nobody, it seemed, had had the guts to tell her the Mitchison reign was over.

'I've been here since before the war,' she whined, much subdued now that somebody had finally hit her and she realised she was capable of being hurt. 'It's not fair, heavin' me out. I've looked after the Purple Parrot since old man Mitchison put me in charge back in 1943. This place has been my life.'

'And a right shit hole you've made of it,' Queenie observed. 'Pack your bags, Hettie. You're history.'

As the weeks passed big changes were made. Jack began to have misgivings about Queenie's approach to the business. He had expected her to be keen; he knew she had organisational talent and would make a lot of changes. But the scale of her reforms was away beyond anything he expected. Or wanted.

'Look, I don't see us competing with the top end of the vice industry,' he told her. 'The idea is to have a good solid little earner – something discreet, well-run, profitable. That's all.'

Queenie was indignant.

'Are you tellin' me I'm doin' it wrong, then?'

'Your ideas are a bit on the big side, that's all I'm saying.'

'How?' she demanded. 'Tell me how I'm thinking too big.'

'Firing all the girls the way you did. That was bloody drastic for a start. And what's all this with the ceiling mirrors and peepholes and the rest of it? The Purple Parrot's a simple knocking shop, Queenie. A place where a bloke goes if the wife cuts his rations, or if he's too grotesque to get himself a wife in the first place. This isn't Mayfair, for Christ's sake.'

Queenie's indignation rocketed.

'A knocking shop is what it *used* to be,' she pointed out. 'A scruffy old shag parlour. I'm givin' it a bit of class.'

'That's what I'm getting at – '

'Class draws cash. I've recruited new girls, girls that really are girls, not clapped-out painted-up grannies. And the mirrors and spyholes are there to bring in the kind of trade the place missed out on before. Sex is like grub, Jack. Not everybody's content to sit down to a plate of meat and two veg. There's gourmets about, men with money to spend on the right menu.'

Jack didn't withdraw his objections, but in the interests of peace he stopped voicing them so strongly. He was too busy to argue, anyway. The Festival of Britain was underway. They were set to extract capital from that operation.

As an attempt to boost public morale and to show the rest of the world that Britain was making a great post-war recovery, the festival didn't, in the view of many people, come anywhere near fitting the bill. The government's idea was to echo the Great Exhibition, which was held exactly one hundred years earlier. But you only had to look at the old prints and postcards to see that this effort fell laughably short of the flair and splendour of the original. It had cost eleven-and-a-half million pounds to put together, yet to Jack and a lot of other people it looked like a big shabby fairground.

The main display was the saddest imaginable attempt at promoting Britain's image. It stood on a blitzed slum, a twenty-seven acre site on a stretch of the south bank between Waterloo Bridge and Westminster Bridge. There was a building called the Dome of Discovery that resembled a huge upside-down saucer and was said to have the largest unsupported roof in the world. It looked like something out of an old Buster Crabbe movie. There were pavilions all over the place with banners above the doors which read 'The Land of Britain', 'The Country', 'Minerals of the Island', 'Sea and Ships' and 'Transport'; the exhibits inside were chaotic, poorly conceived and vastly inferior to the displays at the Victoria and Albert and the South Kensington Science Museum. A meaningless object called the Skylon stood like a huge upended metal bobbin for people to stare at and shake their heads. As a crowning tribute to cack-handed planning there was a grubby old railway viaduct, intact and unadorned, running through the centre of the exhibition ground. Anybody knew that too many cooks spoiled the broth; there had been so many cooks on this project that the broth had vanished as designers, planners and wrong-headed architects had a go at stirring the pot. The Festival of Britain was a mess.

But as a source of income there had been nothing to equal it for thirty years. Hordes of visitors came from overseas and from other parts of Britain. London was full of wide-eyed strangers loaded with gullibility and cash. Then there were traders who rented stalls to sell tea and coffee, sandwiches, souvenirs, regional crafts, books and magazines, fish and chips. The festival organisers stood to make money. So did the interlopers.

Dozens of visitors looking for lodgings were interviewed in a number of smart-looking tents with ACCOMMODATION OFFICER in official-looking letters on the banners outside. The visitors' names and cash deposits were taken in exchange for bookings in hotels and boarding houses all over central London. The bookings turned out to be worthless. The tents were never in position for more than two hours at a time, and never on consecutive days. In the first week Jack raked off £800 from that operation alone.

Stall traders and contractors, meanwhile, were being encouraged to take out insurance against loss and damage to merchandise and equipment. If they queried the need for insurance they were soon shown that it really was a good idea, especially if they planned to stay on the site for any longer than a couple of days. Major contractors were made to understand how especially vulnerable they were. Martin Weir was overseer and co-ordinator on the insurance scheme; he logged first-week takings in excess of £2000.

Queenie, whose enterprising commercial streak was hardening daily, decided to put eight girls on overlapping beats around the festival ground; rooms in nearby hotels had been organised on an hourly-rent basis, and for the less affluent punters there was the special facility of stand-up quickies under the viaduct. The girls did brisk business. Only one was arrested, and she never actually reached the police station. In the squad car she made the two arresting officers an offer they could hardly refuse, and half an hour later she was back on duty near the phallic Skylon.

By the time the Festival of Britain was over, the Kanes had been forced to hide money under floorboards and up disused chimneys. And more was rolling in. The territory so loosely managed by Frog Mitchison had turned into a goldmine under Jack's administration. There were four separate bookmaking operations catering to as many levels of affluence among the punters; a new gambling club flourished in the upstairs room at The Bell; protection was a growing industry in the commercial districts; The Dominoes, renovated and extended, did a healthy trade in spite of an overall twenty per cent rise in prices; the Purple Parrot regularly turned away customers, while money-lending and lifting-and-shifting brought in enough on their own to satisfy any entrepreneur.

'We could sit back from here on,' Jack remarked as he finished his first Sunday dinner at the new house in Rotherhithe. 'The whole operation's turning over like a machine. All we have to do is keep the management tight and alert.'

'There's still a lot needs to be done,' Queenie said, scooping rice pudding into young Danny's mouth. 'We've got the foundation, Jack. What we have to do now is build on it.'

Her use of the word 'we' troubled Jack. 'We' and 'our'. At night she would lie beside him in bed and talk about 'our' operation, 'our' approach to handling this or that difficulty, the way 'we' should administer matters of policy. At her gentle but relentless insistence he had let her take over the running of the money-lending side. She had moved in on management at The Dominoes without being asked, and in recent weeks she had hired-and-fired bookies' runners and only announced what she had done afterwards. Clearly, Queenie regarded herself as a part-ner. Jack didn't like that. He'd never had a partner. He liked to head his enterprises. Airchie Cairns had recog-nised that and so did Martin Weir, who was happy to leave administration and policy-making entirely to Jack.

'What do you mean, build on it?' he asked now, watching Danny gulp down the pudding and open his mouth for more, like a greedy fledgling. Jack disap-proved; the kid was two now, he should be feeding himself. 'We expand automatically. Growth is happening to us, we don't have to *take* new ground, or break any. We just grow into it. You talk like we'd still got a struggle on our hands.'

Queenie looked at him. He wondered if he imagined it, or if her eyes really had gone harder in the past year.

'If you hang on to that attitude,' she said, 'some geezer with a lot of ambition's goin' to walk all over you, the way you did with Frog Mitchison.'

'Like hell.'

Jack saw his elder son, four-year-old Frank, studying him, his head on one side, chewing slowly. He was a self-contained kid, given to a lot more silence than Queenie believed was healthy. Jack winked at him and he smiled. He had a lovely smile. Watching the boy grow, Jack had sporadic fantasies about being an ordinary father, the kind who took the kids into the park with a ball on a Sunday. Frank was smart with a ball, according to Martin

Weir. He showed signs of good physical co-ordination. Maybe he'd be a footballer when he grew up.

'Hard is as hard does,' Queenie said. 'You can't rest on your laurels. How long do you think it'd take for the word to get round that you're in semi-retirement, just minding your patch, like some tame old lion? I'll tell you somethin' for nothin', Jack – them Noonans at the Isle of Dogs are the ones to watch. One sign of softness and they'll be over here chewing your bollocks before you know it.'

That was another thing. Her coarseness. At one time he had found it amusing, even endearing. Now it was like sandpaper on his nerve ends.

'Nobody's going to think I've gone soft.'

'You have to keep remindin' them you're not.'

'What – beat the shit out of firms at random, once a fortnight, just to prove I can still do it? Is that what you think I should do?'

'You know what I mean,' Queenie said. 'You're supposed to work at a business, not sit on it till it smothers. You talked about carving out some territory. All the way from where we were to where we are now. Remember? I don't see much sign of it happenin'.'

'But it is hapening,' Jack said. For Frank's sake he tried to sound patient and reasonable. The boy got upset when voices were raised. 'We're expanding, I don't need to do any carving. I just told you that. The process is automatic, just as long as we keep our operation under a tight rein.'

'Rivers of blood,' Queenie said darkly. 'It's all most of them understand. You got where you are by hammerin' your way there. You broke heads. That got you respect.'

'And now I've got it, I'll hang on to it.'

'You can try.'

Jack put his hands flat on the table and glared at his wife.

'Queenie,' he said, 'just let me get on with doing what I was doing for years before I met you. Let me use my own judgement. And since it's Sunday and supposed to be my day off, let's talk about something else, eh?'

The metallic eyes flashed at him.

211

'Right. Fine. Tell you what . . .' Queenie put down her knife and fork and pushed back her chair. 'You talk to the kids, eh? Tell them about your dreams for a quiet life. I've got a problem at the Purple Parrot that wants sortin' out. One of us should be crackin' the whip where it's needed, whether you think so or not.'

Alone with the boys, Jack took Frank on his knee and encouraged Danny to finish his pudding on his own. Upstairs he heard music from Martin Weir's flat.

'Come on, Danny. Eat it all up. Then we can go and bother Uncle Martin for a while.'

Martin was as fastidious about his environment as he was over his personal grooming. For this flat, an entire floor of the Victorian end-of-terrace house, he had bought new furniture, carpets, and curtains. He liked traditional designs and rich autumnal shades – rust-brown, dark orange, mossy green. Jack wished to God that Queenie had half Martin's taste. The house downstairs was loud with primary colours and littered with spindly-legged tables and chairs.

'I'm glad you came up,' Martin said. 'I've been having a fret about something since Friday. I've spent half this morning debating whether I should tell you or not. Now you're here, it's decided me. Sit down, Jack. I'll get us some beer. The boys could demolish a glass of orangeade, I dare say.'

The men settled into comfortable armchairs by a tall window that faced the river. In another sunny corner the boys occupied themselves with toys Martin kept for their visits.

'It's a grand day,' Jack sighed.

The sun shone warm across his knees. He put his head back against the soft upholstery and gazed at the light filtering through brown hessian curtains. This was nice. It relaxed him.

'So what's the problem, Martin?'

'It's not a problem yet.' Martin sipped his beer slowly, staring at the river. 'It's none of my business, either, as it happens. But we can't be islands all the time, much as we might like to be.'

'You'd certainly like to be, wouldn't you?'

'It's a precious dream,' Martin said. 'Just me, on my ownsome. On a private mountain, maybe. But nothing too wild or primitive.' He laughed softly. 'I'll have to price some mountains.' He put down the glass and sat back, lacing his fingers. 'It's Fred Carey I'm on about, Jack. Our new card man.'

'I hope you're not going to tell me he's doing us.'

'Where business is concerned he's all right. No problems there. No problems anywhere, yet, as I said. But the way things are going . . .'

Fred Carey was a dealer in the new gambling club. He was a gifted card mechanic with two years' experience in a West-End club that had been closed after a few visits by the police. In Fred's hands the second-deal was invisible. He could stack a pack in front of the punters and make it look like a shuffle. Fred was young and eager. He took orders and never did less than the management required of him.

'Spit it out, then,' Jack said.

'He's got eyes for Queenie.'

Jack tried to imagine it. Looked at objectively – and he could certainly look at her that way – Queenie was unsubtle, flashy, a woman nearly thirty-five and looking every day of it, in spite of the make-up she trowelled on her face before she ever let the world look at her. Fred was well-mannered, he spoke and dressed quietly and he couldn't be more than twenty. The images didn't fit together.

'Are you sure?'

'I'm positive,' Martin said. 'If I'd even a fraction of doubt I wouldn't raise the subject. I've watched him. Whenever Queenie's around he's all over her. I know when a bloke's got the itch for a woman. I'd say Fred's *very* itchy.' Martin picked up his drink again. 'It could be a small thing, not important at all. He gets no encouragement, so it might just fizzle out for want of nourishment.'

213

'But you still thought it was worth mentioning.'

'After I did my homework.' Martin sipped his beer and savoured it for a moment. 'When he was up West he had a heavy affair with another dealer's wife. It ended badly. The woman got a couple of black eyes, Fred got warned off. She was older than him. Her general description's a match for Queenie's.'

'I see.'

'He's one of those lads, Jack. We've both known them.'

'In love with their mothers.'

'Something like that.'

Jack valued Martin's rating of a situation. His instinct for its importance was usually accurate, regardless of appearances.

'The fact that matters here,' he said, 'is that Fred has a tendency to get obsessed. The woman up West was the third one in his history with the same specification, and in all three cases he made a lot of trouble. Woman number two didn't want to know, but he made a pest of himself just the same. A *big* pest.'

'So you think I should do something about him before he gets out of first gear?'

'Aye, that's what I think. For the sake of appearances.'

'Has anybody else noticed, then?' Jack said.

'I think they're beginning to. The sharp-eyed ones. The rest of them will, too, before long.'

And nothing can be worse for the boss's prestige, Jack thought, than the staff knowing something he doesn't. Especially something involving his wife. He remembered what Queenie had said earlier about hanging on to his hard-won respect. Here was an irony and a half.

'I'll have a word in his ear,' Jack said.

'You don't mind me mentioning it?'

'I'm glad you did, before it got complicated.'

They sat in silence for a while. Slowly, it began to dawn on Jack that he hadn't felt jealousy. Surely there should have been some kind of reaction? Something deep in the stomach, a wrench of male-animal response to another man sniffing round his woman? But no, apart from simply knowing it wasn't the kind of thing to stand for, and that it would be bad for his prestige to let it go on, he had felt nothing.

He thought back. Had he ever felt jealousy where Queenie was concerned? Often. In the courting days, and in the first couple of years they were married, he had come close to clipping other men for the familiar way they spoke to her, or even the appraising way some of them looked at her. But that had died away. She wasn't that precious to him any more. In fact she was more of a bloody nuisance than anything else, lately. She made him uneasy. In the overall picture of his life, she amounted to something entirely different from what she had been at the start.

He could just about face it. Queenie was a threat.

He gulped down his beer, washing away the thought.

'Another one?' Martin said.

'I think I fancy a whisky.'

That night, when the boys were bedded down and Queenie had taken a bath, she came into the lounge where Jack was stretched out reading the *News of the World*. She sat down in the armchair opposite his, drawing the folds of her green velvet housecoat about her.

'There's been a bit of trouble at the Purple Parrot,' she announced.

'So you said before you flounced out at dinner time,' Jack said, remaining behind the paper.

'It's something you should know about.'

It was his day, he decided, for being told things he ought to know.

'What?'

'We've had a threat.'

Jack lowered the newspaper.

'From the police, you mean?'

'No. The Walsh gang.'

He stared at her. Beyond his surprise was a small observation, a response to his thoughts earlier in the day: *It doesn't give me pleasure to look at her any more.*

215

'We don't have a beef with the Walsh gang,' he said.

'We do now. They put a fire bomb in the basement last night.'

Jack found it hard to believe. A thing like that took the Walsh boys out of their league.

'Didn't do much damage, mind you. The pratts dumped it through the window over the sink. Scorched a bit of paint on the wall, that's all. The point is, they meant to do damage.'

'Just hold on a minute.' Jack folded his arms and leaned forward. 'This happened *last night*? How come you've waited till now to tell me?'

'I thought I could handle it without bothering you.'

'Christ on a crutch . . .'

'I'm in charge over there, right?' Queenie squeaked. 'I'm allowed to use my initiative. That's the way I've always understood it.'

'We're talking about a fire bomb here. Not some tart getting out of line or a punter turning stroppy. You're supposed to tell me when you get real aggravation, Queenie. The serious stuff is strictly for me or Martin to handle. What the hell did you reckon you could do?'

'Let the bastards know they wouldn't get away with it, for a start. And I did.'

'Tell me about it,' Jack said, holding down his temper.

'Not much to tell. Benny Walsh has been comin' to the place a few times lately. He fancies that little blonde, Myra. God knows why. Any road, last night about nine he shows up, well pissed, and he demands to see Myra. Betty on the desk tells him it's not on, Myra's booked solid. There's three other girls free, he can have his pick. But no, it had to be Myra. So round about then Betty sent for me. I went down and I told him staight – no Myra, so pick somebody else or bugger off.'

'Jesus,' Jack breathed. 'You said that to a hothead like Benny Walsh, when he was drunk?'

'Bloody right I did.'

'And he cut up rough, because you said it in front of

other punters and showed him up. Am I getting the picture?'

'So? What did I do that was wrong? There's no favourites in my place. A punter's a punter, that's that. Just because Benny Walsh has got a gang, just because he's got a couple of transport firms stitched up, and two or three other numbers runnin', that don't make him somethin' special, not in my book.'

'And I suppose you said that to him, too, did you?'

'More or less,' Queenie said. 'In the end I had to get both bouncers to sling him out. This morning Betty rings and tells me about the fire bomb. It doesn't need a genius to work out who did it.'

'And what did you do when you went out today?'

'Nipped round to the pub where Walsh hangs out. I told him I knew who tried to fire the place but cocked it up. I told him he's in the shit right up to his bumpers for doin' that.'

Jack was nodding.

'And you told him that in front of his cronies, did you?'

'Yeah.'

'Brilliant.' Jack stood up. 'So you reckon I should know about all this, now you've practically started a war. Great.'

'What's up?' Queenie demanded. 'Scared of Walsh, are you?'

'No. I'm not scared of him. I wouldn't be scared of ten of him. But I don't need trouble with him. If you'd handled him right in the first place, soothed him a bit, given him a couple of drinks on the house – '

'I'm not goin' to suck up to no piss-squit villain like *him* . . .'

'He was drunk, for Christ's sake. Where's the sense in making a drunk man look small in front of other people? He'd be mad, anybody'd be mad. I bet he nearly shit himself this morning when he remembered he'd stuck that bomb in the basement. It could have stopped there, even. He could have been given time to come round and apologise. But no. You had to go and show him up a second time. Now he's got to respond. What else can he do?'

'Well, you're up to that, aren't you? You can handle it.'

'You're a bloody troublemaker, Queenie.'

She shot to her feet, eyes blazing.

'I don't understand you!' she yelled. 'You've gone soft! Since when were you scared of a fight?'

'I'm not scared of a fight – '

'Hah! Still callin' yourself a man, are you?'

For just a second he could have hit her. Instead he gripped the back of a chair and watched her stride out of the room.

The next evening he stopped by the gambling club above The Bell. Fred Carey wasn't there. He asked the manager, Tosh Whitfield, what time Fred woud be in.

'He won't be in, Guv,' Tosh said. 'He's finished. Didn't you know?'

Jack had a sensation that was getting familiar, the awareness of something nameless hovering in the air, ready to burst all over him.

'No, I didn't know. What happened?'

'Your missus gave him the bullet.'

'When?'

'Saturday night. She dropped in here on her way to the Purple Parrot. I don't know the details, she just fired him.'

'Tosh,' Jack said, 'look me in the eye and say that again. If you dare. Since when don't you know the details of anything that happens in here?'

Tosh coloured.

'Well . . .'

'Well what?'

'It was kind of personal.'

'Tell me anyway. If you don't want to go the same way as Fred, that is.'

Tosh cleared his throat.

'Mrs Kane took him on one side and told him she didn't like the way he'd been playin' up to her. She said she'd been thinkin' about it, wonderin' if she should tell you. But she'd decided not to, not for now. If he ever bothered her again, though, she'd let you know and you'd have his balls for bracelets.'

Jack sighed quietly.

'Cheers, Tosh.'

He didn't want to think, to reflect, to do anything but stay at a distance from his temper until it was safe to approach it again. He went to the door with Tosh at his heels.

'Don't mention I asked about this,' he said, pulling open the door.

'Of course not, Guv.'

'If anybody's looking for me in the next half hour, tell them I'm at Benny Walsh's garage. Just popping round to put out a fire.'

He went downstairs and walked slowly across the road to the car, taking deep breaths, trying to ignore a nagging ache in his chest.

THIRTEEN

Time passed in fretful chunks. There seemed to be no gaps, no comfortable breathing spaces as each event overlapped the next. Other people's envy, mischief, and territorial greed obliged Jack to defend his turf – and his rate of expansion – against three major outfits over a four-year stretch. Hand on heart, he could never swear he *knew* Queenie had engineered half the trouble, but he was sure she had, anyway. Of all her compulsions, the urge to keep him on his toes, perpetually proving himself, seemed to have priority.

'Winners behave like winners,' she told Martin Weir, justifying her increasing aggression. 'If you want, you take. Nothin' gets given.'

By the time the sixties began a lot had been taken. A south-of-the-river fruit and vegetable consortium fell to the Kane mob when Queenie's spies discovered that the outfit's principal shareholder was a paedophile. The word got round like lightning. Fellow shareholders, community leaders and a vindictive commander at Scotland Yard all received the news in an anonymous letter, accompanied by a lot of nasty documentary evidence. The man was persuaded to sign over his holding to Jack in exchange for safe passage to Holland. Within a month a lot of market vendors and high street traders, mostly in the area of Rotherhithe and Southwark Park, found themselves obliged to buy their merchandise from the consortium. Or else.

Not long after that Tony Morrisey, a meat-canner and small-time racketeer operating out of Wapping, misread the signs and decided that Jack Kane was getting ready to spread his little empire across the river. Tony sent a raiding party into Rotherhithe to spread discouragement. They came back in much poorer shape than they had set out. Jack Kane and Martin Weir followed up with a visit to Tony Morrisey. To ensure a lasting peace, he was persuaded to lay on facilities for long-term storage of goods that needed to 'cool' before they were trickled on to the market. A lot of Jack's warehousing problems were solved at a stroke.

Late in 1960, the news of Hugh Gaitskell's fight with the Labour militants in Scarborough was overshadowed for a couple of days by a story the papers called The Battle of Brunel Road. It was a brief, bloody inter-gang conflict that won Jack a two-mile stretch to the east of Rotherhithe. As he moved in to convert the existing operation, an accidental overspill into territory further east set another fight going. He won that one, too. The prize was a modest protection network, a couple of gambling enterprises and another brothel for Queenie to tamper with and improve. The cost was an uncomfortable increase in police attention.

The law, of course, could prove nothing against Jack or his people. Alibis abounded, witnesses didn't exist, evidence was always scarce and *always* ambiguous. But the lawmen could harass. They could impede. A zealous detective decided that if the police couldn't nail the cocky jock, other authorities should be given the chance. Officers of the Inland Revenue and Customs and Excise were alerted and briefed. They moved into Rotherhithe and set up an investigations unit in an office above the Labour Exchange.

Within the privacy of the four blue-and-white painted walls, the leader of the Inland Revenue side of the investigation, Mr Hewison, confronted Jack and stated his intentions clearly.

'I know your financial records are falsified,' he said. 'Your file has been studied carefully and tentative conclusions have been reached. I intend to prosecute you for

221

tax evasion. It's what I came down here to do and I won't go away until I've got a solid case. Do you understand that?'

Jack sat opposite the desk with his hands folded. He looked calm, confident. He wore a silver-grey suit, grey broadcloth shirt and a dark-red silk tie. He was impeccably barbered. Everything visible about him emphasised his distance from the rumpled, ragged-tempered, vindictive man opposite.

'I said do you understand that, Mr Kane?'

'You know, it's been bothering me,' Jack said, keeping the blue eyes wide and steady, 'I've been sitting here thinking, racking my brain – but I've got it now.'

'I beg your pardon?'

'You're a dead ringer for Raymond Burr. Has anybody ever told you?'

Hewison's neck coloured.

'I'd advise you to take me seriously.'

'How could I help it? You're Perry Mason to the life. Everybody takes old Perry seriously.'

Hewison's jaw churned as he opened a folder in front of him. He lifted a clipped sheaf of papers and waggled them in front of Jack.

'Copies of your bank statements,' he said. 'I want to go over the deposit columns of each one with you, item by item.'

'Some mistake, there,' Jack said.

'What do you mean?'

'I haven't got a bank account.'

'Not in your own name, no . . .' Hewison smiled thinly. 'We intend to prove that these accounts, three of them, represent moneys banked by you during the past five years.'

'No sense going ahead with this,' Jack said, shaking his head. 'I can't talk about something that isn't mine and that I know nothing about.'

'I've already told you – we intend to prove these accounts are yours.'

'Fine. When you prove they're mine we'll talk about

222

them. We can stand at the window and look at the blue moon while we're doing it.'

Hewison's conflict was visible. Jack understood. The bank manager, Mr Temple, was a cautious little man. Since he was both cautious *and* nervous, the enquiries by the Inland Revenue must have made him sweat; he would have been prevented – because of his caution – from telling any outright lies about the accounts. But Jack knew Temple would never reveal whose money that was. He would never break, although Hewison obviously believed he would. No threats from the Revenue men could top the dark warnings issued by Martin Weir when he opened the accounts. Mr Temple would vacillate, he would hum and haw, but he would never reveal whose accounts those were.

'I can force this issue,' Hewison warned, slapping the papers back into the file.

'I'm sure you can do lots of things. But you can't prove I have bank accounts when I don't have any at all.'

'We'll see what we shall see, eh? I think we can move on to the matter of your income, meanwhile. How much did you earn last year, Mr Kane?'

'Not a lot. The stalls are a bit up and down these days. I make a living, but that's about it.'

Hewison stared at him.

'Do you expect anybody to believe this ridiculous claim of yours?'

'What claim's that?'

'You know what I mean. You say your sole earnings come from an antique stall and another one selling secondhand books.'

'That's right.'

'Do you think I'm stupid?'

'I don't know anything about you,' Jack said, his face expressionless.

'Look at the clothes you wear. The car you drive.'

'I save up for my clothes,' Jack said. 'The car's loaned by an old friend. He lets me use it from time to time. It's part of his hire fleet.'

'It's part of the hire fleet at Apex Motors. Which you happen to own.'

Now it was Jack who stared.

'Who told you that?'

'Never mind who told me,' Hewison snapped. 'It's something else we're going to prove. That, and the fact that you draw income from more than twenty different enterprises in the Rotherhithe and Dartford districts.'

'I don't want you to think I'm being rude,' Jack said, making a show of swallowing amusement, 'but I really think you're wasting the taxpayers' time on this enquiry of yours. I mean *me*, running a car hire firm – where would I get the money to do something like that?'

Five minutes later Mr Hewison withdrew grumpily, no doubt intending to lean on Mr Temple at the bank. His seat behind the desk was promptly taken by Commander Harbottle from Customs and Excise. He was an entirely different individual. He looked more positive, less prone to bluster. He was quietly sure of himself. A dedicated man, Jack thought.

'I won't keep you, Mr Kane,' he said, after he had introduced himself. 'I just want a quick word with you while you're here. I'm conducting an extensive investigation into your affairs, I'm sure you know that already. It'll take me several weeks to complete my enquiries. In the meantime, I want to give you the opportunity to come along here and make a full statement about any irregularities in your activities – irregularities that could be the concern of the Customs, that is. Go away and think about it for now. I want you to be absolutely sure of your ground before you do anything. I'll put you under no undue pressure, I promise you that.'

'Well, it's very kind of you, but – '

'If you should decide there are no irregularities we ought to know about,' Harbottle went on, 'and we discover there *are* . . .' He pursed his lips for a moment, looking Jack straight in the eyes. 'It'll go very badly for you. I'll press for maximum penalties. And I'll get them.

224

It'll be vindictive, Mr Kane. I'd much rather be some-where else, doing more interesting work. I don't like having to come over the river to rummage through the dirty linen of a shitty little Glasgow crook. If you make the job any harder for me than it needs to be, I'll use all the pressure I can to see they put you away for years. And I do mean years. OK?'

'Aye, fine,' Jack said, nodding. 'Fine.'

He went straight from the enquiry headquarters to his office over at The Bell. For a while he just sat behind the desk, thinking. Inland Revenue was no worry, he decided. They had practically nothing to go on and they would gain no more while they were in Rotherhithe.

Customs and Excise was something else. Before he had gone out that morning he was confident there would be no danger of the enquiry turning up anything. But now he had laid eyes on the impressively determined Com-mander Harbottle he wasn't so sure. Jack had met men of that cut before. Quiet crusaders. They were always hard and tenacious, the kind who put in an extra bit of effort, the type of men who took the job personally. They fuelled their endeavours with resentment and a strong capacity for spite.

Jack knew he could resist Harbottle. Whatever the pressure, he wouldn't break. But what about his people? What about all the minor characters that Harbottle would root out and talk to, the gofers who weren't used to being interrogated by experts? Without meaning to, they could put him in the shit up to his eyebrows.

He looked at his watch and decided to call Martin Weir across for an urgent conference. He reached for the telephone and felt a surge of pain along his arm. It jolted the muscles and deadened his fingers. After a second it shifted and swelled in his armpit. Another second and it was burning. He sat back, making himself breathe slowly. It would pass. It always did.

'Jesus . . .'

Needling pain fluttered across his chest. His stomach churned and he belched sour gas. He had suffered the identical symptoms maybe a dozen times in two years. They always came at odd moments, at times of no particular physical stress or unusual movement. Jack closed his eyes, tried not to wonder if Harbottle's abrasive intrusion on his life had brought on the upset.

'It'll go away,' he whispered.

He reminded himself that his will was in charge; a body was obliged to obey a mind like his. He had improved his self-awareness enough to be sure of that much.

Men with a governing passion dictate the rules.

The formula couldn't hold forever, but he believed it prolonged life. He coughed. His throat was dry and his shirt collar felt too tight. He undid it, feeling sweat on his neck. Focus the mind, he told himself. The governing passion, think of that. It was a fervency for control of his life and all he touched.

Concentrate on that.

A man who wanted less than dominion over his life was less than a man.

Believe it!

He thought of his sons, ultimate solace. The boys grown and in charge, carrying the business forward, a powerful extension of their father, skilled to a knife edge by all Jack Kane would teach them.

The pain began to slacken. His stomach eased and the fluttering in his chest faded. He sat still, breathing through his mouth. He would wait until he was in command again, until his body ticked to the beat of his will. Then, when he was ready, he would have Martin Weir in here and plan a little hell for Commander Harbottle. The prospect was a tonic in itself.

'I've always heard the Customs are mustard,' Martin said. 'It's a pity we've got tangled with them, Jack. A bad pity.'

'Blame the papers. If the Brunel Road caper hadn't got reported the way it did, the coppers would never have got so involved, and if they'd kept their noses out, the government types wouldn't be here now. But they are here. So we've got to decide what needs doing.'

'There's always the hope they'll come up with nothing. I know you're worried about some of our people letting things slip, but I think they're sounder than maybe you believe.'

Jack did a drum roll with his fingertips on the desktop.

'You're right. There's a hope. But do you know what I believe? A man that lives on hope can easily die of starvation. Hopes aren't a patch on certainties. You should only lean on hope when there's no alternative. The more I think about this, the more I want the whole investigation stopped – Inland Revenue, Customs, the lot.'

Martin was looking at Jack strangely. Jack noticed.

'What's up?' he said.

'Are you feeling all right?'

'Sure. I feel fine.'

'You're a hell of a colour.'

'You keep your bloody racialism to yourself, pal. I promise I'll be a better shade when we get this wee problem sorted out.'

'Right,' Martin nodded. 'What's the strength of this Commander Harbottle, then?'

'He's a tough bastard. Experienced, determined, all the bad things that get his kind promoted. He's dead set on nailing me. I don't think personal threats would make much impression on him. If I took him somewhere quiet and hammered him, he'd make sure that whoever took his place would come at me twice as hard.'

'Have you any ideas for handling him?'

'One,' Jack said.

He gave Martin an outline. Martin said he thought it might work. He also said he didn't like it.

'Neither do I. But I don't see any option. So. The first thing we need to do is get all the info on Harbottle. Home background, off-duty habits, everything.'

'That should be easy enough.'

'We need to do it fast, Martin. He looks like a nifty mover himself.'

'I'll get started,' Martin said.

Jack thought over the plan again when Martin had gone. It was something he hadn't used before. There were limits, after all, and sailing near them gave him an uneasy sensation, a feeling that he was besmirching himself.

Which was a laugh, he thought. When had he last been clean?

He soothed himself with the thought that, if the scheme worked, he would never use it again. He hoped he would never *want* to use it again, or ever have such certainty that nothing less would do the job. Harbottle meant business, and Jack knew a man who could handle business when he saw one. So, for his determination, for his dedication to doing his job to the best of his ability, the commander would be caused some anguish. It would never be possible to let the man know, afterwards, that Jack Kane wasn't such a loathsome, vile, debased heap of scum as he would soon appear to be. Harbottle would never know that Jack had no intention, ever, of fulfilling the kind of promise he was soon to make.

Martin's intelligence-gathering and ground preparation took two days. He came up with the kind of information Jack had been praying for. Commander Harbottle had a dream of a background. It made him as vulnerable as a day-old puppy.

Three days after the interview in the office above the Labour Exchange, Jack appeared in the lounge bar of a Chiswick pub called the Drover's Arms. It was what he called a corduroy-and-cravat place, twee and cosy, with an abundance of polished brass and waxed mahogany, full of off-duty business types smoking pipes and conferring in voices far too loud for the distances they had to cover.

Jack armed himself with a pint and hovered by the open fireplace. For a while he pretended to read the framed music hall posters while he listened to a conversation about the current state of art and literature. Things were in a state of flux, it seemed. According to a chap called Rupert – *Rupert* – Lawrence Durrell's new book, *Clea*, was an unmitigated disaster. Robert Bolt's film *A Man for all Seasons* was something of a consolation, but there was still that awful Picasso exhibition at the Tate to agonise over.

'Have you seen Visconti's *Rocco and his Brothers*?' another man asked.

'You mean *Rocco e i sui fratelli*?' Rupert said. 'Oh yes, we caught it last year in Milan. Not bad, not bad . . .'

It's a whole different world out here, Jack thought. He turned and saw Commander Harbottle walk in. There was a flashing memory of waiting in a Maryhill pub for a man to arrive. This wouldn't be quite the same.

When Harbottle had his gin and tonic he began to cross the room towards a clutch of men chatting by the door to the public bar. Jack moved briskly, intercepting him.

'Commander,' he said, smiling brightly. 'I'm glad I caught you.'

For a second Harbottle looked confused, then his expression cleared.

'What the hell are you doing here?'

'I wanted a word with you. I hope you don't mind me breaking into your leisure time. It won't take a minute. I won't detain you any longer than you kept me. Can we stand over there by the door, where nobody can eavesdrop?'

Jack moved away before he got a reply. Harbottle followed him.

'How did you know I'd be in here?' he demanded.

'It's your local. I checked. You come in here at this time every night. You have three gee-and-tees, you chat to the boys for a while, then you go home again.'

Harbottle put down his glass on the window ledge. He turned to face Jack in a way that put his back to the rest of the room. He raised one finger and held it an inch from Jack's chin.

'Before you utter another word,' he said, 'I'll fill you in on what I think you're up to. You want to make a deal. Or you're going to be stupid enough to threaten me. Either way, Mr Kane, you're wasting your time. And mine.'

'Well . . .' Jack shrugged. 'I sort of guessed you'd catch

on straight away. But that doesn't matter. It doesn't change anything.'

'You seem very sure of yourself.' Harbottle's delivery was cold, dismissive. It was easy to tell he despised Jack, and just as easy to guess how much he liked the power his job gave him. 'We'll see how your confidence holds up when I put this little encounter into my report.'

'Oh, you won't do that,' Jack said amiably.

There was a flash of caution in Harbottle's eyes. It was gone as fast as it came. He was supremely sure of himself. He had heard it all, seen it all. Life held no surprises.

'You'd be wise to save your shabby menace for your own kind, Mr Kane. I can see you for the trash you are. Now excuse me.'

Harbottle picked up his glass and moved away.

'It was Julie I came to talk about,' Jack said.

Harbottle froze, turned.

'I beg your pardon?'

'I had to find some way to make you back-pedal, if you know what I mean.'

As Harbottle moved close again Jack noticed the coiled anger in him. He would fight, he would do it here if necessary.

'It's not that I've much to hide from your investigation,' Jack went on. 'But I get the feeling you want to damage me whatever you turn up. You'd want to do it even if you found nothing. That's right, isn't it, Commander?'

'You mentioned my daughter's name,' Harbottle said.

'Yes. Julie. A nice wee girl, I'm told. Not that I've seen her myself. I'll never see her, because I'll never go anywhere near her.'

'You've overshot,' Harbottle said quietly through his teeth. 'You've said enough to hang yourself. I'll definitely get you now. By any means at all.'

'But I didn't say anything – '

'You'll learn, you shit, that you don't turn your gutter tactics on people like me and get away with it.' Harbottle continued to speak quietly, but his voice shook with

230

anger. 'How *dare* you threaten me. By this time tomorrow, you'll wish you'd never had the lunatic audacity to come here. Go home, Mr Kane. Say your goodbyes to your family.'

'What do you mean?'

'You're going to jail, that's what I mean. The arresting officer will read out the charge to you. And the charge will be proved in court.'

'If I didn't have more respect for the Customs and Excise service,' Jack said, 'I'd swear you're thinking about faking a case against me.'

'Certain ends justify certain means.'

Jack sighed.

'You go to a lot of trouble to cause yourself pain,' he said. 'Poor Julie, eh? Does she mean that little to you?'

Now it looked like Harbottle would hit Jack. The anger was drawing back his lips, showing his clenched teeth.

'Settle down,' Jack said. His manner had changed. He squared his shoulders. 'If you think you can take me on, then you're daft. You might be a handy big lad but you've not had enough practice. I've mangled bigger men than you for fun.'

'I don't doubt it.'

'Just shut your face, Harbottle. We'll forget all the footwork now. I'll explain how things are. You're out to nail me. I'm out to stop you doing that. I'm prepared to go to lengths you can't even imagine. At any time, no matter where I am, I can have your daughter picked up and taken away.'

'Have you any idea what *I* can do?'

'Nothing,' Jack snapped. 'Nothing to shield yourself and your wife from a lot of heartbreak. You're from the civilised world, Commander. You've got limits. Constraints. I have no fucking limits. If you don't let up on me, little Julie gets spirited away. You can't stop it happening, not if you put a twenty-four-hour guard on her. If it takes a year, *two* years, I'll get her, and you'll never prove I did it. And here's the most solemn promise I'll ever make. If I get done by you for anything at all, or

231

by anybody else and I suspect it was your doing, I'll have your sweet little girl put through the kind of hell no child should ever know about. And then I'll have her killed.'

Harbottle's hand flew up and Jack caught it. He twisted the wrist sharply, making the man gasp with pain.

'You bastard,' he hissed. 'If you so much as – '

'Don't threaten me,' Jack said. 'And don't be crazy enough to think I'm bluffing. I can get to you or yours any time I like. I've left a bit of proof for you.'

'What do you mean?'

'When you go home, take a look at your daughter's raincoat. You'll find a tiny white cross chalked on the back, near the left shoulder. It was put there to show you how easy it is to get close without being noticed.' Jack put down his glass. 'I'm going now. Tomorrow, I want to hear the whole investigation's been called off.'

Jack didn't go straight home. It was a bright warm evening and the thought of being indoors with Queenie stifled him. He drove out to Ealing, taking it steadily, still feeling echoes of pain in his chest. He parked the car on a dirt road on the outskirts of a little wood he had discovered years earlier, a place where he used to bring the boys and where young Frank had started going alone when he was ten or eleven.

Jack wandered in among the trees, breathing deeply, touching the rough bark as he made his way to the centre. He paused to look at the tracery of leaves and branches above his head. It was a canopy, translucent green, holding in the mossy smells and dusty, glittering puffs of leaf mould. One day, long after he had stopped coming here, Frank admitted to his father that he once fell into an overgrown pond and almost drowned. Even after his nightmare five minutes fighting with tangles of reed and water grass, he had felt the wood to be a friendly place, a shelter. Dozens of times he had sat on a velvety hummock near the centre, reading adventure stories in a shaft of bright light from a break in the foliage. He had told Jack it was an enchanted place. Jack believed his son had an instinct for detecting enchanted things. He didn't agree with Queenie when she said Frank was too much of a romancer.

As he came out on the far side of the wood clouds were gathering. After a few minutes it began to rain. He felt light warm drops on his face and hands. He took a rising hill path that led in a circle to where the car was parked. The evening was unbelievably quiet. He trod steadily, hearing the soft crunch of dried earth under his shoes.

I am poured out like water, and all my bones are out of joint: my heart is like wax; it is melted in the midst of my bowels . . .

Nothing like the Old Testament for pinpointing a misery. For more than a month during his third year in Barlinnie, he had been attacked by moods and feelings that Uncle Brian diagnosed as spiritual unrest. Jack thought that was putting it mildly. He experienced such emotional pandemonium that he had turned to the Bible for an answer, or at least reassurance. But the messages there had no comfort for a baddie like him: *There is a way which seemeth right unto a man, but the end thereof are the ways of death*. He had abandoned the idea of religion as solace, but the stern texts remained with him.

As he walked he thought over the evening again, point by point. He hated what he had done, hated it more than he had thought he would. But there it was, that was life, such things had to be done. When it was necessary to keep peril from turning to disaster, you had to neutralise the source of peril.

When he got back to the car he paused with the key in the door, wondering if the ploy with Harbottle had worked. For a while he'd been certain it had; now he couldn't be sure. He was sure of nothing, he decided, getting into the car. Nothing except that he felt old, and tired, and fairly worthless.

When he got home Queenie was in the living room with Beattie Douglas, one of her old cronies and now manageress at The Dominoes. They were locked in conversation and hardly seemed to notice Jack. He decided to go to bed.

'He doesn't look at all well,' Beattie said, waggling her carroty head. 'Has he been under the weather?'

'He's just tired.' Queenie looked at the closed door. 'Or at least I think he is. I'm not sure.' She looked at Beattie. 'Look, you're a friend of mine. You can keep a confidence, can't you?'

'Of course I can.'

'Well . . .' Queenie examined the flawless red enamel on her thumbnail. 'It's not an easy thing to talk about, but some things shouldn't be bottled up. They can harm you if you don't get them out in the air.'

'Right,' Beattie said. 'Definitely.'

'I don't regard myself as a woman who's overly demandin',' Queenie said. 'I'm not one of those females that think about nothin' but the sexual side of marriage.'

'I'm sure you're not.'

'Even so, there's things I can't help noticin'. Changes in certain patterns.' Queenie took a sip from her brandy glass. 'Jack doesn't . . . He doesn't bother any more. He hasn't for at least eight months.'

Beattie thought about that.

'Maybe it's overwork,' she offered.

'Maybe. But I don't think so. He waits until I'm sleepin', or until he thinks I am, before he comes to bed.' Queenie looked at Beattie with hurt eyes. 'I can't imagine what's wrong. Neither one of us is too old. God knows I'm not, anyway.'

The confidential tone was giving way to a soulful squeak.

'Maybe he just doesn't fancy me any more. That could be it. He's got too used to me. Or he's gettin' drawn in another direction.'

'Oh, surely not . . .'

'How do I know what he does when he's out and about? Look at the state the country's in these days. It's all sex, sex, sex. The girls I've got workin' for me aren't takin' a fraction of what they used to bring in – because men can get it anywhere for nothin' these days. Who's to say Jack's not helpin' himself to a bit of spare some place else?'

'I'm sure you're jumpin' to conclusions.'

'Am I? I've tried to tell myself that, but I'm not convinced. I mean, *eight months*, Beattie. I don't know what you consider normal . . .'

She paused expectantly.

'Well . . .' Beattie shrugged. 'A couple of times a week, I suppose.'

'There you are, then. Don't you think I'm entitled to be concerned?'

'Yeah, I suppose you are, love.'

'Maybe there's a straightforward explanation,' Queenie said. 'It could be somethin' medical. I can't make myself believe that, though.' She sighed heavily. 'Surely it's not selfish of me to expect what any married woman's entitled to?'

'God, no.'

'I've complained, in a roundabout way, but he just says he's tired, or he's under the weather. Maybe I should demand to know what's goin' on. You know, tackle him straight out.'

'Would that maybe not make things worse? I mean if Jack started to feel he was obliged to do his stuff . . .'

'But he *is* under a bleedin' obligation,' Queenie snapped. 'The marriage service is clear on *that* point. He knew what his duties were when he took them vows.'

She accepted a cigarette from Beattie and sat back with it, the smoke billowing around her. She never drew on a cigarette like other people, she took short serial puffs, like someone trying to keep a pipe lit.

'I'll tell you this much,' she said, 'it would just serve Jack right if I had an affair. I wouldn't have to put in any effort. I can tell by the way some men look at me.'

'But you wouldn't do anything like that, would you?'

'Why not? I can't let things carry on the way they are. If my old man, for whatever reason, can't or won't pay proper attention to me, then I might have to find my satisfaction some place else. Wouldn't you?'

'I don't think so,' Beattie said.

'Hah! That's how you feel now.' Queenie blew smoke

235

into the air above her head. 'If you were a neglected wife you might feel different.' She paused, flicking ash absently into an onyx ashtray. 'Would you think bad of me if I took up with another bloke?'

'I'd try to be understandin',' Beattie said.

'Yeah, I'm sure you would. You're a good friend, Beattie. But other people would crucify me. It would be jealousy, mind you. More women want to have a bit on the side than their husbands realise. But mostly they haven't the courage. I'd be hated for remindin' them of their own cold feet.'

Beattie looked troubled.

'If Jack ever found out . . .'

'He'd kill the bloke,' Queenie said.

'He might kill you, too.'

'No, he wouldn't.' Queenie shook her head firmly. 'He might think he'd want to for a while, but he wouldn't. Boil it all down, Beattie, and the fact is, that man needs me. He'd be nothin' without me. And he knows it.'

At ten the following morning a telegram arrived for Jack. He wasn't there so Queenie opened it.

CROWN INVESTIGATION OF YOUR AFFAIRS SUSPENDED AS OF THIS DATE. FURTHER ACTION NOT ANTICIPATED.

'That'll please him,' Queenie muttered: 'If anythin' will, any more.'

236

FOURTEEN

The fear of death set in some time between 1965, following Jack's first full-blown heart attack, and the summer of 1967. Its approach had been insidious, there was no way to tell when vague disquiet had hardened into terror.

It was always worst in the hour before daylight. Jack would wake in the dark, listening, confirming life was still there. The precarious feeling came over him then, as the minutes passed and the curtains began to show faint light.

His end was one day nearer.

The thought devastated him. This time yesterday he'd had one day more than he had now; tomorrow there would be one less than now. On it would go, the relentless drain on time left, until it was all gone and he would pass into the darkness forever. A lot of events could be avoided, but not that one. The certainty made him shake: one day, soon, he wouldn't exist.

Drink helped. He started quite early now, around noon, kicking off with a couple of vodkas to dull the edge, staying topped up until evening, when he could settle down to getting properly stewed. No matter how much he drank, though, he couldn't kill off the sober awakening, the terrible morning time when he felt his mortality like a delicate wounded thing, fluttering in his chest and along his veins.

Jack wished he could be like Martin Weir. Martin didn't look at the world the way most people did. He stayed detached from everyday life. He did his job with patience and thoroughness and when he wasn't working he withdrew. For years now he had lived alone in a three-storey terrace house on Redriff Road. He never entertained, rarely visited. On a single occasion Jack had sounded him out on his views on ageing and death, Martin said he had no fears. There was something mysterious on the other side; no living soul had ever come near to knowing what it was, but he was convinced it was there. Religion, in his view, was a load of crap concocted to make us believe there was no such thing as death. There was no need to invent such a thing, because the other side existed anyway.

Jack wished he believed that. But he couldn't. His own certainty told him there was only black emptiness ahead, a sightless and soundless pit. Life, as far as he could tell, was completely pointless.

On a particularly tremulous and humid July morning, after lying awake for half an hour gazing forward to his own extinction, Jack heaved himself out of bed, suddenly convinced that the only way to handle these doom-laden dawns was to counterbalance them with as much pleasure as he could suck from his life.

For months he had been seeing a girl in Stepney, a hairdresser called Shirley. It was a furtive relationship which Jack approached on tiptoe. He had embarked on it, and others in the past few years, because of boredom and low self-esteem. The affair with Shirley was therapy for his ego. It was a diversion, too, but so far it could hardly be called a pleasure. So sod all that, he thought this morning. He was going to have fun while he still could. It was Shirley's day off; he would collect her and they would spend the day up West.

His plan hit an obstacle as soon as he got downstairs. Martin Weir was at the door. He looked worried.

'Queenie's in the papers,' he said as they went to the living room. He held out a copy of the *Daily Express*. 'I've just read it.'

Jack took the paper. His eye skimmed down the page: a smiling Patrick Gordon Walker was pictured next to the man he was to replace as Secretary of State, glum-faced

Anthony Crosland; there was a summary of the inquiry findings on the 1966 Aberfan disaster; a picture of a housewife beaming at a new cooker was printed above the news that natural gas was now being piped freely from the North Sea; at the bottom of the page a heading said 'Police are the Real Crooks claims Battling Ma Kane.'

'Oh, Christ . . .'

Jack sat down and spread the paper on the table.

Mrs Queenie Kane, a tough south London club operator known to friends and foes as Ma Kane, yesterday told our reporter that crooked policemen were a bigger threat to the public than people like her, who only tried to provide a service for hard-working citizens who like to relax in the evening.

Mrs Kane made her angry remarks outside Elgin Street magistrates' court, where assault charges against her were dismissed when the main prosecution witness failed to appear.

'This case never should have been brought,' she told us. 'It was only because I wouldn't let coppers into my place for free that the charges got trumped up. I'd warn anybody who has dealings with the police – make sure you've got witnesses, or they'll have you stitched up quicker than you can wink.'

Jack pushed the paper away.

'What's she trying to do to us?'

'It's nothing deliberate,' Martin said. 'She opens her mouth without thinking, that's all.'

'For years, *years*, I've put myself out to keep the law round here sweet. Now blabber-gob goes and buggers everything up with one stupid remark. They're not going to stand for this kind of thing. It'll cost us money, or tears.'

Jack stood up and walked through to the kitchen. He came back to the living room.

'No sign of her.' He looked at the paper lying on the table. 'I'm not letting this one pass, Martin. I'm going to talk to her. She can risk her own arse all she likes, but stuff like this involves all of us. Where's she likely to be this morning, do you think?'

'At her office,' Martin said. 'If she's not there, she'll be down at that dance hall on Paradise Street. She spends a lot of time there, lately. She's keen on having the place for her own.'

'She can do what she likes. I just want to make sure that she keeps her trap shut while she's doing it. Do you mind giving me a lift?'

'I was going to offer,' Martin said.

Most of the time Jack tried to avoid Queenie. They had separate bedrooms these days and more or less separate careers. While he tended his turf she continued to build little empires, moved in on others and made trouble wherever she could. A bodyguard went around with her now. He was a big lad, very mean, a mouth-breather with a low blink rate. Very few people would care to tangle with him, yet Jack was sure he was afraid of Queenie.

'Well, well, I'm honoured,' she said as Jack walked into her office. 'What brings you here? Come to remind yourself what I look like, have you?'

He glanced around the place. It was a mystery how anybody could work in those surroundings. She had decorated the walls with pink-and-yellow striped paper; the carpet was pale blue and the chair seats were covered with orange nylon fur. Only the desk looked normal, if you ignored the cheap gilt inkstand and the ballpoints disguised as quills with dayglo feathers.

'I read your little bit of press coverage,' Jack said.

She grinned.

'I didn't think it was funny, Queenie. Or smart.'

'I spoke my mind, darlin'. I always speak my mind.'

'You ran off at the mouth, that's what you did. Have you got so soft in the head you think you'll get away with that kind of behaviour?'

'What are you sayin'? That I should be frightened of the fuzz? Is that it? I should be careful or I'll get my wrist smacked?'

'I'm saying you shouldn't go around making trouble for other people. What you do to yourself is your business. Just don't catch the rest of us in the sidewash.'

'Bloody hell.' Queenie sat back in her squeaky swivel chair. 'You're really turnin' chicken, aren't you?'

Jack watched her scowl develop. As she got older she got harder. Moodier, too; she was prone to long threatening silences and bouts of screeching temper. The spaces between the extremes got smaller all the time.

'I made peace with the law,' Jack said. 'There was a price, I paid it and they've stuck to their end of the deal. They give us a lot of space to move, they turn blind eyes. All that'll stop if you start slagging them off to reporters.'

'They asked for it,' Queenie said. 'Bringing that assault charge was sheer rotten spite.'

'They'd no choice. You were too public about it, people saw you. You cracked a punter over the head with a beer bottle in a room full of customers.'

'Oh? Did I? So how come no witnesses showed up at the court? Not even the one I'm supposed to have hit?'

'I'm mystified about that, Queenie. You'd think somebody had threatened them or paid them off, wouldn't you?'

'Think what you like.'

'Listen,' Jack said, 'I'm going down to the station and I'm going to apologise to the Super.'

'Don't make no apologies on my behalf.'

'I'm going to promise him you'll keep your trap shut in future. That might not be enough, there might be a penalty to pay. If there is, I'll pay it. But I'm never going to do it again. You antagonise the law one more time and I'm disowning you. I'll let them know too. You'll lose all the privileges you've got now. They'll shut you down.'

'You reckon?'

'Without my backing you're nothing. It's time you realised that.'

'Bollocks!' Queenie shot to her feet. 'You're tellin' me I'm nothin' without you? Without *you*? In case you haven't noticed, darlin', the days are gone when anybody depended on your cover. It was all over long ago. You're not even a good figurehead any more. You're just a caretaker on your own turf. Who's Jack Kane, eh? Anybody asks, know what they'll get told? He's a has-been. Just another heart case, an old man that gets tired walkin' up a flight of stairs.'

'That's what you think of me, is it?'

'That's what everybody thinks of you.'

He didn't want to defend himself. Not to her. He knew her cruelty was always a reaction to her own pain. He had made her feel undervalued as a woman, so she extracted this price from him. Ridicule and disdain were the only weapons she had against him; why not let her use them? Jack knew that Queenie knew about the other women, younger and prettier than she was, walking rebukes. She knew he would sooner lose himself in the bed of another woman or in a bottle of vodka than spend the time of day anywhere near her. Why shouldn't she hit back, especially when he walked in and invited it?

'Just remember what I said, Queenie.'

He turned and went to the door.

'Where are you off to now, then? Down the pub to get pissed? Time to hide in the bottle again. Get tanked up and pretend?'

'I'm going back home,' he said. 'After I've been to see the police.'

He stepped out and pulled the door shut before she could say anything else. At the foot of the stairs he met his younger son, Danny. He had on a bronze silk mohair suit and a yellow Italian silk shirt. Always the sharpie, young Danny. He didn't smile at his father.

'Been to see Mum, have you?'

Jack nodded.

'What are you doing here?'

'I'm helpin' out.'

It was all Danny would ever admit to doing. Helping out. Jack had been shocked to see him on the door at the Purple Parrot a couple of months before it was sold. Shock wasn't perhaps appropriate – what did Jack expect?

242

How could his son grow up fresh-faced and innocent, given the nature of his parents' business? Even so, it had been sad to see the boy, sixteen at the time, minding the door of a brothel. Sadder to know his mother approved of the way he was shaping. But Danny was his mother's boy, Jack could have changed nothing, even if he had known how.

'I'll see you later,' Jack said.

Danny nodded and went on up the stairs. Already, Jack thought, he's forgotten he spoke to me.

Time makes everything ripe. No man is born wise.

It was written in Jack's round, careful hand near the back of one of the notebooks he had filled during his time in Barlinnie. He hadn't looked in them for years. They were yellowing at the edges now, even though he had kept them in a big manila folder with the flap tucked in. The quotation about time, like so much else in these books, had been picked up from Uncle Brian.

Jack wrote down a lot about time in those days. He had been obsessed with it, with trying to understand. Time puzzled him still. How did something so constant and carefully measured behave so erratically? Why was it that the older he got, the faster time passed?

The people who make the worst use of their time are the first to complain of how little they have.

He had quotes and observations in those books to answer or underline just about every perplexity. Sitting there in the hot air of the attic with the smells of summer coming through the fanlight, he called up distant events with the clarity of recent memory; yet things that happened a year ago were hard to remember. He closed his eyes for a moment, permitting a flash of recall:

Rouken Glen, standing in fragrant grass, tensed, the hatchet flashing away from his hand, arcing and swinging into the trees . . .

He missed Glasgow. No doubt memory had worked its usual distortions, but even so there were certainties about the place, there were times and events he had come to

243

cherish. He had a store of precious images. There was Airchie at sixteen, cheeky-faced, ready for any dare, a right wee villain and the best pal in the world. Mad Harry, using his one arm better than most men could use two. Jessie Young, that smile of hers, the scent of her hair. He could see his mother baking in the tiny living room, his father sitting at the fireside staring haplessly at the coals. Most vividly of all, Jack remembered Annie Kempson, her loveliness, her wickedness in bed. And the hatred in her eyes the last time he saw her.

That sweet pain, memory, lighting and colouring our days . . .

1967. He could scarcely believe it. He was nearly fifty-one. More than half a century gone. Where? He had heard that a man could look back at this age and see everything clear, the road of his life, the meaning. But Jack saw nothing. Just fog. No path, no winding progress from there to here. He had gathered no store of wisdom that he was aware of – he suspected he had lost more than he'd gained. All he had gathered and kept were memories that sometimes brought tears to his eyes, late at night when he lay curled on his side, trying to sleep.

Sitting here, looking through the old notebooks, he wished he'd met Uncle Brian a lot earlier in life. If that had happened, if he'd spent time near a man who placed value on knowledge, a person who thought it was worthwhile to look for something lasting at the centre of life, then maybe, by now, Jack would have found it easier to live with himself.

'What're you doin', Dad?'

Young Frank had stuck his head through the loft door. At twenty he was muscular and broad, a handy boxer with certificates and trophies that attested to his skill as a middleweight. His latest black eye had paled to light mauve and spread around the curve of his cheekbone.

'Sorting through my memories, son.' Jack held up the fattest of the notebooks. 'Remember this?'

Frank came across the loft, stooping to avoid the

beams. He squatted beside his father and took the book. He riffled the pages.

'It's the one you used to read me stories from, right?'

'Well, I used it to help my memory along.'

'The crusades,' Frank said. 'I loved those stories. Couldn't wait for the next one. I used to fall asleep thinking about Jerusalem being attacked by the Moslems, and the Christians defending it. Used to try and draw pictures of the characters you told me about – the Seljuk Turks, Saladin, Sheik Rashid ed-Din Sinan . . .'

Frank handed the book back to Jack.

'When I was a kid I thought the crusaders were great blokes,' he said. 'I'm not so sure now.'

'Just another bunch of villains,' Jack said, nodding. 'But the stories are great, all the same.' He bundled the notebooks and pushed them back into their folder. 'I'll come and look through them again in another five or ten years time.' He stood up. 'Fancy a cuppa?'

They went down to the kitchen. Queenie had left a pile of dishes in the bowl. Frank put on the kettle, spooned tea into the pot and took a dish towel from behind the door.

'You wash,' he said. 'I'll dry.'

They worked in silence, clearing the backlog of washing-up, stacking everything away. When they were finished they sat down to drink their tea.

'Tell me what you've been up to, then,' Jack said. He loved to spend time with his sons. It was a pity Danny wasn't the conversational type. He got fidgety if he had to sit still for more than five minutes. 'Been to the gym today, have you?'

'For an hour. I had to go over and see Father Holmes for a while. He got some leaflets for me.'

Jack sighed. Frank's conflicting activities were bewildering. He could get in a ring and knock six bells out of some Bermondsey bullet-head, then turn right round and put his feet up with a book on spiritual counselling. When he got going about human sinfulness and the problem of personal accountability, he could wear Jack down.

245

'Is he still trying to talk you into being a priest?'

Frank shook his large head slowly.

'He never did, I told you that. All he's done is try to answer my questions. The business about bein' a priest was my own idea.'

'You're not still serious about it, are you?'

'I haven't made up my mind,' Frank said.

'It would mean going back to school, wouldn't it? And that's only the start. You'd have the seminary, all the exams, the years bumming about from one parish to another until they let you have your own, and all for what? At the end of it you'd be poor as a peasant. You'd have to spend the rest of your days listening to people's sweaty confessions. And you wouldn't even have a woman for some kind of consolation. It's unnatural, Frank. You're too healthy for that kind of life.'

Frank laughed.

'You're really shocked at the idea of havin' a son that's a priest, aren't you? I can see your eyes goin' all scary-lookin' when you talk about it.'

'Maybe it's the thought of having a white sheep in the family that upsets me.'

'I'm still only at the thinking stage. There's no need to panic yet.' Frank pointed at the sunlit window. 'It's a big world out there. I thought I might travel for a while, until I'm absolutely sure what I want to do with my life.'

Jack nodded, accepting. There was very little point in arguing with Frank. He was a single-minded young man with concrete integrity. He absolutely refused to work for the firm, he would take no financial help from his father or mother, and he insisted at all times that he be allowed to make his own mistakes his own way. Jack had told Martin Weir that the lad's long-winded views on the importance of a self-made identity would put tits on a cobra.

'As long as you don't come through the front door one day with your collar on back to front and start telling me I should see the error of my ways, I won't do much complaining.'

246

'I don't think I'll be able to stop myself tryin' to redeem you,' Frank said, grinning. 'Or Mum, or our Danny. But I'll keep havin' a go at that whether I go into the priesthood or not.'

'So I'm to have no peace in my old age?'

'None. Not if I can help it.'

Jack smiled, but at the back of his mind there was the almost-impulse to speak, to tell his son he was tormented halfway to hell. But how did you tell these things to your own boy? How could you saddle him with all that?

'Been to see the doc this week?' Frank said.

'Tomorrow.'

'Make sure you go.'

'Don't nag me, son. I'll go.'

He would sooner get into a stand-up confrontation with the Krays, but the doctor insisted he visit him every week so he could monitor the new treatment. Every time Jack came away from the surgery he brought away enough depression to last him the rest of the week. If he were to do everything the old man told him, he would get nothing done. 'Don't exert yourself, Mr Kane. And make sure you get a good night's sleep, every night. Cut down the alcohol, cut it out completely if you can. Your heart's under a lot of pressure. You lead a stressful life and the big pump in your chest has to take all the strain. Remember that. You've only one ticker, you can't have another one.' Jack had begun to think of it as a massive time bomb counting down to zero under his ribs.

Frank went to the sink and rinsed his cup.

'Any idea if Mum'll be back at teatime?' he asked over his shoulder.

'Haven't a clue. She never tells me where she's going, or when she'll get back.'

'I want a word with her about that dance hall she's talkin' about buyin'. The Paradise Club. I think she should leave it alone.'

'How come?'

'There's a lot of mods still use it. If she tries to make changes – '

'Of course she'll make changes. That's one of her big missions in life. Changing things.'

'Well, it could cause a bit of grief. It's like a shrine to some of that crowd. First loves blossomed in that crummy old gaff. It's where they first learned to bop.'

'Your mum can handle a bunch of mods without much trouble.'

'Oh, sure, yeah.' Frank turned from the sink. 'But it's more strife, isn't it? I mean what she needs is less, not more. What good's the place goin' to be to her, anyway?'

'Search me.'

In fact Queenie had explained her plans to Jack in lavish detail, but there was no point telling Frank what she was up to. The Paradise Club was going to be run as the perfect front – that was how Queenie visualised it, anyway. She would co-ordinate her various projects and ventures from the office upstairs. Downstairs the club would be a regular little social centre – old-time dancing, pop nights, country-and-western, discos, amateur talent evenings, afternoon bingo. Queenie said she'd got a good feeling the minute she walked down Paradise Street and saw the place. When Queenie got a good feeling about anything that wasn't actually under her control, it was only a matter of time until she had her hooks in it.

'I'll talk to her about it,' Frank said.

'If you can get her to stand still long enough.'

'I want to talk to her about our Danny, too. She's letting him off with too much.'

'How do you mean?'

'He goes round the 'hithe runnin' up bills in clothes shops and shoe shops and in them poncy barbers he goes to. They let him, because they think it might be unhealthy to refuse. He's a slow payer, when he pays at all. So some of the braver traders, they call up Mum and tell her Danny owes such-and-such, and she sends somebody round to pay the bill. It's not on, is it?'

'I'll have a word with him myself,' Jack said.

'Yeah – but will he listen to you?'

How the world changed, Jack thought. There had been

a time when any person who didn't listen to what Jack Kane told him was assumed, automatically, to be soft in the head, or just tired of living.

'If he doesn't listen, Frank, he'll take the consequences.'

Jack saw the look on Frank's face as he went out. It was the look that said yeah, sure Dad, I'll let you go on thinking you're still the boss.

FIFTEEN

Queenie had a long-standing faith in the power of talismans. Since the age of twelve, when a fortune-teller at a travelling fair gave her a stone engraved with mystical markings, she had clung to the belief that such things would attract luck and ward off misfortune. Later, she began to believe that occult power was invested in places as well as objects. Back in 1967 she had told her friend Beattie that she got the strangest feeling when she first saw the Paradise Club. 'It was the way religious people must feel when they visit a shrine – a sort of sense of power and safety rolled into one. I knew it there and then, Beattie – this was my place, my special talisman, the one I'd been fated to find.'

She had thought of changing the name of the dance hall to the Talisman, but the fact that paradise was already part of the title persuaded her to keep it as it was. Queenie's personal idea of paradise was to be in a position where she had everything her own way, and from the day she made the dance hall her headquarters she felt she was on the road to that special state of grace. With her self-confidence reinforced she embarked on a five-year plan of expansion and consolidation. Her people soon became known as the Paradise Mob.

'Rivers of blood' was a phrase that crossed Queenie's lips many times during that period. Anyone who thought she was being melodramatic had only to look at her record to realise she was describing the upshot of her favourite strategies. Omelettes weren't made without breaking eggs; power would never become a reality without bloodshed. Queenie could cite history to back up her conviction.

Jack was reminded of how things had gone in Glasgow during the thirties. The battles were all-or-nothing, there was no room for compromise; vicious tactics were the only kind; neutral ground became very scarce. He didn't like it. He would have been content to settle down in a benign dictatorship, making a peaceful living, repaying his subjects' allegiance with his protection. He wanted balance; progress was secondary, something that would either take place or not, depending on the currents of events.

But that kind of life was out of the question. Jack was Queenie's husband, after all. They were still looked upon as a team, tarred with the same brush.

'She'll give you more grief than you ever brought on yourself,' young Frank warned him. 'The iniquity of the mother shall be visited upon the father, to misquote Exodus. Watch her, Dad. Try and keep her under some kind of control, for your own sake.'

The warning was issued five days after Frank's twenty-third birthday and two days before he left for Africa. As Jack had known even before he tried, there was no point in trying to argue with Frank about his decision. His mind was made up. Resolution was cemented in position. He was joining the French Foreign Legion.

'You're not even bloody French,' Jack said despairingly.

'The officers are French,' Frank explained. 'The soldiers are mostly foreigners. That's why it's called the Foreign Legion. *Légion Étrangère*, if you want the proper name.'

'They're just a bunch of hired guns,' Jack grunted, 'whatever fancy handles they give themselves.'

'They're an efficient professional army. They've been a presence in every major international conflict since they were founded back in 1831.'

'Sounds like you read that off the leaflet.'

'I did, as a matter of fact.'

'But you're religious, aren't you?' Jack said. 'What does a religious man want to go fighting battles for? You'll be expected to kill people, do you realise that?'

'Life's a lot more complex than catechisms lead us to believe, Dad. I'm drawn to the service of Christ, I can say that in all honesty. But I'm a man of action, too. War is action, and it's in the nature of man. You believe that, don't you?'

'I'm not so sure nowadays.'

'You're not so sure about yourself, and that's maybe because you've come out on the far side of things. You've learned something from your experiences. But you can't deny that people, other people, are aggressive. Maybe war's something in our nature that we're supposed to overcome, or live through till we wear out the impulse – I don't know. It's somethin' in myself that I want to explore. I'm lookin' for answers. I think I'll find a lot of them in the Legion.'

'Couldn't you just join the British Army and find your answers in Aldershot, instead of buggering off to wherever it is?'

'Algeria,' Frank said. 'Sidi bel Abbès. It's not French territory any longer, but there's still a basic training facility there.'

'So what's the point of going all that distance?'

'I want to travel. It's a nice compact solution, if you look at it straight. I join the Legion and I get to find out a lot of things about myself, about other people, too – and I travel.'

No argument, then. At the beginning of September Frank took off for North West Africa. A month later his brother was installed as overseer on the Paradise Mob's gambling operations. Jack wanted to argue about that, too. Talking to Danny himself would be no use, since he only listened to his mother. So Jack confronted Queenie.

'He's not the man for the job,' he told her. 'His temper's a mile too short. It's work for an older man, a wiser head.'

'He can only get wise if he gets a chance to learn

things,' Queenie countered. 'And maybe he is quick-tempered, but he's got the muscle to follow through. Danny can look after himself.'

Jack's heart ached over what was happening to Danny. He had airs and graces, he impersonated the dress and manner of the young business types. But he was trained to be nothing but a hoodlum. The frustration of that alone would damage him. He would go around feeling superior to his peers and he would be rejected by the society he admired. That was a recipe for very damaging loneliness.

'He should have a spell doing desk work, Queenie. Let him learn organisation, bookwork – *patience*. Make him manager of the Paradise Club. Give him some legitimate work to do.'

Queenie was immovable. She knew what she was doing. In her view Danny was being groomed for succession, and she was focussing all her effort on him, since there wasn't the faintest hope that Frank would have anything to do with the business.

'And if you really had his good at heart,' she told Jack, 'you'd be encouragin' him, too, instead of criticisin' everythin' he says or does.'

'I can't encourage him,' Jack said. 'I can't discourage him, either. I have no effect. He doesn't quite believe I exist.'

'Well, you know whose fault that is, don't you?'

'Sure,' Jack said. 'It's your fault. You've deliberately belittled me in Danny's eyes. You've convinced him I'm just some shadow that flits about the place. I'm nothing that matters to him. Nothing.'

'Don't blame me for what you've turned into,' she said.

In the fifth year of Queenie's five-year plan the Paradise Mob ran up against an obstacle when they tried to move in on a stretch of the West Lane district. The obstacle was called Fred Ellis. The three members of Queenie's pioneer group, sent in to size up the turf, were snatched off the street, beaten up and sent back with the message that no further forays should be made on Mr Ellis's territory.

'She's bitten off more than she can chew,' Martin Weir told Jack.

'Is it more than *we* can chew?' Jack said.

'We don't want to try. Ellis has been dormant for years, but he's dormant the way unexploded bombs are dormant. He's old-school, Jack. Pays back every hurt with interest. He's happy to be left with his little bit of turf over there at West Lane, but if anybody so much as hints they're interested in edging in, he'll go off his head. The way he sees it, he never trod on anybody's toes to get what he's got, so nobody has any right to step on his.'

'Queenie's got plans for his whole territory.'

'Well, she might get it, if she tried hard enough. But it'll cost more than it's worth.'

'I think she knows that. But once she makes a move to take something, she won't back off. It's a principle with her now. All we can do, you and me, is mind our own arses.'

Two days later word reached Jack that Queenie's boys had broken up a card school in a warehouse owned by Fred Ellis. They had confiscated the kitty – several hundred pounds of it – and smashed up expensive gaming equipment stored at the warehouse. Ellis had already issued a promise: Jack and Ma Kane wouldn't get away with such an outrage.

Jack went to see Ellis. He had to ask around for a while, but eventually a man was found to take a message, and after twenty minutes Jack was shown into a small room, no more than ten-by-seven, behind a plastic strip curtain at the back of a newsagents. On the wall there was a map of the Rotherhithe district with paper boys' routes marked in red crayon. Newspapers and magazines were stacked in the corners. At a yellow formica topped table a stooped, grey-faced man sat rolling a cigarette between knobbly fingers. He looked up at Jack with hooded, elongated eyes.

'You wanted to see me,' he said, his throat rumbly with phlegm.

'If you're Fred Ellis.'

'That's me. And you're Jack Kane.' Ellis nodded at a tubular metal chair. 'Sit down, if you want.'

Jack sat and they faced each other.

'I know about what happened down here the other night. The business at your card school . . .'

Ellis nodded.

'Don't see how you could avoid knowin', since it was your idea.'

'Not my idea. Mrs Kane's idea. Her operation. It was nothing to do with me.'

Ellis nodded again.

'I've heard she's inclined to be independent.' He narrowed his eyes at Jack. 'How come you can't keep her under control?'

'I don't want to discuss my domestic problems with you, Mr Ellis, but I'll answer that one question. For me to control Queenie, I'd have to stand over her every minute of every day. With a stick.'

'Why don't you do that, then?'

Jack didn't say anything for a minute. He looked about the room.

'Listen,' he said finally, 'I didn't come here to play silly buggers. I wanted you to know that I have no quarrel with you. I've no plans to take or even touch anything that's yours. I wanted you to hear that from my own mouth.'

'Fair enough. I've heard you.' Ellis stuck the unlit rollup into the corner of his mouth and let it dangle there. 'What's the position with you nowadays, anyway? Retired, have you?'

'Not exactly. But since I've been in less than robust health these past few years, I've settled down to a quiet existence. I want it to stay that way.'

'Fine,' Ellis said. 'Control your wife, then, and you can carry on havin' your nice quiet existence.'

Jack sighed.

'Look, I'll say it again. What Queenie gets up to has nothing to do with me.'

'You're responsible for her actions, as far as I'm

concerned.' Ellis lit his cigarette with a rattly old Zippo. He blew the smoke straight at Jack. 'If you were divorced, or even separated, I'd be able to see things different. But you and your old lady aren't split up, are you? You live in the same house. You're a couple. So one of you shares the responsibility for what the other one does. If you don't want any aggravation, make sure she doesn't give me any.'

Jack stood up.

'That's it, then?'

'That's it.'

Jack left.

Walking home, he thought about Ellis and the scale of his operation, about how insignificant the man and his territory would have seemed ten years ago. Ellis himself, in fact, would have meant nothing, he was just another bug, easy to squash if the need arose. But now Jack was worrying about him. So was Martin. And why? The answer was laughable, but also sad. They didn't want any trouble. They wanted to be left in peace – by a third-rate old hoodlum sitting rolling fags at a plastic table at the heart of his crummy empire.

That night Queenie didn't appear at the house until after twelve. Jack had waited up so they could have a showdown about the West Lane business, but she wouldn't talk to him. When he tried to insist she went to her room and slammed the door on him.

The next night was a Friday. On Fridays Jack and Martin foregathered in their own little booth at The Bell. By the time Martin arrived, usually around eight, Jack would be half drunk, which was as drunk as he ever got now, no matter how much he took. This Friday was no different, except that Martin himself showed signs of having taken a few before he got there.

They settled into the buttoned plush seats with a bottle of vodka on the table between them. Martin poured equal measures into the glasses.

'I've got gloomy tidings, Jack.' He replaced the cap on the bottle, turning it slowly, thoughtfully. 'At seven o'clock tonight I collected the minicab take. While I was there big George got a newsflash on the wire. Fred Ellis got hammered. It's a broken legs job. His newsagents was wrecked, too.'

'When?'

'Must have been just before George got the call. Word travels fast among the drivers.'

Jack put his hands on the table and turned his face to the ceiling for a minute. He sighed very slowly.

'Now the shit hits the fan, eh?'

'Any minute now, I should think,' Martin said.

'Who's Ellis's right arm?'

'Lawrence Grady.'

The name was familiar.

'Our Frank fought a Lawrence Grady once. It was a championship event. Frank won, but it was a struggle.'

'It's the same man. He's a hard one, all right. Joined up with Ellis two years ago.'

'He didn't take it too well when Frank won the fight. I was standing at the side of the ring, I saw the look on his face. Pure hate.' Jack swallowed his drink and uncapped the bottle. 'I'm debating now whether I should just go home and exterminate the wife, or if I should stay where I'm comfortable and drink myself to death.' He shook his head at Martin. 'The very thought of strife gives me a headache nowadays. What a thing it is, to get old and peaceable.'

Martin smiled.

'We're greybeards, Jack. I never seriously believed it would happen. I had this conviction I was going to stay young forever. But here I am, getting a fat belly and thin hair and thinking about retiring.'

Jack looked surprised.

'Do you mean that?'

'Aye, it's the God's truth. I think about it all the time, lately. Do you know what I want to do? I want to settle all my affairs here, sell up the house and go back to Edinburgh. I think the heat up there should have died down by now.' He swallowed half of his drink and let

Jack top up the glass. 'How about you? Have you never fancied going back home?'

'I've never stopped thinking about it,' Jack said. 'But I made a very sad discovery a couple of years ago. There's no home to go back to.'

He told Martin about it. It was the first time he had told anyone. On an impulse one morning, after a bleak sleepless night, death-haunted and despairing, he decided to go back to Glasgow. He didn't need to take anything with him, he had money and he could buy what he needed when he got there. He wanted London and everything about it behind him. Finished. He wanted to go home. So he took a taxi to Heathrow. He bought a ticket, boarded a plane and in less than an hour he was there. Glasgow. He was back.

But it was gone. He stood on the Saltmarket, looking about him, more of a stranger here than he'd been in any place. Arriving in London all those years ago hadn't been half as bewildering. It wasn't simply that the city looked different, which he had expected anyway; it was the identity that had changed, the very spirit of the place. The vigour of life that had lived on in his memory wasn't there, either. It had vanished, along with the kind of people who once thronged the streets. There *was* vigour in the tempo of the busy thoroughfares, but it was another kind. It was polite, over-cheerful, desperately bright. Jack suspected it might be a fake. Glasgow was integrating, he thought; it was suppressing its character, the truth of itself. The city was trying to please, instead of letting itself be taken as it was found.

He walked along unfamiliar once-known streets, places where he had lived, played as a boy, got in fights. There was nothing. Not an echo of the old reality. These were forgeries. He went into a pub – the Cockit Hat was gone – and ordered a large brandy. He drank it down and it flared in his throat, providing a legitimate excuse for tears. He caught the evening flight back to Heathrow.

'I hope Edinburgh's still there, Martin.'

'Oh, it will be. It never had much reality to lose in the first place.'

'Have you any thoughts about when you'll go?'

Martin said maybe in a year, two at most.

'I know the place I want to live. It's got wide views, not many houses. I'll be left alone. Perfection, Jack. Pure bliss.'

Jack wished he could get drunker. But this was it, he never got further, short of falling asleep.

'I suppose I'll end my days here in the Smoke,' he said. 'I don't belong here, but I don't belong any other place, either. It's terrible sometimes, realising I've no home.'

Just a shade drunker, he thought, and he could have admitted it was even worse not knowing who he was. He had no image of himself now, it was blurred beyond recognisable shape.

'Tell you what, Martin – on this dark night, with the wrath of Fred Ellis hanging over us in whatever form it'll take – let's murder a bottle of the good stuff. I've a litre of Hine behind the bar.'

They took two hours to drink it. By the last dregs they were both numb, smiling at everybody, snug in their booth. Jack would have liked to stay there forever. He felt cocooned. Everything pleased him, for the present. Even the jukebox. It was playing the current number one, a weird effort called Mouldy Old Dough by a character, or characters, called Lieutenant Pigeon.

Martin pushed himself to his feet and stood with his hands on the table.

'I've got to go, Jack. I'm up early tomorrow.'

'Aw, come on, we'll have a few more. You don't have to pay any attention to the licensing hours. This is our pub, remember?'

'No, got to be moving. I've had too much as it is.'

Martin turned away from the booth. Jack stood up. He couldn't quite feel his legs.

'Hang on. I'll come with you. I've discovered I'm not too good at drinking by myself.'

'You've plenty of company here,' Martin said.

'Good company's not too keen on me, for some reason,' Jack confided in a stage whisper. 'I'm a magnet for chancers. I think I'll go home. I shouldn't have any trouble getting to sleep tonight.'

Outside the pub they stood on the step, inhaling the night.

'I'm leaving the car,' Jack said. 'A walk'll do me good, if I don't bump into too many walls.'

Martin slapped Jack's arm.

'Good night. See you in the morning.'

He stepped on to the pavement. A car across the road drew away from the kerb. Martin waited to let it pass, but it stopped. He stepped into the road as Jack turned and walked the other way. The car moved again, accelerated suddenly, the engine roaring. Martin glanced round a second before the bonnet hit him. He rose in the air, one leg flailing high. Jack stopped, saw Martin's body come down on the far side of the road. The car swerved, made a tyre-ripping U-turn and drove off along the street beside the pub. Jack saw the driver in a stripe of street light, his face tense.

'Christ almighty . . .'

He knew he shouldn't try to run. He did and found he couldn't keep a straight line. He made himself stop, swayed a moment then hurried across the road.

Martin was motionless, his arms up round his head, one leg snapped at the hip and sticking out at his side. Jack reached down and touched the bloodied head. It turned easily. Air escaped the lips in a tiny sigh.

Jack straightened, saw people come across from the pub.

'I'll ring for an ambulance,' a woman called.

'There's no rush,' Jack said, barely loud enough to be heard.

He came back to awareness of place and time with Queenie bustling about the living room.

'You haven't slept,' she said, as if he didn't know. 'Here. Drink this while it's hot.' She put a cup of coffee

260

on the table in front of the couch. 'You should get into bed for a while. You look terrible.'

Jack touched the stubble on his face, looked towards the sunny window. His mouth tasted terrible. He had sat in the same position for hours; now, when he moved, there was a sharp line of pain from his shoulder to the base of his skull. He put both hands on his knees and pushed himself up. Standing, he felt his head begin to throb.

Queenie was rattling about in the hall. She came in with one arm in her jacket. Her make-up was already in place, her hair lacquered into symmetrical waves.

'I'm goin' now,' she said.

Jack turned and looked at her coldly.

'What's on the agenda?'

'Eh?'

'A couple of fire-bombings, maybe?' he said. 'A bit of tarring and feathering? It's your turn, Queenie. You've got Martin killed, you can't stop there. Do something that'll make Fred Ellis bring in the tanks.'

'Don't you go blamin' me for what happened.'

'Who else is to blame?' Jack shook his head. 'You're a bloody tragedy. Have you stopped and thought about yourself, lately? It must be horrible waking up and realising you're Queenie Kane.'

'Now you listen – '

'Shut it,' Jack said, heading for the kitchen. 'I'm in no mood.'

At the sink he splashed water on his face and dabbed it dry with the dish towel. He looked out at the sun on the grass. There had been no thoughts of his own demise this morning. No trembling, wondering how far he was from the pit. Martin was *there*, that was the only focus of his mind. Martin Weir would know now, or not know, depending on which one of them had been right about that place he'd gone.

He turned away from the window sharply.

'Right, then,' he muttered. 'Get moving, Jack.'

He went upstairs. In the bedroom he stripped and

padded naked to the bathroom. He stood under the shower and turned up the heat, standing with his eyes shut, face lifted to the scalding spray. When he felt he couldn't take the heat much longer he turned it higher still and soaped himself, from the crown to the soles of his feet. Unhooking the shower head he applied it to his head, chest, belly, arms and legs. He breathed through his mouth, panting into the steam, hearing the rush of his blood in his ears, feeling the thud in his chest.

When he was dry he used his electric razor, relishing the way it sliced through the wiry stubble, leaving his cheeks and chin smooth pink. He dressed in grey slacks and a pale blue shirt, leaving it open at the neck. He put on black cashmere socks and slipped his feet into glove-soft Italian moccasins, black and buffed to a spotless shine. At the mirror he combed his hair carefully, brushing the sides over his ears. He took his navy-blue wool jacket from the wardrobe, brushed it carefully and put it on.

He stood at the top of the stairs for a minute, going through his bunch of keys, looking for the one that would unlock the old army foot locker out in the garage. Going down to the hall, it occurred to him that the man outside and the one inside were now precisely the same. For the time being, anyway.

At the hospital they were reluctant to let him see Fred Ellis. He was in pain, the nurse explained, and he badly needed to rest. Jack insisted. He wheedled. He wouldn't stay more than a couple of minutes, he promised. His wide blue eyes persuaded the nurse it would do no harm to let him in.

'But please don't tire Mr Ellis.'

'Oh, I won't do that, my love. Word of honour.'

Ellis was in a private room. The ventian blinds were set so that the sunlight was directed on to the floor. He was propped on three pillows, his legs stretched out on half-shell aluminium splints. He winced and reached out for the bell switch as Jack walked in.

'No need to do that, Mr Ellis. I'm here to talk. That's all.'

'I've nothin' to say to you.'

'I'm glad about that. I hate being interrupted.' Jack gripped the rail at the foot of the bed. 'I told you once already, what Queenie's been doing on your turf is no concern of mine. I'd nothing to do with what happened to you last night, either. None of it has been my fight.'

'Yeah,' Ellis croaked. 'Like you say, you told me all that stuff before.'

'But I'm telling you this now – I'm making it my fight. And I'm finishing it. Today. Pass on the word to as many people as need to know. Get your mongrels back on the leash.'

'And how are you goin' to finish it, eh?'

'I'll stop Queenie. After today she'll keep away from West Lane.'

Ellis grunted, his face ashen against the pillows.

'You think that'll finish it, do you? I'm just to forget this.' He pointed at his bandaged legs. 'And forget what's happened to my shop. That's what you think, is it?'

'I don't think you'll forget it, no. But you'll do nothing about it. You've had your bit of vengeance already. More than you deserved. Martin Weir's dead and it was your doing. Quite a price for a wrecked shop and a pair of busted legs, Mr Ellis. The only person that's still due compensation out of this war is *me*. And I'll collect that before today's out, too.'

Jack stood away from the bed.

'That's all I came to say. I'll leave you now.'

He was at the door when Ellis spoke again.

'I'm not lettin' up,' he said hoarsely. 'Don't think that for a minute. This business isn't finished.'

'Yes it is,' Jack said. 'It's best you accept that. If you do anything else that I take personally, I'll kill you.'

He left, certain that Ellis believed him. People always did believe him when he told the absolute truth.

He found Queenie at the Paradise Club. She was in her little office, mumbling into the phone. He waited until she was finished, then he told her what he had told Ellis: the territorial bid was over.

'Shift your attention somewhere else, Queenie. West Lane is out.'

She sat back and stared at him, arms folded defensively.

'Listen,' she said, 'I know you're upset about what happened to Martin. We all are. But don't let it turn your brain. Go home and just relax. It's a nice day, sit out in the garden.'

'I mean what I say. Forget Fred Ellis, forget West Lane.'

'Jack – don't interfere, eh? You're out of your depth.'

The side of his fist hit the desk with such a crash that the phone shot off and landed in the corner. Queenie yelped.

'Get this through your nut!' Jack roared. 'If you or your monkeys make another move against Ellis, you'll get a fight off me like you'd never believe! It's a promise, Queenie! I'll fucking bury you!'

He left while she was still rescuing the telephone. Five minutes later he parked his car on a side street leading off the south end of West Lane. He got out, locked the door and headed for the nearest pub.

The barman was cagey. He knew who Jack was.

'I'm not sure I know any Lawrence Grady,' he said, putting Jack's vodka in front of him.

'Is the guv'nor in, by any chance?' Jack said.

'Yeah, I think so.'

'Ask him if he'd spare me a minute, would you?'

Jack swallowed the vodka while he waited. When the landlord appeared he looked surly, tight-lipped. He was ready to put up resistance.

'What can I do for you, sir?'

'I'm trying to locate Lawrence Grady.'

The landlord shook his head firmly.

'Never heard of him.'

'Yes you have. Just tell me where I can find him. He must hang out somewhere round here.'

The landlord took the measure of Jack's stare. His expression revised itself. A memory was dawning.

'Is he the one that's a boxer, by any chance?'

'That's him.'

'Oh, in that case I do know him – by sight, that is.'

'And where would I be likely to sight him?'

Now the landlord mimed recollection.

'If I'm not mistaken,' he said, 'he goes in the Exeter a lot.'

Jack thanked him and left. The Exeter was at the other end of the road, half a mile away. He went to the car, got in and started the engine. He drove up the road slowly, giving the message time to travel. He was aware that his presence was being noted from the odd window and doorway.

In the pub he ordered another vodka. The place was hot, dampish, smelly. Bronze-green flies came and went. The total atmosphere was one of slovenly neglect. Jack hated dirty pubs, yet he loved the memory of the Cockit Hat, one of the filthiest he'd ever been in.

There were only three men in the place when Jack arrived, but six more arrived, one at a time, in the five minutes it took him to finish his drink. They positioned themselves, in pairs, at a table and at either end of the bar. As expected, Lawrence Grady appeared. He stepped up to the bar and stood a yard from Jack.

'I hear you're looking for me,' he said.

Jack looked at him. Grady was the kind of boxer who took no care to protect his face. He was a mauler with brutality in place of style. His nose was bent and twisted to one side. One ear was thickened and deformed. His lower lip had a deep fissure at the middle and Jack noticed some of his teeth were missing.

'That's right.' Jack raised his hand to catch the barman's attention. 'Another vodka, please.'

'Well?' Grady came closer. 'What do you want?'

Jack glanced around, sketching a strategy. He looked at Grady again.

'It's kind of private. Can we sit down somewhere?' He

pointed to a table near the open door. 'Over there, eh? Where it's cool.'

Grady didn't order a drink. He followed Jack to the table. They sat down. Jack put the fresh drink to his lips, poised the glass and tilted it back smartly, swallowing the lot.

'That's better.' He put down the glass, showed Grady his wide blue eyes. 'I saw you last night,' he said.

'Oh yeah? When was that?'

'A couple of seconds after you ran down my friend Martin Weir.'

Grady's big face wasn't capable of much expression. Even so, it was obvious he wasn't trying for any. He blinked at Jack.

'So? What do you want to talk to me about? Safer drivin'?'

'I had to find you,' Jack said, 'so I could let you know that it hurt me, what you did. You should get punished for it.'

'Is that right?'

Jack nodded. He flicked a glance across the room. Nobody had moved. The layout remained as it was. Two men near, two near enough, the rest not worth considering.

'Who's goin' to punish me then, old man?'

Jack had unbuttoned his jacket. His right hand went inside, gripped the stubby handle of the hatchet slung from his armpit. He looked at the table, trying to look as if he was stuck for an answer. Grady's hands were both on the table now. A bonus. Big fighter's hands, his only tools.

'Me,' Jack said. 'I'm going to punish you.'

'And how are you goin' to do that?'

Jack looked at the ugly face. With the sneer it was even uglier. He thought of Martin, recalled this face behind the wheel of the car, driving away from the crumpled body.

Grady stuck his head forward, hovering over his flattened hands.

'I said, how are you goin' to do that?'

266

'Like this.'

Speed and movement had to co-ordinate. And they did. Jack moved up and back. His hand came out of his jacket. The hatchet went forward and down. Hard. Once on the right hand. Once on the left. Blood and bone spattered before Grady could move. Jack was a foot from the door before anybody else knew what was up.

Grady let out a roar. He jerked up from the chair, hands ruined and dripping. He landed on his knees, vomiting through his teeth. A man shot forward and barred the door with his shoulder. He put out his hands to Jack. The hatchet blade hit him in the mouth. Teeth crunched. As he fell Jack brought the back of the blade down on his shoulder, breaking it.

He was out and round the corner before anybody went after him. He put his head down and ran for all he was worth. As he got to the car the door opened and a big man got out. He had a knife. Jack skidded to a stop, heard the others coming behind him.

Bad odds. He would go down, but he'd take two or three with him. He poised the hatchet, turned.

A voice tore the air.

'Get back! The lot of you! Back! *Fuckin' now*!'

A gun exploded. Five yards from Jack a patch of the road tore open. His pursuers scattered, heading back to the pub. The one with the knife ducked down around the car and galloped away along an alley. Jack looked behind him. Young Danny was leaning on the open door of his own car, halfway up the street. He was holding a twelve-bore. When the others were inside the pub he came away from the car, nodding curtly to his father. He walked past, stood in the middle of the road and took aim. He fired and the whole side window of the pub fell in.

'I think we should go,' Danny said.

They got in their cars. Jack drove behind Danny all the way back to the Paradise Club. At the door he drew up and got out. He leaned on the bonnet, waiting for Danny. As the lad came along the pavement Queenie appeared at the door of the dance hall.

267

'Trouble?' she said, addressing Danny.

He nodded. They both looked at Jack. Reproachfully.

'I got him to tail you,' Queenie said. 'I knew you'd get yourself in bother, the mood you were in.' She turned back to the club. 'Come on, then. Come in and have a drink and settle yourself before you have another bleedin' heart attack.'

Jack watched her waddle in through the door and thought – before he switched off thought entirely – how much kinder it would have been if Ellis's boys had chopped him down where he stood.

SIXTEEN

In the spring of 1973 Jack consulted a Harley Street cardiologist, Dr Anthony Peverill. He was given a thorough examination and a series of cardiovascular function tests that lasted for more than an hour. At the end of it all he was given a cup of tea and invited to sit down in a comfortable armchair in Peverill's office. When he was settled the consultant went behind his desk, flipped through the test printouts, and sighed. He warned Jack, sternly, that he wasn't doing enough to help his heart cope with everyday life.

'The picture that emerges from everything we have done here today,' Peverill said, 'is of a heart and arteries that have been punished too severely and for too long. To know the full extent of the damage and disorder I should put you on a twenty-four-hour stress test, but frankly I don't think you'd stand up to anything so rigorous.'

Peverill didn't hide his impatience. He was a man of sixty, a fine example of what could be accomplished by an organised person determined to last as long as he could. He was firm muscled and tight skinned, with the clear eyes and sound, regular teeth of a motion-picture physician. Peverill looked after his cardiovascular system and wouldn't trouble himself to conceal his disapproval of people who didn't.

'You've a choice, even at this stage,' he told Jack. 'You can live out a normal span, which will involve a lot of changes in the way you conduct your life, or you can carry on as you do at present and drop down dead any time between now and Christmas. I don't exaggerate the case, Mr Kane.'

'I suppose I should make an effort,' Jack said dryly.

'Of course you should.' Peverill clasped his hands, reminding Jack of the judge back in Glasgow years ago, composing himself before he handed down the jail sentence. 'For my part, I'll put you on a course of vasodilators. They're chemical compounds designed to expand the blood vessels, and yours could certainly do with it. I'll also give you something more powerful to use when you get the attacks of shortness of breath. The rest will be up to yourself.'

'What do I do?'

'Change your diet, for a start. That's vitally important. Eat no fried food. Have more fruit and fresh vegetables. Cut your meat intake, have fish and chicken instead. Stop drinking so heavily – I've a feeling alcohol has hurt your liver as well as your arteries.'

Jack knew it had. Some mornings the pain in his liver made him sick.

'Now,' Peverill said, 'dietary reforms aside, I think you should do something about the quality of your inner life – do you have any hobbies or particular enthusiasms?'

Jack said he had none.

'Isn't there something you've always fancied dabbling in, then?'

'Nothing I can think of . . .'

'Fishing? Carpentry, rug-making, anything like that? Think about it when you get home. There must be something that would absorb you. Whatever you think it might be, give it a try. You're too absorbed with yourself, in my opinion. Too broody. That's a bad thing for someone with a heart condition.'

Driving home, Jack wondered if there was any sense in trying to prolong his pointless existence. He had been wondering the same thing, on and off, for months. Apart from a fear of death, he had few reasons for hanging on. He drew no great pleasure from anything. Vodka-numbness was the nicest sensation he knew, now that sex had packed up on him. His life had no area of relish, no region of zest. And he knew damned well that a hobby would make no difference.

A few months earlier, sitting in The Bell with a bottle on the table and a newspaper propped in front of him, he had made a dreamy attempt to work out why he felt so fed up all the time. He concluded, after a lot of thought, that over the years he had made himself a one-purpose man in the process of rendering other people miserable. His life was littered with shadowy deeds and dark after-maths. It was a gloomy thing petering out in uselessness. There simply hadn't been enough sunshine.

That thought came to him again as he swung the car round the end of the street where he lived. *I'm starved of light.*

What was the answer? Was there an antidote? It wasn't as if he could simply turn to the light. He'd no idea where it was. So what could he do? Get monumentally pissed and stay that way until his heart gave out? To do exactly what the doctor said about food and drink would only aggravate the sense of monotony. To ignore the advice would shorten his life. Jack didn't like life much, but he didn't want to die, either.

So what to do, for Christ's sake?

'I'm going away for a while,' he told Queenie that night.

She was at the living-room table with strips of till-roll, invoices, receipts and a calculator. She paused with her finger over the 'plus' button and looked at Jack.

'Away? Where?'

He shrugged.

'You're goin' away, but you don't know where?'

'That's about it, yes.'

'You're a real dynamo when it comes to makin' decisions. How long will you stay for, when you get to wherever it might be?'

'I've no idea. A week, two weeks.'

Queenie went back to her calculator. Jack sank lower

271

in his chair and closed his eyes, trying to think of some place where he might find the light.

Next morning, bathed and shaved, dressed in blazer and flannels, he stood in the hall with his packed bags beside him and looked at the short list of destinations he had made. They were all seaside resorts. After a minute he decided he'd go to Brighton. He had never been there. Of all the places in Britain he had never visited, it was the only one he was curious about any more.

It was raining when he arrived. He had to wait twenty minutes for a taxi. By the time one arrived he was regretting the decision to come here. He told the driver to take him to a good hotel.

After dinner he began to feel better. The Palace was comfortable and the food was good. The sea breezes wafting in from the balcony outside his room reminded him of the time he spent in Blackpool with Airchie. He just hoped the sinus condition wouldn't come back.

That night he stayed late in the bar, talking over the calamitous state of world affairs with an old retired clergyman. He enjoyed himself. Without having any opinions of his own about the problems in Israel, or the endless dilemma of Northern Ireland, he performed a convincing recital of points of view he had picked up from the newspapers. It was the talk itself that mattered, the interaction. He went to his room feeling he'd had a good night. It was only afterwards, settling down to sleep, that he wondered if he was in the process of substituting one kind of pointlessness for another. Was the light really to be found in Brighton?

In the morning he got a guide book from the reception desk and went for a walk. He visited the Royal Pavilion and discovered it was Indian on the outside, Chinese inside. He decided the place was weird. The old fishing port, with its black flint houses, was much better: the marks and traces of real people were there, it was believable and it had heart, although the antique shops were an incongruous touch, and the prices they charged for junk were outrageous.

With an hour to go before lunch he decided to stroll along the promenade. The day was cool but the sun shone, warming his neck and the back of his head. The tangy air made him think of food. He decided he would linger over his lunch and maybe follow it with a couple of drinks in the hotel bar before he took a siesta.

Passing a pub, he made an impulsive revision of his plans. A drink before lunch would be nice. An aperitif, nothing heavy. He went into the pub and looked around. It was homelier than the frontage led him to believe. The carpet was clean, but near the bar it was worn down to the canvas. The wallpaper was bleached where sunlight reached it and the tables, though spotless, were old and chipped. But it was a nice place, nevertheless. Shabby genteel, he thought, seeing an old lady with a pink cardigan and a string of pearls serving behind the bar.

He went forward, smiled, and ordered a large vodka. As the woman poured it into a hand measure he watched the silvery trickle and imagined its dry hot taste on his palate. The sea did sharpen the senses, there was no doubt about that. He paid for the drink and put the glass to his lips almost eagerly. The smell of it, the drink that was supposed to be odourless, made him salivate an instant before he poured some on his tongue. His ears tingled as he swallowed. He must try drinking by the seaside more often, he decided. It was a whole new experience.

He turned and saw a woman on a stool at the end of the bar. His heart lurched. She would be forty, perhaps, a small woman, nicely built with the hint of spectacular breasts beneath her chunky sweater. But it was her face that held him, the even features, the blonde-grey hair combed down straight on either side. She was the spitting image of Annie Kempson.

She turned her head aside sharply. He realised he was staring at her.

Don't hesitate, he told himself. He swallowed a good

273

mouthful of vodka, took a deep breath and moved along the bar.

'Excuse me . . .'

She looked at him. Up close she was even more like Annie.

'You must have thought I was terribly rude,' he said. 'I was staring. I didn't mean to. You gave me a shock, you see . . .'

'I look that bad, do I?' she said, smiling.

'What I mean is, you're the image of someone I used to know. I thought for a second you were her, until I realised she'd be a lot older than you by now.'

'Oh.'

'Can I get you a drink?'

'I've got one, thanks.'

'Well let me top it up.'

He hung on to his smile, playing it persistent but polite. She didn't try to object when he pointed to her glass and asked the old lady to put another one in there.

'My name's Jack, by the way.' Awkward gaps at the start of a chat-up could wreck a man's chances. The flow had to be sustained if he was to develop any speed. 'The friend I mistook you for was called Annie. That's not your name, is it?'

'Lily,' she said.

'And are you on holiday, Lily?'

'No. I live in Brighton.' Her glass was put in front of her again. She picked it up. 'Cheers.'

No wedding ring, Jack noticed, and almost laughed at himself, going through the old routine like this.

'On holiday yourself?' Lily asked him.

'Yes. Bit of an impulse. I suddenly fancied a break.'

'So you came all the way down from Scotland?'

'I left Scotland twenty-seven years ago. I live just up the road, in London.'

It could have died there, for she looked at the clock above the bar and suddenly she was all hurry. She gulped down her drink, taking her cigarettes and lighter off the bar at the same time and dropping them into her handbag.

'You'll have to excuse me Jack.' She slid off the stool. As expected, she was the same height as Annie Kempson. 'I'm a working girl. I'll be late if I don't get a move on.'

'Where do you work?'

'The British Legion Club.'

He had walked past it earier.

'What if I meet you when you finish? We could have a drink, a chat.'

She frowned, thinking. He could see she wasn't pretending.

'Sure,' she said, her face clearing. 'That would be nice.'

'I'll meet you at the club, then.'

'Do you know where it is?'

'I got all the important places sussed-out straight away. What time?'

'Half-six.'

'I'll see you,' Jack said, keeping the smile warm, the eyes wide.

By five o'clock he was getting depressed. Just what in hell was he playing at, he wondered. After the last two humiliations he'd decided that his days with the women were over. Making a play for Lily was just asking for pain. There was always the chance, of course, that he'd be lucky – she might turn out to be one of the three per cent, or whatever the figure was, who weren't interested in sex. Pigs might fly, too. Any female who responded to a chat-up as easily as she did was no stranger to the rituals. Women like that, and especially at that age, could cut up rought when a man didn't perform. They always assumed the failure meant they weren't desirable enough.

At ten past five he wondered if he should go down to the hotel bar and have a quick stun. Or maybe it would be better if he went to the bar, stayed there and didn't turn up at the British Legion at all. He considered that for a while, then scrapped the idea. If he stood her up he'd be bound to bump into her somewhere later. It was Sod's Law.

And anyway, he wanted to see her, whatever the consequences. He'd once had a certainty about Annie that he now felt about this Lily, if less intensely: *She's right for me, she's all the medicine I need.*

She came out of the British Legion at 6:40. Jack noticed she had taken some trouble with her hair, and she was wearing more make-up than before. He asked her to suggest a place where they could have a drink. She took him to an intimate, pink-lit little cocktail bar called Rosie's.

'I've been coming here for years,' Lily said. 'It's the perfect place for drowning your sorrows.'

They sat at a tiny circular table in the corner. Jack had a large brandy, in spite of warnings from Peverill and others that he shouldn't touch the stuff. Lily favoured something called a Fix, made with gin, pineapple syrup, lime juice and a dash of Cointreau.

'So,' Jack said, leaning close, hoping he hadn't over-done the aftershave, 'have you drowned many sorrows in here?'

'More than enough.'

'Man trouble?'

'Sometimes.'

With a little more prompting Lily gave him her history. She was originally from Bristol; a turbulent romance with a soldier made her leave home at seventeen to go and live near his barracks in Wiltshire. There, working as a shop assistant, she transferred her affections to her manager, a married man twelve years her senior. Having successfully broke up the manager's marriage she went to live with him in London. They parted two years later when Lily, twenty-one by then, met an amorous police constable called George who told her he would go out of his mind if she didn't move in with him. They were eventually married in a registry office in High Barnet, where George was stationed. The marriage lasted nine years, then he ran away with a policewoman.

'No kids?' Jack said.

'No, thank God.'

'So when did you come to Brighton?'

'Six months after I knew George had gone for good.

I've been careful not to get too involved with anybody since then.'

'I don't blame you.'

'So now I've given you the lowdown on me,' Lily said, 'it's your turn.'

'You want my story?' Jack made a face. 'I don't think you'd want to know.'

'Why not?'

'Nine years sleeping next to a copper's bound to have conditioned you. Most of my life I've been the opposite of what policemen are supposed to be.'

Lily frowned.

'You're not telling me you're a criminal, are you?'

'I'm afraid so. I don't think I've earned an honest penny in my life.'

'Go on, then,' Lily said, rubbing her hands. 'Tell me all about it.'

Candour was a feature of growing old. Jack had no intention of telling her lies about himself. His account of his life was carefully edited, but what he told her was all true. He sketched his career in Glasgow and London, and he told her about Queenie and Frank and Danny, and made it perfectly clear that he was not a happily married man. As a postscript he confessed that when he was a young man he had done a long stretch in prison. When he had finished Lily looked delighted.

'What an amazing life,' she said. 'I've never known a real crook before. It's another world.'

'I haven't shocked you, then?'

'Not in the least.'

'You're not going to tell me you think my life's been glamorous, are you?'

'No. It doesn't sound very attractive at all. But it hasn't been dull, has it? Most people's lives are terribly dull, Jack. You've missed all that, all the tediousness.'

'Not exactly,' he said. 'Up until yesterday, I was getting my share. The whole backlog.'

'Is that why you're here in Brighton? To try and break the monotony?'

'That's exactly it.'

'Do you think it's working?'

'It's starting to, now I've met you.'

'You have a silver tongue, Sir Jasper.'

They had another drink. Lily began to fill in the details of her recent life. She had no boyfriend, and when she wasn't working she was either to be found having a quiet drink here or in the bar where Jack had met her, or – more often – she would be at home watching television. She lived in a flat, a place that was very important to her. It was her fortress, her retreat, her guarantee of independence. To keep it she had to work hard. She was a waitress at the British Legion and she often moonlighted at the Conservative Club. She admitted it was a very low-key life, but she believed she was content.

'Nothing else matters,' Jack said.

'I know that now. Contentment's everything.' Lily tilted her head, looking closely at Jack. 'Have you ever been a contented man?'

'I don't think so. At odd times, I suppose, but never for long.'

'It's a pity. You've got a face for it. Contentment would look good on you.'

'I bet you say that to all the old crooks.'

'I told you – you're the only old crook I've ever met.'

By the third drink they were comfortable with each other. Jack found no resistance in Lily, she accepted him without visible reservation. He cautioned himself – maybe he was so anxious for her to like him that he was overlooking something, or maybe she was a good actress. And immediately he reproached himself; *for your own good, try to believe this woman is what she appears to be.*

At eight o'clock he asked her if she was hungry.

'Starving,' Lily admitted.

'You're the resident,' Jack said. 'Lead me to a good eating house.'

'Do you like Italian food?'

'I love it.'

They left Rosie's and Lily led the way along quiet

278

winding back streets to a basement restaurant called Il Monello. It was a cramped, candle-lit, garlic-scented delight. The staff were all Italian, three generations of a family from Umbria. They worked hard to make a visit to their restaurant memorable. The menu was extensive and the cooking superb. There was lavish courtesy and an endless stream of jokes from the waiters. A young boy played a guitar and the matriarch circulated endlessly, asking if everything was satisfactory.

Jack and Lily celebrated the happy accident of their meeting with goblets of chianti. The ate huge platefuls of pasta and a main course of Saltimbocca alla Romana. Jack threw dietary caution completely to the winds and had zabaglione for pudding. Then it was coffee and brandy. Then more brandy.

Midnight came and they were the last customers in the place. Nobody made an effort to hurry them. Jack appreciated that. He had become emotional on the brandy; he said he should have travelled more, he had a yen to see people like these in their native surroundings. He told Lily at great length about an Italian called Elliot Rossini who had once saved his life.

When they finally left they walked back along the narrow streets to the promenade, arm in arm as if they had known each other for ages. They stood by the seawall rail, listening to the waves. Jack felt tension edging into his mood.

'I live just round the corner,' Lily said. 'Fancy a coffee? Another little tot of brandy?'

'I should be getting back to the hotel,' Jack said.

He saw the disappointment.

'I *should* be getting back to the hotel, but I'll take you up on your invitation, all the same.'

Lily grabbed his arm again and led him off. Jack put up a silent prayer that when it came to crunch time, she would understand.

The apartment was small and modestly furnished. While Lily was in the kitchen Jack stood in the sitting room, admiring the quiet taste in her few sticks of furniture, in her ornaments and pictures. He thought, rather sadly, of Martin Weir's house, remembering the restful trappings of that solitary man's life. He must tell Lily about Martin. She would be interested.

'Here we are, then.'

She came in from the kitchen with a coffee pot and cups on a tray. She put it down on a side table and went to the sideboard.

'Let's get you a nice brandy.'

'Lord, you're spoiling me . . .'

There was a small framed tapestry hanging on the wall above the sideboard. Jack crossed to look at it, remembering his own, GLASGOW BELONGS TO ME, confiscated long ago by the police.

'My mother did that,' Lily said, uncorking a bottle of Courvoisier. 'She copied the text from the Book of Ruth. She told me it took her months to do. She presented it to my father on the day they were married.'

Jack stood close, impressed by the fine stitching of the letters.

Intreat me not to leave thee, or to return from following after thee: for whither thou goest I will go; and where thou lodgest, I will lodge: thy people shall be my people, and thy God my God: where thou diest, will I die, and there will I be buried: the Lord do so to me, and more also, if ought but death part thee and me.

'That's a beautiful thing,' he said. 'She must have loved your father very much.'

'Yes, she did. But he left her a year after I was born.'

That was incredibly sad to imagine – a woman entirely devoted to her man, devoted to the point of declaring the fact in painstaking needlework, and yet he could walk away from her . . .

'Has it upset you, Jack?'

He realised there were tears in his eyes. He tugged out his handkerchief and dabbed them.

'I swear to God, Lily, there's something about the sea air. It seems to sharpen everything.'

She smiled and squeezed his arm as she handed him his brandy. Jack stared at her face, still astonished at the resemblance to Annie Kempson.

'I'm terribly glad I met you,' he said. 'I mean it. Truly.'

Kissing her was the easiest thing in the world. It just happened. As he closed his arms around her she snuggled close to him, all softness and warmth.

'Would you sooner finish your brandy afterwards?' she whispered.

The moment had come, taking Jack by surprise.

'Lily . . .'

She moved against him and suddenly, miraculously, there was no need for explanation, or regret, or apology. His stirring was real, he wasn't imagining it. This woman was a miracle! He put down his brandy and let her lead him into the bedroom.

By the bed she faced him.

'Let me undress you,' she said.

Dry-mouthed, he stood and watched as she stripped him to the skin. Her movements were slow, matter-of-fact, methodical. She folded every item before she laid it on the dressing table stool. When she was finished she went to the side of the bed and took off her own clothes. Naked, she came to Jack with her arms outstretched.

'God bless you,' he murmured, drawing her close, brimming with more gratitude and plain bliss than she would ever realise.

A week after Jack had left for Brighton Queenie got a postcard.

'He's stoppin' for the rest of the month,' she told Danny over breakfast. 'What the hell's Brighton got that could hold him that long?'

Danny shrugged.

'I thought he didn't like holidays,' he said.

'Not with me, he didn't. The last one we had was twelve years ago, and he cut that one short with some excuse about keepin' an eye on his patch. Ever since then I've never been able to talk him into goin' away.'

'Speakin' of his patch,' Danny said, 'what d'you reckon he's goin' to say when he finds out you've been reorganisin' it?'

'He can say what he likes, darlin'. He can't manage it any more and I'm not goin' to stand by and watch somebody else grab it.'

'He can't be completely out of the game, though. That Grady he went for was a hard sod. He's a right bleedin' mess now. Finished, he is. Dad did that all on his own.'

'Yeah – and he'd have got minced for doin' it, if you hadn't turned up.' Queenie flipped the postcard to the side of the table. 'His days of glory are over, Danny. All he's got are his memories. I dare say that's what he's doin' down at Brighton. Lyin' in a deck chair, dreamin' about the old days.'

'Yeah, well, maybe he is,' Danny said. 'Still, he was a bit of a legend in his time, wasn't he? It's not everybody you can say that about.'

'He's been forgotten already,' Queenie grunted. 'The past is dead. Hatchet Jack's hung up his chopper. In every sense,' she added, scowling.

After the first week Jack moved in with Lily. On the evenings when she worked late he had Chinese or Indian takeaways waiting in the oven when she got back. Other nights they went out to dinner. By the end of the third week they had visited practically every good restaurant in Brighton.

Jack felt years younger. He slept well. There were no early-morning terrors. He made love to Lily nearly every night. The inner and outer man were in focus again, and they were a tight match.

'You've made me a very happy girl,' Lily said one night as they left a cinema where they had been to see *Paint Your Wagon*.

'Don't get me blushing, eh?' Jack said.

'I was sitting in there thinking about it. I thought I was

content before I met you. But it must have been whatsits-name. Suspended animation. Something like that. I feel alive now. All the time. I'm aware of things. And I enjoy myself, I enjoy my job, even. It's all down to you, Jock.' She had taken to calling him that occasionally, ever since he had told her how much it annoyed him. 'But I suppose it's time we faced some grim facts. You've only another week of your holiday to go.'

'I haven't said anything about it because I've been doing some thinking.' Jack pointed at the promenade rail. 'Let's have a lean for a minute.'

They crossed the pavement and stood with their backs to the sea, their elbows propped on the rail. The wind blew Lily's hair across her face. Jack smiled at her.

'You look like a little girl, you know.'

'And you behave like a big boy, I'm happy to say. What's all this thinking been about, then?'

'Us. Naturally. I just couldn't see any good reason why we should be separated. I know we agreed it would be nice if I came down on weekends. But that would make the weekdays miserable for me. And I'd no sooner be here than I'd be thinking, Christ, in a couple of days I'll have to go back. So I've come to a decision. I go back at the end of next week, I hand over everything to Queenie, and I come back down here. For good.'

Lily stared at him.

'You'd do that, would you?'

'Of course I would. I *will*. Unless you think I'll be a nuisance, hanging round you all the time.'

'Don't be daft.'

'Well, I said it because . . .'

'Because of what you were drooling on about the other night. The age difference.'

'Aye, precisely that. I mean, in ten years – '

'Forget it, Jack. Where's the sense in ruining the present with a lot of fretting about the future? People don't get many chances to be happy, do they? We've got the chance and we're taking it. We'll go on taking it for as long as we can.'

When they got back to the flat Jack poured brandy into two glasses and took them to the bedroom. Lily was already there, getting undressed.

'What do you think Queenie'll say about you coming to stay in Brighton?' she said, unhooking her bra.

'She won't say much. She'll be glad to see the back of me, I should think. And look at the present she's getting. My turf. All of it, on a plate. She'll bang that front door behind me so fast she'll have the skin off my heels.'

He put down the glasses on the bedside table and undressed quickly. Lily was under the sheets before him. He grasped her round the waist and drew her cool nakedness on top of him.

'I love you,' he said against her hair. 'Is it all right to say that now?'

'I suppose so. I didn't want you saying it before because I wanted you to be sure.'

He kissed her neck, drew his hands down the smoothness of her sides.

'Have you anything you want to tell me?' he whispered.

'Yes.'

'What?'

'I'm beginning to like you.'

He tickled her mercilessly until she rolled off him, squealing. He turned quickly, pinning her on her back.

'My turn on top tonight,' he said.

She raised her knees on either side of him. Jack felt the silken warmth of her belly as it slid against his. Bliss, he thought. What have I finally done to deserve it?

Lily took his face between her hands and drew him down to kiss her. He tasted the sweetness of her mouth, relished the hungry movement of her tongue. She positioned herself, spreading her legs. Jack lowered his body and felt a tearing pain across his chest.

'Aah! Jesus . . .'

His head buzzed. He felt himself roll over, the pain clamping his ribs. He couldn't breathe. He was dizzy. The pain burned along his neck and up behind his ears. Lily wasn't beside him any more. He saw the overhead light go on. It looked dim and and fuzzy.

'Jack! Jack!'

Her voice was distant, it had an echo. The pain was swelling now, squeezing the air out of him. He tried to push himself up but his body weighed a ton.

'Oh Jack, darling . . .'

He felt her face on his. She was crying. Her hands pressed his chest. He tried to hold them, to comfort her. But he was sliding away, and as he knew that, the pain suddenly went. There was nothing now but a beautiful blue-pink haze. At the centre of it he saw Lily's face, her dear face . . .

He tried to tell her it was all right, he wasn't in pain now, it had passed. But he didn't know how to speak. There was nothing he could do but lie there, seeing the haze get thicker and brighter. He felt strong, even though he couldn't move. Strong, capable, the way he had been before, up in Glasgow . . .

Lily's voice drifted through to him, through the marvellous soothing haze. He thought she was still crying, but she shouldn't. He didn't feel anything. Not a single thing. He was happy. Couldn't she see he was smiling?